Shark

Shark

WILL SELF

Grove Press
New York

For Nick Mercer

D'ailleurs, c'est toujours les autres qui meurent.

– Marcel Duchamp

candle to light you to – Kerr-wangg! *Here comes a chopper-* Kerr-wangggunggggunggg! Lesley, Busner thinks, bloody Lesley playing the Kid's guitar, 'though there ought to be another expression, playing being what Gould does with a Steinway or du Pré with a cell– owowwow-owww! the clawed chord howls in the hallway and tears up the stairs. It's not playing, Busner decides, it's mucking about – that's what he's doing: mucking about with his mucky hands ... one of which throttles the guitar's neck, twisting its steely cords so that they yow-ow-owl. This too Busner suffers, as he also endures the cracklefizzz-tap!-tap!-whine of the flat body ... *Demoiselle de Willesden* ... being laid down on the bare boards of the downstairs back room the Kid and Lesley share ... *not an ideal arrangement, that.* Mercifully, Lesley's *roll-up-stained fingers* ... twiddle the knurled knob of the little Marshall amplifier so the static genie flees ... *I no longer dream of her.* Busner cocks an ear for a while longer – expecting to hear the *pet sounds* of Oscar, the House dog, who often responds to guitar feedback with his own – but there's nothing. The lucky beast, Busner thinks, must've managed to doze through it ... And so he resumes his *'umble task* ... He looks to the claw-footed bathtub, the chipped enamel sides and sea-weedy stains trailing below the taps suggesting to him ... *a tramp steamer* turned *inside out* – his wrinkled fingertips ... *flatibuts* but recently trawled from it, pinch the dimpled handle of the safety razor and twist ... and *twist* ... but it *resists* ... until he receives the support of ... *heavy bombers, massive artillery, a superb logistics system, nearly a thousand helicopters and about ten thousand men* ... – His capacity for recall, Busner believes, has greatly improved since he stopped taking notes during analytic sessions, allowing them instead to develop as they will, freeform, without the imposition of those prejudicial categories *implicit in the Logos* . . . bearing down on all these . . . *wriggling little thoughtfish.* And yet . . . and yet, he muses, can it really be that they call it a fish-hook? Yes! . . . *a fish-hook salient of Cambodia some twenty miles long and ten miles deep* . . . the exact wording returns to him and he sighs, satisfied, as he separates the two halves of the razor's head and eases out the old blade. – You're more likely to cut yourself doing this . . . he thinks, as he bends to fiddle a bit of toilet paper from the wonky roller . . . than shaving. Then he wraps the blade up carefully before, without looking, dropping it into the waste-paper basket underneath the sink. Some slight irregularity in a sound that would anyway be . . . *slight* pulls him up, and Busner squats to ogle the raffia cylinder: it's full to overflowing with twisted brown-paper bags, some of which are red-blotchy. So, he thinks, they've all come on at once, once again, and the cycle has been completed. – He wonders why it is that, although the women all sleep next door, they come tramping up here to change their tampons and sanitary towels – especially since this means they will, at a vulnerable moment, be in close proximity to *the Creep* . . . Then he sighs and, straightening up, eases into another speculation: Hopefully, this'll mean the tension that dominated Friday's house meeting will now be dissipated –. *No*, tension – whether premenstrual or otherwise – doesn't capture it: this was . . . *frenzy Van-der-Graaff crackling* from Irene to Eileen to Maggie to Podge. Saturday saw them all sulking in their separate corners – but then Sunday was, of course . . . *bloody*.

Now, at the start of another week, Busner finds himself futilely yearning for all that electricity to have been earthed by the bedrock *of reasonableness*. Addressing his own worried face in the mirror, he says aloud, We're doin' just great here! in what he imagines is a convincing impersonation of General Shoemaker – then, feeling he hasn't quite got the twang right, he says again, We're doin' just grrreat here! while by way of confirming this greatness he presses on with the job to hand: searching out the little box of razor blades on the wonky, cluttered, dried-toothpaste-blobbed shelf beneath the mirrored cabinet, easing out a fresh one, carefully unwrapping its tissue shroud. As he undertakes these manoeuvres, Busner's penis wheedles its way from the towel inefficiently knotted about his hips to nuzzle against the cold sink. He turns on the tap and twirls his shaving brush on a *circumcised* stub of shaving soap . . . *He knows the temperament of women, and wipes the suds around his face*. A Bakerloo Line train comes clacketing along the embanked track at the end of the back garden, and, even as Busner makes the first judicious stroke, he feels the house rocking on its foundations, pulling and pushing the adjoining properties as the entire one-hundred-and-fifty-yard-long terrace sways and crashes . . . *to nowhere* . . . *Orbicularis oris, buccinator, depressed labii inferioris* . . . Anatomising his own face into naked being, he remembers: What a duffer I was at dissection! – The long, enamel-topped oak bench under cold northern heavens, *Nat-urrral light, gentlemen*, said Roberts, with a vicious rolling of his *r*'s, *Nat-urrral light, gentlemen – and lady* . . . Always there was this grudging admission of Isobel McKechnie's presence on his second pass . . . *because what-everrrr your queasy little tum-tums're telling ye, this is a prrrro-foundly nat-urrral prrrocedure!* Every tutorial, Busner thinks, had begun with this admonition – rote learning resulting from a lifetime of rote teaching. He had no doubt that Roberts was still there, still pacing the worn boards between the benches, still imposing himself between the shaking, white-coated shoulders of first years, and leaning down to point out this or that feature of the human carcasses their scalpels were inefficiently reducing to . . . *trayf.* What was it Marinetti had demanded for his heroic Fascist dinner? *Raw meat torn by trumpet blasts* . . . What was it Roberts had trumpeted every bloody time: *Busss-nerrr, Busss-nerrr, rrrreally, man, ye'll nev-errr get inside the head that way – will ye look at the god-awful bloody mess you're making!* Yes, the god-awful mess – the indignity heaped after death on the corpse that had been lofted over the battlements of Craig House, or perhaps brought by motorised tumbrel from Carstairs, either way: the remains of a mental or criminal defective, of no account, *a burden on the ratepayers*, whose only utility lay in his or her limbs being disarticulated and severed, the head sawn off then thrust . . . *in my face by the bloody Burke! Here comes a chopper to chop off your head!* He smiles, then frowns, at his own *corrugator supercilii* in the listing mirror with its blush of condensation. – He dares to see himself, for a moment, as Roberts must have done: a grinningly inefficient predator with an undershot jaw who swims round *annaround* in a sea of body parts. – The carefree automatism of shaving is over, the tube train has passed and stands loitering by the platform at Dollis Hill, waiting to suck in through its rubber-lipped doors a few stragglers, who, rather than joining the

4

throng on the other platform heading city-wards, are commuting in reverse to Wembley, Harrow and points still further out. Busner's eyes slide to the narrow window – his hand follows, and, as he gropes at the gauzy skirts meant to preserve *my own modesty*, the towel at last quits his hips and flops on to the wet lino. It will, he thinks, be another fine May day, after the sunny weekend that saw them all picnicking in Livingstone Park: Podge . . . *floating and ethereal*, despite the tight binding of her tartan mini-dress to the tartan rug she sat on, and the tartan-patterned thermos beside her. Then there'd been the Creep, floundering into the boating pond – Oscar nipping at his heels – and attempting to board a pedalo by groping its bosomy floats, before Roger Gourevitch got hold of his webbing belt and pulled him away from the shocked, Mivvi-stained faces and feverishly bicycling thighs of its teenage-girl crew. A sunny-bloody-Sunday – to be followed by a *sunny-bloody-Monday*. To an outsider, Zack Busner imagines, it would seem absurd that a community such as this one, with no rules and only the queerest of conventions, the members of which have no occupations – unless, that is, you count the fashioning of mobiles from black thread, wire and dependant gewgaws, and accorded their travels to labour exchanges and hospitals commercial ones – nonetheless responds to the economic cycle: relaxing palpably at the weekend, then becoming increasingly uptight throughout the week – crisis succeeding crisis – until, during the house meeting held every Friday morning, there would invariably be . . . *a dreadful bloody freak-out*. On one of his rare trips into town Busner had been shocked by the blatancy of an advertising slogan: SAME THING, DAY AFTER

5

*DAY — TUBE — WORK — DINNER — WORK — TUBE — ARMCHAIR — TV —
SLEEP — TUBE — WORK. HOW MUCH MORE CAN YOU TAKE? ONE IN
TEN GOES MAD, ONE IN FIVE CRACKS UP* . . . and this mantra stayed
with him — although, after much repetition, it dawned on him:
this ability of capitalism to so accurately identify its own symptoms
was itself . . . *part of the doctor-created disease.* — The house opposite
stares back at Busner through its own . . . *glaucoma tulle*, and he
considers its solidly fanciful form: the three-sided bay windows
on the ground and first floors separated by chunky pilasters . . .
plinths, really — crying out for the honour of aldermen's busts or
hippogryphs — supporting half the vertical section of a tower which,
at roof level, is surmounted by three quarters of a turret, the back of
which is buried in the roof tiles. The whole façade has been recently
painted an unbecoming colour — somewhere between off-white
and pale yellow — that suggests to him the strong likelihood of an
institution yet to come into being that will . . . *one day be ubiquitous.*
Below the twin of his own window heavy Ionic columns frame an
emphatically shut front door. — Busner knows the inhabitants of this
doppelgänger villa by sight — and has also spoken to the patriarch.
He had to, after Eileen — naked and squeezing her dry cracked
nipples as she used them to ventriloquise some verses of the Sermon
on the Mount — had laid her Christ-like Barbie doll in their
window-box manger. He had to explain that Eileen — who had run
up the tiny chiffon robe herself, and glued locks of her own hair on
to the doll's bright-pink nubbin of a chin . . . *clever, really* — was, as
were some of the other new tenants at numbers 117 and 119, rather
unusual, and prone to be a bit, well, distressed from time to time,

but they were all basically harmless and decent people. Diss, Errol Meehan had expostulated, be loo-na-see — and for a moment Zack couldn't tell whether he meant Eileen's behaviour or his own explanation. Either way, Meehan, a member in good standing of the West Indian Ex-Servicemen's Club in Harlesden, who polished his immaculate Ford Consul to a high shine on Sunday afternoons while wearing an equally immaculate blue blazer with lustrous brass buttons and an RAF crest on its breast pocket, seemed hell-bent on being . . . *a pain in the arse*: I give you due warnin', man, don' be vexin' me. If your patients . . . Busner had thought it prudent to foreground his own qualifications . . . be mekkin any more trouble, any at all, den I be callin' down de lot on you. My wife is seer-e-uss-lee poorly — an in-va-leed — an' any dee-stir-bance might well put her over de edge. I can pick up me telly-phone . . . Meehan actually mimed the lifting of this instrument to his cruciferous ear . . . an' speak di-rec-lee wid Sergeant Sealy, de co-mu-nitt-ee relations officer. Lord be my witness . . . Meehan's fine baritone quavered enthusiastically up the scale as he slammed down the non-existent Bakelite and snatched it straight back up again . . . I can get a-holt of Mister Freeson as well, ax him to look into de matter of your pepperworks, certifications, licensings an' so forth. — At the time, although in no doubt about the seriousness of the threat Meehan presented, Zack found himself powerless to mollify the man, transfixed as he was by these magical motions: the body-busyings of that ivory finger dialling the frigid air between them, and the dissipations of his steamy breath as Meehan communicated with his spirit world of MPs and policemen. He backed

7

away to the sunnier side of the street, the Jesus dolly in hand, while his neighbour continued to admonish him: What does go 'round, well, in my ex-peer-i-ence it does come round again. – Then, as now, the nets in the Meehans' top window jerked open to reveal Missus Meehan, who, far from seeming on the brink, from this vantage appeared as robust as the Petrine rock: her great greyish slab of a face framed by these veils, her amorphous bosom thrust forward and bearing on it the Crusading symbol. Then, as now, Missus Meehan seemed about to launch into an Apocalyptic sermon, calling down the star called Wormwood on the miserable whore who had *slouched towards Jerusalem* . . . Months later, still repelled by her husband's very Christian lack of charity, Busner stares across at Missus Meehan and admits aloud, They do have a point – because the underlying equation of the Concept House – as he and Roger Gourevitch have dubbed the community – is insoluble, there being no rules with which to operate on its distressed . . . *often outright hysterical terms.* He sighs, and lets go of his own net curtain, the falling folds of which displace an avocado stone balanced on the rim of a jam jar by three toothpicks inserted in its slimy sides. The stone bobs in the greenish water, tangled in weedy rootlets. Bloody thing! he expostulates as he fiddles it out in the sink, refills the jar, then struggles to reinsert the toothpicks and so achieve once more . . . *this fine equilibrium* – suggestive, he thinks, of some Hindu cosmology . . . *the world is an avocado stone balanced by three toothpicks on the rim of a cosmic jam jar* . . . Although, if this is the case, there are many worlds: for in 117, and next door in 119, he has seen several other avocados germinating. – They are Miriam's doing, of course, another of her attempts to make of the Concept House some sort of home. She and their two sons share a bedroom in 119 on the three nights a week they come over from the Highgate flat, and, although Busner prefers to imagine this is in keeping with the way the community – like any tribal group – has separated according to sex, with prepubescents treated as . . . *effectively female*, he cannot escape the truth, which is that: *I can't stand that creep* . . . this being how she and the other women refer to Claude behind his back, and how he came to be dubbed: the Creep. At any rate, this is what Busner wants to believe: the ascription is *part of the language game we all play*, rather than indicative of the essentialism the women betray when they say such things as, He's bloody creepy, that man, he gives me the complete creeps, or, I hate it when he creeps up on me in that creepy way . . . It is, of course, the Creep who has driven all the women to sleep in a protective huddle in 119, and in periods of still darker reflection Zack finds himself entertaining outright nominalism: the Creep, he worries, may be called the Creep not because he is creepy by nature or because his behaviour is creepy, but due to the fact that in a world of completely unique objects and persons it is he, and he alone, who's the only *100% genuine, solid-gold CREEP!* . . . *Bernie – the bolt, please!* The candy-striper, ripe l'il blondie – she know she done it, an' she done it good. She unzip herself, an' she push up her buzzoom, an' she fiddle with her brassiere so that every goddamn male patient in the day-room who ain't zonked sees all she' got, an' she says, Oh me, oh my, ain't this just the tightest awkwardest orneriest thing . . . ain't it just the tightest awkwardest orneriest thing . . . ain't it . . . – The tube has passed by and the morning traffic on the High Road is a distant swish – so it is, with his hands still spread on the windowsill, the fat and tropic seed suspended between them, that Busner becomes aware of this incantation rising up towards him . . . *creepy, that* . . . just the tightest awkwardest orneriest thing – ain't it, ain't it, ain't it JUST!? – The Creep, in common with many of the seriously disturbed whom Busner has observed, has this occult art of manifesting himself psychically moments – sometimes hours – before he physically appears: a minor mishap such as a dropped matchbox, or a word leaping from dense type, or twigs tapping on a windowpane will provoke the uncanny sensation that he is nearby. Her gams is all nylon shhk-shk, her white wedgies is all click-clack, her ass is so goddamn wrigleyicious you just wanna bite into it – ain't it just! – It's in keeping with this that the Creep's monologuing – which is continuous, uninterrupted by sleep, although impeded by eating and drinking, and only fractionally quieter when he's heavily sedated – should chime with what Zack's thinking about. True, the Creep does live at the Concept House – his boxes full of old electrical engineering manuals, and trendy books by *organic intellectuals* . . . Marcuse, Norman O. Brown, Colin Wilson and also . . . *Ronnie himself* . . . are scattered around the back upstairs bedroom. – So this latest manifestation could be dismissed as mere coincidence, were it not that after yesterday's boating pond incident he'd dashed raving from the park, not returning until now . . . *to eat us all up!* Busner considers for a beat *the oral acquisitive nature of schizophrenia* . . . then, spotting an old bath cube melting on the lino under the claw-footed tub, he squats, picks it up and tosses it experimentally away from himself: Fort, he says, and then louder, Da! – No, he thinks, the Creep hadn't returned yesterday afternoon, or during the long evening, which the communards spent *as usual* barricaded behind the television set. Why . . . Busner niggles at it once again . . . would anyone seize upon the stage name Leif Erickson? – And the Creep had still not come back when, having watched the last three quarters of an hour of Rear Window, holding the Kid's soft and trembling hand, Busner double-locked the front door and finally went to his own bed. He knew the Creep couldn't get into the house anyway: before he'd charged after the pedalo, he'd taken off the bizarre necklace of braided ribbon and keychain he wore round his neck – and from which hangs a scallop shell, a tin opener with a corkscrew attachment, a tiny Japanese transistor radio, his door key, a bear claw and a Tibetan amulet – and coiled it into Podge's lap. – He did this sort of thing, the Creep: singling out one or other of the women for attention, making them – as it were – his favourite for a day or a week, and Zack had to hand it to him, for, no matter how unsettling the background noise of the man's sexuality – an impotent rapist was Busner's own diagnosis, one who'd kill the thing he couldn't make love to – he nonetheless managed, almost always, to behave towards them with exaggerated courtliness: bowing and ushering them through doors, pulling out chairs and fetching things for them as the threnody for one or other of his captious selves – Why does you does that to him? Does you that to him an' I does put you in de coal hole wid de tar baby – continued unabated. It was this gentlemanly ballet, choreographed by the Creep's undoubted charisma, that made the chosen one – no matter how creepy she found him – feel embraced even as she recoiled. The same courtliness would have prevented him from knocking up the house in the night – the same courtliness, and another quality possessed by the Creep that Busner couldn't help but characterise as . . . *an acute sense of self-preservation.* Excepting the occasional wild outburst – and these, if his supposition was correct, might be solely for effect – the Creep always seemed to know precisely how far he could go, and to have, ever-present to his seething awareness . . . *a DMZ over-flown by howling fighter jets* into which he would never venture. In the inkiest, dankest hours of the suburban night, when the rails at the end of the garden had ceased their electro-hum, it was this canniness that Busner suspected was indicative of the deepest and most dreadful truth about the Creep, namely, that, far from being the most seriously disturbed of the Concept House's residents, *he might not be disturbed at all!* Busner's bare arm, sweeping radar-beamishly beneath the tub, has located the bath cube, Da! – but then it is Fort! again, his exclamation sopped up by the lank and balding towels hanging from hooks on the back of the door and absorbed into the crocheted bathmat's damply tufted corolla. He repeats it: Fort – Da! and then, still kneeling, embroiders it: Da-daa-da-da-d'da-daa! while praying fervently that when these Da's are no longer here the Creep won't be either, rather up on some high chaparral thousands of miles from Willesden, booted and horsed, a Winchester thrust into the leather scabbard beside his saddle, his Stetson silhouetted against the Potala Palace of a mesa. *No such luck* . . . Throw de darkie in de coal hole, throw de massa in dere too . . . – Hearing the Creep's weird minstrelsy leak in under the bathroom door, Zack pictures his antagonist quite clearly: he'll be sitting sideways on the mat immediately inside the front door, bracing himself with his big old army boots and his quaking shoulders between the scuffed-white walls papered with a doubly geometric snowflake pattern, his battered brow, with its hairy aurora, knocking against the dull deal certainty of the telephone table, upon which sits the smooth bone-yellow telephone . . . *waiting to ring in a judgement call: Life-to-Death . . . A–D, EeeK!* The postman has yet to come, and so Captain Claude Evenrude, US Army Air Corps (Ret.), awaits him, thick black felt-tip in hand, ready to do his duty – as he sees it – by censoring the enlisted men and women's mail. Usually, one or other of these subordinates will get to the door before the envelopes are thrust through the letterbox and, swinging it open, snatch them from the postman's hand. If they don't manage this, the consequences are postcards upon which the writing has been – seemingly at random – obliterated: here an entire line, there an isolated word – or perhaps a single letter – falling victim to the Creep's black stripes and spots. Not only the message but the picture overleaf suffers: Anne Hathaway's cottage, Leeds Castle – maybe a Kew hothouse or two – will be squeakily defaced, although the Creep reserves his most creative censorship for . . . faces: Beatles mop-tops are dropped on top of the Queen's tiara and a Hitler moustache shaded over her pert top lip. Given a group scene – Brighton bathers, say, or the Household Cavalry trooping the Colour – he will expertly black out all the arms and legs, so that what remains is a smattering of torsos. This is all very annoying – but what's intolerable is that the

Creep slits open envelopes and censors their private contents – also bills, which he subtracts from with his felt-tip and then annotates with a biro, adding complex equations bracketing the few lonely figures he has permitted to survive, so creating . . . *Godly integrals and Satan's differentials, demonstrating the ballistics of heavenly orbs and satanic tridents that will occur – that SHALL OCCUR if I have my way . . . Unless we now take time to make the common pers– pers– pers– . . . Oh, heck, I dunno, y'see in that there is 7, 6, 5, 3, 6-point-1, AM859R45HJ88 turned insie-outsie . . .* This being the sort of thing he says when confronted by Miriam or Radio Gourevitch – the only residents besides Busner who've ever been robust enough to stand up to *the Creep*. – His arm still sweeping for the fort-cube, and oofing with the effort, Busner realises this maddening recollection of monologuing is itself underscored by sing-song rhyming that slips up the stairs: Oh roister-doister li'l oyster, Down in the slimy sea, You ain't so diff'rent lyin' on your shell bed, To the likes of l'il old me, But roister-doister you're somewhat moister, Than I would like to be . . . Perversely, despite everything, Busner believes he'd be content to listen to the Creep all day and for many subsequent ones. He'd ask the others to leave quite coolly, install himself in one of the straight-backed kitchen chairs, put Claude in the one opposite – then he could fully concentrate on *what this man has to tell me* without recourse to the prejudicial pathologies – psychotic, schizophrenic, manic, schizophreniform – that he has steadily abandoned. True, without the compass of orthodox psychiatry or psychoanalytic theory, Busner finds it next to impossible to get a fix as he bobs up and down on Claude's choppy wordsea, its surface criss-crossed by narrative currents swirling into whirlpools of song that subside into glassily superficial doldrums of what might be anecdotage, but beneath which, Busner is convinced, fluxes and refluxes of dangerous repression coldly circulate. This much the anti-psychiatrist will concede: the Creep's soliloquies – and they are certainly this, the dialogic being effected only by mythical figures or imagined characters – display neither the stereotypies nor the overbearing unimagination of those . . . *forced to play the schizo-phrenic game.* On the contrary, the Creep in all he says or does is bewilderingly inventive, never prolix, and repeats himself only for rhetorical effect. He is, Busner thinks not for the first time – it's that pleasing an image – a sort of desert island, upon whose sandy shores others – Radio Gourevitch included – can leave only the impress of their feet, mere dimples that soon enough *are erased by the next neural wave –.* — The *cat-fuck-wail* of the front gate snaps through his reverie – the postman is out there, his canvas sack lashed around his grey suit jacket with a length of sisal, and, as Busner rises dizzily, yanks open the bathroom door and stands naked at the top of the steep and uncarpeted stairs, all these benignant visions desert him. Claude! he cries, and Claude! he shouts louder – but it's to no avail because *the bugger doesn't hear any voices at all!* while the mail has penetrated the flap and been grabbed before Busner has descended five steps. With rapacious efficiency the Creep wields his untrimmed and horny thumbnail to slit open an envelope, register-ing the futile intervention only by turning up his own volume: Ho, darkies, hab you seen de massa, wid de MUFF-TASH ON HE FACE! – he then falls to censoring with a vengeance. Accepting this as a fait accompli, Busner sits down heavily, then rises abruptly *splintered bollocks!* – An important fact about inter-experience – insofar as this can be said to transpire at all with the Creep – that he has kept resolutely to himself, despite urging the other residents to be completely open for *there is nothing to fear*, is that on the one occasion Busner tried wresting the mail from its self-appointed censor he *hit me hard*. A brutal uppercut – learnt where? In bar-room, barracks or Depression-era blackboard jungle – Busner couldn't say. Indeed, he thinks: If I did know, I'd know everything – and, as he caresses the tempered skin of his cheeks, he touches also the memory of this violent coda. – From this angle the Creep appears pitiful: his balding shanks exposed by his hiked-up army-surplus trousers, his knobbly wrists sticking from the frayed ends of his red acrylic rollneck – the wiry U of him whip-lashing as he censors and sings, Ho, darkies, hab you seen de massa, wid de cudgel in he hand . . . And it was that hand that cudgelled Busner . . . *while still holding the felt-tip.* For, when he'd managed to get back upstairs, he saw, reflected in the triptych of mirrors on the mauve-skirted vanity table, side views of bloody rivulets running from the corners of his mouth and a full-frontal of his swelling and *heavily censored* top lip. – Sniffing any-old-iron and acetone, he'd Bloodknocked him-self: Quick, quick, nurse! The screens! although he was scared and his heart shook, Claude having hit him sufficiently hard *to lay me out cold*, the impact taking a big chunk out of Busner's visual field, so that a maroon tide rushed in from its crenulated edges, eating up first the bebop lino's screeching pattern – next his attacker's calmly leering face, its lips *still flapping out words* . . . Then, for a few instants, all that remained afloat in this ruddy tide were Claude's ruined teeth, which were falling out one by one until there was only a single closing-down white dot Jeanie runs towards, while Mumsie's *Fuck off out of it!* scrapes her, an' she scccrapes past the dinosaur wall where she an' Hughie found the T-Rex bone but don't see it coz she don't see nuffin coz the bitch clumped her that hard like the see-eye-enn, see-eye-enn-enn-ay-tee-eye kid done in the film, whippin' round on the footstool she was stood on nude, her skin all glittery where Jeanie had painted it with the Mela-wotsit lotion, an' her face covered with diamond shapes coz the sun was shining straight inter the cottage winder . . . *The bitch!* hit Jeanie that hard that the graze don't bovver her – if I live, she thinks, it'll go all crusty-lumpy an' be sumfing t'pick. If she lives – *an' I ain't blinded*, because Jeanie sees nothing: the puckered silver-green skin of the canal, the poplars shivering on its far bank, the houses up the lane – all are drenched by the reddy-black wave that engulfed her when her mother *smashed me in the gob-da-dum, dee-dum, da-diddly-dum, da-dum, da-dum, da–daaa, da–daaa!* This is what 'appens, Jeanie thinks, when Ollie stops bashing Stan on the nut an' they're both eaten up by the black mouf': *That's all, folks!* – By touch alone she feels her way across the road – the tar's hot and Jeanie is the yogi-bear-man in Look an' Learn, prancing on his flowery bed of bloomin' coals, – then she does a *cray-zee* gate vault over the five-bar and goes all dithery, running in circles, until her feet find a furrow for her and she ploughs along it, her legs scratched and her face stroked sticky by the full-eared wheat. – Still, she sees nothing: not the massy-green superstructure of the *Queen-Lizzy-beth* copse she knows sails ahead of her through the golden wind-streaked rollers, not the high-tension cables she knows stave the sky overhead, *coz I can 'ear 'em singin'* –. She trips and does a forward flip. – When she struggles up, brushing earthy pellets from her T-shirt and shorts, *it's done the trick*, because she can see *the dead man's head* of chert and chalk turned up by the plough, and, lifting her head, the new weathervane on the Butterworths' roof, which Missus Butterworth says is a fighting cock, *see-oh-kew* – although when Jeanie told this to Mumsie, Mumsie laughed her naughty laugh and said, Fucking cock more likely! And Jeanie would laugh the naughty laugh now if Mumsie hadn't tied *a blood bib* round her neck. – She walks on through the time tunnel, waving her arms above her head like what they do on the telly, and doesn't stop until she's deep inside London, which is what Debbie named the copse the day they discovered it, which was the first time Mumsie went to London and didn't come back all night – which was maybe, Jeanie thinks, two summers ago. Anyway, Hughie was littler then and they'd had to half carry him across the field, *'is feet dragging* ... Before that they'd had the two-can dinners: *Debbie'd done 'em in the double-boiler ... opened 'em ... plopped 'em out ... two can-shapes of nosh – bangers an' eggs all stuck togevver by baked beans and steamily glissning ...* Then she forked it all up and the two little 'uns squabbled over the sums: Jeanie said, Free inter four bangers don't go – and Debbie chanted, Dippa-dippa-day-shun my opper-ray-shun, How many trains are there at the stay-shun ... 'til they'd one each – but then Hughie grabbed the last banger *an' stuffed it in 'is gob*, but Debbie just laughed Mumsie's special

Hughie laugh – coz Mumsie loves Hughie more than she loves the girls. She screams at the girls: *You fucking little bitches* and worse – her hatred so high-pitched their ears sing as they run to hide. But even when she's that mad Hughie'll come up to her, no clothes on – coz if Debbie don't dress him Mumsie never bothers – and Mumsie'll cup his bum in one hand and press her cheek against *'is bulgy Biafran belly* . . . Right away she'll be calm – and she'll stay like that, the smoke from her Embassy curling up and around his cherub face. Then she'll take his winkle 'tween her fingers *annuver ciggie* and rubba-dub-dub it. See that, girls, she'll say, that's the family-fucking-jewels, that is, the family-fucking-jewels – 'course, it ain't exactly a World Cup Willie, for that it'd 'ave to 'ave a fucking mane! Then her voice goes all posh and she'll swirl the melty ice cubes in her tumbler, and she'll say, I think Mumsie needs another little drinky-pooh, so which one of you dah-lings is going to get it for her mumsie? – That's on normal days, days when she's shut up *in the shit hole with Miss Hoity-Toity* – which is what she calls Debbie – and *Dumbo*, which is what she *calls me, coz me dippa-dippa-day-shun-adder-noyds-opper-ray-shun went wrong.* Miss Hoity-Toity, up in the girls' bedroom, lying on her tummy on the snot-coloured oval rug, with her ear pressed against the warm throbbing weave of the record player, It took me soo-wo–ooo long to find out! *And I found out* . . . that when you'd stared for long enough at Parlophone going round *annaround* . . . if you lifted the holey bit of board inside the cabinet, you could see the *hot titty-valves glowing – each with a dark nip* . . . Then: curled up in the Chesterfield armchair, drawing patterns in its tawny fur . . . *smoove-light and rough-dark.* Then: making

Sindy dance on the patterns, coz it's only when Sindy sings that the *ringin' of me addernoyds stops*. – But on Fridays, when she gets back from teaching the *mongs* and the *spazzes* in Hemel, Mumsie comes in the cottage door already stripping: off fly her shoes *any old how*, down drops her navy pleated skirt *inna puddle on the floor*. – She yanks Jeanie out of the Chesterfield by her ear and shouts upstairs for Debbie, and together the girls haul in the hip bath from the shed. By the time the kettle's been boiled three times – *coz the immersion's always on the fritz* – and the boiling water's been mixed with a bit of cold in the big galvanised bucket, she's ready for her *gyppo 'andmaidens*. It's a two-girl job, Mumsie's bath – one to stand on the stool so she's high enough to pour, the other to haul the bucket up once it's been refilled and stand back to *take in the show*: watery snakes coiling round her saggy boobs, unravelling into drop-headed worms wiggling over her hips and buttocks, down her swelling belly and burying themselves *in 'er fanny hair* . . . Mumsie, all pink and blotchy, her soapy fingers rubbing the pinker grooves left by her girdle – Mumsie, snorting *like an 'ippo* . . . Oh! that's good, that's so fucking good! and rubbing her boobs . . . an' her fanny all sudsy – Mumsie, calling in her posh voice, Hurry up, gels! and when the next bucket-load plummets down on her steaming shoulders giving a repeat performance *again annagain* until all the *mong-dirt* and the *spazz-shit* has been washed away, and she splashes across the woodblocks to the broken sofa and flings herself into its leather arms, her legs *wide open* and its skirts lifting up so it *farts out mouse droppings an' dust devils* . . . Next Mumsie calls for Drinky-poohs! – In the tiny damp scullery, where plaster falls and the green bottles slip slowly into cobweb veils, Jeanie counts them up to twenty-seven and marvels at how big a deposit they'll get back . . . *when there're sixty-nine.* She lifts the twenty-eighth bottle of VAT 69, uncorks it with a plop! and carefully pours the drinky-pooh – but before squeaking it back in she sniffs the cork and, emboldened, takes a swig that thrusts a flaming tongue down her throat. – In her belly fire *rages like it done at Durrant's, where Gwen's dad works . . . He said the burning chemicals were 'otter than the sun,* and there weren't nothing of the place left when the firemen came *'cept for the front wall . . .* Jeanie's fingers on the scullery wall picker-pattering the plaster, watching whitewash flakes *confetti down* on to the *veils . . . so dreamy . . .* She'd've taken another swig if Mumsie wasn't drumming on the cushions, crying, Drink-ee-poohs! Drink-ee-poohs! – Smelling it on Jeanie's breath, Mumsie grabs her dress and pulls her to her own *burnt front wall.* Didja 'ave a little drinky-pooh, darlin'? She chuckles her naughty chuckle. Didja? An' I betcha yer just loved it, didn'tcha? — Standing deep in the heart of London, by the hut where Mister Jarvis the gamekeeper keeps his stuff, Jeanie thinks: That day was a spazzy day too – and I was mong like today. – Mumsie, with her old Sellotape marks on her soft tummy and the moles on her shoulders, was still bigger than this London – bigger than the real one, bigger likely than the world. Hooking her bra at the front, gagging fat belly lips – she pulled it up, blindfolding *'er big brown nips . . .* She fought her way into her brand-spanking-new Silhouette "X" special girdle, panting and laughing, Don't be afraid, girls, it's just me battle of the bulge! As they sat side by side on her bed, watching her dress, she told them, Cost me forty-one-an'-fucking-sixpence at Peckerwoods in Berko . . . Which was what she called Peterwood's Ladies' Outfitters . . . Fucking shysters – but I'll tell you once, I'll tell you a thousand times, you won't get nowhere with the darker sex 'less you build on a firm-fucking-foundation garment – pass me dress. – She held it against her bosoms, its jet beading *clicketing* against her rings, which she still wore *to keep the pests off* and, grasping its spangly shoulder, she waltzed to the wardrobe and arched her neck and pointed her chin. Mumsie, inside her own black shadow with her hair up in a French twist – Mumsie, with her legs slickly mysterious now they were sheathed in Aristoc dernier 15 seamless mesh "Undergrads". – *Daylight-fucking-robbery*, she'd said, and Jeanie remembers this because that's what it had been: Mumsie, looking at all three of them standing in the cottage door – she laughed her naughty laugh, the one that came with a light slap or a gentle pinch, and she said, Well, well, well – if it ain't Bill, Ben and Little-fucking-Weed, then she ground out her Embassy with her patent toe and got into the Gazelle. The engine hacked into life, the exhaust blew out dirty smoke, and the car *stole 'er away in broad daylight* – over the canal and up the lane to the main road. Jeanie and Hughie ran after it – but all they saw from the humpback bridge were the brake lights winking once, then she was gone. They couldn't believe the Gazelle had done it – stolen Mumsie away in broad daylight. It was their cuddly car, Mumsie said its cloth seats were *like inside a Kanga's pouch*, when she put them in there and drove them bumping over the woodland tracks to Little Gaddesden. Mumsie said the woods were full of real live kangas when the Rothschilds kept the estate to themselves. – The twirling bark crumb caught on an invisible thread . . . The lengthening shadows and the softer sunbeams . . . The bitter taste of sap on their tongues and its stickiness on their hands . . . All that evening they played in the copse, following its secret paths wherever they double-backed through bracken, brambles and nettles. Debbie said, This can be our London – that bush is Selfridges, that one's the Lyons' Corner House in Trafalgar Square, and that one, with its spooky hawthorn arch, is Euston Station. – There was a hut in the dead centre of London surrounded by rusty old bins with a rustier padlock on its door. This, Debbie said, is Mumsie's club, it's where she meets her special friends. Jeanie asked her what these friends were like, were they like the Deacon and Silly Sybil and Jeffers and Kins, who came by the cottage to have drinky-poohs? But Debbie said no, these were much specialer friends – pop stars and film stars and lords and ladies. Inside the club, Debbie said, there was a big mirror ball that spun faster and faster, making everything flash and sparkle – but Jeanie couldn't see it through the dirty little window. It didn't matter, she was enough of a mong then to be comforted, to believe they were all really in London, with Mumsie. – That night, when she hadn't come home after God Save the Queen, and she still hadn't come home ages after that and a big owl was woo-woo-wooing, first Hughie began to cry, then Jeanie. They all ended up together in Mumsie's bed – which was where she found them the next morning when she slammed through the front door, banged up the steep stairs and came reeling in, her tights laddered *to buggery* and a bloodied hanky tied round one hand.

Seeing the three tousled heads on her pillows, she'd cried out, Who the fuck're you? then groaned, Oh, you're my children, aren't you, my flesh-and-bleedin'-blood. She tore off the covers and they flew apart every which way – but Mumsie didn't lash out, she only moaned as she pulled the dress over her head – moaned, a *finger puppet* . . . tottering on stockinged feet, and went on moaning . . . *'til she fell.* – They left her there. Debbie made jam sandwiches and Jeanie filled a VAT 69 bottle with water. They went back to London for the day, where the girls took turns being the Shrimp while Danny leapt out of the bushes with a shandy-tin camera and pretended to take snaps of them. When they got home, Mumsie's black dress, her bra and her Silhouette "X" girdle were all hanging on the line. – The woman in the cottage was a jittery waxwork of Mumsie who didn't shout, only asked Debbie to go get her fags from the nooky shop. When Debbie returned, the little old woman peeled the flimsy strip and pushed the cellophane halfway off and burnt a little hole in this with the tip of her fag. She blew smoke inside and squeezed the cellophane so tiny rings came *piddling outta the 'ole*, and said, See that, Ovaltineys, it's the singin' ringin' smokin' tree – make yer wishes, I'll not refuse you. – Jeanie wanted to ask for the real Mumsie to come back, but she didn't dare, and the waxwork one went on squeezing smoke rings from the cellophane. Then she said, That there's your poor fucking Mumsie, that is – nothing to 'er but smoke an' the holes made by burnt pricks. — That was two summers ago, and Jeanie would go back to the cottage right now if she thought the waxwork Mumsie would be there and not the very real one who'd dragged her from her own bed where she lay *floatin' inna spaceman suit onna asteroid*. – Miss Hoity-Toity was off at Guides. Geddup! Mumsie had screamed, Gedd-the-fuck-up! – Bump-bump-bump, down the stairs gets dragged *Dumbo*, her head stuffed with useless *shit-for-brains* . . . to find Hughie already there, standing shivering on the kitchen flags and naked as usual, but his skin was Cyberman-silvery and his face streaked with tears. Mumsie was so very angry she *spun* as she snatched up plates and slung them in the sink, picked up the tea pot and dumped out the leaves – she spun and she *steamed* . . . she was so full of anger it . . . *'ad to come out some'ow* . . . Finally she said with a robot-voice, Get that nightie off, Dumbo – and when Jeanie was stood naked next to Hughie, Mumsie kicked her feet apart, telling her to reach up tall-as-a-tree. She tweezered apart Jeanie's puppy fat with chipped red nails – under the arms, behind the knees, between her bums – whistling fag smoke while she worked. Jeanie held her breath and her heart bashed at her ribs *againannagainannagain*. – Finally she breathed out. – Ssssscabies, Gordon Bennett, bloody ssscabies, I ain't seen 'em this bad since '46 when the Yid kids'd come over from the Russian sector . . . Lissen, pet . . . Mumsie went on in her specially nice voice, the one she'd last used when they were in the haberdasher's together and she picked out the lovely material with the nasturtium pattern . . . why didn't you say anything, pet, what on earth did you imagine this was? Gently she turned Jeanie's knee so they could both see the livid, lumpy triangle of broken skin on the back of her calf. Jeanie stuttered, I – I dunno, M-Mumsie, I fought it was a rash or sumfing I got in the big field . . . The truth was she knew perfectly well it was much worse than that – but she didn't want to bother her mother, who was always *tray-tray fatty-gay, dahling, Mumsie's tray-tray fatty-gay – so go fetch Mumsie some Noilly, you little prat* . . . It was better to go through the laundry basket if you didn't have a clean pair of socks and wash them in the bathroom sink, and *Swiss roll 'em* in a towel, and hang them out the bedroom window overnight so's to be sure to have something to pull right up to the knee and hide this proof – as if any were needed – that you were a . . . *dirty, stupid, hateful girl.* – Ssscabies, Mumsie hissed again, then: I sees just the one pink 'un on this 'un so straightways I drive into Berko, gets the lotion, comes back and paints 'im up proper. Then I thinks to myself – her grip on Jeanie's knee tightens – which one of my loathsome-bloody-spawn goes up to that fucking farm and plays doctors-and-nurses with that dirty pikey kid. That's not fair! Jeanie screamed inside – she wanted to shout out loud, You done all sorts wiv that lot! 'iding stuff in our shed for 'em – buying them triangle pills offa them. You got medicine from them two old witchy biddies what lives in their chicken 'ouse – black muck inna jam jar. You knocked it back saying, The old ways is the best ways, then you threw it right back up again when we was driving in the car! – Jeanie wanted to shout all this, but she also wanted her leg to survive – to get better, not end up *shrivelled inna brace* . . . D'you know what ssscabies are, my girl? Mumsie hisses on, spittling the bumps and lumps of Jeanie's infested leg. Ssscabies are ickle-lickle buggies that burrow under yer skin. And d'you know what they get up to inside yer? Eh? I'll tellya – they fuck about. That's right – they fuck about, and when they're good an' ready they

26

lay their fucking eggs in you. Well, I tellya what, my filthy little pikey-loving pal, I don't want to be a ssscabies hatchery, so . . . She let fall Jeanie's leg, unbuttoned her dressing gown and reached for the brown bottle . . . – Go get the footstool and put it in the bay where there's plenty of light. I'm gonna paint you proper all in good time, girlie, but first you're gonna do me. — *Rose-moles all in stipple* . . . the Deacon recites when he's pissed – *does 'e mean this?* this lumpy, blotchy leg with the shadows from the shimmering leaves shimmying over it? Jeanie fiddles an evil splinter from the side of the hut that's Mumsie's club. An express train explodes into the cutting at the top of the field, and, although deep down inside London, she sees this: the shock wave bellying out in front of the engine, shattering the haze drowsing above the hot rails. – A ring of taunting teeth and tongues surrounded her at school: Stupid Jeanie's got no brai-ns, Soon she didn't 'ave no vei-ns! – She longed to shout at them, Juss coz I'm a bit deaf it don't mean I'm a spazz! She longed to tell them that sometimes she could see sounds: bass browns and trumpeting purples, screeching pinks and the high-pitched fluting the sunlight made right before Mumsie's fist exploded in her head. Jeanie sets one of the feed buckets upside down on the ground – a featherless chick lies there, its dead body smeared with yolk. Through the dusky pane *Big Chief I-Spy* sees an old gate-leg table, a rotten canvas deckchair, a small bookcase cluttered with jars and tobacco tins – but no sign of Herman . . . *or 'is 'ermits.* Losing her footing on the bucket, Jeanie's shoulder strikes the windowframe and it cracks! open . . . *'Ave no vei-ns, 'ave no vei-ns,* the crows carp in the sky above London. The rough planks fetch her a graze, the latch ssscrapes her tummy – but she's in, tumbling head over heels on to a steamer trunk that, once opened, blows *mouldy old doughhhh* . . . up her nose. It's full of magazines: Club and Playboy and Mayfair (incorporating King). The girl on the cover of Mayfair kneels on a sandy beach wearing only blue gingham check bikini bottoms, her straggly blonde hair whips her honey-skinned shoulders – her face is turned away from what her hands are doing: her metallic-green-varnished nails . . . *grip 'er tits.* Jeanie's nails, each with its dark crescent of dried blood, work their way gingerly over her scabby calf, then begin to pick, *Aaaah* . . . – Shoved in between the magazines there's a thick paper-back – with her free hand Jeanie eases it out: 42 Inches Plus is written on the cover. She riffles the pages – tits balloon and shrink, balloon and shrink again. The glamour models' expressions are *squiffy masks of lippy an' mascara* . . . the riffling stops, and she picks out *dirty bunk-ups* . . . from the uneven type: *wet-pussy, stiff-cock, firm-arse* . . . On the opposite page Mumsie stares at her with furious intent – she's nakeder than all the rest, her boobs saggy balloons *left over from the party.* Jeanie examines Mumsie's skin inch by inch – she knows it as well as she does the immediate vicinity of the cottage: the overgrown garden with its dense and woody hedges, the hamlet of Dudswell, the canal and its towpath, the scraggy fields between this and the main road – the more kempt ones spreading up the hill to the woodland that stretches all the way to Little Gaddesden. She thinks of the bracken-choked hollows up on the common – and she looks at Mumsie's parted thighs, and she says aloud, I done all right, though . . . — She had to begin with at least: she got a saucer and poured the silvermilky lotion into it – she took up the paintbrush Mumsie used for Hughie. Jeanie's model stood on the stool in the bay window and Jeanie began to paint her into lifelikeness with broad strokes across her squishy tummy. There, Mumsie said, and Jeanie twirled the brush into her armpits. Go on, girl, she commanded, slap it on! and Jeanie did, painting greaves on to her mother's shins like the ones the Addressograph workers had when they dressed up as knights for Hemel Carnival. You have an eye, Jeanie Gruber, is what Miss Philbeach at school says – but that was . . . *my undoing*. Because her faithful eye coaxed her steady hand on into fashioning straps and buckles out of the Melathion lotion. The camphor-and-creosote fumes sucked the tears out of that eye, while Mumsie, temporarily soothed, hummed: If I were a rich cow, z-zz-za', zuzza-zzuzza-zzer . . . so soothing Jeanie, who used up the broad skin canvas of Mumsie's back tracing the long and curving feathers of a pair of angelic wings, incorporating into them the scattering of *rose-moles all in stipple* . . . between Mumsie's shoulder blades . . . All day long I'd mooey-mooey-moo, if I was a weal-thy cow –. She stopped, and her diabolical face loomed over her shoulder: What THE FUCK! – She kicked Jeanie and the stool away, strode to the mirror by the front door, turned her back to it, twisted round. – When she does the washing-up, Mumsie unscrews all the rings on the fingers of her right hand. Me knucks, she quips – and it was these that flattened Jeanie's nose, ripped her cheek and slammed her head back so hard that hitting the wall *a bloody mushroom cloud blew up me brain* . . . — Jeanie closes the paperback and shoves it down inside the trunk. There's a bottle of linseed oil on the wonky gate-leg table and a tobacco tin brimming with the maggoty butts of Mister Jarvis's roll-ups – tea mug rings *hula-hoop* across the parched veneer, and in the cluttery corners of the hut spades and mattocks conspire. Snap! a stick snaps right outside – *I'm gonna die like Lesley Ann!* She knows all about it – the graves and the tape recordings and the blondie with the perm . . . *coz the tipsy grown-ups whisper in shouts.* – Jeanie sees herself tucked up in the steamer trunk with the big-boobied dolly birds – Mister Jarvis wheels it along Tring Station's platform on a trolley, City gents ignore him, their newspapers held open in front of their folded faces. Mister Jarvis has always been friendly – taking Jeanie on his rounds when he fills the feed bins, tightening fences with a mole grip and setting traps for foxes. Mister Jarvis wears a bottle-green tweed suit in all weathers and a darker green porkpie hat – he saddle-soaps his leather gaiters, and, if Jeanie sees him first thing in the morning, his boots are freshly shined. If a man works on the land, he says, it don't mean the land 'as t'be on 'im. When he sees Mumsie he raises his hat and says, Good day, Missus Gruber, like he means it – not like Eddie the milkman, who comes into the cottage with the gold and the red top, the orange juice concentrate and the *dinners inna can*, and sits there smoking, using his peaked cap as an ashtray while he sips his tea and his eyes *give Mumsie a grope* before 'aving a fiddle with Debbie, which is *bonkers coz she ain't got her periods yet an' 'er tits're like two gnat bites onna ironing board.* One morning, when milk float and post van coincided on the bridge, Jeanie heard this exchange between Eddie and Mister Fitch, the postman – who looked *like butter wouldn't melt* . . . what with his *Milky Bar Kid hair* and *his Harry Worth glasses*: 'Ad a crack at 'er yet, the Gruber slag? Mister Fitch said. You oughta, she's gagging for it – shagged 'er old man so hard 'e ended up in Broadmoor . . . *In Broadmoor*. – Jeanie goes headfirst through the hut's window, grazing her grazes – soon enough her tormented wails will spool from reel to reel of the Grundig, and Miss Philbeach, pushing the button to kill her off, will say, Now, children, that's what happens to naughties like Jeanie Gruber who run away to London . . . The blood-drenched streets of which she pelts along . . . the brambles arching over Oxford Street tearing her hair . . . the bracken in Tottenham Court Road slapping at her bare thighs with its *pervy fronds* . . . She bashes through the rhododendron bush on the far side of Trafalgar Square and explodes into the wheat field. — Ssssh! she warns Hughie, who's making mud bricks in the back garden with a flowerpot mould. Ssssh! she says again – but his pea-green eyes only widen a bit, as, naked in his silvery ssscabies lotion suit, he piddles water from the rosette of the watering can. Jeanie secretly squirrels under the windows, rising up once to I-Spy at Mumsie, who's also naked, sitting in the Chesterfield, a bottle of Crabbie's within reach and in front of her on the biggest nesting table a pile of newspapers together with this week's copy of New Society: *Catching up on the week's news* . . . she calls what she does every Saturday morning, and . . . *Seeing what's what in my field, 'cause I'd be lost in this cultural-fucking-desert without my New Society* . . . Jeanie pictures Mumsie wandering across her field leaving ssscabies lotion prints on the soft greyish newsprint. Between her fingers her Embassy has mutated into a giant, ember-tipped pencil with which she scorches select phrases or traces classified advertisements with fiery rings. Jeanie doesn't understand how a field can also be a desert. I'm cut off from the world, Mumsie often moans, yet all she ever talks about with the Deacon and Jeffers, Silly Sybil and especially Kins, is the world beyond the canal: *Em-i-ess-ess-i-ess-ess-i-pee-pee-i* – They get Jeanie to stand on a chair and spell *eye-tee* while they fall about laughing – then they get serious, yakkety-yakking about bombs falling on Hanoi, and how disgusting this is, how Mister Wilson oughta do something more about it besides talk, but Jeanie doesn't see how he could . . . *the silly old white-haired man.* She pictures him sitting on the back of a water buffalo splashing about in a paddy field, trying to knock the falling bombs for six with his giant pipe while slitty-eyed kiddies in silky jim-jams and fruit-basket hats bow and bow again . . . *We are Si-am-ese, if you ple-ease.* After a while the grown-ups put another smoochy old record on and all shuffle about in their socks and stockings . . . *Fly me to the moon!* – which gets them talking about the Yanks again – the terrible Yanks this, the bloody awful Yanks that. The Yanks are dropping the bombs on Hanoi, and the Yanks are shooting nig-nogs in Detroit. – The Yanks, Jeanie thinks, must be the grown-ups' grown-ups, coz when they're slagging them off they sound like kids being naughty behind their mumsie's back. – Jeanie presses her ear against the back door's warm green paint and grasps the eight-sided doorknob. She knows every rasp the latch makes and her X-ray specs mean she can also see it . . . *rise an' fall.* In the scullery she touches every third VAT 69 bottle, *which makes nine* . . . This means she should take nine crawl-paces to get to the telephone table, where Mumsie's fat black leather purse will be lolling on the lip of her open handbag. There'll be florins and half-crowns and perhaps a ten-shilling note in it, but Jeanie'll only take ninepence – coz that way Mumsie'll never notice . . . *a stitch in time saves nine, a nine in time* . . . snips that time out – *OUT!* The *ages an' ages an' ages* . . . of ssscabies itch and dusty tickle are gone – never happened: Jeanie is back outside *up on me 'ind legs* and levering herself over the garden wall. She drops down into the musty-dusty tunnel that runs beneath next door's shrubbery – next she's on the towpath, eyes smarting inside the *flash cube* of the noonday sunshine – there's *not a soul about*, and the village slumbers as a great downie of cloud is pulled over it. *Heads up, girls!* Jeanie marches over the humpback bridge and up the lane, past the playing field, where the Batteram boys are playing French cricket, to the nooky shop. Weatherboard walls and a tarpaper roof – whorled old windows covered up inside by cardboard boxes full of mouse traps and fly-papers, Brillo pads and sponges. The nooky shop's warped shelves are tightly packed with boxes of Vim and Daz, loaves of Nimble and Sunblest – none of this interests Jeanie: it's behind the counter that the real stuff lives, not on proper shop shelves but in two old Welsh dressers that're nailed together. The right-hand one houses fags: Guards, Numbers 6 and 10, cool water-falling Consulates and Mumsie's red-striped Embassies – all stacked in any old how, together with tobacco in neat foil-wrapped bricks. The Deacon smokes Old Holborn – and when he's got a new half-ounce, he teases open the triangular flaps taking the greatest care, hum-ming . . . *spit on the mouthy bits of his water-rat beard.* Easing the little brick of sweet-smelling baccy into his tin, he abandons the foiled paper with its picture of a big half-timbered building . . . *like the pub in Waddesdon.* Jeanie knows the Deacon's nickname *is a piss-take*, but, still, there is a holiness about him – he sing-song-sips his VAT 69, and with a vicarish hush intones local indiscretions: bunk-ups, deaded babies, the pikeys' purple hearts, and what "Uncle George" – who answers letters in the Berko Gazette – gets up to in his "Children's Corner". Jeanie keeps the old Old Holborn wrappers in her special hiding place, under the floorboards in the room the girls share – they lie down there, another version of far-off . . . *London.* – The nooky shop's other dresser is lined with large glass jars of lemon bonbons, blackjacks, toffees and the fruit salads which are Jeanie's favourites. On the shelves above are boxes of Bazooka Joe bubble gums and Wrigley's, slabs of Cadbury's chocolate and Fry's Turkish Delight, Mars Bars and the *turdy dollops* of Walnut Whips. On the topmost shelf there's a long *ammo belt* of Barratt's Sherbet Fountains, each yellow-paper-wrapped cartridge of fizziness nipped and plugged with a liquorice fuse. Red-and-black liquorice bootlaces loop from the dresser's hooks, tangled up with elastic necklaces of sweetie beads. – The dressers whisper to Jeanie of the world to come, one of unfettered indulgence: a satchel full of bank notes, an E-Type Jag with its top down *an' filled to the brim wiv wine gums* . . . – She places her thru'pence and her sixpence on a pile of the Tring and District News, and Missus Pile puts her own copy – RAF PIPE BAND'S FLOODLIT CONCERT ENDS HEMEL CARNI-VAL – to one side and, looking up, cries, Oh, my! The state of you, Jeanie, you've bled all down yer shirt an' yer face is all swole . . .

You're one to talk! – Missus Pile's face is *all swole*: apple cheeks and a Superball nose chalky with lavender-smelling powder. Quarter of flyin' saucers, please, Missus Pile, Jeanie says, an' same again of blackjacks an' fruit salads. This'll leave her with a penny in hand – she'll get two liquorice laces, nibbling them will stop her gobbling up the other stuff too quickly. I fell over, she adds lamely, and Missus Pile tut-tuts. – Come in back, Jeanie, I'll clean you up and put some tee-cee-pee on that cut, it'll go septic y'know. – What Missus Pile knows is *what's what*. Missus Pile opens up very early some mornings for Jeanie and Hughie, and knows fine well their coppers have been pinched – Missus Pile sees the pink marks of pinches on Jeanie and watches her traffic-light bruises changing from red to orange to yellow. They're stuck gummily together, the neglected girl and the old widow-woman. No, s'all right fanks, Missus Pile, Jeanie says, as the jar is tilted and flying saucers shuffle into the scoop. Me mum'll sort it out when I get 'ome. That mumsie of yours –. Missus Pile begins emphatically, then equally emphatically stops, because, after all's said and done, *you gotta get along with folk*. – If she could muster the self-control Jeanie would limp back to London before gently unfurling her three tightly twirled paper bags – but she can't. She glances up and down the main road, back down the lane, then scampers behind the bus shelter. So long as she can get in unseen, Jeanie feels safer here than almost anywhere. If people arrive to wait for the bus and sit on the benches with their backs inches from her own, this only pushes her deeper into the jungle of shrubbery, where she fetches up on a rotten old log with the pottery shards of ancient ginger-beer bottles pressed into the dried mud between her plimsolls. *Stupid Jeanie's got no brai-ns, Soon she didn't 'ave no vei-ns!* . . . She lets fall an invisible black rubber ball, and in the time it takes to bounce she's plucked one, two, three, four flying saucers from the bag and *zinged 'em* into her mouth. The rice-paper capsules itch together, sharp rims stabbing the insides of her cheeks – one flies up to the roof of her mouth where it . . . *fitszackerly* – but oh! the stress of not biting when the sweet explosion would kill the ache of her battered cheek, the sting of her grazes and the *fucking ssscabies* . . . itching their way back . . . *inter me brain*. When Mumsie has clumped her this hard she usually goes all nicey-nicey. – In the darker months, limping along the lane, Jeanie will see from a way off the oil lamp Mumsie has placed in the front window, so its buttery shine spreads diamond shapes on the herringbone brick path. The oil lamp is Mumsie's way of saying: It's all right, I'll wrap you up in the woolly rug and chuck you under the chin. The lamp means *the drink that's warm as mink* in front of the fire, while Mumsie sips perry all ladylike and maybe talks wistfully of the holiday they had at Skeggy when Gregor was still with them, and how, when they got back home, it turned out Debbie had *tea-leafed every last knife and fork that come 'er way*, hidden the brightly coloured cutlery in her bit of manky old banky – the yard of flannel Debbie rubbed while she sucked her thumb. At least: It was a yard to begin with! Mumsie would guffaw. But as it got mankier and mankier – what with all her spit an' snot – I'd to trim a bit 'ere anna bit there, 'til all was left was a doll's fucking hanky! – Jeanie presumed the Skeggy incident – which was when she was little, and they all lived on top of a hill in Yorkshire – took place when banky wasn't so manky. Anyway, Debbie doesn't have a manky thing anywhere about her person now – nor does she nick from Mumsie the way Jeanie does. She irons and sweeps and sponges and scrubs – she's always turned out *neat as a pin* in her new Ashlyns uniform, or her Guides uniform, and when she isn't looking after Hughie and Jeanie she babysits for the Cooks or the Scotts, and she mows the Butterworths' verges. She works so hard Mumsie says, *You're a bloody little cappytillist. – Boom!* the alien spaceships are smashed to pieces on the rascally rocks of Planet Jeanie, their sherbet cargo liquefies into sickly torrents, their rice-paper hulls dissolve into . . . *nuffink.* She lets fall again the black rubber ball . . . – In the playground, when she plays jacks with Gwen and Fiona, Jeanie goes . . . *all cack-handed,* fingernails scccraping the asphalt – but here, in her jungle hidey-hole, she's a magician: the invisible ball rises and falls, the flying saucers disappear, then the fruit salads, then all the blackjacks but one. Her mouth is gritty with sugar and sticky with gelatine, her tongue slips in the slops – she looks at the liquorice bootlaces lying on her bare thighs – they do not appeal . . . *Stupid Jeanie's got no brai-ns, Soon she didn't 'ave no vei-ns . . .* She pushes her tongue between lip and gum . . . *Oh sugar! Runny honey, I am my can-dy girl, an' I've 'ad so much sweeties I could eat myself up!* – When Jeanie was Hughie's age, and her baby teeth, riddled with cavities, crumbled in her gums, she still went on nicking from Mumsie's purse, sneaking to the nooky shop and buying marshmallows that she stuffed into the sore bits the way Mister Venables pushed wads of cotton wool in there *when he come at me wiv 'is water drill* – but how can anything that sharp be water? P'raps it's a whirlpool that gets *smaller and minnier and faster* 'til the water turns into *the mole's screwy fingy in Thunderbirds?* Pain *smaller and minnier* until it's Mumsie's fingertips on the nape of Jeanie's neck as she gently brushes her thick, brown curly hair. Touch, *smaller and minnier* until it's sweet honey-runniness – its taste *smaller and minnier* until it's only the thought of wanting it lying on her tongue. – Jeanie's sat still behind the bus shelter for so long that a thrush hops from the hedge and pecks at the sherbet dust with its pretty beak. Jeanie's tears, hot on her cheeks, pitter-patter down on to the waxed-paper wrappers crumpled in her lap. The only sweetie left is a blackjack lurking in the palm of her hand: everything is concentrated into its capsule, the ends of which she pinches between the trembling tips of her trembling fingers – fingers stuck on the ends of her shaky hands, hands that in turn dangle from her *spazzy arms* . . . Arms that . . . *won't fucking keep still*, because they're attached to her heaving shoul-ders. *If I fuck this up, I'm . . . fucked.* She had a 10 mil' get-up first thing, and together with the black bomber, Genie believes this'll make it possible for her to sing songs, hold hands that *ain't shaking*, shout slogans, and spend a long day with Mumsie *without doin' the mad old bitch in* . . . The methadone *would 'old me* – but then there's living and there's merely existing. She exists in her Chinese silk robe in the icy middle of the big first-floor room – wonky straw blinds hide the dirty film of condensation on the windows, and this in turn obscures the hunger-striking trees leaning in the shit-daubed corners of the park. A paraffin heater sends up stinky convection next to a kitchen cabinet topped with fucked-up

38

Formica . . . *I'm all fucked up.* Slowly, Genie sinks down on her haunches, the scarlet silk billowing feebly about her scrawny shoulders, the garish dragon on the back of the robe taking flight for a few moments before crumpling against her pitiful spine. The bare floorboards are rough beneath her bare feet – the big Rasta on the poster she tore off a wall in the Kilburn High Road is . . . *screwing me out* as dark-orange drapes *swish in from the sides.* – Still, Genie manages to hang on to the tiny black capsule pinioned by these *gantries* . . . angled over . . . *alien toes* – long, white and twisted – *Ph-one ho-ome!* But she is home, and the scientific proof is the cat litter tray's moonscape of greyish rubble and brownish boulders. Beside this there's a saucer *licked clean – their tongues're antiseptic,* and she holds on to this fact as, holding fast to the capsule, she haunches towards it. The reek of paraffin is *hell's minge* . . . so she digs her chin into her chest to stop her tears falling on this precision craftiness: the two ends of the capsule ever-so-gently undocked . . . *bum-bum-bum-b'b'bum-bum, bum-bum-bum-b'b'bum-bum . . . under pressure!* The white *sherbet* plumes down on to the dish, together with ping-pinging little silver balls . . . *like cake decorations.* – Some mad old biker once told Genie these were what made black bombers time-release, so if you crushed them up *you'll get the whole hit at once.* Forcing herself level with the fucked-up Formica, Genie spots a teaspoon rimmed with the impurities left behind when . . . *the gear was sucked up.* She gives it a cursory rinse under the spitting tap, dries it on a corner of her robe, then billows back down to the saucer, where she pestles together her . . . *pick 'n' mix,* before spooning it to her dry lips . . . *The shells she sells are surely sea shells* . . . Genie titters bitter dust, and, lest any more be wasted, she gets down on her knees and licks the rest right up. When she peeks through her fringe, Butch the tomcat is sitting a few feet away next to a guitar case *some dipstick left in hock for gear* and staring at her with dumb malevolence. You want some? she taunts. You want some, you fucking moggy? Well, you ain't getting any. She runs the tip of her tongue round the rim of the saucer, purring, Rrrr-Rrrrrr! and when she looks again the cat is gone. The bitter amphetamine trickles down her throat, she swallows, her *ball cock* . . . rises, and she recalls the harbour-master in Nicosia, his cock . . . *pressing into me bum.* — At least it'd been hot there . . . The sun sliding behind the old castle, its softening radiance pouring gently on the oily waters. She'd entered into the charade: allowing his hand to guide one of hers on the shiny knuckles of the steering wheel, while she reached behind with the other and unzipped him. Barry, Mahoney and the others had their folding chairs set up on the front deck, their beers were uncapped and their Bacardi-and-Cokes poured. They were talking their usual yachtie bullshit about force-this and course-that, while Genie felt the complicated network of veins and vessels under the skin of the harbour-master's cock. *Keep 'em dry* . . . Genie's Cambridge education had at least taught her this: Keep 'em dry, even if they say it chafes, and maintain a steady circular motion – the way the men do when hand-cranking the windlasses. The harbour-master's garlic breath flavoured the back of Genie's neck, his hand slid from hers to . . . *twiddle me nip.* She circled his cock with thumb and forefinger to *choke 'im off.* – She didn't want him coming too quick: he might be embarrassed – they often were. Ooh, she'd moaned – You're so bloody big! she'd lied. Gosh! She turned her head to breathily encourage him. – Sensing the gathering storm in the wheelhouse, the fake yachties on deck turned up their own volume, Barry guffawing, Aye-aye, mon cap-i-taine! Touching the peak of his as the peak of the harbour-master's dug into Genie's neck and she registered the spurting against the back of her dress, then the trickling down on to the backs of her legs . . . *THE END – and a really, really 'appy one, as it 'appens.* Because he did the paperwork without asking any awkward questions. – Later, when the funny little chappie had waddled off the yacht and disappeared between the blazing-orange house fronts, Genie had rinsed out her sundress and was draping it over the taffrail when Barry lurched up. You done bloody brilliant, girl, he said, we're home free now. Genie drew down a great draught of the warm air, thinking, Fuck you, arsehole, and said, Gee, thanks, Barry, while Betty-Boop-batting her eyelashes. — The powder has dissolved in her mouth, all that's left is a nasty aftertaste. Genie's heart somersaults sluggishly . . . *Heads up, girls!* The cat comes back, hip-swivelling from the gloomy stairs – and without any ado it squats down in the litter tray and . . . *shits in me face.* Genie's robe has fallen open, and now the silk slips off her shoulders, exposing the crook of her elbow, where *a red liquorice bootlace* . . . writhes . . . *Stupid Jeanie's got no brai-ns, Soon she didn't 'ave no vei-ns!* . . . Her tongue explores the wound inside her cheek her teeth made during the short and terrible night. I could, she thinks, 'ave it all – I feel that ravenous. Yesterday I 'ad hit after hit of gear an' charlie 'til the stash was gone – now I wanna run screaming down Willesden Lane to Bliss, tear the cabinet from the wall, bite through the lock, an' be sitting there hitting up amps an' washing down Tuinals with gulps of linctus when the filth pitches up, drags me off an' bungs me in the cells . . . Where I'd eat my-fucking-self up, 'cause my flesh, my bones, my dumb guts inall – all of it'd be saturated with the stuff. I'd eat an' I'd eat an' I'd eat, and when the screw came all he'd see through the slot'd be my fat-fucking-stomach wobbling on the floor with a few bits of my stupid dyed hair stuck to its sides . . . — Bloody Nora! Mumsie exclaims, Look at the state of it now – look at the state of its hair! She stands in front of the barred doors of the Coronet, under a curled lip of flaking yellow masonry, and sneers out loud at her daughter, who comes clumping along from the tube in her high-top silver DMs. The coach is waiting in the side street, its engine indigesting so it blatts exhaust fumes against the legs of the women who're shoving rucksacks, straw baskets and rolled-up sleeping bags into its luggage compartments. – I thought you weren't gonna make it . . . Mumsie . . . *wheedles on, bloody old man Steptoe, wouldn't mind stuffing a stuffed bear up her jacksie* . . . Is it your coiffure that detained you? This U-turn into the well-spoken is for the benefit of Trot-along-Tina, who's appeared at Mumsie's side, looking shifty . . . *as well she should*, her split ends within *gnawing distance* of her big bared . . . *toothy pegs*. Hi, Genie, she says, what's that you've got under your arm? She's too wired, Genie thinks, to put on her working-class-heroine act, because belying her shapeless donkey jacket Tina's braying like the *well-groomed Surrey show pony she is* . . . Genie *does a Moses*: flourishing the eight ceiling tiles she'd *glued together earlier* and spray-painted grey in their faces. She says: It's a tombstone, obv'. – Tina puts her elbow in her mitt, sucks on a whippet-thin roll-up and says, Oh, yuh, that's bloody excellent, Genie – but Mumsie asks, Who's name have you got on it, then? Peering closer, she reads: GREGOR GRUBER, 1922 TO 1982, and says, What you write that for, Jeanie? He ain't dead – more's the pity! She laughs for Tina's benefit. Genie's about to say, Well, he's fucking dead to me, but the coach driver slams the door of the last luggage compartment and calls over to them, All aboard, ladies – or should I say women. He hauls himself up the stairs and wedges his paunch behind the wheel. His Willie Whitelaw face bears down on them through the windscreen, a supercilious smile plastered across it. – Stuck on the insides of the coach windows are hand-drawn pictures of tubby doves with olive branches in their stubby beaks, and cartoons of Cruise missiles being hacked in half by double-headed battleaxes. There's also a banner strung across the back window, and, craning round in her seat, Genie reads the back-to-front slogan. Embrace the base, she mutters – but Mumsie ignores this. She's beside Genie with a capacious handbag open on her lap, inside of which can be seen . . . *the predictable*: two packets of Embassy, a large bar of Fruit and Nut, and a half-bottle of vodka. Mumsie says, I dunno why you wrote Gregor's name on that thing, Jeanie. I mean, he and I may've had our differences, and he might not've always been the best father to you, but he loves you in his own way. – The coach grinds down to the bottom of Holland Park Avenue and swings on to the Shepherd's Bush roundabout. – London is this to Genie: a cold and filthy present through which the blurry Viennese past

43

is a pudding-faced old woman in a black sack dress drawn tight at the neck with white lace – a plump . . . *stubby-beaked* old woman who, as Jeanie reaches for the plate of sticky little pastries, *slaps my hand – hard* . . . – At least some people speak the truth – in this case, the mad old biker, because, as the coach accelerates past the Grantly Hotel (TV Lounge, H&C in all rooms, £12.50), Genie's heart revs up, and to tranquillise her didgy thoughts she rearranges her bits and bobs, removing half an economising ounce of Golden Virginia and a packet of red Rizla from her jacket and catching them in the netting attached to the seatback in front. – Like I say – Mumsie doesn't know when to *shut-the-fuck up!* – we didn't stick it out together, but we were both young, and with all he'd been through . . . he'd his mental problems . . . *Any man'd 'ave mental problems married to you, what with yer heels tied behind yer 'ead and yer cunt wide open to all comers.* – The women on the coach are of all ages, and, energised by this outing – which, despite its solemnity of purpose, remains a jaunt – they begin to sing, their voices raggedly disunited for a few minutes until they settle . . . *dumb-fucking-cows* . . . for the lowest lyrical denominator of, She'll be coming round the mountain when she comes! (When she comes . . .) She'll be coming round the mountain when she comes . . . Mumsie is at least silenced – but anyway Genie's elsewhere: behind the grotty poster-peeling façade of the Palais, where chopped guitar rhythms slice and dice her hurt and anger . . . *If A-dolph Hitler flew in today* . . . its strings . . . *cutting to the bone* as it *chukka-chukkas* on. She casts a cynical eye over the student lefties . . . *with pimply badges breaking out on their lapels*, and the older women, who all seem to *have lank grey 'air and granny specs.* She wonders if any of them *'ave the chukka-chukka stomach for a ruck* . . . and remembers the flyer Tina pressed on her when she came over to pick up Genie's coach money and her whizz: This is NON-VIOLENT protest, DO NOT BRING any weapons, or even objects – steel combs, wire-cutters, hairpins – that can be seen as OFFENSIVE. DO BRING: flowers, drawings by you and your children, mementoes – such as photographs or handmade headstones of war victims. ALSO plenty of WOOL and STRING to tie them to the fence. DO NOT BRING ANY NON-PRESCRIPTION DRUGS . . . *except, obviously, a bit of hash to chukka-chukka chew on and take the edge off.* – Genie wonders how a feminist collective can have *the brass neck to be this bloody patronising* . . . In the inside pocket of her leathers she's a flick-knife . . . *like any sensible girl-about-town,* and she'd've brought the hammer she keeps on the shelf under the leccy meter but it makes *too much of a bulge.* – Genie glances sideways at Mumsie, who's too cool to sing along and instead sits meditatively French-inhaling her diplomatic smoke, while tapping a screw head in the armrest with a corner of her rolled-gold Ronson: chink-chink, ch'chink . . . Mumsie's hair isn't lank or grey – it's a thick and glossy *mahogany – she should smell of furniture polish* . . . Trimmed short, it understates her precisely plucked dark brows, her neat nose and wide mouth – *generous! That's a fucking joke.* There's more makeup on one of Genie's eyelids than there is . . . *on her entire-fucking-face.* She must be knocking on sixty by now, but she still *knocks it back* . . . seemingly none the worse for this fluid wear . . . *She's prob'ly still gettin' 'er period – she might get knocked up!* Her complexion is clear – the backs of her hands . . .

always a give-away . . . smooth and steady, chink-chink, ch'chink . . .
She wears a blue-and-gold-embroidered tapestry jacket, neat navy-
blue slacks and ankle-high sheepskin-lined boots *snug as* . . . Genie
despises every fibre of her being and would like to pick her apart
. . . *right down to her cold black heart*, then string her up on the
barbed wire of the base's perimeter fence. *Black Irish, that's me* . . .
How many times has Genie heard her mother bandy about this
explanation for her good looks . . . *Yeah, black-bloody-Irish – black-
hearted, pissed-up, foul-mouthed Paddy cunt.* – Genie sees her mother
standing on the top step of County Hall next to the bearded
Provo and Red Ken. – Equally vivid is a vision of Mumsie crouched
down, her steady hands in the boot of a Morris Marina, as she
French-knits red, blue and green wires. *She ain't 'andy like me* . . .
but she'd love to feel the hard rain of horse's heads and bandsmen's
body parts on her face, hear the blast blow a mad fanfare through
the brass instruments before they clink-clank-tinked down on
to the black tarmac that had, in all probability, been laid by . . . *black-
bloody-Irish.* – The coach *chukka-chukka* decelerates past the Fuller's
brewery and Genie smells the dregs in the straights and handles
during those long nights at the White Hart in Little Gaddesden.
The two of them in the kitchenette's neon-lit nook, Mumsie
rinsing, Jeanie drying – and halfway through *my special treat: a fucking Snowball!* the sweet eggyholic smear across her child's lips . . .
no wonder I'm the way I am. The rant gathers pace inside her as the
coach pulls away from the Hogarth Roundabout, and the guitar
chukka-chukka-chop-chops faster and faster. At this moment of
familiar pain, her numb fingers clutching the threadbare heirloom

of blame, Genie has . . . *a weird outta body experience, like on acid* and sees herself clearly: the enraged childish scribbling of her hennaed curls, her *mucked-up mush*, with its silver mascara, heavy black eyeliner, slutty lippy and a concealer that has dried to a whitish mass, only exaggerating the lumpy eruption *I gave a dig to before I left.* – A thrumming bass takes up the beat: *b'bum-bum . . . bum, b'bum-bum . . . bum* – the guitar *chops kindling . . .* and Joe whispers, *Shouldn't go looking for trou-ble, Shouldn't go . . .* But he's not, Genie snaps, back in her own put-upon skin, and loud enough to be heard above When she comes! Eh? – Mumsie plays for time, crumpling her latest Embassy into the awkward ashtray. Come again? Genie near-shouts: Gregor. Gruber. Is. Not. My. Fucking. Father! Mumsie's knucks shred the smoky-tan rags unwinding from her nostrils. I dunno what you're talking about, she says sententiously. He's Debbie's dad, isn't he – and Hughie's the spit of Gregor, so what makes you think 'e ain't yours? Genie takes a deep breath, feeling certain that at last she's blown Mumsie's cover: Moira Fearing, *snide as a nine-bob note . . .* who took Jeanie up to Dacorum College with her, aged about seven . . . — Genie remembers the flags crossed on the wall – she preferred the red one with the golden hammer and sickle. I thought we were enemenies, she said, and Mumsie snorted, Enemies, pet, not pond life – anyway, that's just for show. – Also for show were the beautifully painted wooden eggs, and skittle-shaped wooden dolls that could be eased apart to reveal littler dolls, which in turn could be delivered of littler ones still . . . Jeanie's eyes grew wider and wider, until she clutched the littlest in her hand: a shiny bullet of a baby doll that she wanted more than she'd wanted anything, ever – and that she wouldn't let go of. Mumsie dragged her out back by the bins and clumped her – then she did. Mumsie snarled, You're seven years old, Jeanie, not seven bloody months! She shoved her daughter in the back: You can find your own bloody way home ... Which Jeanie did, trailing along the drowsy summer lanes with the egg she'd nicked earlier ... *stuck down me knicks.* – Mumsie didn't return until late that night, and she went to every other evening of Anglo-Soviet Friendship Week. On the last one she brought home a young lad *couldn't've been more than eighteen* ... who'd sleepy slanted eggshell eyes and the whitest of blond hair. Mumsie said his name was Vaseline, and he sat in the Chesterfield chair *shitting 'imself* ... despite all the tots they'd taken from the bottle of vodka they'd brought back with them. Shitting himself because he was probably a well-brought-up boy, terrified of getting into trouble with the KGB goons they must've had with them, or, if he were KGB himself, probably still more terrified, what with her knucks on his plump young thigh, and her Strangelove-making slurred in his beet-red ear, Do not deny me your essence ... — When she comes! – Genie twists in the seat so she can *screw the bitch right out*: Gruber don't look like me at all – neither do you. You're both small and dark like fucking gnomes – so're Debbie and Hughie, but I'm big and naturally blonde ... Mumsie's fist slow-motion uppercuts, its four gold knucks – purloined signet ring, cheesy half-sovereign, dumb Claddagh and fraudulent wedding band – fiery in the dark grotto Genie's anger has hacked from the coach's beige vinyl and check plush. Genie smells Lucozade burped from behind – sees

48

the Lucozade Building. All at once she's dismayed: her anger's great wave is buckling and breaking beneath her, there's nothing she can do but *soldier on*. Wotcher gonna do, then, Moira, she taunts, beat me up in front of all these nice pacifist women? Or – her fluency emboldens her – are you gonna try and manipulate me like you always do? Thing is, though, Rod – the singsong stops, heads are turning towards them – I'm not your fucking Emu puppet, so DON'T TRY STICKING YOUR FUCKING MITT UP ME! – The tinny p.a. coughs and the driver splutters, I don't give a monkey's if you're cocks or hens, if there's any aggro back there I'll have you all out on the hard shoulder before you can say mutually-assured-bloody-destruction. – Tina's ferrety face lunges between them. He means it, y'know, she says as the coach grumbles on along the Chiswick flyover, and, switching to her *reserve tank of dignity*, Mumsie hauls the bottle of vodka from her handbag, unscrews the cap and says to no one in particular, I think I'll have a little drinky-poohs. When she's taken a ladylike sip, she passes the bottle to Genie, who ostentatiously wipes the mouth with the hem of her T-shirt before taking a mannish slug. She offers it to Tina, who rears away to the back seat, where, to prove what a responsible and jolly steward she is, she tries to start the singing again: The people's flag is deepest red! but she doesn't have any . . . *fellow travellers*. Mumsie says, thick-tongued with pomposity, There's a time and a place, Jeanie, and this is neither. She turns *the eye of the ti-gerrrr* on her daughter, and Genie's so shocked by its dewiness . . . *she can't be fillin' up, can she?* . . . she looks away to the unplace beyond the window: the scrubby brown

49

fields planted with telegraph poles and pylons, a heap of car bones in a wrecker's yard, a slip-road to . . . *nowhere and fucking nothing*. – The two of them sit *outside of time* for the remainder of the journey, passing the Vladivar between them. When at last the coach squeezes through the constipated streets of Newbury and gets bunged up in a long queue of other coaches in a deep lane between a racetrack and a sewage farm, Genie takes the final mouthful, swallows and says, From Varrington, I zink! They both cackle. Mumsie says, This nag ain't going nowhere – let's vamoose. So they gather their stuff and shoulder their way past the other women, who are havering in the aisle as they chorus, I'm gonna talk with the Prince of Peace, I ain't gonna study war no more! Shouldn't that be Princess, Mumsie says, then Tina detains them: We need to meet up with our affinity group, everyone's been allotted their own section of the fence . . . She digs her gnawed nails into Genie's arm . . . And you've gotta write down the legal aid number. Lissen up, sisters! Write this number on your arm with a biro or a marker, Newbury – that's N-E-W-B-U-R-Y – 3-5-1-0-8. Don't write it on a bit of paper and put it in your bag or your pocket – the pigs'll do anything to protect their warmongering Yank mates. Women protesting here have been roughed up, hauled away, strip-searched and – she pauses for effect – worse. Genie stage-whispers, She wishes, and Mumsie laughs her naughty laugh. – They're clambering down from the coach when Tina calls after her, What about your tombstone, Genie? You can 'ave it! Genie calls back. But don't gobble it right up like you do all those other ones you blag! That, Genie thinks, was *inspired* . . . Tina's face goes . . . *redder than her politics*, which is paranoid of her, because no one else will know that tombstone is slang for the Tenuate Dospan diet pills she gets Mummy and Daddy's private doctor to prescribe for her. The driver bats his hairy caterpillar eyebrows at Mumsie and offers her his arm – then recoils as she honks Vladivar in his face together with, Cunting lovely to meet you, fatso. – Every step they take away from the coach is a liberation. Mumsie says, They were a po-faced fucking lot, those Trots, as arm in arm they march up the lane, weaving between the other women, who've spilled out from the stalled vehicles. There are genteel ladies in green wellies and waxed cotton coats – and young student-types with Rasta-style woolly hats. There are fearsome lezzers in leather – some with open cans of McEwen's in *their fat, finger-fucking fists* . . . Genie's cheered by the presence of a few punky chicks, their pink Mohican plumage wobbling as they hobble along – and narked some other women have brought their male children, presumably on the grounds that . . . *their pricks ain't big enough for patriarchy – yet* . . . Mostly she's simply overwhelmed by the great surge of statically charged hair and bright, waterproofed nylon that crackles along the lane, its placards clattering. It hardly matters the day's *turned out crap as-fucking-per*, with the earth's bad breath fouling the hedges. – Mumsie is prattling on: . . . that bloke Allason who was the MP for Berko, I remember him giving a speech all about a missile that could be fired to bring down a nuclear missile – that'd be immediately before or just after the Cuban crisis. Either way, you were very little and Hughie only a baby, and Gregor had had one of his turns and ended up in Claybury – though I said to our Debbie at the time, it ought to've been Broadmoor, which was nearer . . . Besides, Gregor could be a violent sod when it was on 'im . . . *Jee-sus, rabbit-fucking-rabbit* . . . Charitable view'd be it was the temper of the times got to him – I mean, you imagine they're gonna blow the world to buggery now, back then, for a few weeks at least, I was absolutely bloody certain of it. Had it all planned: I was going to drown Hughie in the bath, the rest of us were gonna have to take our chances with Seconal . . . *Decisive old Sophie – made 'er choice, no messing* . . . I'd a big enough stockpile, deffo, but there was no way of knowing how much to –. Mumsie breaks off, because, having passed through a choke point between a pair of cottages, the huddled mass fissions, individual particles shooting off across a wide verge towards the perimeter fence. – There it is . . . *the net we're all caught up in* . . . its chain-link mesh already covered with a mass of handmade cards featuring doves, rainbows, olive branches, CND symbols . . . *all the dumb, predictable stuff.* There are also black-bordered photographs, funeral wreaths and plenty of craftwork banners with sewn-on lettering, a rumpled cladding of sentimentality held together with garden twine, wool, thread *and their bleedin' 'eart strings* . . . Ooh, look, Mumsie says, there's wossissface Thompson – Hughie sent me his pamphlet . . . Tell you what, though, I dunno about written by candlelight, but I certainly had to read the bloody thing by it. Have you got any idea what us teachers have to get by on nowadays? Mumsie accosts a tall old bloke with *a badly drawn dove* of white hair and the face of *a battered eagle*, who shows them his *rotten teeth* . . . as he . . . *opens his beak.* Out comes bad breath and good words: I absolutely assure you that I do, he says, I live entirely on my freelance earnings now, but for years I subsisted on an academic salary, although it has to be admitted –. But whatever it is that *has to be admitted* is *shut out* by a woman who touches his arm and coos, Great to see you here . . . A second *groveller 'omes in on 'im* . . . then a third and a fourth – his white hair flapping, he's spun away from them into the throng. Mumsie gushes . . . *She'll get wet over anything that's got one* . . . I can't wait to phone Hugh and tell him about this – he'll be dead chuffed. Genie says, Well good luck with it, 'cause them old nancies he lives with now never answer the fucking phone . . . The speed and vodka had been keeping her sweet – but the encounter with the smelly old writer has soured it: he reminded her of Kins – and one thing was for sure: *They've both got one*, Hughie had one too – so did all the coppers holding hands along the fence, looking ridiculous in their baggy macs and . . . *bell-end 'elmets*. Besides, what were the missiles that would soon be *sticking it* to the warm silos if not *still more pricks*. The concrete fence posts *are pricks*, the wire strung along their tops *is covered in 'em* – the fog flowing round everyone laps at . . . *pricks* securing the guy ropes of a canvas stockade some *Robina-fucking-Crusoes* have set up, so they can wait however long's necessary before . . . *Man Friday pitches up wiv 'is big black one.* – A small girly ball of auburn curls and freckles in a red rain poncho bursts out from one of the tent doors as they pass and presses a flyer into Mumsie's hand. W-We're having a dragon festival next m-month, she stutters. P-Please m-make your banners at home and bring them on F-February the f-first . . . As they tramp on along the fence, Mumsie reads aloud: The word "dragon" derives from the Chinese meaning to see clearly, she is a very old and powerful life symbol – I didn't know that, Jeanie, did you know that? Genie snarls, No, I didn't fucking know that. Mumsie releases Genie's arm so she can fold the flyer and put it away in her bag. I might, she says, get some of the girls at school to make banners and we could bring them down here – it'd be good for their political education. Genie says, Long as you don't let any of those boys near this place, they'd go berko, they would. Mumsie tut-tuts, You don't know anything about my boys – they're nice boys . . . *Which is why they're in a fucking approved school* . . . Genie thinks back to the dragon festival she celebrated that morning: the dragon's lurid eye, its needle-sharp teeth and golden scales – all of it *puckering up* as the silk subsided between her shoulder blades, and she knelt down on the bare floorboards to lick the white powder from the cat's dish . . . *a very powerful life symbol* . . . *Bumbumbum b'b'bumbum* . . . *Bumbumbum b'b'bumbum* . . . *Under press-ure*! of booze Genie's heart staggers to a crawl – she senses the ssscabies of withdrawal starting to sneak under her skin, and thinks of David . . . *heaviest geezer I know* . . . who *must 'ave a prick like all the rest* . . . — yet came to pick up on Friday wearing fishnets, a pencil skirt and a platinum-blond wig crushed under a wide, floppy-brimmed hat. He sat at the table in the top room concocting his speedball with lock-picking precision, then hunched over *for bloody ages* . . . pushing and pulling the plunger until long after there was anything but blood in the barrel. Finally he pulled out the spike and nibbled up the *red liquorice bootlace* . . . He slinkied over to where Genie had hung one of her tableaux: plastic cowboys and Indians glued on to a photo of Monument Valley torn from an old National Geographic. The caption underneath was IT'S YOUR LOOKOUT! It's my fucking lookout! David had said. The filth'll have me any day now – but in the meantime I'll have this, all right with you, girl? — Mumsie's mask of concern is . . . *in me face.* – I said, you all right, Jeanie, seems you had a bit of a turn . . . Genie finds she is on her knees in the mud . . . *I've shit for brains,* with everything – the fence, the cops, the protesters – wheeling about her head. What is it, she puzzles, this force that keeps pushing all of this stuff – the Yank airmen, their trucks and jets, their TVs and their piled-high pancakes stuck together with maple syrup – against the chain-link until it swells . . . *fishnets fulla flesh.* Genie struggles to her feet, the punctured sole of her Doc Marten pisses out a jet of water, and . . . *it all goes the other way*: the second hand on Mumsie's Timex . . . *sweeps anti-clockwise.* C'mon, Jeanie, she says, it's nearly two – everyone's getting ready. – The implacable *force* is drawing all the women in towards the fence, some *silly moos* hold up pocket mirrors, the idea being to . . . *show Patriarchy its own ugly face.* Others have lit candles – wax spatters as they draw closer and closer, until they are forced *like the pigs* to link arms. Some of the women are singing, We shall ov-er co-ome, We shall over-come! Others chat away regardless. We're in a B&B in a village over that way called Upper Bucklebury, says a chubby middle-aged woman gesturing . . . *wiv 'er goofy teef.* Mine host is a funny old thing with two Pekes – I don't imagine she's got the slightest what we're here for, but then why would anyone come to this part of the world for a weekend in December. I mean to say, it's hardly picturesque . . . Registering the wave of soundlessness sweeping round the base's perimeter, the goofy woman falls silent. Genie staggers – and Mumsie says, Your blood sugar's prob'ly low, then *faffs* in her bag until she comes up with the chocolate. Tearing its wrapper, she snaps off some squares and passes them to her daughter. There you go, meat and two veg'! – The sick-sweet chocolate in Genie's ravaged mouth conjures up this: the dusty plush-puffs ... *tickling me nose*, and the teddy bear marine biologist with granny specs played by Richard Dreyfus, who says, *The digestive system of this creature is very, very slow* ... Too-fucking-right, Genie thinks, I ain't 'ad a shit all week ... Roy Scheider's *bumface* clenches tighter as he snarls, *What is this bite-radius crap?* – And still the fuggy world revolves around her hazy head – the ghostly trees, the bracken's flattened pattern, the scary gorse – all of it growing bigger and clearer, while the goofy woman's arm tightens in Genie's, pulling her upright, and Mumsie's predatory snout lunges right at her, fang-fag jutting from its pursed lips. Genie thinks: When that tooth falls out there'll be another one lit and waiting for her what's grown in behind ... Ten ...! Nine ...! Eight ...! Se-ven ...! the massed women chant, drawing out the delicious agony of the moment all along the nine-mile perimeter of the base ... *a finger circling the clit – not touching.* Six ...! Fi-ive ...! Fouur ...! The lust Genie sees in the women's faces is a lust for death – they want it, she understands, as much as the men who build, arm and aim the missiles ... Th-ree ...! Twooo ...! Wunnn ...! They're *gagging for it* ... their mouths all slack with desire for ... *Cruise cocks.* FREEDOM! The great cry goes up, and right away Genie yanks free of the restraining arms and unties the tapes of his life-vest and the kid – *some poor stupid hick like all the rest* . . . – raises his arms automatically so they slide down and out of the armholes . . . *You're welcome – and would sir like to try another sports coat?* The hands are poised for a moment: Claude sees there's no skin or flesh on them at all, only *cooked* tendons stretched over *white florets of knucklebones* . . . then . . . *it's the last roll of the dice, my friend* . . . and they're gone. – Already ten feet down, sinking fast, the kid's long-sleeved denim shirt twirls about him, his bell-bottomed dungarees whirr, and his pillbox hat oscillates – a white dot hopping from word to word across the sea's screen, *Talk about the moon floatin' in the sky, Lookin' at a lily on a lake* . . . The kid is twenty feet down now, his arms up and circling, his feet down and revolving the other way, his hips swing as he hula-hulas into the deep – that doesn't seem so very deep due to the amazing clarity of the water. Claude experiments, turning his whole head because his eye sockets *are filled with gritty sand* – he sees the sea turn from green to aquamarine to cobalt-blue to silver-blue to silvery to silver-white then vanish completely as . . . *I push my head up her skirt* . . . *Mm–mm, finest ear-protectors a fellow can get – flesh-filled nylons fitted snug to the head and dried with talc* . . . The kid's maybe forty feet down now, yet his dancing plummeting body can still be clearly seen . . . *Happy talk, keep talkin' happy talk.* – At Wright-Patterson combat veterans had told Claude that when their chutes collapsed falling men spun – even as the ship they'd bailed out of flipped up on its wing and spun away from them, while the Kraut fighter that'd scored the hit wheeled away too, so everywhere in the sky could be seen spinning things. *Talk about the moon* . . .

Claude supposes if the sinking kid could only tip his head back he'd see *my face floatin' in the sky* . . . but really it's too late for that – the kid must be nearing . . . *full-fathom-friggin'-five*, and the sunrays – which Claude sees flicker-fingering boots, tin cans and other slowly descending debris – can no longer touch him. The kid has almost reached the Emerald City's limits – Claude wonders what sort of how-d'you-do he'll get from the welcoming committee that circles him, their long grey bodies zigging, zagging and circling evasively. – What're their names? Ah, yes: Ivan Shark, Fury Shark, Admiral Himakito, that Chink shit-bird, Fang, and the sinister Barracuda . . . There's obviously no possibility of Claude warning the kid – let alone saving him – but for his own satisfaction at least he wishes he'd had the patience to decipher that day's Code-O-Graph, a useless mishmash of letters and numerals that, as he watches the first inquisitive shark nuzzle the kid's belly, only spools through his own soggy head *AM859R45HJ88* . . . At least, Claude thinks, I've taken my vitamins, and he feels for the morphine syrettes he took from the emergency packs in the rafts lashed to the bulkhead by the radio room. Reassuringly, they're still in the button-down pocket of his shirt, but how long can it be before the seawater *happy talks* its way up the hypos and ruins all those healthy vie-tay-mines? *All mine . . . this food . . .* Those other lunkheads – the green hands running round *like they were after cooze* . . . and the sad-sack sailors trying to corral all those farm boys, prairie boys and *banjo-pickin' freaks* so's to *herd them over the side* – none of them had the smarts to pick up any supplies before they *took the dive* . . . Yes, Claude snickers to himself, they're all

58

lesser men – men who didn't volunteer for the Secret Squadron, which is why they mostly . . . *flipped their wigs* when the torpedoes hit. – Those who didn't, *flipped 'em* when they saw their ship-mates flying towards them across the tilting deck, the fleshy streamers flayed from their arms and legs flapping in the hot air blasting from the burning fuel . . . *Flipped 'em* at the grotesque sight: the skin angels in flight, behind them flames flaring from the smokestack . . . *Flipped 'em* as the skin angels flocked to the fantail, where, too crazed by pain to recall the layout of their own ship *if they'd known it to begin with*, they slithered about in its dying blood – bilge water, piss and turds from the heads, melted ice cream and still-fizzing soda from the dumb gedunk stand – before launching themselves, screaming, over the taffrail. — Claude had seen them when he was on board, their fledgling wings spread in the hellish light – he'd seen still more of them once he was struggling in the water, as the mass of the sinking ship dragged him back. Although shocked by his searing slide down the hull and the cold impact of the waves, Claude realised: Either his abandonment of the ship had taken a fraction of the time it seemed, or there must be a great host of the skin angels – for there they'd been, high above him, each one silhouetted against the low, scudding clouds for a couple of seconds, then launching into the air, managing maybe two or three futile wing-beats before being swatted by the Indy's slowly revolving screws . . . *Quick, Henry! The Flit!* and crumpling among all the other black flies into the sticky pool of fuel oil that lay . . . *molasses* on the heaving waves . . . — Waves that now cradle Claude . . . *so tenderly . . . Embrace me, You irreplaceable you*, raising him up, then easing him gently down . . . Best not, Claude thinks, get too far down, 'cause then I'll find myself with . . . *roister-doister li'l oyster, Down in the slimy sea, You ain't so diff'rent lyin' on your shell bed, To the likes of l'il ol' me* . . . Excepting that: *Roister-doister you're somewhat moister, Than I would like to –*. What the fuck didja do that for!? The dumb Polack – whose name is Go-recce or something like that – pulls Claude's head from the water, tearing the sweetly salty sheets from his shell bed. Neptune's muffled subaquatic realm is conquered by this: the hurting disc of the noonday sun, the long hard swell of the open ocean, and, on the slope of that swell, the disintegrating chain of men Claude has deprived of a link by untying the kid's life-vest and letting him sink. – Again: What the fuck didja do that for!? Gorecki's two-day stubble rasps against Claude's, his *Chili Williams* life-vest presses into Claude's burnt back, his paddling feet kick at Claude's calves, tearing the saturated skin. I did that – Claude is *thucthinct* through cracked lips – becauth he wath dead. – He-weren't-dead. Gripping Claude's scruff, Gorecki shakes out his own words: I-heared-him-talkin'-when-you-was-untyin'-him! Aww, Claude croaks, giveth a fuckin' retht willya, Gorecki. The kid wath praying – thaying hith latht prayerth. He wath a Catholic thame ath you, and he thought I wath the Chaplain – the Chaplain been by a while back, the kid begun to give up, and the Chaplain went way over there, the kid thaid he couldn't hold out and he wanted to go out praying. What am I gonna do, Gorecki, refuthe a man hith dying whith? It's the most Claude has said to Gorecki in the long hours they've been *spooning . . . In your arms I find love so de-lec-ta-ble, dear, I'm afraid it isn't*

quite re-spec-ta-ble . . . dear . . . and he thinks it may be this talka-
tiveness as much as his explanation that pacifies the Polack, who
lets go of his hair. Claude's gaze sweeps over the beaver heads
of their companions as his hands smuggle the tapes of the kid's
vest behind his back, fumbling them into a knot *that'll do for
now . . .* – Whatever his other *little foibles . . .* Claude comprehends
this crucial fact perfectly well: survival is all about everything
having to do for now. Survival is a jerry-rigged little raft of flotsam
on the ocean wave – and if Gorecki had ridden him harder, Claude
could've euchred him any number of other ways. He might've
pulled rank – although he doubts this would've worked, given their
current communistic situation: officers and enlisted men, swabs
and marines, *all in it together . . . and me the only fly-boy.* Or, Claude
could've fanned out for Gorecki some of the choicer cards he'd
picked up censoring the dumb Polack's mail. – It'd been a strange
realisation, this, that seeped into him during the darkest hours of
their first night together, when, in fear and trembling, Gorecki spilt
the beans on his activities as a cocksman back home in his jerkwater
Pennsylvania steel town: double- and triple-timings he felt the
need to unburden himself of now, hoping, Claude presumed, that a
buoyant conscience might help him stay afloat. Claude didn't let
on he knew all about these *peccadilloes* already – to say sins would
be to . . . *dignify them* – because he'd read Gorecki's letters to these
broads, and, purely for the hell of it, he'd blanked out all the
ham-fisted endearments, while scrawling on the one destined for
Missus Gorecki, You're not the only one, you know, before sealing
and stamping it *kerrr-chunk! you asshole lunk!* PASSED BY NAVAL

CENSOR. Claude knew that for many another man – in particular a mackerel-snapper such as Gorecki – this crazy coincidence would be further confirmation of God's existence – the selfsame God who'd perpetrated this ALMIGHTY FUCK-UP on them all. Not Claude – *not me*. To Claude, Gorecki's secrets were only more of the flotsam folks left lying round for anybody to make use of who was good with his hands – flotsam such as the Very pistol tucked in Claude's belt, the malted-milk tablets and the morphine syrettes in his shirt pockets, and the drowned kid's life-vest he keeps stuck between his thighs – waiting for when Gorecki isn't looking to make the swap. What Claude can do is sneak out the fourth of the syrettes, nip off the cap with his teeth and stab it into his thigh through his pants leg – not because he's in pain – how could he be, when he'd only had the third an hour or so ago – but because *I can* . . . and because he can lie painlessly back on Gorecki's bazoom while . . . *pain is all around*. – A superfluity of pain, seared in the skin, burnt in the flesh and charred in the bones of these sailor-boys. Pain is in the saltwater eating into these wounds, and the sun hammering down on them – most of all, pain is in the vitals of those boys foolish enough to slake their terrible thirst with sea-water, who soon enough begin crazily ranting, then puke their guts out, some so violently they turn full somersaults. Pain is in the fists that fly when one of the boys dies and ten others gather round to fight over who should get his life-vest – not that these crummy pieces of shit are worth having once the penetrating seawater has been sopped up by their kapok stuffing. – You might ath well tie a goddamn thponge on . . . Gorecki's arms tighten round his chest, and the Polack grunts, Wozzat? And it's only then that Claude realises he's croaked aloud, because pain is in those arms around his chest as well – pain is in the legs that grip his hips too. Pain, Claude concludes, is in all human touch, no matter how gently murmurous, *Wiege das Liebchen, In Schlummer ein* . . . – A lover's sleepy breath in the hollow of your neck is a raging flamethrower, a mother's tender caress is the flail of tank tracks, a brother's helping hand is *a bayonet twisted in your guts* . . . With pain so all-encompassing, surely it's better to feel this: the warm numbness spreading out from his leg, and repelling not simply current pain but pain . . . *as yet unborn* . . . *In tiefer Ruh liegt um mich her, Der Waffenbrüder Kreis.* The Chaplain, who'd bullied, slapped and punched the shipwrecked men into tying their vests together, had indeed been hearing the kid's mumbled confession when a sailor on the far side of the circle flipped his wig, firing a service revolver he'd miraculously managed to keep dry. The padre paddled off to deal with this – and Claude let the boy die. It might be kinda funny to tell Gorecki that, yeah, if he wanted to get a fix on it – to read the bottom line – then he might as well know: Claude had killed the dying boy with courtesy. Death had been a sales clerk at Brooks Brothers who helped him out of his life-vest and handed him down into the deep. – Claude had once read an article in the Scientific American about the psychopathic personality. It said the psychopathic killer depersonalises his victim by turning a he or a she into an expendable it about which it's unnecessary to have any human feeling. Yet Claude knew all there was to about the kid: his name and his mom's and pop's names, and his sisters' and brothers' names, and where he went to high school, and the names of the boys he'd snuck into vacant houses with to poke through the lumber in their attics . . . Picking up an ancient ukulele . . . plink-a-plunking a few sad notes . . . *Hullabaloo-loo, Don't . . . bring . . . Lulu!* – Or was this all a lie – had it been Claude himself who hung the garbage on Old Man Olsen's gate, caught frogs in the brook at the back of the overgrown yard, and cried hot tears when he found out that one of the kids he'd played pick-up baseball with . . . *since we were knee-high* had finger-fucked Betty Spiegelman in the back of her brother Ted's rattletrap Ford . . . *The winds blowing . . . the savage old bitch incessantly crying . . . And the strange tears down the cheeks coursing – some drowned fuckin' secret hissing* . . . Anyhoo, the point being that if he'd had his druthers he would've killed the kid hours before, when it became obvious *what a righteous pain in the ass he was* . . . – Close it up there, man! Willya close it up! The Chaplain's cry comes to Claude from a long way off, stirring the thick sludge of painlessness he's lying in. Close it up, man! the Chaplain yells again, and Claude lifts his head from Chili Williams's chest to see the blackened faces of the shipwrecked sailors *polka dots . . . on the . . . bazoom of a wave. Ho, darkies, hab you seen de massa, wid de muff-tash on he face . . .* They'd all been dunked in the thousands of gallons of fuel oil spewed from the ship's ruptured tanks – then, yesterday, when the sun came up, *as if they weren't turpentine niggers already*, they'd deliberately rubbed more on their faces to protect themselves from the tropical sun. Some had tied strips torn from their clothing around their eyes so that blindfolded they faced the fusillade of radiation. Now all that

64

could be done was to . . . *throw de tar babies in de coal hole, throw de massa in dere too* . . . Did Claude really want to embrace the blackened thing that labours towards him, trailing behind it so many more the same, all of them . . . *turned uppity by disaster?* Not. He thinks, I would prefer not to – I'd rather stay away from work for the next few days . . . or years. — *Fat chance of that!* The Old Man does a trick with his hands – taking Claude's arm in a friendly Bing 'n' Bob kinduva way, then pinching puppy fat in his pianist's fingers . . . *He gets me every time.* And every time Martin Evenrude says the same thing: Feel that, kiddo, a span of a twelfth – so sing out, kiddo, sing out after me, Wie sich die Welle, An Welle reiht . . . that means, As wave follows wave, so c'mon, sing it! So Claude does sing out – and, as the Old Man had prophesied on all those walks back uptown from Carnegie Hall, he's never forgotten them: *Fließen die Tränen, Mir ewig erneut* . . . which is also prophetic, because on and on Claude's tears . . . *do flow.* — In the Recital Hall Pop seethed at the bohunk philistines who destroyed his listening pleasure with their papery rattles and moist coughs. He never seemed to see any connection between his own often quite outrageous public behaviour and anyone else's, nor did he ever see the need to mute his vulgarities – the drooly ten-cent cigar, his snap-brim hat with the Aztec band – or to harmonise them with his otherwise studious aestheticism. — As they prowl into the Park, Martin Evenrude stabs at the skyline with his cigar, snarling, Tin-can architecture, Claude, for a tin-pot town . . . The horses rise and fall on the merry-go-round, curvetting waves of cream and scarlet paint frothing with gilt. Tipping his hat back on his big head, and seemingly choosing to ignore the wild incongruity of the coconut palms springing up along the terrace behind the boating pond, Martin says, We'll take the long way back, son. We've sat in the great man's hall, so let's go by his mansion at 91st and Fifth – that way we can stretch our legs, put some of de ol' jelly-roll in 'em . . . – Claude wants to say, I can't, Pop, I'm only here to echelon in this cargo from Midway – I gotta take these down to Tinian Town and get them mimeoed at 20th Air Force Forward HQ –. But when he reaches in his coat pocket for the way-bills, they aren't there. Besides, his father is insistent, pinch-pulling him on at a steady clip as he complains about the sheeny swish Lozenge – which is the joke name he's given the singer of the Schwanengesang: That Lozenge, Claude, why he's a heldentenor – the Met brung him over to sing Tristan, he's got the wrong voice entirely for Lieder! – Pop's two-tones kick up white dust puffs from the crushed coral and quahog roadway, his cigar smoulders in his mottled baloney face. His father, Claude imagines, must've once been a handsome fellow, with a strong jaw, a neat dimpled chin, a sharp-shooting nose and clear blue eyes . . . *but not any more*: thick slices of fat are piled on his plate, and he can't see for the slaw in his eyes – or else he'd notice the Quonsets that've grown up among the Park's stately elms and flowering dogwoods, he'd spot the kinking lizards, and he'd react to the naked men who're lounging about offering up their jungle-rotted crotches to the healing rays of the sun. Moreover, if he were paying any attention, surely Pop, with his *pawshaw for a drop of the ol' aquavit* . . . would spy the group gathered round a drum of aviation fuel who're taking turns at holding an air-compressor hose under its slubbling surface. Good logistics man that Claude is, he's estimated the cost of this cooling method to be seventy-five bucks a can – on the steep side, certainly, but cheaper than persuading a transport pilot to take a case up to twenty thousand feet in his C47, then back down again, fast, which is what Colonel Midgely's staff on Guam do –. Woe to the fugitive! Martin Evenrude breaks in, and his son obediently translates: *Wehe dem Fliehenden* . . . Who sets out into the world . . . *Welt hinaus ziehenden!* Who roams foreign parts . . . But are these foreign parts? Claude wonders, looking over to where the grand mansions and apartment houses should face out from Fifth on to the Park, and seeing instead the shaggy grey-green shrubbery covering Mount Lasso, which undulates in the late-afternoon onshore breeze. – Since Claude flew in to Tinian from Guam a week ago, he's been troubled by these slippages: the past overlaying the present, so that the grid-pattern of roadways laid out by the Seabees suddenly slips down over the familiar shapes of Midtown and Uptown. – It's no help that some smartass also had the neat idea of giving these baking roads – which are steadily being pulverised by the jeeps, trucks and fuel tankers that pound the length and breadth of the island – Manhattan names: Wall Street, Canal Street, 42nd Street, Broadway and . . . Riverside Drive. Claude would also be forced to concede – were he belayed on it – that the torpedo juice hasn't been helping. Since he'd scored a couple of pints off some swabs who'd a gilly-still hidden behind the 212th's tech' area . . . *I can scarcely fuckin' see any more* . . . although they'd sworn to him that they'd double-filtered the hooch. – Who roams foreign parts, his

67

father chants. *Fremde durchmessenden* . . . Claude dutifully recites. Who forgets his fatherland, his father needles, and Claude can't take any more so pulls up short. – Their afternoon stroll has brought them looping over a spur of Mount Lasso, past the Army Hospital on 109th Street, up a perimeter road that runs beside the barbed-wire fence surrounding the Central Bomb Dump. Now they're almost home – home at the six-storey building on Riverside Drive where the Evenrude Family have been the tenants of a cavernous top-floor apartment since they took advantage of the Crash – and Pop's silver-plated trust fund – to move back from Norwalk. Excepting this: there's no apartment block here, its tiled mansard roof nipped by copper-tipped finials, its grey stone façade staring down on to the scary Hooverville on the far side of the streetcar tracks – there're only still more Quonsets that've been pitched so hard into the heavy earth that their footings are buried, more raggedy palms – and a curved signboard mounted on two thick posts . . . *a scythe – or a samurai sword*. Claude shades his eyes from the vicious sun and reads aloud: HEADQUARTERS 509TH COMPOSITE GROUP. Behind the sign there's a barred gate with two MPs lazing guard, beyond them the fence bellies out around a large compound . . . *which is itself within Tinian's compound, sailing on through Pacific waves . . . Heimat vergessenden . . . Mutterhaus hassenden* . . . Claude laughs – and Martin says, You may've enlisted but you don't give a damn about your country any more than you do about the home Mother and I made for you. No! Claude protests. It's not that – it's this sign: this is the outfit I've been palletising cargo for – scads of it, Pop. They've got a big armaments squadron, a troop-carrier squadron

68

and a whole goddamn slew of MPs too. Only yesterday I was down at the harbour offloading this super-heavy bomb hoist we found for 'em over on Midway and had shipped here. This is the hush-hush outfit they're razzing with this poem – he recites: Don't ask about results or such, Unless you wanna get in Dutch, But take it from one who is sure of the score, The 509th is winning the war! Claude, his father says quietly. Yes, Pop? You know I'm dead, don't you, son? Well . . . yeah, I guess so, Pop, I guess so . . . Martin Evenrude takes his time relighting his cigar – he totters on one leg, striking the match on the sole of his two-tone, and Claude is sickened by his father's scrawny shank, its bald shine cinched by a flesh-coloured sock-suspender. He thinks of the garter belt some joker had tied round the toilet bowl in the can of the Liberator he hitched a ride on from Hickam Field to Guam. Lying on a lumped-up cargo of mail sacks and flamethrowers, as the ship gained altitude and the scent of frangipani blossom was replaced by the stench of greasy hessian and aviation fuel, he'd marvelled: So this is what we've become, a fighting force of underwear thieves commanded by panty-waists and policed by snitches . . . *Freunde verlassenden, Folget kein Segen, ach!* his father – the lightest, sweetest, least heroic of tenors – gently lullabies. — A wave slaps Claude in the face, and sobbing the ocean he says, Yeah, I know, Pop: Who forsakes their friends no blessing follows on their way . . . But Martin Evenrude can't hear him – he's already ten feet down and sinking fast. His worsted coat-tails have drifted up to cover his head – while his snappy hat floats up-ended on the surface and his final words are fast dying away in the velvety canyons of his hopped-up son's head:

You're . . . dead . . . toooo . . . – Close it up, man! Close it up! the Chaplain shouts right in Claude's face. He has a sparse blond moustache, through the salt-encrusted strands of which Claude can admire . . . *the resolution of his lip.* Is. That. An. Extra. Vest? the Chaplain wheezes. He himself has none, and has swum to and fro across the sea's buckled deck plates tying the dying boys' life-vests back together so that . . . *the cir-cle will be un-bro-ken, by and by, Lord, by and by . . .* – Give it here, man, give it here! His lustful hands paw at Claude's waist, struggling with . . . *my garter belt – what's a girl to do?* Claude retaliates: shrugging out of his own now useless vest, he tears away from Gorecki's embrace – then, pro-pelling the murdered kid's one before him, he kicks out for the wave crest beyond the wave crest beyond this one . . . — A wave crest beyond which he can see the familiar flying-V pediment of the Fairfield State Hospital Administration Building, supported by its austerely slim white columns, as it slices through the ocean's heaving skin . . . *leaving no wake.* It's crazy to think he'll be able to catch up with the hospital – a delusion that's laid its febrile hands on plenty of the others: Claude's seen it help them out of their uncomfy vests and into the waves' embrace. He's heard their crazy babbling as they've swum off – foolishness concerning the creamily streamlined shapes they could see cruising along the horizon: Luxy hotels with shady patios staffed by smiling waiters serving ice-cold cocktails in glasses choked with fruit. Others of the damned – who Claude considered more inventive – waved their arms vigorously in greeting, then struck out for a passing desert island, shouting to the boys left behind that they could see Esther Williams, naked as the day she was born, frolicking in the crystalline waters of its lagoon. Yet more – the ones Claude reserved his most fulsome contempt for – broke the circle only to dive beneath the surface, because, they cried, they were twice-saved! – For what should they see rising up from the deep but the resurrecting ship, which, as she came, sucked up, through the jagged gashes the torpedoes had torn in her hull, all the dreck – the dud life-rafts, the unused ammo boxes, the matchwood furniture, the pissed-upon mattresses, the three-thousand-times triplicated telexes of never-to-be-fulfilled orders, the tar babies and the skin-fucking-angels – she'd spewed out when she went down. – This may've been the snafu at the end of the world, Claude thinks as he dips and rises, his legs scissoring . . . but how could I know 'til it happened to me exactly how convincing it would be? – There, without question, is the Admin. Building, its white-painted clock tower a lurching crow's nest, its wings wide open to receive him in their warm, red-brick embrace. If he were only Plastic Man he could stretch out an arm, flip his hand round a column . . . *and winch myself in.* Ssshhh-huh, ssshhh-huh, ssshhh-huh – Claude's breath roars in his ears – ssshhh-huh, ssshhh-huh, ssshhh-huh – and then: . . . *the sea's gone!* The sea, with all its multitudinous movements adding up to produce . . . *an absolute stasis.* Claude cannot move his head, and, although his view is *fish-bowled*, there can be no doubt about it . . . *I've arrived*: this is indisputably the association area of Canaan House. Ssshhh-huh, ssshhh-huh, ssshhh-huuuooo . . . Claude's panting clouds floor-boards mellowed by decades of dirt and polish, floorboards that spread all the way to the tall twelve-paned sash windows, with here and there a scrap of carpet floating on their waxy-brown expanse. On these atolls are groups of mismatched chairs – cosy Windsor and Morris, stiffer wicker and Brewster – the habitations of the Canaanites, who, hunched and muttering, perform their ritual sacrifices: setting fire to Philip Morris and R. J. Reynolds, then watching their smoke chiffon up to a coffered sky of cracked and sepia plaster from which hang . . . *eight oblong fluorescent suns. – Why Fairfield?* He might've been rescued by any of the other state institutions and VA hospitals he's patronised over the years – or Lexington, or a drunk tank in a big city lock-up, or indeed Rikers, where he did a twenty-eight-day stretch in '49, or – before his brother, Gertie, wrested away control of Pop's trust and Claude hit the skids – one of the old-style convalescent homes that hung up their shingles to the south of Washington Square. – Such as that quack Doctor Herbert's, where Claude would lie in cloistral repose, loaded on phenobarbital . . . reds . . . MS . . . anything he wanted, in fact, so long as he hit on the good croaker in the approved round-about way. – *And why this particular day – this time?* Chow time, because here comes Claude's doppelgänger, shuffling up the line, his moulded plastic tray in his trembling hand. – Seeing himself like this: stiff creases in his charity blue jeans, his red-and-white knitted ski sweater too tight, his hospital-issue slippers pitifully flip-flopping – Claude feels a compassion he's only ever able to experience when he's . . . *dissociated – yes, I'm dissociating* . . . Dissociating also from the other patients, two of whom, as Claude shuffles on to their chair-island, shuffle discreetly off. – Tears pricking his fixated eyes, Claude thinks, I was a tough guy then, capable of blowing the goddamn snoot off anyone who crossed me, the way I'd mine blown off at OCS. Hell, I'd still grab ass when it came near enough and kick up a ruckus if I was crossed. Things got too wiggy, and they threatened me with the jolt . . . or the knife, I'd bring it right down again, sweet 'n' low – make with the goody-lucid-two-shoes the way they wanted.The belligerent jut of Claude's bearded jaw as he drops into a glider and begins to rock 'n' roll, the digging of his elbow as he wields his plastic spork . . . *my gook-eyed stare* – all of it is expressly calculated to intimidate anybody: stick-body patients, tight-ass shrinks, bullying orderlies, spectral grey ladies and callow candy-stripers . . . *but not this one!* – As the tall young man with the long reddish curls brushed back from his bulging forehead comes striding through the swing door, Claude at last understands why here, and why now: *Gourevitch!* He may be wearing a threadbare pale-blue regulation dressing gown with CT stencilled on its breast, and holding one of the pathetic brown bags new inmates are given to carry their personal effects in, but Claude-with-the-spork makes him . . . *right away.* This is not – no matter what he may've told the intake psychiatrist – a man who hears the voices of entities that cannot be seen. Soon enough after making his acquaintance, Claude realises that such is Gourevitch's colossal self-absorption, he can barely hear the voices of *real, live people who're standing right in front of him.* True, he's wary – his button-black eyes sliding across the faces of his fellow madmen, trying to read them for potential threat – even so Gourevitch heads straight towards easily the most dangerous man in the room, creaks into the rattan chair beside Claude's glider, and, ignoring the masturbatory creaking and cunnilingual slobbering his new companion makes as he paddles back and forth, sporking *shit from my shingle*, sets his brown-paper bag down on the low table in the centre of the crazy little colloquy. Soon enough Claude will find out what's in that brown-paper bag: a blackening banana, a chicken sandwich made for Gourevitch by his still younger *and very sexy* wife and several packets of Winston – contraband he's smuggled past the orderlies who searched him and took his street clothes. Not that this will have been difficult: the Hospital's buildings – which are extensive, and mostly shaped in plan like heavy bombers – are some way out of town, camouflaged by groves of fir and hemlock, although *everybody knows they're here . . .* This tactic of hiding in plain sight is one that Fairfield has – here Claude relies on the jargon of the oppressor – *introjected*, so throughout its mad realm everything that should rightly be covert or furtive is instead out front and blatant: the orderlies sock patients right in the kisser, and there's nothing they can do about it because only other staff are credible witnesses. As for the candy-stripers, since they believe all the male patients have been exiled to sex-free Miltown, they've no shame: unbuttoning their uniform dresses to adjust their twisted brassiere straps, lifting their skirts to straighten their nylons right in front of the fools, who, in point of fact, *are still drooling* – because the patients are also flamboyant extroverts who openly discard such pills, or, if bothering to put them in their mouths, spit them out seconds later in plain view. When served a solution from the dispensary hatch, they sloosh it around and spit it into the dinky paper cup it came in, then drop this into the trash basket with all the rest – so that when the trusty comes along, the frog-legs of his mop scissoring across the *impetigo lino*, he has to sop up all this slop. – Compelled to watch his former self, Claude experiences considerable irritation: Fairfield Claude is trying to put the hex on Gourevitch with his bug-eyed leer, his frantic gobbling and his jackhammer knee. These are *the affectations of a novice . . .* one who imagines he can experiment with the role of madman, pulling it on and peeling it off . . . *a sweat-damp leotard lying on the floor of a walk-up in the East Village, goddamnit!* In the non-place Claude currently inhabits he's becoming aware of these annoyances: an old wooden hat-stand with a watch cap speared on one of its curling prongs and an umbrella sheathed in its tacky scabbard. – Oh, and someone yelling at him: *Claude! Claude!* – Back in Fairfield, Claude snatches Gourevitch's brown bag and, pulling out the banana, starts with the spiel: They say they found it, yeah? Found it with one of these, yeah? A midget sub, yeah? This . . . this is a midget sub, yeah? Gourevitch shrugs non-committally, Fairfield Claude, wise to him and repelled by the fishy swelling of his throat . . . *sooner or later gotta carve him a fuckin' blow-hole!* . . . continues: This is the H-bomb, yeah? Dropped outta a fuckin' boodlie-boo B-52, yeah? I know ALL ABOUT IT, MA-AN, ALL ABOUT IT! He splits the banana's skin with his untrimmed and horny thumbnail and tears it open. You wanna know why I KNOW ALL ABOUT IT? Again, Gourevitch shrugs, and Claude thinks, What a creep, although of what kind – MIS, OSS, Agency or Fed – he cannot be sure. I know all about this STUFF – he picks slimy fibres from the banana peel – about electrical leads that feed through banks of cut-out switches to the proximity fuses

75

buried in this STUFF – he squishes the banana between fingers – AYCH-EE, AYCH-EE arranged in shaped CHARGES – he moulds the pulp into roughly lenticular blobs – fuckin' LENSES, man, focusing the SHOCKWAVE, making sure that it closes in nice and tight into a CRITICAL MASS. He takes the blobs in his hand, squeezes them into a shaking fist that he extends towards Gourevitch's face, the bilious pulp oozing from between his fingers. – You wanna know how I know about THE BOMB, yeah? Goo spatters Gourevitch's dressing gown – he grunts ambiguously. – I know about it because I WAS THERE, MAN, calculating the Godly integral and Satan's differential – that's how I know to track the ballistic orbs and tridents through the heavens, ma-an. – Fairfield Claude's glider carries on creaking, his body rocks, someone claims . . . *there are a thousand million questions about hate and death and war* . . . But the shouting is becoming a drag: it's time to go – Claude gulps down his doppelgänger . . . *introjects him*, and falls to ee-lim-in-ating the seditious and the negative with firm strokes of his pen as he sings: Ho, darkies, hab you seen de massa, Wid de CUDGEL IN HE HAND! – A hand closes over Claude's, and Busner – who's now towelled but still dripping – crouches down beside him in the hall and gently withdraws the letter he's been censoring on his bent knee. Through the wall comes the *highly appropriate* cry, That's what the wall of love is for! Busner slaps the wallpaper and shouts, Some bloody quiet please – IT'S FIRST THING IN THE MORNING! though he knows it's no such thing: there'd been a few too many tins of Worthington's *on stage* last night. Sleep had at first been deep – but eventually the heavy ebb of his bladder had drawn him to the lavatory, and when he lay down once more it had been . . . *full-fathom-five*. Be that as it may . . . Busner thinks, as he holds the sheet of Basildon Bond up to the light shining through the transom . . . there are some advantages to living over the shop. He sees the watermark buried in the notepaper's weave, he registers *de muff-tash on he face*: in fact, several thick felt-tipped muff-taches neatly obliterate the address at the top left, the date top right, the salutation, the entire body of the missive, the valediction bottom left and – assuming the writer had continued pro forma – the first element of his or her signature, so all that remains is a single word, a surname presumably: Lincoln, the *L* with a trailing loop that whips across the page. Busner reconsiders this: It might actually be the place name – or both, in a medievalish sort of way, say, John of Lincoln . . . He summons himself to speak levelly and neutrally with the air of someone who both expects an answer and believes he will receive one: Why did you do this, Claude? But *Gummidge* says *nowt*, only persists in rocking back and forth *rowing to nowhere* . . . his reassumed neck-gear mangling into his lap as he bends, unmangling as he straightens, his *wurzel head* rolling about on his *stuffed-up shoulders*. – Next, and more infuriatingly, he clicks the dial on his little trannie and turns its and his own volume up: I tellya, man, I was THERE, and what I didn't know AT THAT TIME I made it my goddamn business to find out AT A LATER STAGE such as . . . NOW. Find out how the Godly integral fits in . . . Laird & Company must be overcome within ten days if the shipyard is to be saved from closure. This was announced last night following the first meeting of the shipbuilding committee . . . on the holy ballistics – a ball of enriched pee-you no bigger 'n a softball and tampered with, naturally, to intensify the reaction and . . . make immediate representations to the Minister for Employment and Productivity –. *Enough!* Rocking in the hallway of his own head, Zack cannot focus either on the homely newsreader tones or the Creep's nasal honks, so he's overwhelmed by both . . . Kilroy was there – some of it was pretty blue, such as Fuck your slant-eyed mother's cunt . . . of shop stewards will be going to London in the next few days . . . It might be, Busner theorises, slightly hungover lability – or the function of a successful bowel movement, for the longer he listens to the two wordstreams the more they seem to be mingling. He fleetingly entertains the idea that the Creep may be adjusting . . . *my own consciousness!* Deftly tuning it in and out, editing this random word collage into . . . *a surrealistic statement* that, *were I only able to concentrate on it*, would express the fundamental *Logos of experience* –. *Enough!* Busner squats again: Claude, did you read the name on the envelope before you, ah, censored it? Claude, I need to at least let whoever it is know they received a letter, despite their being unable to read it . . . I mean the fact that someone called – he squints at the notepaper again – Lincoln has written to them may mean a lot. – Accompanying Lillibullero on his trannie, Claude sing-songs: Fu-ckyou! Fu-ckyou! Fuck cur-i-osity, We'll fight for the old cunt, fight for the old cunt . . . – Busner senses stirring between his moist thighs and remembers yesterday morning when Miriam came to him in his bed, fully clothed and . . . *smelling of toast.* He remembers her *crumbling* into the warm hollow beside him. — From downstairs there were raucous noises: the Kid screeching, Back up, baby, back up! as Mark walloped spine-jangling chords out of his electric guitar. Zack likes it when their boys play with him, after all, the Kid is only a few years older, and what could be more therapeutic than play? Miriam is unconvinced – whatever sympathy she may have for what they're trying to achieve at the Concept House, she remains, Zack thinks, a victim of her own training. The residents' distress – which he concedes can often be *distressing* – remains for her symptomatic of definable mental pathologies rather than an unusual form of social phenomenology. When the residents are distressed around the boys, Miriam *backs up, baby, backs up!* into an anxiety state – one that may well be maternal, but that he still felt the need to tell her *yet again* ... is probably evidence of her own ... *unresolved attachment trauma*. Maternal! she'd snorted. And why the bloody hell shouldn't I be maternal, Zack? He rose up beside her on one elbow, admiring *her hairy brown mantilla* ... spread on the lacy pillowcase, part of an accouchement set Maurice had given them as a wedding present: fine linen having been superseded at the Highgate flat by easier-to-launder stuff, it's ended up at Chapter Road, enveloping slack old pillows ... *leaking dream-dampened feathers*. With a protestation of bedsprings he lowered himself to lick the butter from her lips. Miriam turned to him, lifting her leg over his hip, pressing herself against him with ... *elemental force*. Stubbornly he'd persisted, coming up for air and to say, Of course you feel maternal, but you wouldn't want to be a Stone Age mother confronting a Space Age child. She reared up at him: Meaning? Meaning, he continued, that there's no illness the residents have,

79

and if they did it wouldn't be catching . . . it wouldn't be contagious. Even people who believe schizophrenia exists don't think that any more – that it's some kind of plague. – All this had *backed up, baby, backed up!* between them many times before – the novelty was this: her taking his hand and pressing it to her breast, his feeling *with lancing intensity* . . . the many dimply depressions made by the machine-made embroidery of her bra through the cable knit of her pullover. She'd breathed buttery into his flaring nostrils and snuggled into him. As he caressed the back of her skull, stroked her rounded shoulders and massaged her slowly rotating hips, he'd exalted in the fine eroticism of a near-naked man together with a fully clothed woman, grappling in suburban daylight. The sexual should always be . . . he sort of thought . . . such up-endings of convention, the chance encounter of *egg-whisks and silk scarves* . . . a perfumed ritual . . . *held in a cupboard under the stairs.* She snuggled in closer, tugging at the bedcovers, trying to get at him, and he savoured the sandalwood talcum powder in the hot crook of her neck – pulling up her pullover, he fluttered his fingers on bare skin. – In the past month there'd been a lot of this: rumpling, rucking up, rummaging, pulling up and pulling down . . . *Surprise-surprise! You shouldn't have* . . . the familiar gifts torn open with fresh expectation. A week before, another torpid Sunday dropsical with rain and overcast by the imminence of her and the boys' departure, Miriam had frog-marched Zack into the bedroom and . . . *debagged me!* In the creaking bed she'd swung back and forth over him, gripping the headboard with both hands, her fringe flapping – and when the younger boy came tapping at the door, she'd leapt from the bed – a barbaric spectacle, turbaned by the lampshade, her breasts flying, her pubic hair beaded with mucus – snapped the key in the lock and viciously hissed, Go away, Danny, darling, Mummy and Daddy are talking! before remounting Zack, grasping his penis, and enveloping it in her vagina with an efficient dispatch that, even as they got going again, Zack continued to find . . . *rather shocking –* although the true shock was this oft-repeated banal and biological insight: A man's desire was an evanescent thing, whereas the depths of Miriam's sexuality remained . . . *unplumbed – at least by me.* — Now, standing in the hallway by the rock 'n' rolling Creep, he concludes that Nachträglichkeit isn't the right analytic concept to apply – but rather *a sort of double-afterwardness* . . . because . . . *she hasn't wanted me like this since before Mark was born.* He turns from the Creep and makes for the living-room door, only to find that *up comes stately Buck Mulligan* . . . and the towel retied about his hips is . . . *sustained by blood and ouns* . . . He leans against the door jamb until . . . *Percy points at the lino* – lino the previous owners had laid in the hall, the kitchen and the toilet, and would doubtless have put down everywhere else had the manufacturer – Zack likes to facetiously hypothesise – not discontinued this particular line because the workers charged with making it had gone on strike, claiming to the tribunal that looking day after day at its maroon rhomboids and beige discs was making them . . . *sick to their stomachs.* Which was how Zack felt after smoking Lesley's strong hash and staring into the squeaky world beneath his feet. Modernity has been *jerry-built* at number 117: polystyrene ceiling tiles cover the old plaster mouldings, clumsily cemented indoor rockeries hide the redundant fireplaces, and the original doors have been replaced with bland slabs. Next door there's at least . . . *a grotty authenticity*. Advancing into the living room, Zack's overwhelmed by a very contemporary messiness: the blue Sifta salt cylinder and the white plates potato-printed with dried tomato ketchup, the empty Worthington's tins and the crumpled cigarette packets. Then there's Clive, who sits cross-legged in the middle of this rubbish with an acoustic guitar in his lap, his balding scalp aimed up at Zack and *censored* with the greasy black strands he's drawn over it. My ex-per-i-ence is my psy-che, My psy-che is my ex-per-i-ence, Clive nasals in Brummie, as his ticcing fingers summon discords from its untuned strings. Then there's the far wall of the room, upon which the same geometric blizzard as in the hall . . . *ever falls*, and an unknown hand has scrawled shakily in biro: GOD IS WITHIN ME AND THEREFORE I AM MY OWN MASTER. This rushes towards Zack, as his visual field expands to include the smoke-stained nets haunting the bay window, the dusty swags of Indian cloth hanging from the back wall and the still furrier television screen that lurks beside them. He staggers, retches and, wondering if he might be having . . . *some dreadful sort of flashback*, presses his hands to his eyes and waits, panting, while phosphenes chase each other's paisley tails and Clive rondels on: My ex-per-i-ence is my psy-che, My psy-che is my ex-per-i-ence . . . until it all thankfully subsides. Whereupon he thrusts the notepaper at Clive and asks, You aren't expecting a letter from anyone called Lincoln by any chance, are you, Clive? – *Flaky notes dandruff to the floor* . . . Clive sets the guitar down among them. Panting, he rises and takes the notepaper, his bloodshot and *exophthalmic* eyes blink as they teletype along the blacked-out lines, he nasals the while: Hmm, hm, yes, yes – stayed on a farm between Lincoln and Market Rasen once ... Mister Treadagar, the farmer-chappie, he'd some faith in me – sent me out after the gappers'd been down the rows with their hoes, said I'd a nose for the one beet shoot uz grows ... – Clive wears a sleeveless Fair Isle sweater and nothing else on his worryingly puce upper body. The paunches of his bare arms waggle. Thankfully, his legs are clad in the blue cotton legs of a regulation Gas Board boiler suit. Secured by a single button, its top half hangs down over his wide arse ... *flayed skin*. Busner notes that Clive's speech, as ever, scans better than his singing – but it's always the same elegy for a life less lived than endured: a hoe's progress from farms to police cells or cottage hospitals, then prison or the long-stay wards of asylums, then back to the fields again, where he committed some piffling crime – pissing openly or pilfering sneakily – and the whole cycle started all over again ... *digging for defeat*. When he came to Willesden, he was carrying a green canvas release bag – inside it there was nothing but a tube of Palmolive shaving cream. Clearly, Busner remarked to Gourevitch, the only rehabilitation they think he needs is to be clean-shaven. – Although Clive, in common with most of the Concept House's residents, attends an outpatient clinic where he receives depot injections of Chlorpromazine that keep him docile for most of the month, Busner tells former colleagues – who visit Willesden either out of curiosity or to gloat with *Schadenfreude aforethought* – that Clive's medication is entirely unnecessary, and he'd be perfectly content without it if he could only live in a pre-industrial society, one decoupled from the relentless assembly line of work and consumption. Not that Zack has actually calculated the life-expectancy of a severely myopic middle-aged man with galloping blood pressure in an era when the only medical specialisation was in horse. Zack does believe Clive, Eileen and Irene hear the voices . . . *they say they do* . . . it's only that he and Roger think these are the internalisation of hectoring conflicts imposed on them by their mummies and daddies – and by the Big Daddy and Mummy of the state admonishing them to *work and be productive*, even as it uses the results of their labour to *stockpile the means of their destruction*. Zack had once sent a postcard to the German philosopher Adorno: a view of a Polaris submarine. On the back he'd sloganised: You say, No poetry after Auschwitz – I say, No love after Hiroshima. Irritatingly, Adorno hadn't replied. – He sent me a postcard once, Mister Treadagar. That were when I were in All Saints at Winson Green, the corner of that card, it were hard. I poked it right in the eye of this bloke what gerron me wick, the prick, an' he starts up blartin' –. Zack takes the corner of the censored letter – which is stiff *but not hard* – and tugs it gently away from Clive. For his maroon jowls and sparse black hair, for his jumbled teeth and the burn scar on his snub nose, for his Homeric attempts to convey in alliterative fits and starts the oddity of his odyssey through life – for all this Busner had loved Clive, loved also all the other Clives he'd encountered banging their heads against padded walls, or counting the raindrops on . . . *windows without views*. He knew it was these Clives – and the tragedy of his brother Henry's mental

84

collapse – that had radicalised him, made him determined to see every patient not as a function of their disease ... *but as a human being.* And it was this striving for humanity ... *and fundamental decency* ... that had brought him to this ... *pretty pass*, where he cordially and unthinkingly despised the ... *human refuse* he'd wadded about himself ... *as a tramp makes his bed.* It might well be that at the Concept House residents received no encouragement to play the parts of either patients or psychiatrists, yet ... *there's still no end to the bloody histrionics!* The living room is at last fully focused and properly configured: there's a mid-ground now, occupied by a three-seater couch covered in fabric the shade and texture of dried porridge, beside it lies a grey-and-white ticking mattress, upon which are scattered several sweat-stained pillows without their cases. The *ticklishness* of escaping feathers, the *fine filigree* of sweat stains – Zack is chilled by the grimness of it all, and as he turns to flee his scrotum *tightens up* ... – The Creep has disappeared from the hall, instead there's Oscar the dog: a black mass of fur and paws squirming and skittering. Inasmuch as he loves anything, Zack believes he may love Oscar – which is why the sight of the dog's muzzle is so angering: one night a month or so ago, Roger Goure-vitch, high on some brain-seasoning bouquet garni, decided to operate on Oscar's muzzle – specifically on the warty excrescence above the right side of the Labrador's worming lip. Zack returned from a meeting of the PA to find the dog supine on the kitchen table, with Gourevitch and Lesley bending over him, both wearing bloodied washing-up gloves. The scalpel in Gourevitch's shaking hand ... *flicked red peas.* Zack slapped Roger ... *hard*, then sutured the wound. With antibiotics from the slightly suspicious vet – it was too early in the year for the claimed lawnmower accident – Oscar was making a full recovery, but he whined if *the Nazi doctor* tried to pet him, and Zack believes Roger's behaviour may've been . . . *the last straw*. Bending to stroke Oscar, he thinks: The RSPCA will come down on us, along with the Meehans' furies . . . Good boy, he says, there's a good fellow! and: Walkies soon, w-w-w-walkies! The . . . *alarm bell* of frying pan clashing with stove makes both man and dog salivate. Others of the residents are up, soon bacon will be frying. Since conditions have started to deteriorate, Zack has taken to rising earlier than the rest, heading downstairs and champing on a couple of rounds of toast while he chokes down that morning's Guardian. Only in these periods of relative calm can he abstract himself from the psychic strangeness of the Concept House and project himself out into the still-stranger and more turbulent world: the world of Operation Prometheus, where nineteen-year-old marines cuddle puppies they've rescued from villages they've burnt to the ground. He can read all about it, then go back upstairs to bathe and shave, before being . . . *shackled to the rock once more* . . . put down his ancient jenny in the field behind Crofut an' Knapp's hat factory, he did, the barnstormer. Five bucks for a spin, he said – an' I'd hoarded all these dimes I got from chores in a mason jar. I was waiting, I guess – waiting for someone to show me the Godly integral and Satan's differential, show 'em to me from the skies . . . Five bucks! Five bucks! An' there's no twiddly-diddly-dee on a 'lastic for this feller, no, siree – up, up an' away we go, an' soon enough I see the roof of the hat factory, I see the railroad bridge over the river, I see the cupola on top of the house where I like to lounge readin' Nick Carter, hand down my pants, apple in my mouth . . . – All this *gnaws away* at Zack in the time it takes him to swing open the translucent glass door to the kitchen and enter. – The Creep, as he monologues, is *twiddly-diddly-deeing* a screwdriver to mend the broken plate-dryer above the cooker. It's a saving grace of the Creep, this: his indefatigable handiness – no job is too large or too small for him, he twiddles, he fiddles and he tweaks, he bolts, bangs and glues – and on several occasions Zack has found him poised precariously on the eaves, replacing a broken tile or mending the wonky guttering. On Tuesdays, when the other residents collect their National Assistance from the post office, he canvases them: Got any chores, my friend, small chores, five-and-dime jobs? For the next hour or three, while he re-hems skirts or solders the straying wires of portable record players, he's quieter – although never entirely silent, his face at once beatific and fearfully strained. It is, Zack often thinks, as if his very survival depended on changing fuses or grouting tiles. – The Creep has lost his red pullover and gained a rag of flowery cravat that's confused with his necklace, so that, as he twiddles, scallop shell, tin opener and amulets tink-tonk against the cooker, while the bacon . . . *frieshhhhh* and the trannie Strines: One little chap, had a mishap, broke off –. An *Aberfan* . . . of dirty dishes has slumped from the draining board into the sink: cereal bowls, saucepans, plates and mugs, all jumbled up with cutlery and other utensils, so that when a train passes the whole mass shifts and vibrates . . . Galloped away to where Joe lay . . . – The four women residents of the Concept House are seated around the kitchen table, all with cigarettes lit: Eileen has her back to the door, Maggie's opposite her, Irene's to the left and Podge to the right. As Busner pauses in the doorway, Podge is saying, I can make collages and paint murals and my name is Fi-o-na, using her teeny fey voice that Radio Gourevitch says is . . . *the china doll persona her repressive mother's white-hot anger has fired inside her*. Zack isn't so sure, although Podge's willed immaturity is . . . *impressive*: She reads the Bunty – which arrives every Wednesday, *piggy-backing* on Busner's Guardian – and carefully snips out the paper outfits, folds the tabs and glues them to the cardboard outlines of . . . *other even teenier girls*. – Irene takes a handful of Podge's thick blonde hair and gushes, Ooh, that's that new Space Age toning you've done, isn't it, luvvie – is it the lunar type or the honeysuckle? Irene's sharp features stab aggressively at Podge – what's left of her own hacked-off hair is hidden by a purple velour scarf bound round her *Nefertiti* head, the ends of which dangle down her arched and bony back. She wears a long tight stretchy black dress – and her chitchat bleeds malice: You're got such super hair, Podge – it's so thick . . . and fat. – Podge preens beneath her withering, while Maggie, face down, knits stolidly on, *clickety-click*, the ends of the needles wiggling either side of her sensible perm, and Eileen – her own hair a slovenly brownish mess – rocks and keens, her nightdress unbuttoned, the injection-moulded-shut mouth of her Barbie Jesus pressed against her parched nipple. – No one in the kitchen pays this any attention, any more than they do the near-naked Busner, who sways, assailed again by the same hallucinatory effect: the SOFT BROWN DEMERARA SUGAR packet on the table, the empty milk bottle, the Sunfresh bottle – all of it surging towards him, as the background of twiddling Creep, tangled net curtain and damp wall expands, so the entirety of Zack's visual field is perversely . . . *impossibly!* . . . in focus: he sees through the window above the sink the overgrown garden, its spindly weeds ignited by sunflash as yet another tube train batters the back of the house. Tracers hiss in from the corners of the steamy, smoky kitchen – he shuts his eyes and the after-image of the garden shines in maroon velvet. He feels a predatory yet impersonal memory hammering at his consciousness *againannagainannagain* . . . a vision he never actually saw – but will never escape from . . . *We'll meet again, don't know where don't know when!* But Zack does know when: *Now, we'll meet again now* – with the plaster dust trickling from the cracks in everything, the walls collapsing, the fragile psyches shattering, and the flesh that contains them shredding into . . . *trayf – all trayf.* Although his Uncle Maurice has told him repeatedly this wasn't so: Walter and Felicia Busner's bodies had been quite intact when they were found. His father's three pieces buttoned into one – his mother's breasts buttoned into another one. It was the shockwave that killed them, and they were buried the very next day in decent plots in the decent Liberal Jewish Cemetery . . . *which is not far from here*, as is Churchill's wartime reserve HQ: an investigative journalist from Red Mole had told Busner how a coal shed between two inconspicuous semis was the entrance to a subterranean maze of offices, bunkrooms and storerooms – a place of greater safety where *the Anti-Semite-in-Chief* could wait out the apocalypse while . . . *the Untermenschen died in their shitty little shelters . . . some su-unny daaay!* – The train has passed and the day is indeed sunny . . . *the trayf fries* and the Creep stops twiddling to turn it. Busner says, I'm afraid this didn't make it past our house censor. He passes the letter to Irene, who barely glances at the blacked-out lines before handing it to Maggie, who sets down her knitting to examine it closely before shaking her head dismissively. Eileen won't stop nursing Barbie Jesus to look – but Podge flaps the notepaper and squeaks, Ooh! This is funny! Didja do this, Claude – did you? Didja leave Lincoln 'cause it's the same as the biccie or what? Busner thinks, It's always food with Podge . . . Her nickname is itself a pained self-ascription: *Ooh, I'm so podgy!* And if he weren't done with such pathologising he'd diagnose her as . . . *a classic hysterical anorexic.* The Creep, who's still twiddling at the plate-dryer, responds to Podge by turning up his volume: The Shaeffer boys ate crullers for breakfast, and my how we let 'em have it – Mother said it was so dé-class-é . . . Still, crullers is circular, and cookies is circular – pancakes too. Anyway you look at it, most sweet things are either circular or there's a circular process to makin' 'em . . . Pop and me used to make the ice cream on the back porch, hand-crankin' that old bucket freezer, round and round it went – my how it gobbled up big grains of . . . gobbled up big . . . big . . . – Being lost for words is not, Busner thinks, something the Creep is used to: he ceases to screw the plate-dryer, drops the screwdriver and lunges for the canister of Saxa on the table . . . *a boy chasing a chicken!* – W-W-What's this?! W-What's this?! he cries, brandishing it – his scrawny neck is corded, his crazy necklace spins . . . *hypnotising the women.* Busner says, Salt, it's called salt,

Claude – and, retrieving the letter, he stalks out of the kitchen via a side door beside the stuttering fridge. – And enters what was probably once a scullery-cum-laundry room, but which Lesley and the Kid have converted into a crash pad, with coconut matting on the floor and Indian hangings pinned up on all four walls and the ceiling as well. Through a ragged rip a single low-watt green bulb hangs down, bathing the mildewed mattresses, a slew of superhero comics, the Kid's amplifier, his guitar and the Kid himself in an aqueous *brinelight* that ripples on his troubled hair. The hair, Busner thinks, says it all: it's thick, blond, and was once upon a time cut and styled with a sensible side-parting. However, the days of hitch-hiking and the months of squatting have seen turbulent new growth. Now the Kid's haircut floats on these waves . . . *an empty life-jacket* that no longer saves . . . *his parents' respectability from drowning.* Sitting either side of him on the edge of the mattress pile, very close, so all six knees touch, are Lesley and Radio Gourevitch. As Busner appears a polythene bag vanishes into the pocket of Lesley's leather waistcoat . . . *Fort – Da!* Busner elects to ignore this, as he does the obviously conspiratorial nature of their huddle and the smirks on the two older men's faces. Hi, man, Lesley hails him, while Gourevitch only flutters the fingers flying a roll-up up to perch on his lips. The Kid guiltily squeaks, Hi! and Zack hears the Creep's trannie in the kitchen: a vast work of pop-orchestral portentousness piddling out from its dinky box, accompanied by this tinny cry, That's where I'm gonna go when I die! Zack thinks: Asinine as it is, anything's easier listening than Radio Gourevitch. – The tension between the two men is far more savage than any of the other residents' mutual antagonisms. More savage, and more corrosive of the community than the women's revulsion towards the Creep – revulsion Zack feels should properly be directed at Roger, since Claude is his baby, his pet project, one he happened upon serendipitously when he was doing the work he'd believed would make his name. Without his association with Claude Evenrude, Zack doubted Roger would've got anywhere much in his career – he'd be another pill-pushing psychiatrist . . . *with a theoretical axe to grind*. Instead, the fortuitous escalation of the Vietnam War reignited public interest in Claude's story – and Roger was on hand to tell it. In the States, Roger Gourevitch went on air, at first simply to discuss the traumas of war, but soon enough he was the media's favoured pundit for all opinion fringe-psychological, a position he retained – indeed, enhanced – when he crossed the pond. Zack imagines there to be a sort of Bat Phone beneath a glass dome at Broadcasting House for producers who need to reach . . . *the fearless fink-fighter*: the monster of vanity Zack has dubbed . . . *Radio Gourevitch*. Taxied in from Willesden, Radio Gourevitch obliges by pronouncing on the sanity of Rothko and Ojukwu, or the likely behaviour of newly sexually liberated eighteen-year-olds, or mop-tops but lately manumitted from their fab' slavery. The kitchen-sink pop-opera climaxes, then fades out in a last trumping of tuba-kazoos and an angelic strumming of bass Jews' harps. What's eating you, Zack? Gourevitch asks. His tones are teak and well carpented, *a sailor's trunk with polished brass fittings*. You look like Tarzan would if he'd been told Cheetah was, uh, cheating on him. Lesley sniggers, and Zack says, Yeah, Rodge, I am being cheated on – but not by Miriam, Miriam is . . . — How, he wonders, did it come to this? When they'd first met – both barefoot doctors at Kingsley Hall – Zack had seen in Roger Gourevitch someone he believed complemented him perfectly: *the twanging yang to my still-callow ying-tong-iddle-i-po* . . . Inseparable, they'd sparred together, thrown the I Ching together, and gone on three-day benders beginning at the Scotch of St James and ending at dawn on Mayfair rooftops where the dolly birds floating on gossamer wings chorused with cut-glass accents. All this time they . . . *chewed it over*: together they gashed open the bloated belly of the West and yanked out its half-digested incorporations, munched their way through any remaining repressions and spat out its worthless projections. With his arm around Roger's broad shoulders, feeling the heat of each other's psychic energy as their faces almost touched, Zack had become convinced that they – and they alone – possessed the X-ray vision needed to see through the pseudo-events that surrounded them . . . *in the fibrillating heartland of sclerotic capitalism*. Together they'd reached the exhilarating conclusion that, far from Ronnie being the best and most radical proponent of an existential and phenomenological approach to so-called mental illness, *he hadn't gone far enough!* — . . . cool. – Zack looks at his erstwhile blood brother, at his high and noble forehead with its aurora of red curls, at his prominent cheekbones with their fiery Victorian sideboards, and thinks: hot – Miriam had the hots for Roger, we all did – Maurice included. But was this surprising? He had charisma, Roger, and he was a force of nature, thrashing his way through the tepid lagoon of London's psychoanalysts. — Roger and I, Zack had said to Miriam, are thinking of setting up a place of our own – a therapeutic community, that is. We rather feel Ronnie's lost his way . . . a bit. And Miriam said . . . *didn't she?* . . . That's a good idea. – After Sunday lunch, at Uncle Maurice's, once the boys had got down from the table and gone to lark about in the garden, Zack raised the tricky business: Roger Gourevitch and I would like to open a sort of clinic . . . We feel we could offer distressed patients a more, um, humane environment than they get in ordinary mental hospitals –. Maurice interrupted, a forked sliver of beef perturbed by his gestures: I thought that's what your Scottish chap was all about, absolute freedom, no drugs or other treatments, everyone pitching in? Yes, Zack explained patiently, that's what he set out to do, but, to be frank, he's become rather a victim of his own rhetoric and the whole thing has turned into something of a personality cult. Besides which, he can be terribly overbearing. – Miriam had laughed, That Ronnie! He's awfully authoritarian about anarchy – utterly unyielding when it comes to a total lack of restraint. Maurice laughed as well, and dabbed with his napkin the neat moustache pinned on his handsome donkey's face. Then he sat back in his chair while Missus Mac cleared the heavy gold-rimmed plates. In the past two or three years Zack had begun to notice this nimbus of anachronism forming around his uncle. Maurice had always seemed so with it, what with his fast cars and his brittle theatrical friends. But the gilded oval of the portrait hung behind him now framed a pre-war head: the hair Brilliantined, the collar starched, the spotted silk tie Eton-knotted. Maurice's very dialogue was dated: Here's

94

how! was his toast, and gin his poison, while what he feared above all things was people . . . *banging on*. Fidgeting with his rolled-up napkin, sliding it in and out of its silver ring, Zack had thought: He's probably rumbled already that I'm going to touch him . . . Yet Maurice was as elliptically discreet as always, only asking, D'you think you might be able to have Henry to stay there? And Zack, who hadn't entertained this possibility for an instant, blustered, Well . . . ye-es, I suppose so . . . Maurice said, Good. – Then, after pudding, when Miriam had curled up on the settee to gain Insight from the Sunday Times, Zack joined his uncle in the bright study, with its glassy gaiety of playbills: There's a Girl in My Soup! which, in Maurice's case, was . . . *not remotely likely*. There was no *beating about the bush* . . . Maurice unscrewed the cap of his Parker, raised a querying eyebrow, then wrote out a cheque for £35,000 to buy the two dilapidated properties on Chapter Road, cash down. Zack had sat there, stunned by his own temerity – the fat numerals hanging in the air, together with the soft rrrrip of the torn perforations, until Maurice fanned them away with the cheque. Taking it, Zack didn't know which way to look – Danny La Rue, it appeared, had been at the Palace with Roy Hudd, and Missus Mac hadn't emptied the smoking stand, which was full of his uncle's Du Maurier butts. Maurice, *ever tactful*, had said, There're strong rumours on the horizon of a merger between Forte's and A. N. Other. Nothing in the bag yet – by no means a dead cert' – but I do hold a fair number of shares . . . He laughed: Anyway, it wouldn't matter one jot if I'd to write it off entirely – suppose I'd to live down to a regular some-thing every week, spin it out a bit, it'd still be a very generous something . . . This didn't assuage his nephew, who tried to hand back the cheque, but Maurice hee-hawed gently, twisted his moustache and shook his long face – all that was required to silence one already so heavily indebted . . . — *And this is how I've repaid him!* There on the mattress pile sits Gourevitch and his leather-breeked henchman. In between them sits the Kid – Christopher 'Kit' Titmuss – guileless . . . *and stuffed full of their salacious plotting*. The Kid, now *a pyjama case* . . . but recently . . . *a basket one*, whom Gourevitch had picked out from among all the raffia tat the hippies flogged in Gandalf's Garden. The Kid had gone on the run from Uppingham, and such was his momentum he'd travelled full-pelt from public school into the power circle of the Aetherians. Gourevitch – who collected the confected arcana of the age the way Jungians coined archetypes, and who now referred to himself as a yogibod *with no irony at all!* carried the Kid back to Willesden and listened to him intently as he raved: The Great Cosmic Master was due . . . Satellite No. 3 would be brought into orbit, and those – such as the Kid – who'd evolved their cosmic consciousness would join together in a great spiritual push, lifting their bodies by psychic power alone up to the satellite, which would set course for Mars Sector 6, where they'd all dwell in peace and love with Master Aetherius and the Master Jesus . . . You're not bloody LISTEN-ING! Busner shouted at Gourevitch when he enthused about the limitless possibilities of the liberated mind to discover new and viable syncretisms. Recalling the expression on Gourevitch's face – a topological oxymoron, since Roger was simultaneously full of himself . . . *and hopelessly spaced out* – Zack now realises this was the precise moment when they stopped talking meaningfully to one another at all. Their nights in white satin had been ripped to shreds . . . *trayf* . . . and Roger fully metamorphosed into Radio Gourevitch, a one-man pirate station, moored in this suburban backwater and continuing to broadcast at full strength whether or not anyone was listening. – There was also the problem of sex. Roger had always been . . . *libidinous, aren't we all?* . . . but his powerful body began to writhe with the unearthly flexions of the Kundalini spirit, and after swallowing a couple of nigger minstrels Lesley had given him he spent most of one Friday morning house meeting sitting cross-legged, clutching his crotch and chanting, My dick is God, God is my dick . . . over and over again, until Zack had thought he would *stick my fingers in his eyes, my thumb in his third one and tear his bloody head off!* – Skinning up and smoking a little shit – this Zack hadn't minded, and with two or three of the residents, in the right surroundings and carefully guided, he believed LSD could have therapeutic benefits. He'd read Osmond and Smythies, and, while he thought the stuff about psychoses being caused by metabolic malfunction of the adrenal gland was . . . *balls*, he did find the successes they reported treating chronic alcoholics credible. There was a point, Busner had found, in the psychedelic journey when the ego consumed itself . . . *an ouroboric process*, whereby the tail of earthly desire was choked down by its own avaricious head. Safely shepherded through this dark and terrifying psychic defile, the day-tripper became aware his neuroses were a featherweight contingency rather than a heavyweight and unalterable given. True, within days – or weeks at most – the residents who'd undertaken the therapy tended to slide back into the mire of their maladies, but this was only to be expected: the social pressure to conform to the insane game was so very strong. However, they'd never discussed any rules for drug use in the house – any more than he and Gourevitch had had an espoused policy on sexual relations . . . *Why would we? Common sense should surely prevail.* — But that was before John Lesley landed on them, a Jumbo jet overloaded with Pakki and Red Leb', Rocky and Nepalese temple balls, its erratic pilot wired on dexies, yellow bellies, mandies, prellies and black bombers. Speed – Busner had deployed San Franciscan sententiousness – kills. And Radio Gourevitch had . . . *whined at my interference*: Aw, shucks, ma-an, don't tell me you didn't pop a little pep when you were sweating the books in med' school –. Besides, Lesley had chipped in, everything's cut with speed nowadays, why'd you think these chappies look so bloody happy? And he shook the cereal box in time as he chanted, Snap! Crackle! and Pop! Then he squinted at the small print and said, What the hell's riboflavin anyway? This was the previous autumn, when the three of them had been seated around the kitchen table on better terms. It was shortly after Lesley had joined the Concept House with the preposterous title of Multimedia Coordinator – Lesley, with his ank-on-a-thong and his lank hair weeping sebaceously on to his habitually bare and spotty shoulders, *I've only myself to blame for.* Zack had picked him up one night when he'd been at Finch's, roughing it. Lesley, he realised later, must've been smoothing it – because he was wearing a clean shirt and his hair had been washed within the week. He'd looked sharp and was drinking modest halves of Double

Diamond. – But, again, with clear hindsight Zack saw a tachycardic blur: Lesley had been propped up against the bar by pills, as he dropped the Shrimp, Terry, Stanley and Antonioni with a sort of aplomb, then spoke of his own photography and film-making – largely amateur, of course – and told of wildcat recording sessions: planting microphones in the soft palate of Esalen primal-screaming sessions, or insinuating them into Keith Richards's guitar case – *You can 'ear 'im shooting up back stage, ma-an* . . . There'd also been the noise-activated devices that, fairy-like, he had pushed under Beat pillows, so that, come daylight, Alex, William and Allen could listen back to their own freewheeling sleep talk. – Emboldened . . . *no, drunk* . . . Zack had traced his own counter-cultural map on to Lesley's: they'd coincided at the Congress for the Dialectics of Liberation, where Lesley had been minding Stokely Carmichael . . . *a gone spade, ma-an* . . . and Zack had breached the analytic confessional by bragging that he'd had at least one of the Angries on his couch. – Still smarting from a row with Miriam during which she'd *characteristically belittled me*, Zack had so enjoyed reinventing a louche and possibly dangerous persona for himself that he'd invited Lesley home to Willesden on the spot — only to end up with . . . *this*: he and Radio Gourevitch in cahoots, nuzzling up with the hapless Kid under the Bodhi trees bellying and the lotuses looping . . . *in the veggie light* – the three of them participants in . . . *a perpetual bed-in timed by a broken floral clock*. At least Zack could now acknowledge this harsh truth about himself: I was charmed by him, just as I was charmed four years ago by Roger. They both made me feel I was accepted – a younger boy invited to play the big ones' game. – Another Bakerloo Line train has passed, offloading its freight of silence – and it's on to this vacuous heap that Busner drops his bombshell: What's in that plastic bag? The three buddy-sattvas look up at him brazenly, and Lesley conjures the ear of the bag back out of his pocket . . . *then the whole white rabbit.* S'blotters, man, he lisps, I made 'em up with my little dropper –. Yeah, yeah, Radio Gourevitch says, you go from place to place, man – you're Johnny Acidseed. Oh, I see, LSD, Busner says, and, revolted by his own prefectural tone, he lifts one foot nonchalantly from the itchy coconut matting to scratch it with the big toenail of the other. It's a super-strong batch, Lesley says, super-strong and super-pure – I got it from this gone spade down at the Hippy Hotel –. I wish, Busner remarks facetiously, that all these gone spades really would be . . . gone. At this Gourevitch *levitates* from the mattress. Upright, he assumes all of his asinine hipster pomposity: he's fully dressed in a caramel-coloured leather jacket, cavalry twill trousers, cowboy boots with Cuban heels and a thin nylon jumper the obscene colour of crêpe bandages, from the rollneck of which his Adam's apple . . . *prolapses* while he blathers, Yeah, beautiful day, Zack, totally peachy. We – my good friends here and myself, that is – thought we'd go on a journey to celebrate the vernal return, a sea cruise, maybe – or a plane flight –. He means, the Kid is emboldened to interrupt, we're gonna take a trip. Radio Gourevitch's face . . . *is right in mine.* Zack stares deep into the emptiness of Roger's demonic eyes, while he hears muffled enthusiasm coming from the kitchen: This has been Johnnie Walker playing down the Radio 1 chart for this week, and that was Norman Greenbaum in at num–. I'm numb, Busner thinks, that's what I am: numb – and powerless to resist all these Johnnies . . . – He's certain Gourevitch has had sex with Podge – he's a hunch Lesley has too. He wouldn't be surprised if they'd *interfered* . . . with Irene and Eileen as well –. We need, Gourevitch pleads, to have some kind of a showdown round here, kick out the jams, shake up the snow globe – there're circles within circles, my friend, and it follows, counter-clockwise, there're repressions within repressions. Y'know how it goes, Zack: Jack and Jill, up that goddamn hill – but what if she don't wanna get a pail of water, man? What if she feels he's pressuring her to get it – he makes like it's a . . . a . . . mutual decision, but has she ever been given a real choice, maybe she doesn't dig water? Busner says testily, Yes, yes, I know all this – it's classic double-bind stuff, so what? Gourevitch rolls his shoulders and yawns eggily in Zack's face: So what, Zack? So what? You slay me with your so whats – your so whats explode in my face, man, poof! Poofs of indifference, that's what they are, a poisonous, radioactive indifference that, like, goes off whenever you get too close . . . Throughout this speech Busner stares, paralysed, at the *radome* of Gourevitch's forehead, even as this loudhailing alerts him that: *The predator is already inside – what defences I had are long since breached!* . . . f'rinstance –. For instance, what? Zack says, and Radio Gourevitch, running both his hands through his igneous locks, turns up his volume: Yesterday, man! In the park – I shoulda never gone after Claude like that, but you made me do it! I coulda majorly freaked him out – traumatised him! He coulda thought he'd been checked back into the goddamn Graybar Hotel! But Rodge, Zack says, Claude was about to . . . to pounce on those girls on the pedalo, you must appreciate that we're already on thin ice here as it is. The Meehans over the road – they're just itching to call the police on us. Zack says this, and he gives his freshly shaven chin a Socratic stroke before continuing: Are you sure under the circumstances that it's wise for us –. Yes, Gourevitch spittles, yes! It's the acme of wisdom, Zack – the antagonism between us is tearing this community to pieces. You and me, you and I . . . we gotta stop playing the alpha-male game – we need har-mo-ny, we need to dissolve our fragile egos into a group mind, and we gotta get everyone on the same plane –. Everyone? – Busner doesn't feel humiliated, standing there in his towel – the *Evo-Stik on my balls* happened a long time since. He moves to where the window is hidden by still more Bodhisattvas, all of them *on the same plane*, and, pulling them apart, he opens the catch. Out there, on the broken concrete, Oscar is coincidentally licking his balls . . . *faithful yet with beast*. Busner takes a deep breath and turns back to the trio in the room: When you say everyone, Roger, who exactly has had one of these, um, blotters? Gourevitch looks shifty – and shifts from heel to heel. Well, obviously it ain't just me 'n' you, Zack, the bad vibes are ricocheting all round the saloon – the chicks've all got it in for Claude, they'd murder him if we – he waves a leafy hand in the bulb-light . . . *and it spirals down* – weren't here to keep the peace. Ah, yes! Zack thinks, it always circles back to the Creep, whatever else he may be he remains Roger's baby. — The tale of their meeting was Radio Gourevitch's foundational myth: the fledgling yogibod was doing his part of the research that led to On Feigning Insanity in Mental Institutions. Zack had of course read the paper – it'd been a cause célèbre – but the list of co-authors' names took up an entire page in Science, Roger being just one among scores of pseudo-patients ... *though probably not the only pseudo-therapist*. Playing the giddy ox at some ghastly state institution in Connecticut, the young Doctor Gourevitch had come upon Lieutenant Claude Evenrude, once the target-spotter for the Enola Gay, latterly – or so he had managed to convince Roger – a political prisoner, held in asylums and prisons because of his principled objection to the bomb. That, and also his near-psychotic reaction to the horrors he had not simply witnessed, but actually helped to cause. – Wouldn't yours! Roger had gripped Zack's wrist with passionate intensity, and his isotopic eyes had smouldered on the drunken night when he first told him the tale. Wouldn't your conscience burn, Zack, wouldn't it? No wonder the poor guy's so disturbed, out of all those aircrew – and there were scads of 'em, three B-29s on each mission, more than a hundred men altogether – he's the only goddamn one to stand up to the Man and say, no, this was bad, this was wrong! Didja know, for the first few years after he was sucked into the system, he was still sending his separation pay to the victims! Sure, it never got there – but when I sprung him from Fairfield I got a stack of these pathetic crinkled-up brown envelopes from Admin. Claude had scrawled For the People of Hiroshima and Nagasaki on 'em, and trusted to the goodness of the US Post Office to do the rest. Poor sap! *Poor sap indeed* ... but what a beneficent friend he had in Rodge, who secured his release and had only begun to make his *dancing bear* pay for his keep – by dragging him from TV studio to radio studio to tell of his ordeal – when Evenrude *went on the lam.* – I couldn't blame him – he'd been through hell since getting busted in '52 for a stick-up that was actually a cry for help – I mean, Claude was armed with a zucchini inna sock ferchrissakes . . . – Following his own Hippocratic muse and generously funded by his wife's money – Caroline Gourevitch was some kind of department-store heiress – Gourevitch teleported from New to Olde England in order to undertake analytic training at the Tavistock. Then, a year or so ago, shortly after the Chapter Road houses had been bought, and the two of them were casting around for suitable residents . . . *could it have been fate, or simply an amazing coincidence?* After all, it defied any logic that they'd found each other once, let alone twice – yet there Evenrude jolly-well was, burbling about the bubble-glass Wurlitzer jukebox in the opulent squat behind the Langham Hotel that was one of the stations on the underground railway for GI deserters. Gourevitch had gone there to look for prospective tenants among the genuinely shell shocked and the Marvellous fantasists with their tall tales of dumping napalm from helicopter doors. Returning to Willesden with the motormouth in tow, Gourevitch was . . . *happy as Larry.* His explanation for how Evenrude had come to be there – C'mon, if you felt yourself to be permanently deserting from an Imperialist warmongering army, who'd you pick to hang out with, especially in a strange city? – rang increasingly false to Busner, who, as the drivel-filled days turned into weeks that, full up with gloopy monody, burst, splattering his logorrhoea across entire months, saw that Roger-and-Claude was a . . . *freaky creep of nature,* incorporating in a single entity all the madness and guile the pair shared.

Busner also came to believe the repulsion the Concept House women felt for the Creep – and their mysterious attraction to Gourevitch – was also a function of this sinister dyadic nature. — So, Zack groans, you've given LSD to Claude, what an absolutely tip-top idea – a wizard-bloody-wheeze. What possible good can come of it? You, Roger . . . you . . . surely you understand quite how . . . disturbed Claude is? He isn't about to experience a meaningful ego-death – he doesn't know where his ego ends and anyone else's beg–. You mustn't tease me, teasing is what meanies do . . . Next door in the kitchen, Podge's dolly-voice quavers above the wittering of the Creep and his trannie . . . and you're all frightful meanies, but it doesn't matter 'cause I'm like the Rainbow Girls, I'm going to go through the Spectrum Door to the invisible universe on the other side of the rainbow – Rodge and Johnny and Kit're taking me there, and you could've come too . . . She slides down half an octave into pained maturity *as the elasticised string retracts into her plastic back* . . . if you weren't such fucking arseholes! Cowed by this hysterical bulletin, Radio Gourevitch has been pushed to the back of the room. Trying for blithe, he fidgets with the machine head of the Kid's guitar, then says, She's an adult, Zack, she's got the right to make her own decisions – what exactly is the concept in this Concept House if it ain't that? — Busner has no doubts about Podge's adulthood. He's worked hard to excise from his memory the episode about a fortnight ago when, no one else being available, at her insistence, he'd put her to bed: Podgie so-o sleepy, Podgie wants bye-byes now . . . In the back bedroom of 119 she shares with Maggie, Podge drew her tartan mini-dress over her head and thrust out her flat belly, a sign he should un-button the jeans she also wore. He had stooped to the Snoopy patch on her knee, smelling minty toothpaste and the heady reek of TCP . . . *What was I thinking of?* Certainly not any notions of organic repression, as he tugged at her waistband, exposing the inverted triangle of her panties. A record player had started up in the next room *I smelt blossom but the branches were bare* . . . and his whole hot head had been caught unawares when she stepped out of one trouser leg and swung hers over *my shoulder, You need someone who's older* . . . and, gripping his hair in both her hands, rubbed her pubis lustfully against his face. When he toppled over backwards, she went with him, still gripping and rubbing while moaning, Fuck me in my hole, put your cock in my hole . . . To detach from her jerking cage seemed for elongated moments to be impossible – then he managed it: twisting her bony hips so they lay rasping on the boards, their bodies still conjoined but his mouth now ungummed. Stick it in! Stick it in! she ordered him, mysteriously possessed by the embittered spirit of the RSM who'd bellowed at Zack during rifle training, and meaning . . . *the blunt bayonet fixed in my groin.* Busner's National Service had ended shortly afterwards – cut off by a strangulated hernia, but in the poky bedroom the straw dummy was still twisting . . . *foam on her lips* as he'd slammed the door behind him and held its knob tight. Behind it parade-ground barks became waste-ground moans, then, know-ing perfectly well he shouldn't, *for nothing protects her virtue stronger than sickness*, he peeked back inside, only to see Podge – now naked except for the fan belt of her panties stretched between her juddering calves – *robot-crab-walking to nowhere* . . . on one of the rumpled single beds. – He'd shut the door again, retreated across the landing, down the stairs, out the front door, into 117, gone to the fridge, got out a packet of Family Choice sausages Miriam had bought at the Tesco's on the High Road that afternoon, opened out the waxed-paper packet and thrust his throbbing penis between their pinkly piebald skins. 3/2d they had cost – with the need to economise he noticed such things . . . *3/2d* . . . *3/2* . . . *3* into *2 doesn't go, let alone Roger, Lesley and me into* . . . *Podge.* His own behaviour had been . . . *highly reprehensible*, the sausage rolling . . . *disturbing.* But at least he had resisted the oceanic pull of Podge's raging lust — and it's with his own restraint self-righteously in mind that he rounds on Roger: What the bloody hell makes you think –. Then equally emphatically Zack stops, because to raise this matter of Podge's ability to consent would be to . . . *drag the whole filthy business up*: a corpse pulled from dank waters, with mucus-smeared eels jostling for precedence as they exited through its eye sockets . . . *three into two doesn't go* . . . Lesley says, The point is, yeah, that we're all heading through the Spectrum Door – me, Rodge, the Kid here, Claude and Podge too. 'Course, it'd be super-cool if everyone else'd come along with us, but Podge can be the chicks' sorta spokeswoman . . . or delegate – that sorta thing. Zack looks down on the Multimedia Coordinator and reflects that, yes, there is *a sorta truth* in his job title, because that's what Lesley does: channel sounds and visions deep inside vulnerable psyches. Then he turns to Roger Gourevitch and says, What about me? Roger props the Kid's guitar carefully against the amplifier and turns to him. You? he says, you're it, Zack – you're the berries. We don't go nowhere with-out you, man – you're the Howdy-Doody man, we're only puppets. Lesley has fiddled from filmy folds a tiny postage stamp of blotting paper that he now holds out to Zack on the palm of his hand . . . *the black spot!* Zack recoils: Oh, no, I really don't think so! I'd better be the, um, guide for this one, chaps, keep things under control, make sure the setting is safe – no visitors, that sort of thing. Besides, if this stuff is as potent as you say, John, you may well need me to go down to Brody's . . . again. — Why it's necessary to remind them of this incident Busner cannot imagine – unless it's that they think . . . *I was so shocked or drunk I don't remember* the model psychosis the pair of them had induced in Irene – which was how Gourevitch had justified giving her LSD. *A ridiculous, foolhardy idea!* because whether you labelled this condition mental illness or not, Irene was permanently in a model psychosis, racketing around the Concept House, her velour scarves and gypsy shawls flying in the slipstream of her eurhythmic lunacy: I am the wind, darlings! I am the sky and the clouds too! I am the birds, darlings – see me swoop and dive! *And see her nest*, which is what Irene did at the very zenith of the trip's parabola, after sneaking away from Gourevitch and Lesley to remove all the light bulbs from the bedrooms. – When he got back from the pub, Zack found her naked and brooding in the airing cupboard, her buttocks and thighs covered in blood. It was patently useless getting Gourevitch and Lesley to deal with the situation – they were squirming around on the living-room floor of 117 . . . *caterpillars who'd eaten their own toadstool.* So once he'd been to the chemist – where the pharmacist was young, compliant . . .

and female to boot – Zack injected all three of them with Chlor-promazine. As soon as the astral pilots were back on the ground, he'd suggested to them ... *in no uncertain terms* ... that they stay there. — Well, yes, Gourevitch says, we're not about to forget that friggin' Nazi-jackboot bring-down, now are we ... But if things get a bit screwy again, you can fill us out another little RX –. What! Busner cries, you must be bonkers, Roger – you expect me to walk into a suburban chemist completely intoxicated by an illegal drug and hand them a prescription that's at best professionally dubious? Caroline-bloody-Coon won't save my bacon: it's a recipe for getting oneself struck off! *The Nabob sobs on* ... Anyway, it's completely academic, Roger, because I'm not taking one of these bloody things – no matter how gone the spade who sold it to Lesley was. – He senatorially hitches his towel higher on his hips and turns to leave – only then recalling why he came in to begin with: Any of you chaps know anything about this? He gives the censored letter to Lesley, who glances at it cursorily, then passes it to Radio Goure-vitch. Roger takes his time, holding the notepaper under the green light, his lips pursed, humming – clearly he's going to come up with some *claptrap about Claude's discourse of negation* ... Then the Kid taps on the letter from below and says, Um, Lincoln ... I recognise that handwriting, that's Michael Lincoln ... Oh, Busner says, and who's he when he's at home? The Kid looks at his bare feet shamefacedly, muttering, He's, um ... he's my guardian y'see, and I think he might be coming to visit me. Busner looks at the Kid, who's already sweaty in his cheesecloth shirt. Why, he thinks meanly, would anyone want to visit that face full of pimples and bum fluff? But he says, Well, let's hope he doesn't pitch up today, shall we? I don't imagine anyone's guar–. And breaks off because Irene has . . . *batted into the room.* She leans, panting, in the doorway, although Busner has the nauseating sensation that . . . *she's flown straight into my face!* Chris, Chris, she pants, there's a phone call for you . . . Only then do they all realise that for the past few minutes the telephone has been ringing, its Answer-me! Answer-me! echoing in the hall, each insistent peal . . . *eating into us* and cranking up the tension between them still more. Busner sighs, Gourevitch too – Lesley gives a yelping laugh. Irene says, It's someone called Lincoln, Chris, he says he's in a phone box and he hasn't got much change . . . In the hall the Kid picks up the receiver and presses it to his ear, she can hear the long fetch of his sigh and pictures Maurice holding the instrument with one manicured hand, while the other wields a toothpick to spear a cube of Turkish delight. Maurice says, He isn't going to arrange for Henry to stay in Willesden, is he, my dear? Miriam thinks, If I carry on pressing the phone this hard against my ear, it'll knit with my skull . . . But she only says: No, Uncle, I don't believe he is . . . — Miriam calls her husband's uncle, Uncle, not because she hasn't enough uncles and aunts of her own, but, on the contrary, because she has . . . *too bloody many of them!* Uncles bald as eggs who wear open-toed sandals, drive Austin 7s and canvas for Jeremy Thorpe – others who import Meissen to premises beneath the arches of Broad Street Station, and who, when she was a little girl, took her deep in there, among the resinous packing cases, and pulled out pink-and-white shepherdesses for her to admire, lying on . . . *their afterbirth of frizzy straw.* Miriam has yet more uncles, including apostates who have married out: there's one who has a goatee, does something utterly unacceptable in the motor trade and is married to a bottle-blonde from Leicester. Then there are the aunts – some with crazy two-tone hair, their wigs are . . . *that bloody obvious,* and others, less pious, who still Marcel and *smoke like billy-o,* cigarettes, cheroots as well – and there's an especially scary pipe-smoking one: Tante Mitzi, whose corsetted bulk and deep, curved creases from lip to chin earned her the nickname the Boar from Miriam's brother Felix. Ach! the Boar would exclaim each time she relit her trumpet-shaped meerschaum. Now I am burrrning ze Turk! Tante Mitzi's exaggeratedly rolled r's are, Miriam's always feels, proof of her ineradicably . . . *schweinish nature.* This despite her having been the first of Miriam's mother's siblings to have left, fleeing Berlin following her active participation in the *Sparrrtakusaufstand* . . . a blooding which cost her her left leg – or so the Boar madly claims, each time she removes the tin of Presbyterian Mixture from the small cedar-wood box bolted to the steel spavins of the prosthetic leg Onkel Herschel made for her. Madly, because Miriam and the other children – including Boopsie, the youngest – all remember perfectly well when it was cut off. It was inevitable, given such a large family – many of whom were either doctors or other kinds of physiological technicians – that these squeamish matters were the subject of noisy debate. There was Onkel Hermann, the much teased osteopath, Tante Frieda, the openly derided naturopath, and of course Onkel Herschel, who, having providentially made a small fortune during the war from the manufacture and sale of prosthetic limbs – mostly to wingless airmen – was deferred to in person, then derided behind his hunched back. – At the Shabbat supper the children, tipsy from the dregs of the Kiddush cup, drowsy from the singing of prayers, their eyes widened by candlelight and smarting from the tobacco smoke, had listened in awe as their mother glee-fully described how difficult it'd been to cut off her aunt's leg. Meira Gross took the oiled braiding of the challah and, tearing it in half, illustrated how she'd squeezed plaque from Mitzi's clamped arteries that was: So thick! Toothpaste from a tube wouldn't be thicker . . . And the tissue itself: riddled – I say riddled with necrosis. You pay attention kiddy-winkies, and every time you see Tante put her pipe in her mouth imagine it like this: the white meerschaum is her leg, the amber mouthpiece is the rotten tissue – pure rot! — I'd so hoped, Maurice continues, that he'd find space there for Henry, the hospital he's in at the moment is so very grim and gloomy-seeming . . . Miriam, gripping the phone still tighter, thinks, What should I tell him? That Zack's so deluded now he thinks not just that it's impossible for either of you to help his brother, but that you actually caused his schizophrenia to begin with? And she also wonders: What loyalty should I have to this silliness in Willes-den? – To begin with she'd thought of it as a sort of compensation for her husband: an opportunity for him to have a wider family, as she did, with eccentric onkels and tantes of his own – she'd never taken the house's concept seriously, hoping it would all *blow over – but now it looks as if it'll blow everything else down first* . . . Perhaps, she thinks, I should tell Maurice to put the properties on the market – he'd do it if I asked. – She cherishes their telephone calls, which have become more frequent in the past six months: they help to distance her experience, making of the Concept House some sort of child's collage: the sticky-backed residents licked and stuck down . . . *on to the appalling wallpaper.* Zack's idea had been for them to do their own decorating – to do it for them, he said, was to paint them back into the institutional corner. Miriam bought brushes, emulsions, glosses, rollers: the residents ignored them with teenage hauteur, preferring to Sellotape posters and maps on to the walls, scrawl loopy slogans across the crumbling plaster, and coat every kitchen surface with spilt tea and bacon fat. The kitchen in 119 had never been properly equipped, and besides *the patients* – as Miriam called them in the locked ward of her own mind – preferred to congregate in the one foetid place, the better to cultivate . . . *their noxious antagonisms.* – Fleeing all this on Sunday afternoons, Miriam would drive the wheezing Hillman back to Highgate via Swiss Cottage. Parking under the elegantly marine superstructure of John Barnes, she'd hustle the boys down the Finchley Road to the baths. – Yesterday, she'd changed and joined them in the almost empty Priory pool. Her eyes smarting with chlorine, her groin nipped by her too-tight costume, she'd swum a few desultory widths while Mark and Daniel duck-dived for heavy black rubber bricks. Looking up to the windows high overhead, she'd discovered them . . . *fitted with prismatic bars.* How circumscribed, she thought, our lives have become – or perhaps they always were. – Now, she grips the receiver still tighter and stutters, I d-do so v-value these conversations, Uncle . . . *Two-Way Family Favourites* . . . Now-now . . . Maurice's snout noses in her ear – he's homed in on her, from Hampstead to Highgate, guided by GPO cabling implanted *in his cerebral cortex.* She imagines what the sheen of his silk suit might feel like against her skin – which is *idiocy* . . . as idiotic as it'd be to speak to her mother about her marital problems. Strength and honour may be Meira's clothing, but when she *openeth her mouth* any wisdom concerns improvements in the *abdomino-perineal route of rectal incision* – it being a given that what *fear and trembling* Miriam might experience could always be rationally dispelled by her surgeon mother's *steadiness and bravery* . . . Now-now . . . Again, Maurice *touches me at a distance.* He's dapper and ever-contained in his smooth tailored suits, while his nephew is a tuftiness of tweedy jacket and hairy neckwear. – Nevertheless they have this in common: *they're both sharks* . . . if by this are understood creatures that are *shy and solitary until predatory* . . . For them any intimacy will always consist in *going in for the kill* . . . Yesterday afternoon in the pool, when the boys had surfaced beneath her, gargling with laughter, their dorsal spines *rasping* her back and thighs, she was reminded of what it felt like to have them *bumping and boring* – first in her womb, then at her breast. Miriam thought: This is it, this is the oceanic cocktail we all swim in: one part masculine urine to one of female chlorine, one part aggression to one of passivity. – This is why she's confused by her own behaviour. Why, she thinks as Maurice murmurs, why am I leaping on Zack in this slutty fashion? It made no sense at all when . . . *I'm utterly fagged out with looking after the boys.* Bored as well, and still more *magnificently bored* by the pettiness of her daily tasks: picking at the oakum of dried corn-flakes, smoothing pillowcases that no one ever sees, preparing kosher sausages *for the little pricks* . . . and mopping up those little pricks' *constant piddlings on the lavatory floor.* I've qualified as a psychiatrist, she thinks, only to suffer this mindless roundabout: *Time for bed, Zebedee says* . . . Miriam replaces the receiver on its cradle – Maurice, his framed playbills, his unspotted blotter, his polished manner, *it all slides smoothly away* . . . She's left facing her own muddled face, which stares warily at her from the scrap of mirror she's propped on the tiered plant stand – which is empty except for a couple of avocado bulbs *waiting to blast off* . . . and an alien succulent. – Last Shabbat the old family home was all but deserted. Besides Miriam's parents there'd been Tante Mitzi and a freckled, ginger cousin arrived from Aberdeen to train as an optometrist. Her father read the Jewish Chronicle at the table – her mother *scrimshawed* in the *ivory air* the fine cuts necessary for *a successful nerve transplant* . . . – But do I want him to feel something, Miriam ponders, or is it my own numbness I cannot stand? Do I want him to cleave to me, or do I want us cleft asunder? She picks up the cardboard box she'd left beside the plant stand a week or so ago and sorts through *these nerveless things* . . . shoe-polish tins, spare laces, *horny shoehorns, cartilaginous cloths* . . . She picks up a brush and playfully – or crazily? – buffs her nails the caramel brown of the boys' school sandals. I can't . . . she wearies . . . I can't go on tidying things up – another baby'll finish me off. – Already that morning she'd tidied up the letter Doctor Horder had written her with the results of the pregnancy test he'd done. Miriam interleaved it in the pages of a copy of the Ham & High and shoved . . . *the local news* well down into the dustbin the Busners share with the Fowlers in Flat 3. Looking at her filthy nails, Miriam decides: I'll tell him sooner rather than later – perhaps as soon as this afternoon . . . – And the thought of an unscheduled return to the Concept House with *this dagger held before me . . .* is . . . *thrilling.* She shivers in her ski pants, and considers, Was this the power that I really sought: my right of frost, death and life's privilege? – She remembers the previous morning, when, after rising up from the bed in 119, she'd had to get right back down on her knees again, to watch her bile swing lazily into the toilet bowl. Next door, before she'd gone into Zack's bedroom, she'd flopped forward on to the even more emetic lino in the bathroom of 117. After she was purged Miriam noticed the waste-paper basket under the sink cluttered up with brown-paper bags *full of the harpies' blood . . .* Possibly, Miriam considers, it was this driving me on: they were all cursed and so I had to be sure. – Now, with leaky tap and ticking clock duetting *tick-drip-tock* in the flat's undersea gloom, she feels it . . . *already threshing inside me,* its flukes brushing the sides of her womb with . . . *a phylogenetic flip.* – Yes, she'll pick up the boys in their pinkish blazers and caps from the stucco villa that calls itself preparatory . . . *for what?* But beforehand she'll have another swim at Swiss Cottage . . . *because there's nothing to fear now.* — Eet ees an unequal battle, I zeenk, the marine biologist said, bracing himself against the wheelhouse. Each an' ev'ry year zee 'uman beens zey keel many zousands – meelions p'raps, keel zem many times ownlee to cut off zee dorsal feen like thees – he snatched the serrated dagger from his rubber belt and vigorously mimed this barbarism – ownlee to deescard zee mortally wounded feesh . . . He cast aside the invisible *feesh,* and the camera followed it into the Calypso's churning wake. – Sitting in the spun-sugar smoke of the Neasden Ritz, Miriam mused: Cousteau must have special lessons so as to speak English like a joke Frog. She pictured him – together with Chevalier, M., and Distel, S., their bare and hairy adult knees crunched up behind a long desk while they diligently copied out mispronunciations. – All this, purely in order to tell us . . . *there's nuzzing to fear* if you observe a few basic rules: don't swim at dawn or dusk, which is when they feed, don't swim in the murky water at river mouths or in ports, don't thrash about and, most importantly, *do not sweem eef you 'ave zee bleeding.* – No, indeed, don't dive into the sea when you should be stepping into a mikveh – not unless, that is, you're happy . . . *to be snaffled up.* Yes, indeed – she'll swim in the pool with no fear, then she'll decompress in the Cosmo, breathing in aerated cream with her strudel as she listens to the helium squeaks of the ageing Viennese. Afterwards she'll take a turn along the decks of John Barnes and have a peek in the maternity section . . . *no harm in that*, before picking up the boys and heading for Willesden. – . . . *Tick-drip-tock* . . . *Toute la pluie tombe sur moi* . . . *It's torture*, but Miriam determinedly resists imagining what her husband is doing or saying *right now* . . . because he effortlessly withholds such empathy . . . *from me.* – She chucks the shoe brush at the plant stand and an avocado stone trembles on its toothpicks. Bitterly, Miriam ruminates on the way the Concept House and its crazy residents have taken over her husband's life. – The trip to the Ritz, one long planned as a break *for the two of us, alone*, was scuppered at the last moment when Roger . . . *the selfish beast* . . . suddenly announced he couldn't babysit because he had to attend a Love Feast at the Krishna Consciousness Society in Bury Place . . . *purely as an observer, I won't be eating*. It was out of the question to leave the boys at Chapter Road with the Creep creeping around – besides, the very thought of taking any responsibility for them sent Irene, Eileen, Podge and Maggie into . . . *a hysterical tizzy*. In the end Miriam bowed to the inevitable: Claude came with them, sitting erect in the back seat of the car and sighting at the sodium streetlamps through the hole in his tin opener as he burbled, Goddamn it, sailor, dog down those hatches, this ain't a game of wiffle ball – we're a fighting ship . . . – In the cinema, when the Cousteau short began with the startling blue waves of the Pacific breaking against the screen, he moaned and shrank down in his seat until he was on the floor. Where he remained, and was at least silent, apart from the occasional bizarre ejaculation: Get up sky aft – that's where the rafts are! Or moaned hymnal couplet: To the old rugged cross I'll ev-er be true, Its shame and reproach gladly bear . . . which summoned up shushes from the other patrons. Throughout all this Zack had sat, either wilfully ignoring it or, Miriam thought – knowing him as she did – simply oblivious. During the main feature the Creep struggled back up and stayed *blissfully silent* as he stared into the sun-burnished American deserts framed by the Deco seashell of the proscenium. As she took sideways glances at his under-slung jaw and weedy locks, it had seemed to Miriam that Lieutenant Claude Evenrude, US Army Air Force (Ret.), had shining eyes. Could it be, she speculated, he too has the tapetum lucidum Cousteau said was shared by creepy cats and scaredy feesh? – In the car, on the way back, Miriam concentrated hard on the Creep's verbal bouillabaisse: It's a dime to go to the movies, only a dime – cross the river by the railroad bridge, or dangerouser go with Barney in the big old scow with the putt-putt one-lung motor . . . We-ell, I'm hip about time, ma-an, but I gotta yank the strap and see if that ol' mag-nee-togo will go-go . . . And for the first time in all the hours she'd spent listening to him, she began to appreciate *an informational exchange* was taking place, as the Creep integrated the recent past with what, presumably, was his own distant one. In this too, she thought, he was following Cousteau's beeg feesh, whose arteries wove a rete mirabile that allowed them to equalise their muscle temperature and so sweem on across the cold dark oceans. – Along Dudden Hill Lane, under the railway bridge and into Chapter Road, Miriam, lackadaising upon the dreary sodden house fronts, thought of woodland bogs where slimy tree trunks clustered, their undersides barnacled with finely edged funguses . . . – When they pulled up outside 117 the lights were on and blazing through the bay window. In the living room Miriam found all the residents save Lesley sprawled either on the mattress or the cushions they'd pulled from the sofa. They were drinking mugs of Clive's rancid-smelling homebrew, a harmonica entreated from the television, while Podge burnt her split ends with a Swan Vesta and sang to their acrid fizzle, Lloyd George knew my fa-a-rther, Father knew Lloyd George . . . The only upright people in the room were her sons, who, buttoned into their striped pyjamas, sat ornamentally on straight-backed chairs to either side of the rockery chimneypiece, each with an Airfix model airplane on his lap. Miriam identified the planes – a Superfortress and a

Lancaster, both Second World War long-range bombers – before she did the boys who cradled them. This was because Mark's hobbies were nothing of the sort, rather . . . *full-blown obsessions* with which . . . *in a creepy manner* he tormented anyone who would listen. The Creep had barged past her into the room, keening: When you get to the right place and it's the right time and you're with the right people . . . but Miriam ignored this – she'd spotted Maggie's red-and-green-striped moab on Daniel's tousled head, and was so incensed she shouted, What the bloody hell have you got that on for? His words booming through the station and squeezing beneath an upside-down mushroom-shaped . . . *thing*, which, as Michael starts towards his brother, intent on shutting him up *before there's any bother*, reveals itself to be an enormous khaki tarpaulin lashed to the roof trusses high overhead. In there, Michael assumes, are the wicked steel fragments of the bomb casing, thousands of glass shards, pounds of dust, dirt and pigeon droppings – the whole mass of it an explosion that's been arrested, dangling over the heads of the scurrying people, one that will bide its time patiently – for days if necessary – until it finally . . . *goes off*. Again Peter ejaculates: I say, what the bloody hell have you got that on for? – There are still twenty yards of the concourse for Michael to cross . . . *a Jordan to wade through* . . . and, try as he might, he's certain . . . *I cannot reach him before he's smited by the Angel of the Lord* . . . An avenger that could be a gent with an umbrella, or a belligerent Tommy, or a Doré demon that comes swooping down from the campanile of Westminster Cathedral to bank between the departures board and W. H. Smith's, its bat wings brushing the advertisement

BILE BEANS FOR RADIANT HEALTH . . . An avenger that might perfectly well . . . *be me*. – His anxiety is misplaced: slouching soldiery, sidling cockneys and parading office workers simply change step and turn to the left or the right so as to avoid the substantial bulk of Peter De'Ath, who stands, his walking stick brandished in greeting, wearing a hairy bottle-green tweed jacket his brother doesn't recognise, a cricketing pullover he does and mud-spattered grey flannel Oxford bags, within the ample folds of which Michael knows Peter's legs will be set in a twisted stance, one that, while superficially ungainly, is nevertheless a rock-steady platform from which fine cuts, savage hooks and shattering cover drives can be unleashed. While barely moving on the tennis court, Peter can unwind a fiendish backhand – or, by taking a long stride, tip the ball into a lethal drop volley. In a squash court he wriggles his octopus arm and the black rubber bubble detonates against the wall – but, most of all, on tee or green, in bunker or rough, he can drive, chip and putt to such devastating effect that their father . . . *who loves exactitude in all things, not at all the imprecision of his own flesh and blood* . . . cannot help but favour the older son over the younger one, whatever their political differences. – The brothers meet, and Michael feels first . . . *the bone of my bones*, and only after this the unfamiliar calluses on Peter's palm. He wonders if his brother can also sense the changes wrought in his own fingers by the plying of dividers, the flicking of switches and clips – and the tremor that's always there nowadays, an echo of the shuddering control column, which, as he hauls it back to climb, makes of Michael . . . *a marionette*, enlivened by the wires passed through wing and fuselage from ailerons, flaps and rudders played upon by the wind. – Well, well, well, this is a bally business, Peter says, I'd heard about it, of course, from the old people, but you didn't write yourself – ashamed? Michael says, I don't think I can bear it, Ape, if you're going to bang on at me. – He deploys their mutual nickname deliberately – each dubs the other Ape . . . *we're two sides of the same simian* – hoping thereby to drag Peter back to their nursery, and out on to the heath, where, throughout endless skylarking evenings, they played two-boy test matches, each standing proxy for eleven men: *Chapman, Wyatt, Peebles and Hammond were all him – Bond, Merkel and de Klerk, all me* . . . Bumbly keeping score in a wide-brimmed umpire's hat she'd ordered especially from Lillywhites. – Peter releases his brother's hand, and over his heathery hill of a shoulder, Michael sees a placard that's been put up on a pillar: it's a crudely painted map of the surrounding streets, showing the location of the public shelters. THEN GO TODAY! is its injunction and he thinks, That covers most contingencies . . . Peter's bottom lip is moist, as always – but his wide cheeks and broad, high brow are sunburnt, while his thin black hair is so long it curls up *artistically* from his grubby collar. His heavy and colossal old brogues are recognisably from Sirbert's stock, shoes laid down shortly before the General Strike on the basis that *Northampton pygmies would cease production* . . . and . . . *we might be giants*. – How long're you going to be up in town? Michael says – before rushing on: I've a seventy-two-hour pass, I've to report to ITW 10 at Withernsea by 0800 Sunday, so I expect I'll have to head off in good time on Saturday evening, trains being the way they are – spent six bloody hours in a siding at Didcot on the way up to town yesterday. – Peter's only response to this busying bulletin is to suck his bottom lip redder and wetter as he prods the stone flags with his stick . . . *seeking a better lie*. Michael persists: Shall we take in a flick – or a feed, or a show, or all three? Sirbert gave me a sub' so we can swank it a little if you fancy, Kins. – Peter – as in Peterkins Custard, so Peterkins, which has been abbreviated to Kins, and is what family and friends alike call him – at last shakes himself heavily. Michael thinks of Louis, the De'Ath family's Old English sheepdog, and for a moment imagines it is he, *back from the grave* with bloodshot eyes, who's awakening to the clatteration of pigeons' wings and the shrilling of . . . *hard peas in steamy spittle*. But it's Kins who is growling yet again: What the bloody hell have you got that on for? His tone no longer comically belligerent but wondering — and Michael Lincoln wonders the same thing thirty years later, as he steps from the bank of telephone boxes beside the Grosvenor Hotel and peers through sepia smut and bluish diesel smoke towards where they'd rendezvoused . . . *What the bloody hell did I have that uniform on for?* And as he walks away across the chilly nave of the station, which is steeped in the cabbagey smell of recently departed crowds, he self-sermonises: What if I'd known then what I knew later, what then? And if I'd had the compassion I pride myself on now – an empty pride, emptier than any other – would I have seen things any differently? *No!* He stands before the gaping hole of the vehicle exit on to Buckingham Palace Road and the sunsplash drenches everything in a ghastly luminescence, revealing the very cracks in the secretaries' makeup as they mince past in their maxis, and setting fire to the chromium trim of the taxis drawn up at the rank. – Michael's head swims, wobbles, falls back – his eyes . . . *lift up to the Lord*, but he sees only dirty old glass soaring above, patched here and there with squares of chipboard . . . *Underneath the ar-ches, We dream our dreams away* . . . – But these aren't dreams – they're daymares that are always close to him. —— Close to Michael in the Worthing stopper as it crept along beside the cement works towards Hove. He tried to distract himself by reading the Land Agent's prospectus for the vacant building in Covent Garden . . . *another home on high – a seventh heaven.* But the phantoms crept back and were more intrusive on the London train, jostling in the corridors, pushing into the crowded compartments, and either squeezing between the living commuters – who rattled their newspapers and played their patience, entirely oblivious – or plopping right down on to their unsuspecting laps, while more of their hideously disfigured kind lay in the luggage racks. Always there's the moaning: a low susurration deeper and more persistent than any human in pain. It is, Michael has often thought, the agony of the earth herself – the sound she makes when her soft flesh is sliced through by the rails, and spikes are driven into her muscles and sinews so that she may be *crucified on the sleepers* . . . —— Only at one or other of the five nursing homes he's founded and now runs is Michael free from the attentions of these *revenants* . . . he pushes this archaism at them, hoping it will remove them in time, if not in space . . . *but it never sticks.* At the Lincoln Homes – which are part communities and part rehabilitation centres for ex-servicemen – there's always plenty of tortured flesh . . . *for me to feast my eyes on.* The livid burns smouldering in the day-rooms for three decades alight, while in the aquarial sun porches the amputees' fins flip – and, notwith-standing graft upon graft, nothing ever covers up the inflictions made by bullet, shell and shrapnel on the fly-boys who lie, swatted, on the couches of the physiotherapy suites. Among these eternally wounded men Michael finds himself unburdened of his compassion by the weight of their suffering . . . *the Homes are the fulcrum* . . . and . . . *there all is in equipoise.* – It had been like this for years now, as he made his ward rounds from Shoreham to Bexhill to Banstead to Royston to Torbay, then travelled anti-clockwise, speaking at schools and universities, Rotary Clubs and chambers of commerce – anywhere, in fact, *I can rattle my tin* . . . in front of . . . *anyone who'll listen.* He keeps a small room in all of the homes, each equipped with a put-me-up, so when he isn't in residence it can be used for an office. Otherwise, there were a few personal effects, some sticks of furniture from the Cyrenians . . . *worse than utility* . . . and framed photographs of Bonhoeffer, de Chardin and Schweitzer – men he'd once thought of as . . . *kindred spirits – but not any more.* Not nowadays, with the skin angels flocking more and more densely, starvelings coming home to roost – while for Michael . . . *there's no home for me in this world*, although this had not been a freely made choice: *I cannot abide these bloody cripples!* His then wife had screamed at some crucial turning point in the fifties, when they struggled every day to put food on the table, and there weren't enough hands on deck to swab all the filthy commodes and shitty bottoms. And yet she wasn't a selfish woman – far from it. It was simply that *she wanted sweeter-smelling and prettier children with less tormented dreams* . . . As for Michael, he could only abide with the bloody cripples, for, if he was their beneficent father, he was also their prodigal son, ever-returning with his pockets empty of all but hope. – His natal home he hardly ever visited: he'd no wish to expose himself to his own father's naked absence of feeling, no longer covered up by his mother's sentimental flounces . . . *because Bumbly's not scoring any more – Bumbly's headed back to the pavilion . . .* — He was forsaken on the London train, and, as the coaches chuntered across the Ouse Valley viaduct, the skin angels drew closer and closer, their flapping translucency blocking his view of rich green fields, dew-sparkly in the early-morning spring sunlight. He stumbled from the compartment, and, since this was a Pullman service, made his way to the restaurant, where an overweight waiter, his thick buttery paunch oozing from under his short stained white jacket, silver-served him kippers *with forceps* . . . from . . . *a surgical salver.* – The flak embedded in Michael's shoulder at Wilhelmshaven had smarted – while the portly City brokers and civil servants who sat all around him maintained a steady and aggrieved mutteration . . . *always taxation*, as they tucked sausage stubs into their prudent mouths. They're the right age, Michael thought, to've been through the show, surely there's one I might hold on to, one that can stop me from falling? But he knew: the plummet would never end . . . *I've got no home on high*, while the only flyers who could stay in this dizzying formation were the skin angels. – Accelerating through Redhill, then Purley Oaks and Croydon – as all those years ago another train had clattered through the western suburbs, albeit much more slowly – Michael remembered de Gaulle's inspiriting fatalism: *We who go on fighting are all more or less sentenced to death anyway* . . . — In the first few years after the war he'd consulted eminent doctors, who'd referred him to compassionate psychiatrists. They hadn't helped. He'd also made several visits to a modish psychoanalyst, who was long-haired and self-regardingly dishevelled in a brown corduroy suit. The analyst asked Michael *againannagain* . . . whether Bumbly had breastfed him . . . *which was idiotic*, and if she'd cuddled him often . . . *the very idea!* However, the analyst had no sig' int. when it came to the skin angels with their alien faces. Michael thought he might've been able to bear it if he'd recognised them – if it'd been Tufty, Claus, Jimmy, Jimp, Jacko, Hobbles, the Scamp, Smalls, Dotty, Tommo, Taffy, the Barrel – or indeed any or all of the spare bods he'd served with who'd gone for a Burton and remained in the celestial saloon, playing crib, throwing darts and, with cries of Here's how! . . . *drunk themselves stony* until they'd petrified into memorials of their own truncated lives. But it wasn't their faces that haunted him – and it wasn't their victims' faces either. On that day – the day the skin angels alighted on him and commenced their vampiric feeding – there'd been a photo of Rita Hayworth torn from a movie magazine stuck to the bulkhead at the back of the cockpit . . . *breastfeeding*, and he'd curled the sweet tongue of chewing gum he was offered into his dry mouth, and he'd taken a look through the Norden bombsight out of courtesy to the proud bombardier, but he hadn't done anything at all himself – only watched. Perhaps the narcissistic shrink would've said this in itself was a form of doing – this voyeurism, and as culpably perverse as any sadism. But how could you desire to watch what you'd never seen before, never so much as entertained the existence of before: these others, these Windmill girls who cavorted for him in skimpy skin skirts . . . *torn from their own bellies* and who, batting their lidless eyes in their baked faces, seduced him *againannagain*, while silently screamingly entreating him with their lipless mouths . . . *We are Jap-a-nese, if you ple-ease* . . . — The commuters who boarded the train at Ealing and Park Royal had stayed silent as the grave, although Michael knew, from speaking to evacuees in Chippenham and men who returned to Hullavington after leave, that in town the nattering about the air raids was incessant. The windows of the third-class compartment were heavily misted, and he employed his battledress cuff to rub a little bomb-damage sight into being. It was the same on cold mornings before the ground crew swung the propeller: he sat in the Tiger Moth trainer rubbing the Perspex windscreen with the fleecy cuff of his flight jacket, then they took off to do bumps and circuits over the pristine Wiltshire fields. – There were ugly heaps of clods at the backs of the railwaymen's cottages along the track, and beside them the corrugated-iron sheds the householders were supposed to take shelter in – here and there a cottage had been pulled by the Luftwaffe *quite painlessly* . . . leaving behind . . . *a gingivitis of rubble.* Michael had been able to persuade himself his curiosity was . . . *really rather academic*, or, more accurately, that it was *an interest appropriate to a professional when examining his competitors' handiwork.* – Then, as the train skulked past the barges in Paddington Basin, the walls of blackened moss drew closer, and rising up behind them he saw the boarding houses alongside Queen Mary's, their cliff faces grimy and guano-dashed. One, he thought, has been . . . *especially cleft for me* – all seven storeys, from the garret to the cellar, while . . . *from thy wounded side flows* . . . water spattering over a staircase doubling back into nowhere. Worse than this was the po poised on a tilted scrap of remaining floor – worse still the wardrobe door flapping in the breeze, opening to reveal short-sleeved summer frocks still hanging inside, then shutting, then opening again. – It may've been this *peek-a-boo* . . . or possibly the rosewater of the girls belted into gabardine beside him, but, as Michael gazed upon the bombed-out boarding house . . . *I was resurrected.* His fingers had twitched – their nerve endings remembering the joyous slide from prickling nylon to smooth skin, then the glide inside the moist woollen leg . . . *of her blackouts.* Michael, pressing his copy of John o'London's Weekly down *hard* on his lap, revisited the incomparable feeling of holding *all of her* in the palm of his hand as she rocked back and forth, giving excited little yips. – Surrounding them in the dark orchard garden of the Three Feathers at Sherston were other agitated couples: WAAFs, local girls, Princess Marys – in the absence of any artificial sources they'd been attracted to the mooning light of the officer trainees' faces and the whiteness . . . *of our unsullied hands,* and so . . . *we fed on one another's unrationed faces . . . When apples are ripe and ready for plucking, Girls of sixteen are ready for* –. It had, Michael thought, been incomparable with the Sherston girl, because such a thing had never happened to him before – how could it? The only females detained in the knapped-flint compound on the downs were Matron and the headmaster's wife – neither of whom had any more allure than the school sow. Instead there'd been Monk minimus, who came to Michael's study most evenings, where, in his faggish capacity, he made toast and . . . *never kissed me any other way* than lovingly. — *Brained* by the bright light boring in from the Buckingham Palace Road, Michael gropes through the shining strips of his memories, memories that interfere with insight's invisible beam. It isn't until he's leaning against Dumbo that he realises this is the small cinema that used to show newsreels, and where on the morning he'd met his brother he'd sat in the sixpenny seats watching footage taken in the aftermath of the raids on the City and the Docks. – It's a testimony, Michael thinks as he sniffs the yawning station's halitosis, to . . . something . . . that I remember an image from that film better than anything I personally witnessed in the Blitz. – A double-decker had driven into a shell crater in Lombard Street, nevertheless the commentary remained a breezy *City-gents-put-aside-their-toppers-and-brollies-to-help-passengers-to-safety!* Michael also finds it significant that: The interpretation I place on it to this day is that the baby elephant bus had blundered into a pit the clever Nazi cavemen had dug during the night, and covered up with a tarmac-coloured tarpaulin . . . He forces himself upright – the kipper that slithered across his tongue on the Brighton Belle is yet with him . . . *sickening, smoky and oily.* For routine assurance he pats down the pockets of the pinstripe suit he wears for going up to town: *wallet, keys, pipe, tobacco pouch, matches* . . . just as before each sortie he'd pat down the pockets of his Sidcot and check the rest of his kit: *rations, oxygen tube, Webley side-arm, harness, parachute, gloves, pear drops? No pear drops!* Such had been the clouds of superstition they all barrelled blindly through that no one item or action could be accorded greater importance than any other – pear drops mattered as much as parachute, because where would you be in the icy turbulence of wind and death without those sweet strings of saliva *to hang on to* . . . The smirched station pigeons wheel about Michael's head, and the still-filthier station wheels about them. He staggers, and would fall if it weren't for one of the cabbies, who's been standing chatting and smoking with his mates, coming up to *take the old man's arm* . . . You all right, guv? he says, a grinning leprechaun, more freckle than face, with a shock of ginger hair. You all right, guv? he says again. You look like you're 'aving a bit of a turn. Michael wants to scream, I'M NOT EVEN FIFTY! but recovers himself by taking out his wallet, and from this unfolds a sheet of paper. I'm quite all right, he says, but thank you, honestly – and, actually, I need a cab if you're for hire. Do you know this address? The cabby looks at the paper, Dick-van-Dykily scratching his head. Chapter Road NW2, he says, that's up Willesden way, guv. I should fink we'll make it so long as there ain't too many Mick bombers about. – In the back of the cab Michael *fills the sunlit conservatory* with a convolvulus of pipe smoke, and thinks, How strange we met at Victoria that day, but of course, it'd been because that's where we took the train to school . . . And where they returned to at the end of each term, fleeing Jencks the malevolent mathematics master, who, hypoxic in his brainstarver collar, *hacked at our shins with a hockey* stick. It makes sense, Michael feels, to think of himself as being on a sortie . . . *of sorts*: rumbling up Park Lane past the new American skyscraper, on his way to *liberate this lad* . . . the son of one of his Shoreham residents who's a decent enough chap, *although quite unable to cope*. But then why should he be able to, what with his leg left behind on a Normandy beach, marriage to a difficult woman who he says drinks – and, of course, his own morphine addiction. The boy has bolted from school several times before – but never for this long. And now he's got himself mixed up with some self-styled revolutionary psychiatrist who has a hippy commune . . . *in Willesden of all places*. Michael wonders how easy it'll be to detach Christopher – if the garbled letter he sent to his father is anything to go by, he's powerfully in thrall to this bloody man Busner. Still, there are some young men, Michael knows, who can be very easily swayed . . . *from their deepest and most sincere convictions*. He grips the bowl of his pipe so tightly his hand shakes, burning tobacco shreds . . . *whip me – more mortification*. He remembers praying all night on the cold stone of the altar at Winchester Cathedral . . . *there was no revelation* – only an openly contemptuous sexton who shooed him out into the cloisters, lest his deranged expression frighten the arriving choristers. *And yet . . . And yet . . .* if only he could've seen what Kins saw that September morning – seen himself through his brother's eyes – then perhaps Tufty, Claus, Jimmy, Jimp, Jacko, Hobbles, the Scamp, Smalls, Dotty, Tommo, Taffy and the Barrel . . . *would all still be alive*. And not only them, there were all those omas and fartis, onkels and tantes, who, shaking the fine dust from their overcoats and their furs, would draw back into their lungs the air the blast had sucked out . . . *when I did my bit for the Morgenthau Plan*. As for the flayed angels, maybe they'd zip up their skin Sidcots and, patting down their pockets, discover heart, liver, lungs and lights . . . *all once more safely housed* – so they were full of life's *CONCENTRATED FOOD*, whereas he feels *parched* and his furred tongue cleaves to the roof of his mouth – there's the young squirt, bold as bloody brass, clad in a blue-grey uniform, a soppy, eager expression on his pink face, and a forage cap floating on his blond kiss curls. Kins thinks, I'm too bloody bilious to choke down a bloody bile bean, and calls out to Michael, What the bloody hell have you got that on for? his tone gently joshing, then he makes his way across the concourse, swinging his stick when there's enough room to do so – which there mostly is because on this Thursday morning the crowds are keeping away, terrified, no doubt, by That Man's threat to raze their city . . . *by night, by day, whensoever it pleaseth him.* Kins isn't afraid of Hitler – or of tuppeny-ha'penny patriots taking exception to his civvies. He's amused by Michael's appalled expression – clearly he expects everything to stop: the porters lined up for the chase to round on Kins, clerks and secretary girls too, and for him to become . . . *Actaeon, run down then torn apart by the dogs of war.* So, purely to twit him, Kins sings out again, What the bloody hell have you got that on for? — Kins believes himself to be inured – no longer afraid of man or beast. Since arriving back in town a fortnight before, he's discovered an appetite – and an unexpected aptitude – for this *live-wire stuff.* An Anderson has been delivered direct from the Ministry to Blackheath . . . *there have to be some benefits to being a big bug in Whitehall*, but Daggett, the odd-job man, has enlisted in the Engineers, while Kins lacks the aptitude – and Sirbert the time – to erect the thing. So it lies stacked in the front garden next to Sirbert's old handmade Indian clubs, and when the sirens by the station start up, sending their wails surging up the hill to echo over the heath, Sirbert, Bumbly and Kins retreat beneath the dining-room table. There they await the airborne flotilla's low rubba-rubba-rubba, a noise that penetrates the heavy black mahogany and throbs into them where they lie, propped up on bolsters, playing a . . . *rubber-rubber-rubber or three* of bridge by candlelight, and sipping cocktails of an asperity to gladden Lord Woolton's heart – six parts Nicholson's Gin . . . *It's clear, it's good!* to one of Vermouth – cocktails Bumbly has dubbed Bombshells. – *Sirbert says* . . . is a little tease that Bumbly and her sons share behind his monolithic back, never to his face. Since the raids began, coincident with Kins's return from the country, *Sirbert says* the chances of any one Londoner being either injured or killed on any given night remain reassuringly constant: in the region of one in fifteen thousand, with the possible exception of those unfortunate enough to be in the slum areas around the docks. When the wind was from the north they could all smell the vile stench of burning chemicals . . . *stronger and more astringent than gin*, but *Sirbert says* . . . based on his own readily available data – stressing that he relies on nothing not in the public domain – he calculates there's a greater chance of one being killed during a raid by spent anti-aircraft ordinance, a gravity-stricken night fighter, or fire engines and ambulances rushing to the scene. In other words, Sirbert says, we've more likelihood of kicking the bucket due to what's called blue-on-blue actions than because of anything Herr Goering has chucked at us. – There's no justification, *Sirbert says* . . . for putting the leaf in the table when there are only the three of them to dine, so it's with a chair leg digging into his back that Kins becomes painfully aware of these demotic expressions diluting his father's normally standard English – a flow that increases as the dumm-dumm-d'dumm-dumm of the barrage gathers in intensity, and the liquid bombshells are poured down Sirbert's long stiff neck. – When the all-clear sounded two nights ago . . . *unless I was so tiddly I imagined it*, Sirbert actually said, Go an 'ave a butchers, willyer, Kins. I shan't bovver to haul meself up 'til Bumbly's made 'er free 'earts. The very idea that Sirbert might be afraid is preposterous – although why, given his cool assessment of the probabilities, he bothers to fold his long form into this purely symbolic shelter also perplexes his eldest son. Kins has entertained the idea that Sirbert might be doing it in order to comfort Bumbly. Since the incident in the farmyard, with Annette . . . *by the light of a haar-vest mooon!* . . . Kins has tried to factor into his parents' relations his own mounting passions. It's difficult, though, because the proposition that Sir Albert should ever have done to Lady De'Ath – whose sobriquet derives as much from her plump dirigible form . . . *always bumbling into things* . . . as it does from her wistfully spirituous absent-mindedness – what Kins wishes fervently to do to Annette is still more preposterous. Although when he considers it – as he does, now, wending through the drab travellers towards his absurdly dressed brother – there's been an all-round softening in Sirbert's usually adamant demeanour since his elder son returned. Not that Kins was expecting any brow-beating or other unpleasantness, for that . . . *isn't the way between us*. It could be Sirbert has intimations of . . . *what happened to me* – but this Kins doubts. The gulf separating father and son in terms of political philosophy is very wide indeed, but it's bridged in many places by . . . *bridge*, which both play to championship standard. It's also soared over, in perfect arcs, by the golf balls they strike to perfection. On the increasingly rare occasions they play in a four together, their respective partners are the true irritant, for the De'Aths are scratch golfers. – They did, of course, debate the matters of the day, however their positions were by now so well entrenched hostilities were confined to the occasional, largely symbolic salvo of opinion. And when Kins tipped up at the house, explaining such was the general laxness of the establishment he had simply . . . *leant my hoe against the barn and, well, sort of wandered off* . . . Sirbert merely took a short break from mixing his morning messery to recap the principles advanced by Locke in his Second Treatise, before drily observing that – contra Mister Churchill, whose own opinions were invariably partis pris – it seemed to him England's finest hour was exemplified not by the martial spirit of the general population – surely a given in a fight to the death – but by the wholesale restraint of a government which tolerated the pacifists' dissent, rather than stringing them up from the nearest lamp-post. – As to what Kins intended to do now that he'd abandoned his experiment in Tolstoyan communism, Sirbert was equally dégagé. Kins explained *yet again* that his tribunal had placed no restrictions or conditions on him at all – and Sirbert seized on this as an opening, fitting in a potted lecture on the inherent arbitrariness of all arbitration, before pressing into his son's hand a Gestetnered paper summarising his own application of certain mathematical algorithms to the problems of distributive justice. – They were seated in the drawing room, an elongated space stretching from the bow windows at the front of the house to the glassed-in balcony at the back, and divided by high double doors that are always open. This is the territory Kins's parents fight over – but it's a silent battle fought only with things: he's never heard either of them so much as raise their voice. Bumbly is constantly trying to soften – with vases of flowers, silk cushions and embroidered cloths – the awkward contours of those objects that are deposited on the heavy Edwardian furniture by her husband's tidal preoccupations. To call Sirbert's interests anything as joyful as enthusiasms would, Kins felt, be a profound mistake. Looking about him at the sticky coils of capacitors, the transparent teats of valves and a series of heavy zinc-encased batteries – one of which, with utter insensitivity, had been placed on his mother's spindle-legged escritoire – he was appalled by his father's relentless single-mindedness. The accumulator man visits the house daily – and Sirbert said: The radio waves resonate in the ears of the just and the unjust. – This wasn't, Kins knew, intended to be humorous, but was a reference to the hours Sirbert spends, deep into each resonating night, re-jigging his powerful homemade radiogram so he can listen to German, Italian, French and – on those occasions when the sun spots behave – Russian wireless transmissions. It may very well be, Sirbert continued almost coyly, that your brother is being instructed in radio operation now he's been compelled to join the service. Kins wouldn't be baited. – Since learning that Michael's tribunal – acting exactly contrary to his own – had refused any exemption at all, he'd pressed his father for more information, but Sirbert had proved implacable: You say, Peter, your own refusal to serve King and Country is a matter of conscience, and I think we can credit your brother's conscience with giving him as much trouble as yours does. We must agree that, while *Astra inclinant, sed non obligant*, in Michael's case he's so clearly necessitated in so much of what he does, we should acknowledge his freedom to say what he wants to say to whom he wishes to say it, eh? — Maybe so, Kins thinks, but there's no harm in asking, and so, staring at the silvery wing that's sewn to his brother's pigeon-grey breast, he does so once more: What the bloody hell've you got that fancy-dress uniform on for? Then he takes Michael's hand, shakes it warmly, links it to his own arm, wheels them both round, and off they set at a brisk pace past the *faggot* of destinations piled up by the departure board, past the porters *straining at the economical leash* . . . up from the station's undersea gloom and towards the bright surface of war-torn London, to where there floats along every gutter a newsstand folded out of Picture Posts and Home Chats, and all the paper-sellers cry out, Ben-nar-ezzz surr-vi-verzzz! – Kins takes in the gas-mask bag hanging from Michael's shoulder and is on the point of saying something contemptuous, but checks himself: Have you been by the Paragon already? He rattles on: Obviously I didn't quite make it back last night – those banshees start a'wailin', old man, and everything goes to pot by way of buses, trains and cabs. I'd've strolled back, taken in the show, but everybody gets frightfully officious during a raid – shouting at one and so forth . . . Besides, one might easily trip over a hose and biff one's nose. – The crowds start to press in on them, and before long there's no further headway to be made towards Parliament Square. Kins says, Apparently there were some incendiaries dropped on the Army & Navy warehouse in Greycoat Place, p'raps Jerry thought it was the actual Army and Navy! He laughs at his own joke, mirth soon dispelled when they're diverted towards Petty France by . . . pettifogging tyrants! – Michael smells the stale beer on his brother's breath, and suspects he may still be tight – wonders also if the reason Kins keeps such a grip on him is so he can maintain this morale-sapping flow – The ARPs're nothing but little Hitlers – they'd be perfectly satisfied really if he were the big boss here – under the protection of his brother's RAF uniform. Certainly they don't attract any attention, most of those they pass – clerking types, junior civil servants, secretary girls – have weepy exhausted eyes, and their mouths are tightened by the effort required to keep their jaws jutting. Everyone's too preoccupied to take exception to the sight of two apish pals, arm in arm, out for a stroll. — Ape had been the Lancing boys' nickname for Kins's housemaster, a balding man whose tonsure, pot belly and permanently exposed yellow teeth would've been an embarrassment of riches for schoolroom satirists, were he not such a kindly fellow. The Ape had been gassed at Ypres – or so the boys whispered among themselves while he whistled gerunds – yet he'd none of the twisted cynicism of other masters who'd served. Happiness, the Ape fluted from his high desk, his gown completely enfolding him, is a by-product of existence in the way that coke is a by-product of coal – you cannot obtain happiness directly, you must mine, sort, ship and finally consume the hard and dirty business of life before you're granted a little piece of it. – A by-product of the Ape's wounds was surely his swing-armed and bowlegged gait, his rounded shoulders and the asthmatic sough he made as he sipped the air to see if it was breathable. The De'Ath boys, only a year apart, and pressed into sympathy by their odd and secluded childhood, noticed that they also shared these characteristics with the Ape – although not so well combined with his affability or quiet piety – so they took to calling each other Ape in affectionate remonstrance. – Happiness is a by-product, Ape. – I know, Ape, I know, and the Holy Ghost is a by-product of the Trinity. Beyond this simian similarity there's hardly any resemblance between the two. Michael cannot fathom from which branch of the family tree his ripe looks have fallen – the flaxen hair, the creamery complexion, the firmly dimpled chin. Bumbly's people are certainly fair, but, judging by the foxed ovals of their faded studio portraits, these gentle country parsons and dotty spinsters had always been dough-faced and weak-featured, while the current generation – Uncle Martini, the remittance man, Uncle Melville, the DC in Nyasaland – have the distracted appearance of men . . . *out of kilter with the times.* As for Sirbert's line, there's so very much of him in Kins – the Baroque dome of his forehead, the spear-point of his nose, the heavy cheeks with their insidious veining – it's no wonder there was . . . .*nothing left over.* Michael has entertained the idea . . . *I may be some throwback,* although he can muster no evidence, his grandfather being long departed, and his grand-mother encountered only once, when, on a tour of the links courses along the Dorsetshire coast, Sirbert having unexpectedly kept the driver on, they motored into Devon for a day and paid a call on a peculiar bundle of black silks in a tiny whitewashed cottage. Ignoring Kins and Sirbert, the old woman had stroked Michael's hair, chucked his chin and clucked, Ain't 'e the spit, ain't 'e the bloomin' spit . . . while an indeterminately younger boss-eyed woman sat on a stool by the low window, the drool from her open mouth tangling in the thread she pulled as she sewed the simplest of samplers: a single word, misspelt by blue cross-stitching, JEBUS. – That these were Sirbert's mother and sister Michael realised much later and purely circumstantially – for his father said nothing. It had been the first summer . . . *when I was eleven* that his father had begun to engage Michael in conversation at all, Sirbert viewing intercourse with men as only really appropriate on the golf course or at the bridge table, and with women solely the latter. By the age of ten, Kins . . . *my Irish twin* could play every convention there was, and so received paternal favour . . . *doubled and then redoubled*. Albeit this mostly consisted of Sirbert saying, Are you completely certain you can make four diamonds? while the boy stared furiously into the fan of his cards. – There'd been little sociability beyond this at the family home, and there was less still during the vacs when the boys returned first from prep school, and thereafter from Lancing College. Sirbert had a loathing for that sort of carry-on. He had raised his voice to Bumbly on just one occasion that Michael could recall, when she'd accepted a dinner invitation on their behalf without consulting him, imagining since it came from such a powerful personage . . . *the Beaver himself, I think*, her husband would forgo his usual cocktail, one mixed – Michael had assumed for a long time – from two parts rectitude to one of outright disdain. You silly woman! he'd cried – and Missus Haines scuttled away to hide in the cupboard beneath the stairs. Don't you realise, he boomed on, his face engorged, that if we go there they may very well form the expectation they should come here! — The brothers stand beside the . . . *Sirberts-upon-Sirberts* . . . of sandbags piled up by the entrance to St James's Park tube station. Michael's eye strokes their prickly sacking, then slides up the smooth sooty sandstone *laid down aeons before Ussher's world began* . . . to rove the rigid folds of the skirted figure sitting on the pediment . . . *a bearded lady Jesus who I daresay wears no blackouts!* He turns to Kins: So, what's it to be – I see the Karloff's still on at the Paramount . . . His brother sneers: I see you've secured yourself a cushy commission. Michael softly admonishes him, Ape, I don't think I'll stand it if . . . Ape, please . . . ZZZZZZZZUM! Kins swipes his stick across the façade. This rotten pile, he says, would be just the ticket for you and your United Airmen, eh? Unfortunately you've come from your HQ in Basra a little precipitately, eh? After all – he pulls his younger brother on – the wandering sickness is still very much abroad. What was the timing Wells proposed for civilisation's collapse and resurrection? Ah, yes, I remember it now: social vitality begins to return in 1967 and the pestilence finally ceases in May 1970. Very factual when it comes to his fantasy, is Master Herbert, however, like all systematisers he prefers the bigger picture, doesn't want to bother himself with fiddly little details such as how the BLOODY HELL DO WE WEATHER THE NEXT THIRTY YEARS! Breathing heavily, Kins pulls up short and tugs a pack of Tenners from his jacket pocket. Gasper lit, he puffs away with both hands on his hips while declaiming: War can be a stimulating thing – and you can always do with stimulus! – Not having his brother's perfect recall for words, any more than he does Sirbert's for figures, Michael doesn't remember the line. In place of their flat certitude he has only these swelling sensations: *sweet Aero bubbles suddenly sickly* . . . as the Hawker Hart banks hard right, drops into an air pocket, then is lifted, so it soars up and around in a thermal carrying him and PO Murgatroyd out over the downs in a widening circle. Far below there's the soft seethe of beeches and the azure-and-brown roundel of the dew pond at Chanctonbury Ring. – It's the flying, Kins, Michael says as they shamble on up the lane that debouches into St Anne's Gate, not the dying. Dying! Kins snorts. I should've thought it was the killing that'd bother you more, Ape – the Ape I knew was a vegetarian beast, not at all happy with killing in the main . . . They stroll on along Birdcage Walk and turn into the park. – At the Lyons' in Trafalgar Square, Michael watches moodily as Sirbert's sub' starts to disappear by the forkful into Kins's ever-moist mouth. There is something, he thinks, rather sickening about the concentration his brother brings to bear on making little bite-sized sandwiches of egg white, bacon and fried bread, then mopping up the yolky grease in . . . *widening circles*. Charles the First's dainty horse is mounted on a thick cloud of steam and fag smoke – beyond this Michael can make out the Whitehall Theatre, while to the right a barrage balloon *bumbles* obscenely against the opening of Admiralty Arch as some AA types cack-handedly winch it aloft. *Sirbert* . . . *Bumbly* . . . *Kins* . . . Everyone except me, Michael reflects, gets a nickname . . . which was why, when one was bestowed on him at the OTU, he felt his conscience . . . *crumble a bit more*. Links, the chaps call him, or Creamy, by reason of the biscuit that shares his nom de guerre. — The De'Ath Watch, a weekly round-up of cinema visits and sports fixtures, appeared during the Easter and summer vacs. To begin with it was a single typewritten page, but soon enough it was four, then eight, and multiple copies were cranked out on the Gestetner in Sirbert's study. Kins had written the review of Things to Come, and Michael had typed the stencil. Kins's dismissal of the flick had been trenchant: Like the work of speculative fiction on which it is based, this film demonstrates the shallowness of a socialistic ethic when it is divorced from any Christian morality. Raymond Massey's performance seeks to establish as incontestable the patently threadbare idea that the only foundation necessary for civilisation is a stiff enough lip . . . *or words to that effect*. This was when Kins was seventeen. Three years later he'd be the only person Michael knew – besides Sirbert – who wasn't surprised when Commissar Molotov and Herr von Ribbentrop declared their respective nations . . . *desirous of strengthening the cause of peace*. Kins had been Publisher, Editor and Chief Correspondent of the De'Ath Watch – Michael was compositor and ginger-beer boy. As the sun set and the shadow of the All Saints' steeple stretched across the heath, Kins would still be hitting Michael's perfectly adequate deliveries . . . *all over the shop*. It'd been more humiliating on the golf course – by the time they were fourteen and fifteen Kins was awarding his younger brother six strokes . . . *and still thrashing me*. At Lancing, Michael should *by all that's sacred* have been more popular: he was a good average chap in the classroom, and a solid player at rugger. Kins by contrast was . . . *an oddball*, who wouldn't play rugger or footer at all, and made letter-perfect translations from Cicero and Demosthenes. Worse still . . . *surely* . . . when they both joined the sixth, Kins cold-shouldered his peers – instead of gathering with them at the common-room settle on winter evenings to toast bread on twists of barbed wire, as Michael did, he hid himself away in his study – *the Anchorite* they called him – and palled up still more with Ape, who prepared him for confirmation, and with a history master called Venables, who was *a terrific Bolshie*. All this, yet still Kins . . . *got their vote*. He was so very popular that when he set himself up as the College's very own Steel-Maitland, the resolution was easily passed that none of them would fight for . . . *anything much*. Michael had been the most energetic of canvassers: he'd do anything for his revered older brother and fears . . . *I still might*. The pale-blue Oxford entrance paper had a single-word question on it: Why? Michael felt the compulsion to write an essay explaining he'd applied purely in order to be closer to Kins. – They'd gone up together the previous autumn, and at last the gap that had been widening between them since Highers was confirmed. Parting on Beaumont Street, Kins brayed in terribly accented French, C'est magnifique, mais n'est ce pas la gare . . . then turned on his heel, heading towards Balliol. – At the beginning of the long vac Kins and Venables bought a banger from a grocer in Kemptown for a tenner and had it shipped to Dieppe on the Newhaven packet. Winched down into the white dust, they'd hammered along . . . *underneath the ar-ches* of the planes, a Grande Armée of two, so rapidly mobilised that they soon reached the limits of Michael's imagination. He pictured them sitting at Parisian café tables, drinking cloudy Pernods, while they watched ladies of high fashion and drooping garters promenade . . . *with their lapdogs and lobsters.* The stiffly prosaic truths were cartes postales, the first showing the table decoration of the Place de la Bastille with model motor-cars revolving round it. Michael pored over this for evidence of loose morals and discovered only the long hoardings exposed on the rooftops – SAVON CADUM pour la Toilette – flanked by electrified cherubs. Kins had written: Smooth crossing, Bumbly . . . the banger, christened in her honour . . . running well. Fell in last night with two Germans who stood us a drink! One was Manager of Berlin Chemicals en route to do business with Imperial Airways. Address here, Hotel Burgundy, 8 rue Duphot. – Address there: The Paragon, Blackheath, where, having been passed over for the trip, Michael spent the whole summer – apart from a short walking tour of the Suffolk coast with some pals from the Corps. He chanced his arm at the tennis club, and in the evenings swayed away from Gwen Cudlip's embrace at gramophone parties . . . *I can't give you the ocean – or deep and tender devotion* . . . thankful his one decent pair of white flannels at least had . . . *substantial pleats* . . . *These fragments I have shored against my ruins* . . . — Whozzat? Kins has finished his breakfast and pats his *sluggish* bottom lip with the triangle of a paper napkin. To be frank I don't altogether fancy a flick, he says, screeching his chair back. Nor a show, got in the way of spending rather a lot of time in the great outdoors when I was with the CLTA wallahs, seems I lived out there in the wilderness forever –. Kins does a lousy Clark Gable and his brother thinks, I myself could do a better Loretta Young, then remembers the De'Ath Watch gave the flick two out of a possible four stars, then interrupts: Where did you spend last night? Kins grins apishly at the girl who's plastered their scrap of a bill to the sticky tabletop. All in good time, Ape, he says. – Time, Kins thought, had been a by-product of the coal he'd found in the bunker in the mews off the Euston Road – a bunker that . . . *rather counter-intuitively* was also full of damp clods, though it hadn't rained for days . . . *with the exception of bombs.* Kins supposed some Camden sparrow had dumped the clayey earth in there when he dug in a galvanised nest for his own brood – or possibly it was for the quality in the mansion blocks. Either way, it made a satisfactory settee for . . . *my struwwely self.* For the last half-hour of the barrage it'd all felt curiously personal – each bomb with *Der Kins* painted on it. In the coal hole he regretted his behaviour – if he hadn't overstepped the mark he might still be up in the top-floor flat of the Nash Terrace which Annette shared with her pal Doreen. When the raid began, he fed the girls Sirbert's hard data, before extinguishing the electric and opening the curtains. He'd watched scarcely able to contain his excitement, as a stick of incendiaries falling somewhere to the north of the Mappin Terraces lit up the freshly dug allotments on Primrose Hill. Doreen had hurried off down to the basement – but Annette, Kins was persuaded, shared his exultation in these . . . *the trumpets of Jericho,* and when she buried her face in his chest . . . *I pawed her breasts.* — At Collow Abbey Farm, Feydeau, an old contemptible of the movement, arrives to speak to the trainees. Squinting at Kins through the lamp smoke, he says, De'Ath, eh – putting heavy emphasis on the second syllable. I knew a very fine young fellow by the name of Stanley Death, who was killed in the last war, any relation of yours? And Kins, repelled by the pubic protuberance of the old proselytiser's wagging beard, bridles: No, not that I know of . . . and hopes it'll end there – but Feydeau's not to be so easily subdued. Earlier he'd made some rather pointed comments about how community living appeals to a certain sort of person, usually comfortably reared, as an Elysium in which, without having to do anything in particular about it, he feels the burden of existence will be lifted from his shoulders . . . and now he *prates on*: Death is a good old English peasant name that in my experience is frequently left behind – as if it were a smock, hung on a lowly peg – when the family begins its social ascent, very often under a new and Frenchified covering –. If you're implying, Kins breaks in, that my old man has cut his cloth to suit his position, then, I'm afraid you nothing at all about him! – And on this peevish, rather than Napoleonic, note, Kins struggles up from the broken rattan chair with a good deal of squeaking, then endures the further humiliation of . . . *a Hardyesque interlude* as he grapples with the two halves of the door, before eventually finding himself in the yard, breathing heavily and trying . . . *to take the long view* between the barns and over the lime woods, to where in the distance the soft light of the new moon silvers the Wolds' grassy haunches. Picking his way gingerly over the well-manured cobbles, Kins draws closer to a long low byre and its . . . *beautiful pong – By faith Noah, being warned of God of things not seen as yet, moved with fear, prepared an ark to the saving of his house.* Kins fights to maintain his footing in the present — had it been days or weeks before, when, by way of being more useful, he'd taken on the task of doing the farm's accounts? And also begun acting as . . . *a rum sort of scribe,* filling out forms and penning personal letters for the unlettered labourers in the neighbourhood. Time – at least of the readily divisible species – had . . . *dissolved.* He wore no wristwatch, no calendar hung in the farm's kitchen, and the clock on the mantel was only intermittently wound. There was no wireless, while his weekly bike expeditions into Market Rasen – where he took communion from the vicar of St Thomas's, a man acquainted with the Reverend Dick, who evinced . . . *at least some sympathy* – became less frequent as the summer wore on, before ceasing entirely. Kins wrote no letters of his own – he'd given his address only to his people, and so received tersely loving postcards from Bumbly in response to his own tersely loving ones. There seemed to be an unstated agreement between all four De'Aths that, as their con-sciences took them in different directions, so it was better for all concerned if . . . *we became heirs of the righteousness that comes by faith.* Saving that there is faith no more – not for Kins. Brockleby, whose beloved Friesians jostle and fart in the byre, has a faith that rises up strong from the furrows. Shortly after Kins's arrival . . . *the singing-bloody-farmer,* in old-fashioned high gaiters, corduroy breeches and a mismatched double-breasted jacket, took him out to the Glebe field, together with Jack Clarke and Bill Smedley, the latter having cycled all the way there from Coventry wearing his window cleaner's overalls. That's faith! Brockleby hosannaed when

Bill turned up – and, as they all squatted down to goggle at the furrows, he intoned, This is white gold, my soulful boys . . . The trio followed his fanatic eyes along the row of little plants groping into the grey May daylight. Looking from the farmer's breeches to *the corduroy field* . . . Kins had realised that the beets interested him . . . *not a bit*. These clutches of tiny leaves on spiky stalks might as well've been . . . *docks, lettuces or ruddy opium* so far as he was concerned. Our role, Brockleby preached on, as pacifists in a time of war such as this, is to plant the seed of a new civilisation within the barbarism of a world hell-bent on destruction. These . . . these are the seedlings of that civilisation, my soulful boys – and when we take our hoes like this – he delved down as his cigarette holder stuck up, and Kins thought that for a pious man Brockleby relied rather a lot on . . . *these Craven "A" crutches* – we remove the weeds choking the little saviours. The men who work the land hereabouts will tell you there's na frim folk as can manage singling, it's too arrud t'make it natty, but I tell you, my soulful boys, we'll make proper clod-hoppers of you all, for, when you untangle these seedlings here . . . gently does it . . . and when you pluck out the weak ones and leave only the single strong shoot . . . thus, you're making it possible for the one true God to grow with vigour in your hearts, same as the one true beet grows in the earth. – Jack Clarke singled well enough, Bill Smedley better still, but Kins, who'd to coil himself down to the ground, found the work back-breaking . . . *and soul destroying*. He wished the beastly beets would fly at him at a decent height, and he were equipped with a fives glove instead of this . . . *bally hoe!* – May handed off to June, June held fast to July.

Kins's hands blistered and burst – his neck burnt and he walked with a permanent stoop, as . . . *With what rapture, With what rapture, With what bally rapture, Gaze we on those glorious scars* . . . The attic room he shared with Jack stank of *his cheesy feet,* and the thin mattress on the iron cot was stuffed with horsehair, so *draught animal that I am, I sleep on others of my kind.* He poured the tepid water from the earthenware ewer over his aching, crusty head and it dribbled down into the earthenware bowl. A corn dolly had been nailed high up on the wall, and when Kins touched it, it crumbled to . . . *chaff.* — Had this been days or weeks before? Kins cannot decide – any more than he comprehends how they all manage to regard the aircraft roaring up from the aerodrome at Goltho with such studied indifference . . . *the thunderbolts of a Babylonian marduk we worship not.* Instead, every evening the gramophone is wound for recitals, and there's Evelyn Dall, or Flanagan and Allen, or Myra Hess playing Jesu, joy of man's desiring to the conchies, together with one or two clod-hoppers who creep in to sit, transfixed as much by the oddity of their fellow listeners . . . *in our grass-stained cricketing pullovers and torn Oxford bags* . . . as by the music's wistfulness. As he cranked the handle, then watched the shellac sheening go round *annaround*, Kins meditated on this: a small dog with its ear cocked tumbling over a horn . . . *the only Victor I'll ever be.* – Each interminable and hurting summer day was somehow succeeded by another, and, as the sun's swords *were beaten into ploughshares*, so Kins's faith – forged during the long walks up on to the downs, matins plainsinging back into evensong – melted away. In its place a white-hot lust boiled through his veins.

He tried thinking of the altar boys wafting their censers – he tried to hear the choristers, their reedy calls and the school chaplain's honked responses. To Kins, surrounded by Brockleby and his Fenland ilk, the College's devotions appeared *higher and higher* . . . and he tried to fix upon that higher purpose – but the smells assailing him emanated from Annette's berry-brown skin, and the bells he heard were his ears ringing as he strained for the slightest note of approval in her monotone. – This, though she was a spirited enough girl, dismissed within weeks of the declaration for speaking openly of her objections to her class in Bromsgrove. Given Annette had been an ILP member since '36 and was also an organiser for the Teachers' Anti-War Movement, Kins assumed she'd take a shine to Jack – he certainly did to her. After all, he was closer to being a proper proletarian, and spoke without a smidgen of the ironical about *the inevitable production of warfare by the capitalistic system*. But they jawed so over doctrinal matters – Kins thought of shop stewards . . . *speechifying on the head of a Woolworth's pin*. Besides, while Jack was handsome enough – with his long, lean form and head of jet-black hair – Kins had his suspicions: for all her mucking in and talk of equality, Annette remained an alderman's daughter. She'd told Kins – with a pride he'd have found . . . *laughable* in anyone else – that her father was a stalwart Rotarian who owned the largest sanitary-ware manufactory in the Midlands. No doubt he also had . . . *all the wholesale prejudices this implied*. — When the farmhouse door opens and she comes out, Kins assumes her aim is to finish off *what the old fraud Feydeau has started* . . . and castigate him for being a public school and Oxford man, circumstances that . . . *are patently beyond my control.* She pauses on the doorstep, straightening her shoulders, tugging down first the one then the other sleeve of her dress, taking time, Kins thinks, to gain her night sight – then she comes towards him calling softly, Kins? Kins? Before she arrives he smells her perfume – a real one she must've put on after her bath. He knows she's bathed today, because this is a twice-weekly ritual the three young women at Collow Abbey Farm undertake together, in the smaller of the two milking parlours, with a great deal of public fetching and carrying of just-boiled water, the aim being to give the men ample warning, so they'll retreat to the home field for footer, or to the millpond for a dip. Annette, Valerie and Ida do their laundry together as well, then carry their moist things to the very end of the orchard to be pegged out to dry. One day Kins came on Ida unexpectedly there, and they stared at each other with the shocked recognition . . . *of minds encountering bodies.* She's a small girl who wears thick spectacles and has a voluptuous figure. Between them were dresses, blouses and smalls hanging from a washing line – as she grabbed brassieres and bloomers, hugging them defensively to her chest, he was sure they both saw the same mirage: the bare breasts, exposed haunches and naked buttocks these scraps should clothe . . . *wobbling in mid-air. Anointed she is, my Sheba* . . . her perfume mingles headily with the sweet reek of dung. The great heat of the day is subsiding, the earth giving it off in *shuddery gasps* . . . Annette wears a sensible-enough frock, over the knee, with a collar and *some sort of embroidery down the front* . . . it's her breasts he's overpoweringly aware of as he gestures at the moon, saying, They should put a big bit of blackout over that if they really want to stop the Luftwaffe finding their targets. His legs go *all dithery* as he awaits her response. Honestly, she says, that man Feydeau is a complete ass . . . Her shoulders are *high and mighty*, her thick auburn hair, unset, lies loose and tousled on her neck. She has *an ironstone* stuck in her throat, and every time she speaks it resonates with *an adenoidal whine* that for Kins lends everything she has to say *an irresistible authority* . . . told us a faintly indecent anecdote. Said he'd met some chap on a London bus, chap says to Feydeau: No civilisation can be secure that wastes its sewage as ours does. Feydeau says to chap: Pray give me an example. Chap continues: The Chinese were a civilisation thousands of years before we were, and they'll remain one when we've blown ourselves to pieces because they return all their . . . excrement to the land! – As Annette's *great heat* . . . subsides, she gives off . . . *shuddery gasps*. Kins starts muttering how Brockleby says there are increased yields to be gained from concerted manuring . . . then takes two steps forward, grasps the back of her head and *spreads* his mouth over hers. – The meals at the farm are simple, although ample and served with plenty of ale and cider. The girls have no interest in camouflaging dishes with suet or pastry, instead bowls piled with steaming swede, potatoes and mangel-wurzels are set before them, *gilded* with their pooled butter ration. When he looks from mouth to mouth around the long refectory table, Kins thinks, Yes, this is a re-creation of a village community such as there was in the middle ages . . . He misses the heavy chocolate cake of his parents' cook, Doris, and her beetling beef, roasted into a carapace of its own juice – but his bowels move easily . . . *and with terrific regularity.* Her belly seethes against his and in the alarming tumult of lips, teeth and tongue, for a second or so it seems to Kins ... *she yields!* — South, towards Bardney and Woodall Spa, the soil is richer and the land ... *rolls* – not on the surface ... *deep below.* The fields open out and out. In some places they're half a mile wide and interspersed by dense copses of lime, beech and elm ... *stately Queen Marys, each a world entire.* Walking here, distractedly fleeing the earnestness of the farm, Kins stumbled upon the bones of a Cistercian abbey, the vertebrae of its pillars scattered across a pasture snarled by vetch and cow parsley, spattered with dung. Flies and midges revolved giddily above the dolloped cowpats, the waywardness of one only emphasising the tight conformity of the rest. He happened there upon a bull in the act of mounting a cow, its earnestness was ... *comical and tragic.* Kins looked once upon the preposterous extent of its penis – then turned away from its bemused and foam-flecked muzzle. – There was no wireless at the farm, no electricity or water from the main either. The buildings were dilapidated, which was why Brockleby and Feydeau had been able to buy the property for a few thou'. When a refugee from the wider world arrived, fresh from the ordeal of his tribunal, he might talk nervily for a day or two about the capitulation of the Netherlands, or the encirclement of the BEF, but soon enough he'd be caught up in workaday farm life, succumb to its Lilliputian captivity, and so fall silent. Kins was responsible for the wall newspaper, which he put up *conscientiously* every other day. Modelled on the De'Ath Watch, Collow Laffs featured reports of eggceptional layers, with whimsical pen-portraits of individual hens. There were testy editorials on the wilfulness of Lincolnshire shorthorns – more emollient ones celebrated the epochal progress of the first farm-bred heifers into Brockleby's precious Friesian herd. Kins tried to give his paper plenty of pep – also intellectual depth: he glossed Mandeville when reporting the bee hives' harvesting, and quoted Ovid in his analysis of silage-making. He commissioned Valerie to illustrate this article, and she produced a vigorous gouache on a bit of old Lincrusta depicting Work Group No. 1 loading up the great galleon of a haywain, with Kins himself – somewhat implausibly – directing their labour from the high poop of its thatching. Collow Laffs was popular with the Community Land Association trainees, whose numbers had swelled to near twenty by midsummer. Brockleby offered them all the same terms: bed, board and thirteen shillings a week. There will be sweat and tears, he told them, but no blood unless you're daft enough to fall into the threshing machine. – There weren't meant to be any bosses as such, yet he still divided them into two working groups: one under Ted Cornwallis, a pugnacious communist and former docker from South Shields, the other answerable to Tiny Procter, a giant and seraphic Quaker. Procter had lost all the toes on his left foot when he was wounded at Passchendaele while serving with the ambulance service. This gave him a precipitate gait: always lurching forwards, saved from falling flat on his rubicund face, Kins hypothesised, only by his irrepressible good humour. The socialistic gravitated to Cornwallis, who stirred them up. War, he sing-songed, is the in-ev-i-table condition of capitalistic pro-duction, laddies. We moost de-velop new modes of mech-a-nis-ation. The Brockhouse trac-tor is only the beginning – the old Imperial master's belly woon't continue t'be swollen by cheap food imports after this war has ended, and it's co-mu-no-ties such as these that'll take up and radicalise the great armies of the unemployed! – A rivalry quickly developed between the two groups – at first good-humoured, then predictably earnest, and eventually verging on hostile. – Each day the trainees toiled in their work groups, and each evening, after their vegetable supper, they separated again to form their own colloquies, each one gathered in the halo of an oil lamp. Kins hung back, looking from face to face, from lips pursed at the ends of hand-rolled cigarettes to teeth clenched on pipe stems. He sidled away from the refectory table into the dark passage, where he stood, muscles stretching and twanging, fingers twining in the soft hush of spider webs, nostrils prickling as he inhaled the old must-makings of beetles and mice. In the back parlour, under a photogravure of Sanssouci ... *how could it've ended up here?* ... Tiny Procter's *Mennonites in Morris chairs* recited their own catechism. For the Quaker, as much as for the communist, agricultural self-sufficiency was merely a means – for him the end was emancipation from interest: Usssury, Procter's boiling face gently hissed, is an unparalleled evil, one that you, my children, will live to see torn up from the land, root and branch ... He spoke as if they were ... *seed already sown*: the printer, the glazier, the boiler-house-keeper and the four wayward students – Kins pictured them planted waist-deep in what was *at best marginal land, the soil claggy and richest in ... stones* ... 250 acres of arable, sixty more of grassland. Kins understood the practicalities, knew from the accounts the farm was only ... *a touch on the right*

157

side: 105 tons of potatoes, 150 of *sugar beastly*, 2½ of dried peas, 12 of wheat, 9 of oats, 6 of barley, 300-odd lambs – and of course Brockleby's beloved Friesians, whose lush udders the singing farmer – as he was known throughout the north of the county – would suck upon . . . *a nightjar in a Norfolk jacket slithering over the damp grass* . . . if he could. This is no super-abundance – no revolutionary bread basket. Kins has read The General Theory – he knows much of it by heart. Havering in the dark corridor, a thoughtful moth drawn to neither flame, he sees Cornwallis's views on employment and Procter's on interest for what they are: *hopelessly naive, and ignorant of the third and prime factor, which is money* . . . — Kins's and Annette's tongues thrash . . . *round annaround* in their coralline cave, scraping against *teethy reefs* . . . He cannot restrain that mutinous part of himself, he's bemused, his muzzle is . . . *foam-flecked*. After so much in the way of vegetables her *meat* is strong in his hands . . . *aitch bone, rump* . . . As he wrestles with her, Kins pedantically notes . . . *for the umpteenth time!* that were Cornwallis not a pacifist, he'd be delighted to have Bevin's ukase, since it'd give him all the control over persons and their property . . . *any revolutionary may desire!* – Is it sheer wantonness or bracing *for an escape attempt* . . . Annette has parted her thighs. Fighting for control, Kins thinks of the dismal week he spent in Oxford after receiving his call-up papers . . . *round annaround I went.* — Never at ease on a bike, as he wobbled off each morning over the cobbles in the Broad, he'd to concentrate on every push of the pedals – then wavering down Holywell Street, then teetering along beside Magdalen, then turning on to the High Street, then huffing his way up it to the Turl, along which he wobbled back towards Balliol. – But once he'd completed one circuit he found he couldn't stop, for the concentration he'd mustered at least muffled the symposium in his head, the rhetorical flights of which were, in essence . . . *balder-dash*, for when it came right down to it there was only the one stark question: *Should I, or shouldn't I?* So long as Kins kept pedalling, kept going round and round the town . . . *the arrow remained in flight.* The prosperous-looking matrons rolling across his path towards the Cornmarket, the blazered hearties aiming for the river, the dons . . . *their black wings flapping* – if he stopped pedalling and made a decision then, all at once, the vividness, the colour and the motion would be drained from this scene, leaving pen strokes sketchily describing their dropping jaws and widening eyes, their outstretched arms and horrified hands, for before them would be standing, astride his bone-shaker, the preposterous figure of *THE MAN WHO SAID HE WOULDN'T FIGHT.* So, even as ARP volunteers were painting thick white lines along the kerbstones and up the walls of these ancient halls, Kins kept on pedalling, *round annaround* . . . he kept on cycling . . . *round annaround.* – The tribunal was held in the Pitt Rivers Museum, an oddity for which no explanation was forthcoming, although Kins intuited this was only the beginning. Wartime – for him, at least – would be characterised by such improvised billets: a trestle table covered with moth-eaten baize, on it, propped against a stack of books, a coat of arms borrowed from some council office that . . . *kept sliding down* and rucking up the cloth . . . *Honi soit qui billiards y pense.* As the chairman harrumphed his way through his opening remarks:

No definition in the Act of conscientious objector per se . . . Convened here rather to assess gradations of sincerity . . . A tricky notion, indeed . . . – He wafted away into slight mystifications of G. E. Moore, the Naturalistic Fallacy, the reductio implicit in any concept of a belief sincerely held. Kins, standing to attention at an odd little lectern, thought, I can win this trick at least. He'd heard tell of the chairman – a blinking little moley-man who wore a queer moustacheless beard – as a fairly typical super-numerary, loosely attached to Teddy Hall, who'd published a single book on Thomas à Kempis so long ago the saint . . . *had checked the proofs himself!* or so Kins's informant quipped. The other panellists he wasn't so sure about. – In the background, display cabinets hulked, their dusty glass obscuring savage clutter: tomahawks and necklaces of cowries, teak masks and bongo-bongo drums fringed with coconut fibre. Closest to Kins sat a lady JP who wore a high-crowned puritanical hat garlanded with a crazy bunch of artificial fruit. Her long powdered chin bathed in its shadow – the glass eyes of the mink tucked up around her bony neck drew the winter day down from the skylight into their cold dead orbs. To concentrate on the chairman's interminable circumlocutions was an athletic feat: his sentences were so long they curled up and up, then curled still more, arching over in the waxed gloom, until their object was finally united with their subject . . . *and eaten by it – in its end is its beginning.* Moreover, try as he might, Kins couldn't subdue a strange trompe-l'œil tic: if he looked away for an instant, then back at the lady JP, her head had shrivelled up and been displaced to one of the display cabinets, shelved there beside those of the two remaining tribunal members, a saturnine reservist colonel and a wisp of a parson whose *gonflé* . . . lower lip suggested to Kins acts of unspeakable . . . *Stiffkeyness.* He kept his own eyes averted from this horror: the three of them, enraged by being *bagged as trophies*, so determined to . . . *enact their own coup.* – D'you not think Christ himself would appreciate the justness of this war? It took a while for Kins to realise the lady JP had addressed him, for her tone was surprisingly warm . . . *Bumbly even* . . . while her long skinny fingers – fidgeting from dusty beaker to smeared carafe, to the coat of arms which she re-propped – seemed to be acting out an inner conflict. The unbending colonel and the end-of-the-pier parson regarded Kins with expressions indicating they too believed this to be the very crux of the matter, and so: *Off I went* . . . giving chapters – Psalms 29, 32, 34 and 37 – and verses therein – 11, 17, 14 and 37. Quoting: *The LORD will give strength unto his people, the LORD will bless his people with peace* . . . Alternating between the Hebrew prophets – *LORD, thou wilt ordain peace for us, for thou also hast wrought all our works in us* – and the Gospels – *Peace I leave with you, my peace I give unto you: not as the world giveth, give I unto to you* . . . At which juncture Kins swept his eyes over the quorum and tugged the end of an invisible mantiple, as he impressed on his judges the unsaid – but for all that *SHOUTED* – message: See! See what all these so-called statesmen and their backroom deals have brought down upon our innocent heads! How they cheered Musso and stood by applauding while he poisoned Abyssinia! How they urged on Chamberlain as he beat Beneš to death with his good old um-ber-ella! – The lady JP was looking *rather down in the mouth* . . . still Kins persisted with Romans, Chapter 14, Verses 17 to 19: *For the kingdom of God is not meat and drink, but righteousness and peace, and joy in the Holy Ghost. For he that in these things serveth Christ is acceptable to God, and approved of by men. Let us therefore follow after the things which make for peace, and things wherewith one may edify another* . . . — Not *meat and drink* . . . but *tongues and spit, as the fighting continues* . . . Each seeking the other's tip so they may . . . *suck each other, an ouroboros the subject of which eats its own object* . . . — There'd been a few more questions. It was established that Kins was a regular communicant, and that, while he'd signed the Reverend Dick's pledge in '37, he saw this: Very much as a logical adjunct to my faith, not a political statement per se. – Kins could guess at the figure he presented: ruddy-cheeked, his dark hair flattened with water and hair oil, his rather beefy upper body draped in studious and unflashy tweed, its thick material hiding the fine balance and magnificent control he could deploy on court and course . . . *not battlefield* . . . The pious and unworldly young man they saw before them, his tie inexpertly knotted . . . *was me*, and if he seemed too clumsy to handle anything with more materiality than a conscience this was . . . *no contrivance — because Lord knows I want to move my hands but cannot!* They hunger after Annette's breasts and sides, her hips and thighs. – Suddenly they break to stand, eyeing each other warily, breathing heavily and hearing the snuffling in the stalls. Annette, her face monochrome in the moonlight . . . *throws me a lifeline* by asking, Were you awfully afraid? and Kins . . . *deflating* . . . *going soft* . . . hauls himself back to the land. Jack Clarke and another trainee remain in custody – Bill

Smedley was packed straight off to join the Nancy Elsies. A blanket of shame has covered Collow Abbey Farm, and . . . *the baseless fabric remains unrent by full and frank discussion.* — Two nights before, tiring of their confabs, bored by their limited selection of gramophone records, the trainees and their mentors had set out on a moth hunt. Kins couldn't remember who'd proposed it – or why they'd all hared heedlessly about the farmhouse and its outbuildings, pulling sheets off beds and gathering together electric torches. *Of course we were a bit tiddly – but even so . . .* Then they marched out together through the recently harvested home field, its stiff hackles scratching their ankles as grasshoppers and mites flew up their trouser legs. It should've occurred to someone the row of currant bushes beside the dried-out pond known as Despond was an ill-starred spot – the Graveneys, *unsympathisers* . . . lived a quarter-mile beyond, hunched in their *Maginot Line manor house* beside the Wragby Road, and armed with one of the few telephones in the district. The torches were implanted in the cracking earth by the bushes' roots and the sheets were flung on top of them, and the . . . *great globe was drawn down into these cloudy chambers,* over the eerily glowing billows of which inched . . . *the bamboozled muons and positrons,* their antennae twitching, their tattered wings fluttering. They were all there, the CLTA crowd: Brockleby, Cornwallis and Procter – their wives, their older children and their disciples. All fell silent at the eerie sight, and quietly moved to form their own orbit around the pulsing, illuminated bushes – a circle that . . . *too late!* realised it too had been encircled by the . . . *bloody warmongers!* Whose powerful electric lamps . . . *smashed on!* The cosmological model was *annihilated*, to be replaced by *a scrawny boy*, his carbuncular neck loose in his battledress, his teeth bared, who stared furiously at Kins over the quivering point of his fixed bayonet. All the Tommies had been racked by nerves – the one confronting Cornwallis actually pricked him. When the enraged ex-docker – temporarily abandoning his own principles – made to give his assailant a clip round the ear, he was immediately surrounded by three more, whose bellicosity was rather compromised by their having to struggle with their rifle bolts. Cornwallis held his hands up, clawed at the air and gave a howl, Kins supplying the line from his archive: He's remembering the time when he was a wolf and other people and other places never existed. Kins's Tommy chattered, Wh-What the 'ell 're you on about, m-mate? And, as with the tribunal, Kins gave him chapter and verse: The Call of the Wild, 1935, starring Clark Gable, Loretta Young and Jack Oakie –. He would've continued – since there was laughter on all sides and the tension was draining away – but an officer strode forward at that point and tore the sheets from the bushes. *For eternity* . . . the torch beams pierced the darkness, light tunnels along which the moths whirred as they struggled to reorientate themselves. Then they were smouldering in the stubble and the officer was shouting, What the bloody hell is going on here?! Who the bloody hell are you people? – Later, Kins concluded it was puzzlement rather than the rifles that had made the CLTA party so compliant. How had the Army detachment managed to creep up on them so stealthily . . . *seems as if I've lived out here in this wilderness forever.* When they were jolting along in the back of the lorry, it did occur to him that the conchies, having learnt to ignore the air-planes roaring aloft at all hours from RAF Goltho, had probably, quite unconsciously, placed the Army lorries in the same ignorable category. – At Despond, Brockleby took his time coming forward, and when he did he was nonchalantly screwing a Craven "A" into the end of his amber holder. The singing farmer softly serenaded the officer – who looked old enough to be a regular and probably hadn't much to do in this rural backwater but cultivate his own zeal. That's all very well, Mister Brockleby, he said. For my own part I don't doubt you are who you say, but the Station Commander is another matter, he'll want to know what manner of fools he has on the doorstep of his airfield . . . The officer's voice began to creep up the scale, the anticipation of his superior's grievance stimulating his own . . . a malicious meddling fool, or merely one who thinks it a bit of a lark to show the enemy precisely where we are on the brink of a bloody invasion! – After that Brockleby's Lincoln-green treacling couldn't smooth things over: the officer all but frog-marched him to the road, his men chivvying the others along in their wake. The women and children were allowed to return to the farm on foot. When they arrived, they discovered the Tommies had already up-ended the stripped beds and emptied out all the cupboards. Out in the barns – Kins found this comical because *it was something they'd seen done in the flicks* – they were pitch-forking the loose fodder with their bayonets. A pair of binoculars, two Box Brownies and two shotguns were confiscated. The officer was still in high dudgeon, and when Jack Clarke couldn't produce any papers he acted . . . *precisely as any jumped-up little fascist would* and held

165

them collectively responsible. As they were being loaded back on to the lorry, Jack kept on at him: For heaven's sake, Captain Smyth, I'd have to've been here since W. G. batted for the MCC in order to acquire my accent – and I'd've had to mug up like a bastard to've gained my mastery of Wisden. Go on, man, try me out, I can give you any Test match result for the last twenty years, every innings, if that's what you want . . . But Smyth was not to be drawn, so off they went, the lorry with its slitted headlamps purring throatily along the dark lanes . . . *a big cat, its belly stuffed after happy hunting.* In the back, pacifists and warmongers sat jolting . . . *un-der-neath the ar-ches!* but, rather than being allowed to dream his life away, Kins was . . . *viciously ragged.* Seated opposite him was one of the older Tommies, whose chubby cheeks and lumpy nose forced *Syd Walker* . . . from Kins's deck of cigarette cards . . . *a hundred stars of British cinema.* The Tommy confirmed his own knowledge of this resemblance by removing his bayonet from its scabbard, catching its point in the floppy skirts of Kins's cricketing pullover and pulling the hem so as to oblige its wearer to lean in to his leering face. I killed the cunt! he spat – and his mates guffawed. It was the first time Kins had ever heard the epithet spoken aloud, and such was his feverish shame he wondered whether it might abracadabra that part of Annette . . . *a grin without its pussy* . . . into the thickening atmosphere. Blushing heavily, Kins spluttered, Wh-What the d-devil d'you mean by that? And Syd Walker smashed Kins's cut-glass with his mockery: W-Wot ve devil do I mean by vat? Well-well, wot 'ave we 'ere, lads – you must fink you're some sorta dis-cunt vi-cunt swannin' abaht safe in your cunt-tree funk-hole while us lot bash the square 'til it's time to get our fucking bollocks shot off! – The pronounced indifference of the other Tommies – who were more taken up with whether they'd get a weekend pass and, if so, which local pubs would be most congenial for a prolonged soaking – stopped Syd Walker from getting any uglier . . . *than he was already.* Jack Clarke, who was sitting next to Kins – and who, as a deserter, had much more to fear – gave Kins's shoulder a brief squeeze and whispered, Buck up, man. For the remainder of the journey Kins faced down his tormentor's sallies with stony indifference. But at Louth, when the lorry pulled up in the courtyard of the police station and once more the conchies were chivvied out at rifle point, Kins . . . *began to lose my stuffing.* They were booked in by a bull-necked desk sergeant who bellowed his orders, then locked up two or three to a cell. The last thing Kins saw before the door clanged shut was Captain Smyth, who, he now realised, wasn't much older than him, and who bore – with the addition of a futile blond moustache – a disturbing resemblance to . . . *Michael's fag at Lancing.* – In the coolly carbolic interior of the unlit cell Kins said to his companions, I'll stand – then he tripped over a bucket and the stench of urine and vomit soon made the confined space . . . *unendurable.* The others didn't have to endure it for that long: Syd Walker, along with a cadaverous and diffident constable, came to fetch Finlay – a bookish, reserved Scot with whom Kins had played the occasional game of chess. An hour or so passed in silence . . . *we'd never developed any rapport* . . . before they returned for Briggs, a warehouseman from the West Country Kins had been accustomed to gently patronising – he'd taken the Molotov–Ribbentrop Pact . . .

perrsonal, like. Kins was left to his own miserable devices, the spillage from the bucket *manured* his imagination . . . *the singing farmer would approve*, so visions of what was being done to the other conchies – things that in due course . . . *will be done to me!* . . . sprouted up before his eyes, and, for once, singling came easily as he nipped off the weedier possibilities – a tongue-lashing, a beating, a debagging – to leave the one healthy certainty: dawn was being dragged unresistingly into being with each muffled bing-bong! of the town hall clock, and the quarter-hour would arrive that brought with it the leaning stake, the stained gravel, the handcuffs and the blindfold soaked with the impotent tears of those who had gone before him. *Rationally* . . . Kins knew this to be . . . *poppycock of the first order*, yet no sooner had he wrestled his imaginings into submission than Syd Walker returned, slid open the Judas and added his filth to the general ordure: Yellow-belly, he spat. Lily-livered conchie and Fucking pansy . . . If he could've mustered the necessary sang-froid, Kins would've remarked on the floweriness of this language – as it was, he only quailed while he was told, You, you're less than fucking British, which is why we're gonna do for you soon as cock crows. – The dated expression set Kins wondering: Was there an inky-pinky spider somewhere in the cell, whose doughty example would . . . *put some backbone in the Bruce?* For now he truly was *in a funk-hole*, nearly giving way and screaming back at Syd Walker, Don't you realise who I am?! My pater'll have your guts for garters – I insist you put a trunk call through to his Ministry right away! – It was the thought of Sirbert's embarrassment that restrained him – but when he was alone again he got to pondering: I've never seen him embarrassed in my life. Indeed, while his father's thoughts had always been an open book . . . *much pored over* and frequently declaimed from, his elder son had no apprehension of his feelings at all . . . *Flush'd is his brow, through every vein, In azure tide the currents strain, And undistinguish'd accents broke, The awful silence ere he spoke.* Now considering it with a clarity borne of pitiful resignation, Kins decided that if Sirbert had any feelings at all . . . *he must keep them in a locked ministerial box.* This was Kins's epiphany: his father might be adept at putting on a show, but he'd probably no greater sympathy . . . *than a tree or a rock.* – Moreover, if his own physical cowardice was a hive burning under his skin, Sirbert – being nerveless – had no comparable feelings, so neither balked at the necessity of dishing out death from a safe remove – as he'd done at the Arsenal during the last war, and was ably doing right now as the Beaver's PPS – or so much as gave it a thought that he might be *hee-hawing* . . . while others . . . *roared into the slaughter.* The repellent smoothness of Sirbert's hairless calves when he pulled up his stockings and tied the laces of his golf shoes, the ugly varicosity that wormed purplish behind his knees – these were proof he was incarnate, although, in common with Our Saviour, Sirbert had . . . *risen without trace.* But that was where the resemblance ended. All this time Kins had been mystified: why was it he was unable to deploy the one weapon allowed him – prayer. Now he understood: his God had never been a meek, mild, silky-bearded ephebe, but a clean-shaven Old Testament bully, who took every trick his partner won for his own . . . *and the Devil take the hindmost.* Kins had never imagined himself to be a physical coward before − now he saw there'd been a thick yellow streak running through the persistence with which he'd skived off footer and mitched rugger. There was also the studiousness with which he'd avoided the RSM who'd taught the Lancing boys the noble art ... *of sadomasochism,* encouraging them to spar with their guards scarcely up so as to invite their opponent's blows ... *in a manly and virile fashion.* All became clear: it was not − as he'd assumed, knowing of the pashes older and younger boys shared − the homo overtones of such activities that repulsed him, it wasn't *wily Grecian love* ... but ... *forthright Roman contact* he couldn't abide. And if this were the case, might what Syd Walker condemned him for also be true? All this pledging, pontificating and piety had really been ... *an awful pose.* The old Sirbertian religion had, Kins now acknowledged, been no leap of faith, but rather ... *finely factored for risk,* a matter of Pascalian wagers within *still more Pascalian wagers.* When Kins and Michael were boys ... *Our Father encouraged us to bet on the duration of the sermon.* Kins had never doubted Sirbert's sincere belief in certain aspects of the Christian deity: the ones he believed he shared, each having been made in the other's image. *Why dost thou hide thyself in clouds, From every searching Eye, Why darkness and obscurity, In all thy words and laws ... Thrice I denied him before the cock crowed ...* So when Syd Walker finally beckoned him from the cell and with slapstick digs and pricks drove him into an office where an elderly and corpulent man sat wrapped in an unseasonable blue Melton overcoat, Kins was fully prepared ... *to recant all and become a fighting heretic, if necessary.* It wasn't. The bull-necked desk sergeant held Kins's certificate upright between the tips of his fingers. Bugger off now, laddie, he said to Syd Walker. Your OC has been held up a fair while now – you're ruddy lucky I don't get him to put you on a two-five-two for . . . ah, mislaying this one. – Squeezing past the rooted Kins, Syd Walker gave a final smirk . . . *for my eyes only* . . . and brought his martial heel down hard on cowardly toes. After that he was gone, leaving Kins to grimace at the rolltop desk, a calendar advertising Emco Farm Suppliers of Caister, a hat-stand and an open but barred window, through which early-morning sunlight *drained* into the room. A quart-bottle of Watneys Ale and a glass sat on the blotter beside the sergeant's zebra-striped cuff. The fat old man sighed heavily, then wheezed: I've no time at all for you bloody conchies. If I'd a free hand, that ass Brockleby's set-up'd be shut down pronto and the lot of you'd be rounded up. After that, if you weren't disposed to do your bit, well . . . He sighed again, still more heavily, and, struggling round on the squeaking swivel chair, poured some ale into the glass and took a gulp. Aaah! Theatrical satisfaction, Kins felt, was of a piece with the man's spotted bow tie and the antique nippers hanging from a tri-colour ribbon pinned to his jacket collar. You'll have a quick wet? The old man gestured with the bottle, and when the sergeant declined, he finally confirmed: I'd have you shot. Now . . . he ran on *blind to his casual savagery* . . . take your lousy bit of paper and bugger off. You. Are. Free. – he gave each of the words sardonic emphasis – To. Go. – In the courtyard behind the police station a cockerel was rooting in some straw and a corporal was slamming the lorry's tailgate. Captain Smyth leant out from its cab and called to Kins, I say, d'you want a lift back to Holton? Shielding his eyes, Kins called back, No, thanks all the same, I'd as soon stretch my legs . . . For the first five miles or so he suffered the torment of this remonstrance: *You snivelling idiot, you could've at least given him a proper wigging!* – By mid-morning he'd come down off the hills and was labouring across the fields, too fagged to do anything but follow furrows that tended in roughly the right direction. He came upon an old woman who was . . . *a bit touched*: a living oddmedodd who stood by the hawthorn hedge screening her tiny tumbledown cottage from the sunken lane. Her outspread apron filled with crumbs, she brought down on her head an unkindness of crows, which limped across the beech-mast to stare one-sidedly at this . . . *carrion in waiting*. She pumped water into an old tin that Kins drained and she refilled several times, then she went to her hen house of curling tar paper and withdrew two speckled eggs that, still warm, she introduced to his hand. – He went on with the eggs in the tin, and an hour or so later waded out through the hip-high waving wheat to a shrub-choked marl pit. Hiding on the shore of this sunken island, he filled the old tin with tea-brown water, put together a tiny pyre of bark bits and very slowly hard-boiled the eggs. Sitting there, the fire still smouldering between his out-stretched legs, Kins twisted the first egg, unscrewing the white meat from its ends so it fell to lie steaming on the grass . . . *an armistice, at last, with Blefuscu*. He thought of Bryant & May – very old gentlemen, he assumed, Victorian benefactors with a penchant for fallen women . . . *and turning them into match girls*. He thought of his Solomon at Louth . . . *some lordly Lieutenant or acceptably*

Oddfellow . . . and, taking the hot naked egg in his hand, slit its perfect translucent skin with a dirty fingernail, marvelling: I've never done anything quite so satisfying before – prob'ly never will again. The egg's atomic core steamed . . . *with all the pungency of coition*, and in its yellow core Kins discovered a blood-red speck of fertilisation. — He's sat for so long a thrush hops from the hedge and pecks at the puzzlement of shell bits with its pretty beak. Lifting his head from the mess in his hands, Kins sees, *Gains-boroughised* by foliage, a V-formation of airplanes stammering over-head. *I'm n-not as ig-ig-ignorant as my comrades imagine* . . . Kins has studied a chart in the Daily Mail, so identifies these medium-range twin-engine bombers to be Whitleys . . . *by their Jew-boy noses.* The thrush scats – Kins hunkers forward to watch as the V-flight recedes over copse after copse. He licks his palm, savouring the sweat-salted egg dregs, and waits for . . . *the ill-omened Trinity* to be gone – only to see the aircraft turn in a wide circle, smut filthying from their engines. Grasping that Goltho will be . . . *the fix'd foot* at the centre of this aerial geometry, Kins appreciates . . . *I must be almost home.* Then the fat old eggman repeats on him: *You. Are. Free. To. Go* . . . whereas Jack Clarke has been *singled out* from the formation that *hedge-hopped over the beet fields.* Besides, in Kins's breast – sharply angled *as heartburn* – there's this shameful know-ledge he'll keep . . . *to mine own self*: rock by name, each time Syd Walker's bayonet thrust through the Judas . . . *I was petrified – then shattered.* Of course, Kins muses as he wades on through the wheat, there may well be such a coward lurking inside every one of them – in Syd Walker and in Captain Smyth, in the desk sergeant and in

Brockleby, in all the veterans of Wipers *coughing over their shove ha'penny* . . . Is it, he wonders, that they don't see this craven part of their natures and so wreak their fear on others? Or is it crasser: *because secrecy gains females' loud applause?* – The crooked elbow of an old oak bough leans on a broken fence, and, with a pang of recognition . . . *that's a valediction*, Kins sees he's reached Collow Abbey Farm. He should seek Annette out – she'll be waiting for him in among the worn bricks, the rotten wattle, the splintered laths and all the other jetsam . . . *of our floating world – but nobodaddy's not coming* and yer mummy's not coming neither. – He stands by the window rolling a joint in a skin the same colour as the blinds . . . *Rizla Wheetstraw*, Genie's so weak . . . *I can't move*, so remains . . . *crucified*, her tormented arms *nailed down* to the rough grain of the massive and heavy table that Hughie bish-bosh-bodged up out of railway sleepers during one of his increasingly rare visits. Genie makes still rarer ones to the Cambridgeshire village where her disturbed younger brother has ended up, plink-a-plunketing on his acoustic guitar . . . *My babe don't stand no cheatin', My babe* . . . in a grotty semi beside a muddy river lined with sobbing willows. His landlady is fatter than anyone Genie's ever seen before in her life – five or six distinct tubs of solidified lard, the topmost . . . *wiv makeup on it: foundation for skin, lipstick for lips, mascara an' eyeliner to make eyes* . . . The fat woman – whose name is Karen Rastrick – takes Hughie's social and doles out his medication. — The one night Genie stayed there she was . . . *freaked right out* by the steady stream of couples who came to see Old Mother Rastrick. Yokels with bleached-blond mullets and bunches of keys draped over the bulges in their faded jeans. Sitting beside them on the broken-down sofa were their young yokel wives, who'd the same . . . *bow-wow-wow hairdos*. Girls who in any other place would be *fat and manky* . . . looked slim and presentable. Old Mother Rastrick got Hughie to shift a stack of cat-pissed-upon newspapers from the top of a wicker hamper and . . . *get out me 'erbals*. She gave the yokel couples roots and dried leaves, told them how to crush and pound them. They listened respectfully, then divvied up a fiver, or the lad said he'd bring some firewood by . . . *on the morrow*. Up in Hughie's room, Genie laughed uneasily: What the fuck, is she some kind of witch or what? And Hughie, smiling . . . *for the first time in ages* . . . said, No what about it, she's a witch, but a white one. — I wonder, Genie thinks, if he uses her reinforced commode? Then she says to David: No offence, but what the fuck d'you know about my mummy? He laughs . . . *not an 'appy sound* . . . and, opening the patent-leather handbag he wears dangling round his neck by its gold-chain strap, he puts the rolled joint away and takes out a gun. None taken, he says, while using its muzzle – which is too long and slim, surely for a real one . . . *p'raps iss just a target whatsit* – to prise out the blind so he can . . .'*ave a gander* down into the . . . *bloody orangeyness* of the street below. I always think, David says, things get a lot realer when the shooters come out. Genie numbles, I dunno what you mean, mate. Half the hit was more than enough: her lips are swollen and prickling from the coke, while her head is wrapped in the smack's bitter lagging. – In some distant and maximally neglected part of the house, *iss notta squat, iss 'ousing 'sociation*, under the cork-covered top of a laundry box she scavenged from a skip, Genie's racing heart lies wrapped up in a soiled tea towel printed with a Welsh dragon – it stalls for half a dizzying beat, then races again. What I'm driving at, David continues in his strange half-posh, half-geezer accent, is that you've got to stand on your own two feet. – He comes back to the table and resumes his own plastic stacking chair. He puts the gun on the table and props his long powdered chin on the platform of his interlaced fingers. He looks at her through wide green lenses. – For an intelligent man, Genie thinks – and everyone says he is – David . . . *don't 'alf mouth some dumb clichés.* You take my situation, he continues. You're a crim' so basically there's no law to protect you – thass obvious. Then, in the course of doin' a bit of work, you 'appens to waste a copper. Well, now the law wants to fucking crucify you . . . He talks in clichés, Genie thinks . . . *an' iss always about 'imself.* Next up, to cap it all, you got the sheer-bloody-balls to leg it from the cells just before your case is up. Hey, sinner-man, where you gonna run to now? The chaps? I don't-fucking-think-so – they'll grass you up quicker than they can wipe their hairy arses. He carefully shrugs off his coat, which is shaggy . . . *some sorta synfetic fur.* He must, Genie thinks, be mad if he thinks it's a disguise . . . *'e'd stand out a mile from the Paddies along the 'igh Road.* Under the coat David wears a lilac blouse with ruffles down the front . . . *but no fake boobs – an' 'e's whippet-thin.* Give us the works, willya, he says, and Genie rouses herself to *tong* . . . the syringe lying beside . . . *my setting* with her thumb and forefinger. – She remembers a handful of shifts she did waiting at Simpson's-in-the-Strand. When Genie went into the storeroom to try on the itsy-bitsy black nylon dress with its *white cotton cunt-rag* . . . of an apron, the dago maître d' followed her . . . *and tonged my arse.* She knew his bullshit about his invalid wife was *exactly that* . . . and he knew hers about being silver service was . . . *same again.* The onion sacks were rough and hard and knobbly . . . *I'm always at the parties in kitchens,* she thinks aloud – and David says, You what? and Genie says, Nuffink, juss finkin about standing on me own two feet. David holds the syringe – a third, glossier one – between his Revlon lips as he unbuttons the blouse's ruffled cuff. Genie says, You're not really gonna hit that up, are you? I might have hep' or all sorts . . . *inna paper bag from the nooky shop . . . Pontefract cakes . . . the free-decker biggie an' the aniseedy one wiv the little sugar balls . . .* Genie may be stoned, but David's strong resemblance to . . . *someone famous* has been bothering her. Now he's expertly twisted the handbag's strap around his . . . *stained-glass* arm, and probed with the needle in the pit of his elbow, she gets it: the blond page-boy wig, the floppy-brimmed felt hat, the pink-framed and bug-eye green shades . . . *it's Brian Jones!* Because David isn't trying to look like a woman – *'e's trying to look like a man trying to look like a woman* . . . Genie puzzles over this confusion as David pushes in the plunger . . . *all that claret* mysteriously robbing his face of its remaining colour. *He's pretty enough for a bird* . . . with his refined nose and flirty lashes . . . *He's outrageous, he screams and he bawls . . . let yerself go-o-wo!* – She was Jeanie until 1972, then she began to write GENIE with different-coloured felt-tips. Next she doodled her way round GENIE, turning it into a flower's stamen . . . *with daggers for petals* –. Oof! he says, withdrawing the needle, and immediately ducks to suck the thick black streamer of blood. Genie says to the dimpled crown of his hat: What about the other geezer, whassisface – Waldorf? Then curses herself *You fucking mong!* for such lairiness, because of all the heavy blokes who score off her, David is indisputably the heaviest – heavier than the ex-SAS nutter who came with them on the Lebanon run, heavier than the South African gingernut pimps who sold her in Cambridge. Heavier than the Dilly-boy thugs Trouget brings into Mumsie's club – rough trade, Mumsie says, the painter pays to . . . *beat the shit out of him.* David shows his heaviness by walking into Genie's top room *an' pullin' me paintings off the walls.* Genie thinks this is a worse violation than anything he could do to her physically – anyway, David's probably queer . . . *like Trouget* . . . and if he were to fuck her it'd probably only be . . . *for the hell of it,* or else he'd go all soppy – queers did when they did it with a woman. She pictures David opening the passenger door of a metallic-blue beach buggy plastered with daisy decals for her. She pictures him driving her away along a Kilburn High Road . . . *gone tropical,* with white sand banked up against the scuzzy shop windows and palm trees bursting through the flobbed-upon pavements. Genie's wearing a travelling outfit from Sindy's Bazaar: a pink party dress with a twist flare, white lace edgings, bow-tie loop belt and matching Alice band . . . *and underneath* a blue nylon petticoat edged in more white lace with pink flowers . . . *and deeper down* matching blue-and-white nylon lace bra and panties . . . *and deeper still* David's . . . *matching pearly-whites ready to bite 'em off* . . . Genie sees the hole smashed in the abandoned fishing boat's hull, sees her own severed head wobble into view, its dead eyes staring stupidly back at her, its slag's mouth open and the words felt-tip-doodling out: *When Genie comes around and sings a happy song of summ-errr* . . . The money Barry gave her for the smuggling trip is long gone . . . *all twenty grand of it – mostly straight up me sleeve*, and the two keys of hash she nicked are gone as well. All she's left to show for it are the canvases stacked against the walls of the downstairs room she calls . . . *my stew-di-o*, and the half-squeezed tubes of acrylic paint worming on the bare boards or nesting in balls of stained rags. – Sweat trickles from beneath David's blond bangs, and Genie thinks, He must have a stash of cash somewhere – he could help me. She needs help, she owes . . . *every-fucking-body*: Bantock, the big Jamaican geezer who lays ounces of gear on her – and Joe Levy who does the same with coke. She's already borrowed to pay them off . . . *and the loan sharks are circling*. For now they're only curious – nosing out from the urban murk to see what manner of creature she is. There's been a petrol bomb through the window – only a small one . . . *never mind* . . . and a dead squirrel nailed to the front door . . . *least it weren't the moggy*. Soon, however . . . *they'll smell blood an' zero in fer it*. Genie looks at the gun lying on the table – it has a dull blue-shine barrel and a brown grip that *looks like plastic*. Life, Genie thinks, is stretched so thin – it doesn't . . . *take Allsorts, it ain't a biggie* . . . it's stretched out right around the world, *a triple-decker*: thin sea, thinner land, thinnest of all . . . *the sky*. It's a shell, this life, and through the cracks in it the darkness is forever . . . *leaking*. The paraffin heater's stink catches in her throat – outside, *where the pissed-up Paddies 'owl*, it's cold enough, but inside it's hot, because she lit the heater at dusk when she got up. Between five and seven she served at least fifteen punters – when there was a lull she laid a fire of chair legs and splintered orange boxes in the grate and lit it. The thin dry pieces of wood caught and crackled – kneeling, watching, thinking not of her own childhood but of someone happier's, she saw a spider leg wiggle through a crack, followed by another, *a third, a fourth* . . . The wee beastie pulled its body laboriously after them, and *inky-pinked* into incandescence. David puts his hand to his face and sweeps it all off – shades, wig, hat – to reveal slicked-black back and sides, a foundation mask with Revlon lips and mascara eyelids scorched on to it. In an odd little-girly voice he says, I've only one life so I prefer to live it as a blonde . . . Then in his normal one: What about that fucking slag, Waldorf? Sue says when the filth thought they done him – by which I mean they thought they done me – one of 'em still stuck his piece right between her eyes, like this – he picks up the gun and, with hands upside down and back to front, levels it at the bridge of his refined nose – and screamed, OK, COCKSUCKER! Which is a laugh, really – a complete fucking blast. – Genie's fingers have sidled of their own accord over to the pack of Bensons and are *inky-pinkying* one out. David leaps up, rubs his hands on his black sateen matador pants, stretches to his full six feet and says, 'Cause she never sucks cock, Sue, never. I can give you that on the best authority: my own. As for Waldorf, they think he's a bloody civilian and I ain't about to put 'em straight, y'see, Genie . . . He circles round behind her and, lifting a greasy bunch of her curls with one hand, lays his other palm on her hot throbbing neck. The gun is still in plain view – her cigarette wags, amplifying the fishy twitches of

Genie's nerveless lips. She knows enough to . . . *keep still an' keep shtum* . . . She's been done over for her stash enough times to understand this: *kicking off only gets you . . . a kicking* . . . iss all about i-den-titty, innit. – Why d'you say that, David? – The hair falls, he dances back in front of her, snatches up the gun and strikes a . . . *harder-they-fucking-come* pose, aiming at the big poster of Dennis Bovell nailed to the crumbling plaster. Don't be dumb, Genie, he says. You may be smacked out of your mind, but don't act like it's a tiny fucking one – like I say, it's all about identity: Babylon come looking for me and they get that toe-rag instead! David sings: They blew his mind out inna car . . . then says: Right location too . . . He sticks the muzzle in his mouth and yodels: as it 'appens, guys and girls . . . then taps ash from the trigger guard. You've gotta understand, he says, it weren't really that they thought Waldorf was me – it was fucking Sue! See – he snags the wig with the gun-sight – she's a blonde, she's tall, she's a known associate, so the stupid cunts stake out her gaff, they clock me going about my business, they see her farting around – and they know I'm a master of bloody disguise so they reach the obviously wrong conclusion: she's me. Waldorf – the pistol droops and the wig flops back on to the table – he was just in the wrong place at the wrong fucking time. It was a blue-on-blue action – mistaken i-den-titty, yeah? But what you gotta understand, girl, is that nobody – and I mean ab-so-lute-ly nobody – is who anyone thinks they are. – His face . . . *back in mine* . . . is plucked eyebrows . . . *cemetery gates*, and the *red ironwork* of veins in his bugging eyes. He ticks them off on his lock-picker's fingers: The dingo ain't a dingo, it's a religious nutter, the terrorists ain't terrorists, they're freedom-fucking-fighters, the shrink ain't a shrink, he's a fucking nut-job. As for that other nut-job, the one they nabbed in Her Maj's boo-doir, he ain't just some pond life chancing his arm, oh no – she asked him up, didn't she, 'cause if there's one thing a queen likes it's a bit of rough. We all like a bit of rough –. David stops short and consults his wrist . . . *'ands an' chins – they're always too big, that's 'ow you spot a trannie.* Stupid me, he resumes, I never wear a watch – he plucks up the wig – I'd know that about myself if I'd any idea who the fuck I was. What's the time? – Genie looks over at the sink, where a Teasmade sits on the crusted draining board. She has to stagger up and limp halfway there before she can read the clockface set between its cracked china columns: 8.15, she says . . . *and that's the time it's always been. We got your message on the ra-di-o, Conditions normal and you're coming home* . . . The synthesisers tootle an accompaniment as David reassumes his disguise . . . *doodle-oodle-oodlie-oo, doodle-oodle-oodlie-oo* . . . over and maddeningly over again . . . *doodle-oodle-oodlie-oo, doodle-oodle-oodlie-oo* . . . aimlessly again . . . *boodle-oodle-boodlie-oo, boodle-oodle-boodlie-oo* . . . Genie thinks: I'd welcome the bullet – I'd enjoy watching all the boodles and boos spurting outta my cracked china bonce . . . *Deathsmade.* – He's kitted out and standing by the stairs . . . *ready for the drop.* Your gaff's a right shit-hole, he says, kicking at the charred laths rising up to the smutty ceiling. For myself, I want to have it with 'em somewhere with a bit of class – Kensington or Knightsbridge, fitted kitchen, en suite, all mod-fucking-cons, me serving Pina Coladas to the Old Bill . . . He looks her full in the face – his eyes are *deeply submerged* in his green shades. He says, You think I dunno I'm on my way out, girl . . . I'm brown bread, I am – fucking toast. That's why I don't give a shit about shooting up your manky claret, you sad little slag. – He pulls down his hat brim and shifts his handbag so it dangles, a patent-leather medallion, from the gold chain buried in his synthetic chest. I'll let myself out, he says, but Genie follows him down the five flights, his high heels chattering as they . . . *chew the 'ouse a new arsehole.* – Through this tight aperture she sees: bloodstains from carelessly flushed works spattering the staircase – worse, the potty by her never-made bed she pisses in when she can't make it to the bog – and worst of all the open wardrobe door that reveals dresses she'll never wear . . .*'cause they're short-sleeved.* – She unlocks the front door, shoots the bolts, and the January night scours their faces. David flattens against the porch wall, then skips to the other side. She sees what he does: split black plastic bags, a squeezed half-lemon, a crushed milk carton, dented bins, a wild shrubbery tossing in the wind. Genie hugs the meagreness inside her dressing gown *my sad tits*, which, when surprised in the bathroom mirror, are . . . *old men's chins*. A single streetlamp has pitched its orange flysheet over the park gates . . . *Where the fuck's Mister Tumnus?* – David turns back to Genie, and, grabbing her chin roughly between his thumb and forefinger, he lilts, I want your bod-y, I want it in parts, I want your thighs and hips – I want your tender lips, I want your bod-y – I'm not a queer – I want your tender heart, I want your tits that sag . . . I want 'em all wrapped up . . . inside BLACK PLASTIC BAGS –. He's gone. Struggling with the door, she almost blacks out. She thinks: Mumsie's not coming and thank fuck for that – as for Daddy, who's 'e when 'e's at 'ome? – At the top of the house she crashes on a broken-down old couch . . . *golden syrup* of time . . . *dripples*, her eyes ooze over to the Teasmade: it persists with 8.15. Broke, she thinks, it must be broke. She sings aloud, Conditions normal and we're coming home! – But what was normal? When you're little, she supposes, you don't know nothing else. — Miss Philbeach, whose nose twisted at a peculiar angle . . . *deformed, really* . . . taught them domestic science at the two-room primary in Little Gaddesden. One time it was elderflower wine: they mixed up the ingredients, let it sit. Weeks later they took turns helping her to pour it out of the demijohn, through a funnel and into flat, clear-glass medicine bottles – Miss gave them one each to take home to their parents. On the way Jeanie and Hughie did the sums and drank one between them. When the sweet green juice was gone . . . *we thought we could speak Oddle-Poddle*, which was what they did, stagger-zagging back along the lanes to the cottage, where they found . . . *Big-fucking-Weed* with Mumsie, who laughed uproariously as they came tottering up the garden path. Well, she said, whose idea was this, then? Was it you, Bill? She grabbed Jeanie's chin roughly. Or was it you, Ben? Hughie's she only gave a gentle tweak. Kins hovered in the background, a thin smile stitched across his . . . *stuffed scarecrow face*. Cray-zee kids, Mumsie said approvingly, and Kins, shuffling his big stupid feet, said something non-committal . . . *Weeee-eeed!* He was around a lot at that time – always prepared to run errands for Mumsie and her cray-zee kids. Kins, Mumsie would order him, drive us over to . . . *here or there – pretty much anywhere that took her fancy, 'cause she was pissed* – and, 'though he must've been as well, *you could never tell with him, 'e 'ad a head for it*. He'd pull on his soft leather driving gloves – his knuckles showed white through the holes . . . *crotchless panties*. He drove his sharkish Rover 2000, *which smelt of Trebor mints and Windo-fucking-lene*, with fanatic care, his traffic-cone nose close to the windscreen, his rounded shoulders . . . *more rounder*, his ape arms . . . *bent*. It'd been . . . *a flappy-wappy day* – which was what they called them. You had to give Mumsie this much: when the mood took her she was a dedicated laundress. Sheets, blouses, pillowcases, knickers . . . *all spotless*. The cottage might be a tip you had to . . . *Twister through*, placing your feet in the small patches left between dirty dishes and drink spillages, but there in the middle of it all would be a hanky pressed, folded and . . . *crying out for snotty panky*. — Kins drove them through the outskirts of Hemel to St Christopher's, a new comp' of glass and concrete H-blocks with a bleak playing field across which blew . . . *the wind from nowhere*. In the corner of this, set well apart, was a crap-looking prefab': the special unit for difficult pupils Mumsie had set up, and which was the first of its kind in the country – a piece of information she took immense pride in shoving at . . . *all comers*. The grown-ups clustered by a chain-link fence with a banner tied to it, and chattered loudly over its . . . *flappy-wappy*. Jeanie and Hughie had been around the unit enough to get over any repulsion – now they found the mongs' and spazzers' groans and gurns, their gargoyle faces, *fucking hilarious*. They liked to be chased . . . *and we liked chasing 'em* – around the ragged goal nets . . . *the ragged rascals ran*. I was jealous, Genie thinks, she loved them kids more than she's ever loved me . . .

Mumsie and Kins hung on to sausage rolls while they talked to a tall blonde woman wearing an ethnic dress of many colours . . . *her astounding clothing took the bis-cuit, Quite the smoothest person in the dis-trict* . . . 'cause the other parents all looked like their spazzy kids, and this was . . . *disturbing*. Round and around they chased the mongs, zeroing in on the witch's hat roundabout, which they jumped on and off, making it rock and squeal . . . *Help! Not just anybod-y!* – Someone would've rigged up a record player to a crappy tannoy . . . *they always did that* . . . and there would've been crappy-flappy bunting as well. Woozy and knock-kneed, their heads spinning, Jeanie and Hughie staggered away to skulk by the table where the tombola prizes were set out: Emva Cream Sherry, Quality Streets, a tin of Saxon Car Wax, each on its own little wooden plinth . . . *like they were a big-fucking-deal*. Eventually, *bored outta our tiny minds*, they took the half-bottle of Gordon's gin . . . *an' did fer at least half of it in the school bogs*. The juniper fumes were . . . *disinfectant cubes* plucked from the dribbling urinals and . . . *rammed up our noses*. Hughie began puking right away . . . *he was only five*. Jeanie left him to it and reeled back to the playground equipment – the *shand* pit, the *shee-shaw sheahorsh* . . . and the climbing frame . . . *it took some bottle* to haul herself up, bar after bar, before she stood right at the top, legs spread . . . *Olga-fucking-Korbut* while the mongs gathered below, their eyes wide, their upside-down mouths open. – I should, she thinks, have shouted, Mind yer Ps an' Qs! because the puke – when it came in rhythmic surges – had been watery except for these *carroty bits – What did I 'ave for breakfast?* or brekker, as Kins called it. — Sometimes he stayed at the cottage – not in Mumsie's bedroom, but tucked up in blankets on the sofa – or, if he didn't make it that far, stretched out in the Chesterfield armchair with a bedspread chucked over his long legs. When the kids were getting ready for school, there he'd be: *a canary in candlewick*, who'd wake up and be *chirpy enough* . . . as he ducked under the low beams in the kitchen, opening cupboards and drawers, stewing tea and burning toast. Once he made Nesquik for her . . . *wiv five spoonfuls!* She sat stirring the sludge and watched, repelled, as he ate toast: buttering a small corner, coating it with Golden Shred, then bringing the little bite-sized sandwich up to *'is rabbity teeth*. Of all . . . *'er casual fucks*, Kins repelled Jeanie the most: his nervous tic of rubbing his thumbs on his fingers, his voice *a flem plum* lodged in his throat, his ever-wet lips and always moist eyes, the way he cleared his throat with a *Harrumph!* The way his shoulders were permanently hunched *from talking down to Munchkins*, so his head stuck out from this *shell* . . . while he . . . *munched 'is dandelions – fucking tortoise.* As she grew older, and especially after she'd *come on*, Jeanie's revulsion only increased. She could see that to others he might be good-looking enough . . . *for an old man*: his nose was straight, his chin firm, his eyes clear-sky-blue – but she saw through to the inside: she knew who Kins really was . . . *Desperate Dan, desperate for cuddles from Mumsie-wumsie* . . . and this made him ugly. Over time, her repulsion settled down sootily on . . . *his skin*, its snowy pallor scattered with freckles and reddish moles that, as he slumped despondently in the kitchen, she fixated on through the mesh of his dingy string vests. Genie hated Kins's skin most of all because it was a puckered carrier bag full of Kins's wanting flesh – and she hated this wanting flesh because it coddled Kins's . . . *yearning 'eart.* – Years later, when she'd get back from weeks away – crashing on the floors of squats, or travelling with the Convoy – her own skin browned by dirt and sun, her hair thick with grease, her eyes *shattered mirrors* and her head *all over the shop – in trees an' flowers an' both 'alves of a worm*, she'd be appalled to find him palely loitering – still there . . . *still lapping up whatever she dished out.* On his wounded face the same soppy expression – the one Jeanie saw as her puke spurted into the mongs' faces, the one she saw – her bare leg outstretched, her Converse basketball boot arched – just before she tumbled, her head boinging off the bars once, twice, *fuck knows how many times* . . . only that it was a miracle she was still alive when she reached the ground and he came shambling up at a run to disentangle her from the climbing frame's steel embrace. — Someone is yanking the string that rattles the tin against the window. It'll be One-Armed Mickey, Genie thinks, because *'e's more regular than any clockwork.* She ought to haul herself up from the old couch, drag herself down the stairs, shoot the bolts, turn the keys and *serve 'im up 'is poxy little dollop.* She doesn't move: the memories are within and without now: *tapeworms* . . . curling in one eye and out the other, in one whistling adenoidal ear *an' out the uvver.* — It was Kins who took her to the carnival in his sharkish car. That was the summer Mumsie stopped sending her with Gregor and the others to visit Omi Maria in Vienna. She remembers . . . *traction engines, and some bint got up as Lady Godiva inna flesh-coloured body-stocking.* Kins held her hand as the parade passed by: there were floats with people wearing giant papier-mâché animal heads on them, others with dolly birds doing the twist in their swimming costumes. She sees them ... *coming round again*: the enormous weighing scales on the Co-op float and the jolly lifeboat men got up in bright orange sou'westers and oilskins. Everybody was waving ... *Hello, hello – good-fucking-bye* ... and Kins lifted her – he was so strong, try as she might Jeanie couldn't stop him from ... *clamping my cunt against the back of 'is neck*. It was from this clammy lookout she'd seen the Royal Flush ... *the Yanks' fighters an' ours togevver* ... howl overhead, fanning out as they released *red, white an' blue puke trails*. Kins carried her on through the crowds to the showground, *'is cheek sandpapering my thigh*, where they watched the Blue Stars marching up and down, oompahing ... *the Damn-fucking-busters*, the bandsmen at the head turning on their heels and being swallowed up by the ones behind. Then Kins and Jeanie went on a swing boat, and after that heard a speech given by *some nob wiv a dirty-great gold chain* – Genie can even remember his name: *Sir Aubrey-bloody-Burke* ... because this coincidence had appealed to Kins's simple nature, so the rest of the afternoon he kept muttering to himself, *Burke of Berkhamsted* ... and giving one of his ... *sad little titters*. When they arrived back at the cottage, and he'd limboed under the heavy oak lintel, he said it to Mumsie: *Burke of Berkhamsted* – and she'd said, You're the fucking berk, before *splapping 'im in the mush*. That was Kins: always ... *feeding the 'and that bit 'im*. — One-Armed Mickey, a *gyppo-faced sparrer* of a man, hops in the hall, the empty arm of his donkey jacket slapping the broken screen of an old television Genie had hauled out of a skip weeks ago and heaved home. In her buzzing state she'd intended to use it as part of an artwork, but it never made it further. I was gonna get two bags, Genie, Mickey says, but if you let me 'ave a quarter I'll settle up Tuesday . . . Sensing her utter indifference, he *tweets on*: All right, is you? Is you alrightee? And yer mum, she alrightee too? – There's . . . *no 'arm in Mickey*, Genie titters. – I ain't seen the cow since Christmas. – Which is what she'll say to the filth if they come looking for David Martin. She stands, swaying slightly, and thinking how strange it is that 'armless Mickey now occupies the exact same space so recently vacated by the armed robber – if she squints she can see the psychic energy David left behind, a Ready Brek outline . . . *fizzling in the gloom – This is the way we go to thieve onna cold and frosty mor-ning!* – Her stash is a teddy-bear pyjama case that slumps on her unmade bed. Honey right to the bottom, she whispers as she gropes in its guts. Back downstairs, Mickey unfolds the square of glossy paper. No offence, he says, and Genie mutters, None taken . . . *because that's what the cow mooed.* —– It'd been Christmas Eve. They were sitting on the wonky stools next to the ornately engraved tin-plated cash register occupying one end of the Plantation Club's bar – Mumsie's club! The magical realm Jeanie had dreamt of, with its film stars and millionaires with their flashing teeth and glittering eyes, all dancing in the rays shining from the mirror ball! This was what it'd turned out to be: a poky room above a bankrupt coffee importer's off Wardour Street, full of dusty tat and stinking of beer-soaked carpet. The Plantation Club – a zombies' graveyard where the undead drink themselves back to sodden life. The Plantation Club – where Mumsie felt so at home among the vicious hacks and maudlin old queens she'd no qualms

about asking her daughter, *granted, inna roundabout way*, to prostitute herself in order to pay her bar bill. It's not like we haven't made
our little arrangements in the past, Mumsie had coaxed, swirling
the drinky-pooh in her hand so its ice cubes . . . *tink-fucking-tinked*.
The Plantation's owner, Val, was slumped on his stool, his pitted
red shnozz aimed at his slack lap, his white hair with its nicotine
highlights wreathing his shiny temples. The Roman in bloody
Britain, Genie thought – but what she said to Mumsie was, None
taken. – Hilary, the barman, his skinny denim rump pushed out
and the dish cloth stuck in his belt wagging, wiped a patch of the
window clearish and, peering down into Blore Court, said, Poof's
on 'is way up. Mumsie kept on: You done it with the Poof . . .
Which was true enough: Genie had done it with the Dog and
McCluskey too – she'd done it with Barry as well, which was why
he'd offered her the Lebanon caper. The only non-queer Plantation
regular she hadn't done it with was the Martian – and no one really
knew which side he batted for anyway. It'd been like this since
Genie had reached . . . *the age of fucking consent*: she was allowed to
relax in the Plantation, absorb its restful fatalism – there was no
desperation here . . .*'cause their gear's on tap* – but towards the end
of the month, when there were still a few drinking days before
Mumsie got her pay packet, the grim pantomime would begin:
Val would hold Mumsie's latest IOU up to the sardonic light bulb.
Ooh, he'd meanly grate, your handwriting ain't half gone wonky,
Mumsie – girlie of your advancing years oughta get her eyes tested,
you prob'ly need some ogle-fakes. – Mumsie, the hard-won G&T
cradled between her bangly wrists, would look defeated for a

moment . . . *tiny, frail and old*, then she'd pull herself together and jiggle her tits so her reading glasses – which hung on a length of fine chain – did a disembodied dance. I've got readers, she'd say, you miserable tight-fisted cunt. Val, depressing a key on the register so the cash drawer shot out, lifted a spring-hinged clip and rummaged in one of the compartments. Well, in that case, dearie, he'd say, you can see the old Jewish piano's already chock-fucking-full of your worthless promises. This is the last one: no payback, no more drinky-poohs, I'm running a going concern, not a fucking charity! Then he'd add the IOU and release the clip so it . . . *thwacked*. Mumsie, disconsolate, would leave the bar and come over to Genie, her *lyin' eyes* . . . shining with tears . . . *of self-pity*, her *fat arse wagging* . . . submissively. Shooing away the Dog – who was always sniffing around Genie trying to *cock 'is leg* – Mumsie would begin pimping: So-and-so isn't a very happy chappie, she'd say, wifey's a bit of a ball-breaker, he can't be getting any – and him with plenty of readies . . . A girl could do worse for herself than give him a bit of company – shouldn't be too strenuous . . . He's knocking on sixty – and not with a brass nob if you get my drift. Girl'd prob'ly get a good dinner inall – Rules, maybe, or L'Escargot . . . Girl could do with feeding up anyway . . . She'd squeeze Genie's thigh appraisingly . . . no meat 'angin' on that bone, nothing much for a chap to get 'is teeth into. At this point Mumsie would resurrect her naughty laugh . . . *as if we was in cahoots* . . . followed by her posh voice: Actually, I'm reliably informed he's a breast man! — Genie sighs and Mickey looks up from his quarter-g. You alrightee? he says, but she's lost again — wandering along Oxford Street from Tottenham

Court Road, taking the long way round by Regent Street simply in order . . . *to make myself feel bad.* From time to time she pauses and presses her numb nose against plate glass, thinking: Better in than out. Better in with all that cosy fakery than out here with the touts, the Three-Card-Monte men, the beggars . . . *and the pimps.* The crowds shuffle along wet pavements under the outsized baubles strung between the buildings – and as they shuffle they . . . *tread in the runny shit* of lurid reflections. *Better in* . . . with the butter biscuits spilling from tartan tins to scatter across tartan blankets, *better in* . . . with wax fruit and mince pies frosted with icing sugar, *better in* . . . with an extravagantly embroidered stocking hung from a fireplace with a fire effect, *better in* . . . among elaborately wrapped boxes full of *fuck-all*, but still: *better in* . . . with side plates and matching cutlery, and electric candles with a dummy child poised waiting to blow them *out – in!* to a life she's not only never known, but can scarcely imagine. Genie wonders if she could eat the giant baubles, eat the shoppers, eat the fancy department stores and all their stock. – The hunger she's kept at bay with smack and coke and methadone and speed and booze is gnawing away at her . . . *from inside,* its snout tucked under her ribcage, its sickle-shaped jaws wide open, its many rows of angular teeth sawing away at her broken heart, her filthy lungs, her *stupid slow-witted brain* . . . When she's staggered through the mazy streets, limped down Wardour Street, turned into Blore Court, climbed the stairs, pushed the tatty baize-covered door, and is finally . . . *in,* Val says: Look what the cunt's dragged in – *and not in a nice way.* Genie stands there, swaying, looking at the stinking hypocrite — and remembering the evening she and Mumsie had got back from Greenham Common and Val guffawed, Ban the bomb! What you two need is a cruise missile apiece up your fucking jacksies! *In* . . . Val's guzzling neck his Adam's apple rose and fell . . . *a dirty works* pushing *in* his vodka fix – yet he'd the brass neck to whinily croak: I don't want no junkies in 'ere, this is a respectable-fucking-house – you're barred! – Barred, because she served no purpose — although the day after Boxing Day she did: propped up in a straight-backed padded chair, hosed down and made up *with a full coat of slap*, her skinniness hidden in a red silk Chinese dress with white and yellow chrysanths embroidered on it . . . *and long sleeves, obviously*. Her hair up, with a real chrysanth . . . *stuck in it*, while on the other side of the table the punter sat, his belly pushing apart the vertical stripes of his shirt, the four pockets in his tan suede safari jacket stuffed with Dunhill fags, Dunhill lighter, wallet . . . *and extra rubber johnnies in case I'd forgot*. Ignoring the waiter – who, although obviously repelled by this very odd couple, was angling towards the ice bucket – the punter took out the bottle of 'poo and topped up Genie's glass. I don't know why I do that, he said, straight into the waiter's furious face, but I always do. – All around them in the restaurant the other diners . . . *mindless fucking sterotypes*, who'd driven their Cavaliers in from Hendon for supper and a show, looked on, secretly delighted by this *little shop of horrors*, because it gave them a dirty thrill to see the fat old lecher and his painted whore, right after Christmas as well . . . *'aving it in So-ho-ho!* Sitting there, waiting woozily to poke giggles into the punter's pauses, Genie thought back to the Plant-ation and Mumsie's pinched and avid face. She wondered what might've happened if she'd the bottle to say: No! – That single-syllable shot straight into Mumsie's mouth, piercing the steel cylinders in which were compressed all the carbon dioxide from all the scotch and sodas and vodka and tonics she'd ever drunk . . . *and,* *BOOM!* a righteous explosion: Mumsie's brains dripping from the leaves of the money plant Val gloats over, Mumsie's false teeth pinging into the bottles of Merrydown and Harp on the shelves behind the bar, Mumsie's blood staining the Christmas cards, colouring in the cartoon one showing Santa, trousers round his ankles, *dumping a steaming plum pudding. No!* – She hadn't got that bottle, only the champagne one, and another – then the crappy hotel in Bayswater, where he'd taken a room not much bigger than the double bed, a bed *'ollowed out* by the pneumatic hammering of . . . *soft cocks into dry cunts.* A hot room, where she'd spent the next three hours, at first with her dress raised up round her waist, as – watching himself intently in the mirror – the punter ever so gently stroked the most sensitive parts of her: the soft flesh-swell where her buttocks flowed into her thighs. A-ha, the punter said judiciously, and, No-ho, when she tried to move his hand some-where more obvious, or get her own on his cock so she could *finish* *'im off.* Take your panties off and sit there, the punter said, and because he had the face of a nasty tomcat – all stringy whiskers and snaggly teeth – she did as he instructed, sitting on the cane-bottomed chair until he told her, Enough. She passed the remainder of her sentence with him purring as he traced the raised pattern of welts – breaking off occasionally to take another pawful of salted peanuts from the big bag he'd bought in Soho. *Black pussy, white pussy, pink pussy, blue, The name of the game is Little Boy Blue* . . . Nyum-nyum, he nibbled, his salted breath stinging her. Now I'd like, he said, to put my mouth where my money is . . . Genie held the dress tightly bunched. Her belly was full of potatoes dauphinoise and steak . . . *well done* — she'd managed to button her Trevia skirt over her puppy fat, but it was *so tight it's given me a second insie.* – Genie's in the *poxy* back bedroom of the *poxy* little two-up, two-down they'd moved into in town. Skinhead Moonstomp jitters from the Dansette Debbie abandoned when she fled to teacher-training college, and Genie fluffs up her feather-cut in the mirror, her tummy . . . *sucked in.* No need for all those extra rooms now that Miss Hoity-Toity's buggered off, Mumsie had said. The Chester-field wing armchair had come with them to Berkhamsted. While the removal men in their *parcel-paper coats* were loading up the van, it stood on the verge outside the cottage – its legs looked *scrawny*, its old-gold upholstery – the backdrop for so many brightly painted visions – *filthy, it shoulda scuttled sideways into the canal for shame* . . . Mumsie'll be sitting on it *right now* . . . downstairs in the front room . . . *what's 'ad nuffink done to it* since they arrived. There's a flamenco dancer bunching up her skirts on the Artex wall, a pair of castanets dangling from a nail hammered into the one opposite. Hughie, Genie knows, will be lying on the floor, his hooky nose and tumbling brown curls cameoed by the double loops of his Matchbox Superfast track, around which shoots a metallic-purple toy car. Shot by the Superbeschleuniger, it loop-the-loops, click-clacks through the Superfast Doppel-Rundenzähler, leaps over the Sprung durch den Feuerreifen, then skitters across the raspberry-ripple lino before crashing into the bare tootsies of *she*, who, as she'd helped him to slot it together on Christmas Day, taught Hughie these German words purely in order to show off that she really can *speak the lingo.* Heil Hitler! Genie cries, standing on the third step up – she's one hand raised and two fingers of the other on her top lip. She smells of acetone and Bacardi. Mumsie lifts her sleek head from her magazine and examines her *through rings of bright water.* You look like a tart, she says approvingly. — At Ashlyns, where Genie's sunk deep in the U-stream with the cockney kids from the Percy Bilton Estate, she sits *cramped up* . . . as Mister Watts draws his snake on the board. In less than a year, he says, you'll be leaving this school – and you ignoramuses remain utterly incapable of reciting your times tables. Genie knows he's saying this because she reads the shapes his lips make – but she can't hear him, only the dull hubbub of chair-scrape and the snot bubbling in seventy nostrils. She'd had the operations when she was little, and endured for years their *afterpuff* of cotton-wool ear-muffs, but her hearing never improved *that much* . . . *I'm in mono* . . . She could listen to one thing at a time: the Dansette, Mumsie's voice, the jets wobble-boarding overhead – but when Adam had laid her down on his parents' fitted carpet, with her head carefully positioned between their huge Grundig speakers, she still couldn't hear Jimi's wah-wah guitar *shoot straight through my 'ead* . . . which is what he said she should . . . *experience.* It simply *buggered off* . . . then boomeranged back as Adam's hand squirmed up her skirt and his fingers plucked . . . *at me knickers.* – This she does hear: Thwack! Mister Watts's steel ruler cracked down on the desk, and then the slaves' lament, One times el-ev-en is el-ev-en . . . This she does feel: his breath tickling her neck – followed by the poisonous Thwack! across the back of her calf — she touches the *Superfast* welt it made as Mumsie says again: You look like a tart – not that anyone'd want to have a crack at yer. Genie smiles – she know this isn't true: black sixteen-hole DMs, white thighs, black pleated skirt, white Ben Sherman, black Harrington . . . *I look the biz.* Down the shops on a Saturday afternoon – out round the pubs after dark, sipping from Coke tins and waiting for Billy the greaser to . . . *top 'em up wiv Bacardi* . . . At weekends Genie is a Berko boot girl *out on the razz*, and spazzes who've been taking the piss all week – *Watch my lips, Jeanie Gruber, You-Are-Shit* – shut up when she and her mates swagger by. Genie's bullies have no real appetite . . . *for a bit of aggro*, they're *wet-knickered bitches* . . . whose knees go all rubbery as they . . . *near piss themselves, coz they fink we might be tooled up.* — That morning, in the Kardomah, flipping through Jackie, search-ing for the Marc Bolan pinup . . .*'e looks like Hughie – it'd be incest . . .* Genie had stopped at a cartoon strip: You do not like the thought of war, earth girl, speech-bubbled a hunk called Gemal, his cloak was flung back over his shoulder, his muscly bicep clasped by a leather armlet, yet we delight in it. If you were to be my woman, you would be proud to be loved by such a great Warrior! And Genie thought: I ain't ever gonna be your woman, you dirty hippy coon – 'sides, I love the thought of war an' I could take you any time I want! Mumsie lowered her copy of Spare Rib, her expression serious, like it was whenever she'd been teaching . . . *or raising 'er conscious-ness.* She covered up Gemal and the earth girl with her cup of cappuccino and, taking a spoonful of sugar, trickled it down on to the froth – the white granules hovered on the white foam, then sank through it, creating a brownish gash that instantly resealed. See that, girl, Mumsie said, see all those little pricks tearing themselves a new fanny . . . Genie laughed, but Mumsie pursed her lips and said, That's holy deadlock, that is Jeanie: some sweet-talking prick making a cunt out of you, night and day if they get the chance. That's what we call sexism nowadays – and that's what it was like with Gregor, he couldn't stop pawing at me – this in spite of his mental health problems . . . *Always Gregor to me but Your Father to the others.* Mumsie folded her Spare Rib and tapped the page: See this woman here, she followed a bunch of brasses round the West End, in and out of knocking shops, up and down the back stairs of the Regent Palace. What did she con-clude? I'll read it you: Men'll continue to need prostitutes so long as there's an inhibition on sex, while women will continue to sell their bodies while they're denied an equal right to financial independence . . . So, take my advice, girl, give marriage a wide berth – whoring's honester. I never took a penny offa Gregor once he'd left us, I got my own . . . *'til I was old enough to get it for you* . . . — Collapsed back on the couch, Genie marvels at this: while so much of her life has . . . *gone up in smoke*, Mumsie's words exhale through the years, smarting her eyes — then dragging her back into a typical Jackie horoscope she once weepily read: *You'll find it hard to stick with one fella when you could have fun with so many, and you're tempted to play the field while you're getting away with it* . . . She remembers the pathetic pen pals who signed their letters *David Cassidy*

Fan, *S.W.A.L.K.*... and the chain letters ... *that mustn't be broke*, and the nice girls with poodle hair they styled *with their Pifco Go-Girl hairdryers* ... But Genie hadn't been a nice girl at all: she didn't fancy fellas from afar, or moon into the mirror. *I so want this job, but I don't stand a chance with skin like mine* ... Because: *I never wanted a fucking job.* As for her skin, *If I could've I'd've popped my plukes in their complacent faces! Stu-pid Genie's got no brai-ns, Now she ain't got no vei-ns* ... But back then, *in Berko*, back then: *I 'ad the brains, I was the ring leader of the tormentors* ... While the nice girls were nerving themselves to sneak into the rerun of Up the Chastity Belt at the Rex, the Berko boot girls were pelting down the High Street with the landlord of the King's Arms in fat pursuit, crying, *You yobbos!* They'd regroup by the phone boxes to drink Double Diamond ... *which was all we'd addaway* ... fall about laughing and make some calls so that *shazzam!* the greasers'd be there, revving their bikes, spurting forward, braking, spurting forward again, leather legs *bending* as they absorbed the shock. — One-Armed Mickey is long gone ... The *nail* of charred paper detaches from the long *finger of ash* ... Genie thinks of a picture in the Guinness Book of Records of the longest fingernails in the world spiralling from a mandarin's hands. Such a world there'd once been! Full up with such super things! Now there were only the cats scratching in their litter tray ... *they'll eat my face if I go over* ... and the twigs scratching against the windowpane in the wind, and her left hand ... *a mind of its own* ... that scratches the place the punter touched, scratches it hard and harder ... *the longest fingernails in the world* hungry for flesh and blood. She thinks:

I pulled my skirt right up and I swung my leg right over, I wish I could've stayed on the back of Adam's bike forever, a Norton Commando *Moves like a cat an' 'e knows how to ride her* . . . the petrol tank mirror-shiny and — flashing under the streetlamps, folding the road in on itself as he sticks his knee out, cries, Lean! and they heel into the roundabout at the top of the London Road, her bare knee almost touching the tarmac, his hair lashing her face, the pistons hammering up through the saddle, her heart hammering through her Harrington and his leather jacket to meet his hammering heart – the grass and the bushes and the road and the lights and the night . . . *a smear of fear* that she can smell . . . *powerful as petrol*, which she breathes more and more of as they lean more, the big bike thundering round the roundabout . . . *againannagain* its tremendous torque dragging the earth round on its axis, ratcheting up the sun *faster and faster . . . Allll-rrright, get ready – here we go! Little Boy Blue come blow up your horn, The sheep's in the meadow and the cows in the corn, Ai-yai-yaaaa!* – Until cold, cold dawn comes drum-rolling over that meadow, driving before it the cool breeze that blows the singed curtains through the open window of the council semi at Potten End the greasers have squatted, then trashed. The pitiless day finds them out, kneeling on a mattress in the front room, *one flying duck on the wall, two dead on the floor* . . . Adam's black fingernails on her white buttons, his brown fingertips *on my browner nips*, as he lilts, *The little beauties, the little beauties* . . . while her heart hammers *fit to bust*, because at some point in that wild and beautiful night *I'd done some dexies he give me.* She sucks in her tummy as he unbuttons her Trevia skirt . . . *insies go outsie* . . .

Where's the boy looks after the sheep, he's under the haystack with Little Bo Peep, Ai-yai-yaaaa! Kins pushes all that's left of the shattered door – and it swings, admitting him to . . . *the last-fucking-chance saloon.* He's every inch the chap, in his tweed cap and sheepskin car coat . . . *coz he's the boy who looks after Little Bo Peep, an' he's shaking an' he looks like he's gonna puke, his fat face all white and veiny* . . . — Out on the churned-up handkerchief of lawn the white Rover's radiator nuzzled at one of the bikes . . . *ready to take a bite.* In the car, still shaking, Kins had said, Button your blouse – which made her laugh, then choke — as she chokes now, smelling the sickly acridity of her own burning skin – she flaps her hand and the sparks of her fly . . . *and die – I musta nodded out* . . . She struggles to stay in it — the Rover rumbling along the lane, Kins praying to the wheel, and her teenage self laughing as she pulls apart her Ben Sherman and thrusts her goose-pimpled breasts against his suede arm. You want 'em, don'tcha? that's what I said . . . *You want 'em, don'tcha?* Kins's arm jerked away, the car skidded, rose up the bank, stalled. In the sudden stillness the Rover's engine ticked, its radiator hissed . . . *We shoulda fucked and kissed . . . maybe* . . . Instead he groped his own woolly cleavage, pulled out his wallet and from this withdrew a *Happy Families card* . . . Saying nothing, he passed it to her. Before taking it, she buttoned herself up primly – then she looked at smiling Kins in check sports jacket and brown trousers, standing with a boy a couple of years younger than Genie balanced on his big feet, and a boy a year or two younger than him balancing on those smaller feet, and a third, still smaller boy . . . *stacked on top.* The boys wore the same school-uniform-grey Aertex shirts, maroon-striped ties and grey shorts. Big hands on smaller shoulders, smaller hands on littler shoulders ... *littler hands on littlest shoulders*. The squashed Moroccan leather pouf, the framed watercolour, the piled-up photo-cubes on the sideboard in the background – all these unfamiliar things confirmed for Genie the closeness that hair, eyes and noses all ... *screamed*. What was it Mumsie had said about Kins? *A brilliant man – the biggest waste of brain power I've ever seen*. What was it Kins did for money? Something that gave him enough free time to fritter his days away chasing round after her. *A sociology lecturer*, Mumsie had said ... *together with some private means*. And the wife? *A castrating bitch and a harridan – like all wives, always* ... He took a small block of wood covered with chammy leather out of the glove box and, beginning with a small circular portion, methodically wiped the whole windscreen. They saw a hawthorn hedge in the mist – there were still some berries on it but these were dead and shrivelled up, while streamers of cassette tape caught in the thorns *glittered and gleamed*. Kins said in a high, hysterical voice, This ... this is all I have, and Michael says, What the devil d'you mean by that? They're in Wardour Street, standing staring up at St Anne's: its charred campanile has been plopped atop a tower so generally *beaten about and done in* the most plausible explanation is that it was *built but lately from the rubble*. Kins looks malevolently at a pair of red caps who've detained a soldier by the Queen's stage door and are asking for his pay book. He resumes: I mean all I have now is London – specifically Soho. Michael exclaims, What rot, Ape! You're beginning to give me the absolute bloody pip. — From the

Lyons' they'd gone to a fleapit on Haymarket, where Goodbye, Mister Chips was showing. His belly full, Kins fell asleep halfway through the first reel, his snores – his brother thought – making a mockery of the flick's sentiments: for here was the star pupil bored into unconsciousness by Robert Donat's tear-jerking performance. The cinema was surprisingly full for a matinee, and Kins's snoring buzzed above canoodling couples' smacking lips and shuddery breathing. They shushed and tutted – but Michael couldn't rouse him, and when he dug him in the ribs Kins inexplicably muttered, I killed the count ... Blinking in Piccadilly ... *and looking like one* ... Kins insisted on a corpse reviver at the Café Royal – so Michael saw more of Sirbert's sub' poured out: two parts cognac to one of calvados and another of vermouth. Standing at the bar in his egregious civvies, Kins twined the ticker-tape from the chittering machine through his clumsy fingers and boomed, It's all balls – war balls and peace balls, love balls and bloody hateful balls ... Michael couldn't understand why the serving officers – and there were many present – didn't loft him on top of the bar, hitch a brocade drapery cord round his sunburnt neck ... *and bring down the curtain on his performance* ... Time was I'd've ticked anyone off for such specious reasoning – a diallelus, don'tcha know, that allows 'em to claim that since A caused B, and B led to C, it follows that C must've produced A. But y'know, now I see these wallahs' point: love – love is indeed a product of hate – not a by-product, Ape, but a direct one. We love in order to hate – and so it follows, ceteris paribus, we hate in order to love. Kins ... Michael chided, but he wouldn't be deflected: I say that the current hostilities are evidence of the same circularity . . . Michael looked away from his brother's flushed face – through the bottom of his raised beer glass he spied out cream-and-gilt cherubs preening in patinated mirrors, and *an obvious nancy-boy* wearing a cream silk shirt, peach-coloured tie and white corduroy trousers, who he . . . *raked with fire from nose to stern – always attack on the beam if you can.* Kins persevered: We declare war in order to make peace, and no doubt – in the fullness of Mister Roosevelt's time – we will make war again . . . The corpse that's been revived is not the Kins he'd known – *no, idolised – had a pash on quite as bad as Monk minimus did on me.* This Kins is pie-eyed, certainly, but beneath his ebullient crust *something ugly is fulminating.* — Michael says again: The absolute bloody pip! and Kins, sighing, takes him by the arm and leads him around the corner away from the bombed-out church. Has it ever occurred to you, Ape, Kins says, that when you kiss a girl – and I mean a truly ripping girl, one you've deep feelings for – that everything, by which I mean every single thing – not just your hopes and your feelings and all that rot, but every thing: your people and their place, your books and your sports togs, your prayer book and your pipe – every thing is inside that girl's mouth being minutely sensed by hundreds upon thousands of nerve-endings. Your tongue and hers, your lips and hers –. He stops, seeing the consternation on Michael's face. Does it bother you, Ape, Kins says, my talking like this? – No, not exactly, Ape – Michael lets go of his gas-mask bag, which at all times he finds he's *petting nervously* – it's only that I'm wondering . . . *what the hell's come over you!* . . . where're we heading to now? — Simmy, whom Michael had teamed up with to swot for their pilot's exams, got his posting first: a Spitfire squadron in Scotland. This station's remoteness from the big show was at least compensated for: he'd be flying single-engine fighters, which was what everyone at the OTU yearned to do – the honourable form of combat, knightly and mano-a-mano. There was this, and Michael supposed there'd also be good links courses – and possibly some grouse shooting. Stopping by Hullavington on his way north, Simmy confessed he hadn't spent his five-day leave with his people on the Sussex coast . . . *it's quieter than the grave, old man – picture villas with picture windows picturing more villas with picture windows, and no bathing to be had unless you fancy getting your balls blown off by a mine* . . . but with some *t'rific girls* who by day were living statues in a nearly nude revue at the Whitehall, and by night were occupied . . . *rather more energetically.* I told 'em to keep an eye out for you, Simmy had said as he hefted his leg into the mono-cocque of his Armstrong Siddeley, and Michael thought: Lucky bugger! – He'd almost suggested to Kins they pop round to the stage door when they were in the Whitehall's vicinity, but his brother's mood seemed . . . *so volatile.* There was also this other business to conclude: the orders folded into the pocket of his battledress . . . *my wings awaiteth me – and they're not angelic ones.* He'd only spoken the truth – but not all of it: he was to report to Withernsea. However, if the grapevine was anything to go by, this meant he was destined for heavy bombers – most likely Whitleys. His compensation would be more personal: most of the squadrons were up in Lincolnshire – he was reliably informed there was one at Goltho, only a couple of miles from the CLTA outfit at Collow

Abbey Farm. *We'll be near-neighbours . . . popping round to see each other . . . drinking sharp cider in the shadow of haystacks . . .* He imagined a rekindling of their close fraternal relationship – and through this agency a funny sort of *matchmaking of RAF men and conchies . . .* Of course, when Michael analysed this pipe-dream it was . . . *utter tosh*, nearly as ridiculous as the visit he'd paid to the town hall shortly before enlisting. The Registrar seemed totally uninterested, asking him only to be so good as to sign here . . . and there . . . and there also, before rubber-stamping De'Ath to death. Then he used a rusty dipper to copperplate in, Lincoln. — Now, observing his red-faced brother, who's squinting at the an ornate antique clock through the strips of tape on a jeweller's window, Michael doubts there will ever be *a right time* to reveal the extent of his romanticism, his imagining that . . . *I could in some peculiar way stay beside you tending the peaceful garden, even as I rode Pegasus aloft with a saddlebag full of HE* . . . Kins says, We're going to the pub, you silly-billy, but such are our prehistoric licensing laws – they order these matters, don'tcha know, far better in both Frances, unoccupied as well as Marianne enchained – there's little point in hurrying. You don't need to be conversant with the Eleatic paradoxes to understand the peculiarities of British boozers: we may go as swiftly as we like, we'll only cover half the distance to the Marquess of Granby, then half the remaining distance, then half of that distance in turn – just as opening time is miserably and endlessly deferred, so will our arrival be. Better we maintain the tortoise's slow and steady progress towards its favoured dandelion patch. And is it? Michael asks. Is it what? Kins snaps back. Is it your preferred . . . dandelion patch, the Marquess of Granby? I have, Kins says, no favourites as such, rather, I love 'em all: the Granby and the Beer House, the Burglars' Rest and the Black Horse. We might venture so far as the Wheatsheaf – if, that is, you're in the mood for a strenuous hike – Kins brandishes his stick – Though I'll have to insist on stopping at the Highlander on the way to take on the necessary, ah, ballast. – Tightening his arm in Kins's, Michael brings their *slow and steady progress* . . . to a complete halt: Is this what you want, Ape, this pub crawl? I mean, you seemed a bit stinko at Victoria and now you're getting plastered again –. – Don't be deceived – Kins brings his hot face to within inches of his brother's – by my proposed itinerary: this is a pub crawl in outline only, while the libations are purely incidental. No! this is a quest! – He yanks them on, declaiming, I must find the lovely maiden, clothed in white samite, and lay my poor aching horn in her tender lap! – In the Highlander, which smells of fried onions, there's no bitter on tap, so they have bottled ale instead. Michael sits powerless to exit his brother's dramatics . . . *He is the Hands of Orlac, I sit and watch while they play.* Mine host, whose waxed moustaches echo the oiled wings of his centre-parted hair, says, D'liveries are gettin' erratic to say the least, gentlemen. Dray hoss lay right down in Warren Street – shell shocked they say. First on 'is knees 'fore 'is back legs go – then 'e rolls over gentle like, but 'is great weight cracks the shafts. Drayman gets down, goes to see what's wrong – hoss is stone-fucking-dead without a mark on 'im, an' that's a big and noble beast. Kins says, sotto voce, As if size had anything to do with it. – He's spinning a coaster between his thick fingers, and when it stops Michael's momentarily taken by this small irony: GUINNESS GIVES YOU STRENGTH! before Kins says out of his blue fag smoke: She's a t'riffic kid, Annette, I'd like you to meet her. Funny thing, though, for a serious girl she's running with a rather fast crowd. – Michael thinks of the Dornier that was shot down during the raid that damaged Buckingham Palace. There was a photograph in the Express of its anodised wing lying in the wreckage . . . *white and severed – the Hand of Orlac.* He says casually, Have you seen much of her since you both came up to town? And Kins grabs his wrist: You don't get it at all, Ape, I can't possibly see anything of her: I'm inside her mouth! – In the oaken cave of the Marquess of Granby, the potman, wearing a holey reefer jersey, puts up the blackout boards: I'd be obliged if you gentlemen move temporarily like . . . And at the bar they swank it with scotch and sodas. Kins says, On my way through Lincolnshire I holed up for a day near a village called Helpringham – and they were very helping of him, I can tell you. It's Fen country, you see, divided up by long drainage channels into a sort of enormous chess board – a bugger to find your way through, had me stumbling around like the White Knight . . . — In the morning, when they'd met at breakfast, there'd been considerable awkwardness, Annette announcing *out of the blue* that a friend of a friend had offered her some sort of job in London working with refugees, and on balance she thought it was probably for the best if she took it. Best for whom? Kins said ungraciously – then, to hide his upset, he went out into the farmyard and began to pace up and down, picking up tools and letting them fall with dull tinks and cretinous clanks. She came out ten minutes or so later, packed and ready to go . . . *obviously it'd all been set up in advance.* The post van pulled up at the gates, and Annette said, Cheery-oh, then, and held out her hand *in a comradely sort of way.* Kins pulled himself together and asked for her address, said he'd write, and held on to her hand until she took it away from him and picked up her case with it. After that he paced some more, and picked up a hoe with the intention of going off somewhere to do *a little ineffectual weeding* . . . But then, as he told Sirbert . . . *I simply leant my hoe against the barn and, well, sort of wandered off.* He stopped in the attic room for as long as it took to stuff some underwear in his knapsack, to finger the faded muslin of the curtains and to scrutinise the flies taking off and landing on the airy strip of the window. He took four apples sticky with juice from the bowl in the kitchen – then he slipped away into the inky shadows under the lime hedge, thinking of Fox and how he'd walked abroad in solitary places for many days, and sat in hollow trees and lonesome spots until night came on. Kins, stopping by the gamekeeper's pole to touch the shot-pulped breasts of buzzards and hawks, understood this: *I am the Anti-Fox, a man of sorrows in a time when the Lord has ceased His suffering on my behalf and left me to my own* . . . At dusk, when the sun threw a half-halo above the horizon that was *simply ghastly* in its perfection, he found himself passing by the Cistercian abbey's broken masonry, and there were plump pigeons coming in to roost: streamlined gunmetal bodies rotating as their wings remained *absolutely still.* But Kins kept on, seeing the half-halo of Syd Walker's tin hat rising up from behind every hedge, hearing him cry out, I'll kill you – you cunt! – In the starless night, with the mothering moon bumbling ineffectually along behind the clouds, Kins blundered into fences, barking his shins, and tore his flesh on rapacious brambles – then at dawn, filthy and bleeding, the familiar racket of some farm dogs – two barking low, one falsetto howling – told him he'd proceeded in a great and useless circle. He lay most of the day on a bed of wood sorrel, *God's broken green typography* spreading between the lines of trees in a perfectly square plantation. He slept intermittently, waking often to the ignominy that . . . *I lack the spunk to throttle a hen pheasant on its nest.* And he drank stump water and ate unripe berries, so that dusk found him out being . . . *spasmodically moved by my bowels.* He went on, his soiled thighs chafing, until as night descended he came upon the Witham and was able to follow its manmade banks under a sky . . . *yellowing to black.* He watched closely as the river's algal bloom *consumed everything – earth and sky* alike absorbed into its *snaking intestine.* Before at last, the umpteen-thousandth footfall supplied the necessary pressure, the rude mechanicals did their capering business, and *the byss and the abyss swopped places!* — After that, he tells Michael, navigation became altogether easier, d'you see? What with the land stretched across the sky and the stars beneath my feet, I'd only to set my course at a consistent tangent to the rising and setting of the moon in order to head south. Kins takes a swig of his scotch and continues: Which I did at a fair old pace for several hours, before dawn spoilt it all by flipping everything right side up — slipping on runny dung he was flung *into the drink.* Swans closed on him, spitting suspiciously, and when he'd floundered away from their wing-beats he found the cold hard nostrils of a shotgun . . .

thrust into my nose. — Kins downs the last of his whisky and sets the glass down, clack! He grips Michael's sleeve: Don'tcha see, Ape, this was my baptism of fire . . . my Waterloo! After what'd happened at Louth, I'd been crawling about on my yellow belly for days – but climbing out of that drain, as it were under fire, I regained my self-possession. I said to the fellow, absolutely calmly – Kins comes to attention and takes off John Snagge – I'm in the mobile infantry, don't you know your own? – But Michael has no knowledge of what happened in Louth. In the corner of the saloon bar a small pugnacious blonde is fending off an unsmiling man sporting a fire-watcher's arm band. You said you'd take me for spag' bol' at Fava's, she cries, but now I find you've not been straight at all! Michael thinks: Kins isn't being straight with me at all . . . Then his sozzled thoughts begin tripping over their own feet: How strange it is that Kins manages to veer in and out of drunkenness without spilling a drop of dialogue . . . And how bally typical it is that he doesn't bother to ask *about my own tribul . . . tribunala-tions . . .* – They leave the Highlander and crawl on past dunes of sandbags . . . *towards the next oasis of booze.* Michael adjures himself severely: It's less than honest to blame Kins, after all: he never expected me to observe such protocols. — Michael had registered with the local labour exchange in Blackheath. He didn't want to queer Kins's pitch, believing the coincidence of conscientious brothers might test the Oxford tribunal's patience. The chairman of the South London Tribunal had the look of a vegetarian cross-word compiler: faint toothbrush moustache, sparse mousy hair, non-existent shoulders and greenish buck teeth. The bronze cross and swords of the Croix de Guerre he wore on his jacket lapel seemed as preposterous to Michael as . . . *my own ability to identify it as such*. The chairman's small white hands scuttled among the papers he had in front of him. Be a man! he squeaked suddenly. You certainly seem to have the necessary capacity – an air cadet at your public school, and now at the varsity. How the devil d'you square this with such whole-hogging pacifism? Taken aback, Michael blustered, I simply like flying, sir, always have . . . The whole business of being up in the air – getting things in the air. When I was younger it was kites and model airplanes, that sort of thing . . . He'd tried to adopt an unmartial bearing – he wanted to avert his eyes from the chairman's, but was worried this might seem . . . *sly*. Standing there on the highly polished floor, he flinched as sunlight *exploded* against the high windows of the Council Chamber, then his eyes went from the handle of one window to the rods corkscrewing up into the complicated system of ratchets and levers used to open its . . . *top flaps*. The chairman inveighed, D'you imagine His Majesty's air force exists solely in order for you to go fly a kite at the expense of the British tax payer? – N-no, absolutely not, sir – it's simply . . . in the context of peacetime, I confess, I regarded it as on a par with any other sporting activity, such as . . . such as . . . golf. – *Yaroo!* On the town hall steps Michael gave himself an imaginary *kick in the pants*, then he drove *the Fat Owl of the Remove* through the teeming Greenwich streets and into the park with imaginary swipes of Quelch's cane. He was stunned by his own passivity. He'd failed to raise the matter of the speech he'd delivered only months before at the British Peace Assembly – the text of which was actually in the chairman's paws. Nor had he summoned any of the Bible quotations he'd carefully memorised to confirm his . . . *whole-hogging piety.* He'd also neglected to call his living reference, Teddy Tippett from the CBCO, who, commiserating with him before taking the train back to London Bridge, said: They're notorious for their carping and bullying, this lot – haven't to our knowledge granted a single unconditional since their first sitting. Even so, a flat-out non-exemp' in your case is a bit bloody thick – you'll appeal, I s'pose? But Michael didn't say anything – at that moment a ghostly aircraftman cried Contact! and his insides began turning over. – When the chairman had sneered at him: There are lads of your age who're embarking from Folkestone right this moment to defend you, you blackguard – how does that make you feel? Michael wanted to say: It makes me feel pretty damn unlucky, given were I a couple of weeks younger I wouldn't've received my call-up . . . Instead he'd closely observed the sunlight touching the clerk's whiskers . . . *dripping solder.* – There were navvies smoking through their tea break at the building site on the corner of Roan Street – and further along dockers jostled into the pubs to sling pints down before the hooter went and they'd to scamper back through the foot tunnel to Millwall. The burnt-molasses breeze was blowing from Silvertown as Michael dived into the covered market and encountered a detachment of cadets taking a short cut back to the College. Making his own way up towards the Observatory, Michael chanced upon a . . . *tea bush terracing* of freshly dug slit trenches, some planted with school kids being put through a practice drill. All of it made him think in a confused way of how the coming hostilities would fuse together thousands of perfectly arbitrary decisions – such as the one his tribunal had made – into a mighty ball of leaden bureaucratic *muddling through* – a ball that would roll down on top of them *all*, crushing them *all* with monstrous and implacable inertia. What if he were to appeal and, instead of standing there mutely, prate on about the exploitation of the common man by forces beyond his control – or lay claim to an exemplary holiness? The end result would, he felt sure, be the same: no donkey ride or palm leaves – no punchy Pilot or Judy Jesus, only the stamp of ill-fitting boots on wobbly cobbles ... *nostrils clogging with wet wool.* He'd already heard about men in orders who were ... *taking them*, and, as he stood at the top of the hill beneath *tossing white altar candles* of flowering chestnuts, this was given to him: *I cannot bear the mark of Cain ...* – for surely, that's what it would be: an *I* for Individualist, branded on the forehead that *you'd bear for the rest of your days.* Michael received this unction, and also a vision of his brother, shambling by night from village to village, unkempt and unloved, not just for the duration of the war, *however long that might be*, but *forever – a body without a heart, a brain without a mind, missing every part.* He gazed over the tight parquetry of Cubitt Town and Millwall and pictured the coming attack: *all* the individual airplanes subsumed in a single swarm that swept round the bend in the river from Tilbury and buzzed past the inlet of Barking Creek, while oblivious to it *all* the stevedores, their jolly wives and their Ah, Bisto! kids went on happily singing in *all* the corner pubs: *Then they hear the rumble on the floor. It's a big surprise they're waiting for, And all the couples form a ring, For miles around you'll hear them sing* –. Then the city *does a somerset* so *all* the porter in *all* the pint pots *drops* on to the smoke-browned ceilings, and *all* the cellar hatches burst open: *Roll out the barrel! We'll 'ave a barrel of fun!* – It will be a total annihilation, that's what every futurist worth his salt – the Coles, Huxleys and Wellses of this world – have been predicting for years, so why not propel yourself above it . . . *white, whirling thistledown.* Why not choose, at least, the manner of your own Daedalus death, if not its place . . . *or time?* – That evening, Missus Pelham, the cook, served cold meats and cold roast potatoes. Just us, Sirbert said – Bumbly was out at a charitable function organised by one of his colleagues, an occurrence rare enough to be . . . *worrying.* Michael supposed in the normal run of things a father might be expected to discuss the tribunal's decision, and what plans his son had in the light of it. Placing a red ministerial box on the floor by the dumb waiter, Sirbert said: Tact should have the same root as taciturn if etymology had any logic to it – then proceeded to work through supper, his mechanical-grey eyes *processing* sheet after sheet of paper, his pen's nib making green-ink annotations so neat and minute that, observing him from the far end of the dining table, it seemed unlikely to Michael that they were consciously willed at all. He knew Sirbert was having troubles with Nuffield – he hadn't forgiven or forgotten the dispute over shadow factories. He wondered whether it would be *politic* to remark that at least the motor-car manufacturer was now acting with *a certain probity,* enlisted in the public service . . . *gratis.* Watching his father at work, he thought better of it: Sirbert's reluctance to speak of Whitehall went beyond mere professionalism . . . *in my father's house there are many mansions* . . . all of them converted into shadow factories and shadow offices, all of them staffed by clerks and secretaries. All of them *disbarred from interdepartmental chitchat*. Michael, who had since infancy seen his father perform two or more tasks simultaneously, only now fully formed a thought that must for years *have been embryonic inside me*. The truth was *Sirbert simply has no understanding of what it might be like to be anyone but him*. Yes, yes, he did a good job of normal human intercourse, smiling when others laughed, appearing touched when they wept – however, this was a product of rigorous analysis and the amassing of vast quantities of data. Deep in the Sirbertian brain box, there was, Michael imagined, a deftly constructed model of the house. And in this there was a reconstruction of the very room in which they currently sat, complete with balsa-wood furniture, felt rug, a dumb waiter operated by a length of twine, and clever little Sirbert and Michael dolls finicked into being out of pipe cleaners, wax blobs and cotton-wool puffs. As he flicked at his papers, Sirbert manipulated these puppets, furnishing them with a repertoire of hypothetical remarks, so were his son to say anything at all, it would already have been anticipated, and the answer would rise *naturally enough* to his beetroot-stained lips. Sirbert barely ate – Michael did so heartily, then slept more soundly than he had since his call-up arrived. Slept in the attic bedroom he still shared on occasion with Kins – slept in one of the complicated and unwieldly folding beds that, when Sirbert bought them in the twenties, had been advertised as the latest in space-saving convenience. These were great oak-sided cabinets that disgorged iron bedsteads with tormented sproings – every maid the De'Aths took on complained of being nipped by them. Lying full stretch, Michael could see through the open double doors to the old nursery, and instead of dwelling on the pig-sticking of *my whole-hogging pacifism*, he decided to inventory its contents . . . *by way of a sedative.* Tea chests and steamer trunks had been piled up into a stepped Aztec pyramid that fitted in under the sloping roof. In these were balls and cups, spinning tops and hoops, mah-jong and Ludo sets, croquet mallets and hoops, cut-down golf clubs and carpet bowls, boxing gloves and cricket pads – all the impedimenta that had cluttered up their busily isolated childhoods. Deep in the core of the mound – although requiring the skills of a Schliemann to disinter them – would, Michael thought, be the large collection of lead soldiers amassed by the three De'Ath males. Sirbert had been as enthusiastic as his sons, and would appear punctually after nursery tea on Fridays with a Britains box in his coat pocket from which he'd extract fusiliers, dragoons or artillery men, adding them directly into whichever column was currently attacking the bastion. This ugly-looking fortification was Sirbert's handiwork: the towers turned on his small lathe, then glued to a wooden base. Around these he'd built up successive layers of papier mâché, painted brown and grey, until – to his own satisfaction at least – he'd effected a resemblance to Edinburgh Castle's volcanic mound. Sirbert directed the match-stick volleys fired by spring-loaded guns – Sirbert organised the levees of reinforcements. Sirbert knelt in his striped trousers, his sharp nose . . . *harrowing* through the ranks, his godly fingers pinching out the unfit whose paint had been chipped, or the wounded whose extremities had been bent. He and Kins would've discarded these casualties altogether were it not that Michael pleaded for their lives. So they grudgingly allowed him to set up a field hospital behind the lines, in a toy farmhouse left over from more bucolical play. Each time he lifted the roof to add a newly wounded soldier to their recumbent ranks, Michael would be re-infuriated by the way the toy soldiers' oblong bases and rigid stances prevented them from ... *lying down properly*. A Scots Guards bugler – in red coat, yellow tartan trews and pith helmet – was especially troublesome. His shoulder joint – a simple pinion – was broken by one of the marbles Sirbert used for heavy ordinance, until, following what almost amounted to a row, Kins persuaded him that they were contrary to the spirit of the Geneva treaties. My, my, Sirbert had snarled, a proper little Dunant I have on my hands. Michael repaired the bugler with some fuse wire, but Sirbert wouldn't let him be returned to the fray. To allay his younger son's sense of injustice ... *it's not fair!* ... he came home the following evening with a whole box of buglers, enough for a *ridiculous tootling platoon*. Their shiny uniformity repelled Michael – by then he'd fallen a little in love with his own bugler's imperfections, and he spent more and more time with him at the field hospital while the others got on with the war. The Scots Guard became a sort of one-man welcoming committee: as the farmhouse roof rose and a new patient was lowered down, he lifted his battered bugle to his chipped lips ... *and tootled*, he lifted his battered bugle to his chipped lips ... *and tootled*. – The bastion would be in the nursery pyramid – the bugler would too, entombed together with every issue of the De'Ath Watch, Kins's carefully ordered back numbers of Night and Day and Film Fun, and Michael's of Model Maker. Somewhere near the apex of all this stuff, Michael pictured Darsing, the straw-stuffed Old English sheep dog that the brothers had cuddled when they were babes. A Bumbly relative had once painted Kins holding Darsing. She was a dotty maiden aunt who spoke to the boys through the agency of her glove puppet – a creepy silk-robed mandarin with long lacquered fingernails she called Sonny Jim – and she'd rendered the little boy with bright pink cheeks and pouting lips surrounded by blond tresses, so he appeared rather less lifelike than the dog. This queer memento was doubtless also somewhere in the house . . . *for nothing's ever discarded.* – At breakfast, Sirbert sat sipping his messery and sorting through a cardboard box full of linen-bound octavo notebooks. Fascinating, he said, I do believe your maternal grandfather catalogued in these every single household expenditure – right down to, and including, individual stamps – made between 1853 and his death. Michael produced the noises Sirbert had *undoubtedly anticipated*, then, without saying anything, went off to see the recruiting sergeant. He'd expected . . . *what?* A thoroughgoing bollocking perhaps – but there was simply his muddling absorption into the great ball of blue-grey serge. A fortnight later he was pulled out of the trench he was digging and told to go wash up. In the latrine he rinsed the earth and dried urine from his hands – in between unmerciful raggings the regulars had shown this much decency . . . *and told us piss was the best blister prevention.* After that he picked up a travel warrant from the base commander's office. At the Selection Board no one seemed to have the slightest interest in any youthful idealism he might once have evinced, nor any knowledge of tribunal decisions. All they cared about was . . . Golf? the wing commander asked – on his long top lip perched a dappled moustache . . . *thrush's breast*. Yes, sir, Michael answered. The wing commander gently pressed him, Decent handicap? Well – Michael shook his head regretfully – only a five or a six, I'm afraid, sir . . . He had almost blurted out: My brother's scratch! Shuffling his papers, the wing commander said, Five, six – good as scratch so far as we're concerned. Important thing is we've people who can keep their eye in – that and the habit of command, obviously. How many hours d'you have? Michael said, Twenty-seven, sir, most of them in Oxfords. The wing commander sought clarification: Twin-engined? And after Michael supplied this, he puffed out his . . . *breast hair* and said, Jolly good, you'll only need another hundred-odd, then we'll give you some wings! – It had all seemed to be going . . . *swimmingly*, until the man sitting next to the wing commander stated: You were at Lancing. Michael replied tentatively, Yes, anticipating some snobbery – after all . . . *it was hardly top-drawer*. Instead the man said, Time was the service thought the only necessary qualification to command men in action was a decent public school education, but we don't see it in those terms any more. There're already Poles trickling over from the Continent – men who've flown in combat. We've got some pretty wild colonials queuing up to do their bit – Americans as well. The last thing we need are first-eleven heroes wet behind the ears who imagine they're going to be batting in some thrilling match . . .

The man was jowly, and, although clean-shaven and well-dressed, he had a dissolute air – a pale-yellow silk handkerchief *spurted* from his breast pocket, while he held his cigarette cupped in his palm so his knuckles *smouldered*. Later, when he rose awkwardly to shake this hand, Michael was shocked to discover how short its owner was, no more than five feet with peculiar blocky built-up shoes. Registering Michael's consternation, the man had said, quite blandly, Feet chewed off by a Camel's prop in '18 – my own bloody fault entirely, boffins couldn't be expected to synchronise blades so bodies passed through 'em – only bullets. Michael saluted him, the wing commander and the third member of the Board, a Fleet Air Arm officer in blue and brass — then, in the stark stairwell, he took two quick steps and, launching himself at the brown-paper X on the window . . . *Going out? Look out – Blackout!* . . . crashed out into the starker daylight. Banking hard, Michael came back round through the cloud of glassy shards towards the bland façade of Adastral House. The brass hats were standing by the broken window, commenting favourably on his coolness. He saluted them again before rapidly gaining altitude and passing over the tiled peaks of the Aldwych. He set a southerly course by . . . *dead reckoning*, and presently reached the extremities of London, where the coagulations of Croydon and Carshalton untangled into arterial roads winding through downland valleys. – Michael flew away from the Selection Board through space *and time* to the Channel, where he saw spread out beneath him *a magnificent diorama*: steamers and merchantmen, their decks teeming with the Expeditionary Force as they smashed through the waves in a welter of *valiant spray!* towards the tricolour of blue sea, red land and white sky. – But, as he dipped down to buzz the hopeful faces, his victory roll *tore the flesh from them*, leaving behind only grinning skulls rattling in tin helmets. Now he heard the Stukas' whistling howl as they circled above the piles of *human ordure* dumped on the beaches ahead . . . *carrion* that took it in turns to swoop low . . . *and feed*. Losing height, Michael checked the fuel gauge: there was a noxious smell in the *cockpit of my head* while knees dug sharply into his ribcage. Twisting round, he saw this *dissolute teddy bear* squatting on his angelic back: *Winnie!* with his sewn-on red button of a nose, his spit-damp cigar stuck between his two stuck-up fingers . . . *Winnie!* who, as they stalled and began to spin down to the ground, cried out, I'll 'ave a Baby Guinness! — Wh-What? Michael is flummoxed – the Marquess has filled up so rapidly that in between deciding to go to the bar and standing to do so, the intervening fifteen feet has been packed out with *a queer crowd*: a mixture of Guardsmen and *obvious homos* . . . all of whom seem to be . . . *getting on famously*. Then there's this very young girl, who a moment ago plonked down on the pew seat between the two brothers and without any ado applied her heavily lipsticked mouth to Kins's damp lips . . . *a real smacker* . . . then said, I'll 'ave a Baby Guinness! Her red nails dig into Michael's sleeve, her merry green eyes invite his into her unbuttoned blouse. Her *habit of command* is easily explained: *she's two pips up!* Kins says, Moira, this is my brother, Michael, he's with the United Airmen don'tcha know. And Moira says, Ooh, 'e can bail out with me any time he fancies. – By the time Michael has relayed their drinks back from the bar, his seat has been taken by a sallow-faced man wearing a heavy overcoat with a lamb's-wool collar and an Astrakhan hat that he touches lightly with his splayed fingers . . . *as if he were raising it*. I do wery much beg your pardon, zir, he says. His accent is mushily foreign, but he makes no attempt to move, only sits there . . . *insolently* touching things: his flowing Lavallière cravat, his sunken cheeks, and then Kins's arm – his brother cries, Get your mitts off me, Kraeplin! before turning to the girl: Well, have you seen her this evening? Moira says, She was in the Burglars' 'alf an hour ago, but you'll 'ave to be sharpish if you want to nab 'er – she's with that thumping bore, Willie Mackeson. Kins moans, Oooh, I'd like to slosh that Mackeson, the stout bastard! Kraeplin strikes a parliamentarian pose, fingers *petting his woolly lapels* . . . Mit ze eggstream gravity of ze international situation, he says, wiolence cannot be contemplated! Then he *Winnies on* . . . Ve haff vwelcomed ze Czech Provisional Government into our bed, unt ve haff made ze restoration of Czech plezzures vun of our principal vorr aimz! All three laugh crazily – Moira drains her Baby Guinness and cries, Chin-chin! as she rubs the brown fluid from her *sharp little chin* with a handkerchief pulled from the sleeve of her tight black jacket. Hooding her finger in cotton, she says, Ooh, lookit yer, then rubs at the red lipstick on Kins's pouting lips. Michael sits, ashamed of all their foolery. They should, he thinks, take a turn on the bloody parade ground – bit of square-bashing'd knock 'em into shape! Then he too is embarrassed by his own . . . *cod*, and the hollow sound of his own propagandising: *We'll show the Nazzies what Britons can do when we really roll up our sleeves!* Still, this Moira is awfully false and pretentious, while as for Kraeplin, Michael doesn't know what to make of him: *What is he, some Bethnal Green kike pretending to be a refugee?* The high-backed pews press them all *closer and closer* . . . and the advertisement plastered on the dull mocha wall is . . . *upsetting.* I'll Take Cover in a Bols! cries a khaki-uniformed lemon, running down the street towards a gigantic and salvational yellow bottle. One of the Guardsmen at the bar cries out, The Luft-fucker's flying boot was stuck on a chimney pot! And in the close atmosphere Michael can see the drinkers' beery guffaws . . . *plain as iron filings round a vulcanite rod.* From a far-off place, *stinking of pot' permanganate,* comes the fluting execration of Mister Etchingham, *gassed at Wipers,* who always compounded his own torture by his choice of words: *Stop your bally gassin', boys! You're black men – d'you see it? Lotus eaters! Circe's swine! Idle savages, only too happy to lie there gassin', hopin' the breadfruit will drop into your bally gassin' mouths!* – They catch up with the girl Kins is chasing after in another pub that might be the Wheatsheaf. Annette's tall with broad shoulders and elbows that stick out at exaggerated angles no matter how she arranges them. Her reddy-auburn hair has been set severely into two side curtains and a rolled pelmet, and her strong features *declaim woodenly* from the stage of her face. Everything about her *speaks volumes* . . . of . . . *Methodist sermons, coal tar soap and cold tapioca.* Michael cannot *for the life of me* imagine what she's doing with such a louche crowd – nor what his brother can possibly see in her. Kins sits with his head tilted back against a patch of tartan inset in the oak panelling, he's yet another fag lit, and he shouts smoke at Annette, together with the rest of the story he had begun to tell Michael several pubs earlier: T'was the gamekeeper, of course! I'd to own up to what I was! He'd've bloody well shot me if I hadn't! *Every phrase has to be flung across the ever-widening gulf between him . . . and everyone else.* Here's the thing! He approved! Yes, approved! Poor bugger'd been at Dunkirk – a tank-basher! – Annette has a tight smile and the expression of a DC observing the jiggy-jiggy dancing of some . . . *idle savages.* It was plain to Michael as soon as he saw her . . . *she's N. B. G.* The chap with her, Mackeson, has white-blond hair lying lank on his collar, and washed-out eyes that swim about behind the thick lenses of his horn-rimmed spectacles. He was introduced to Michael as one of the organisers of a programme to help refugees. With medical care, Annette explained, and – she drew the words out proudly – psy-cho-log-ical supp-ort . . . It's plain as day that in the contest for her affections *Kins has already lost.* Nevertheless, he keeps on with his shouting: The officers all piled into a staff car! Not so much as a cheery-bye to their men! They were down at the port and taken off before the Nazzies even got there! That's what my gamekeeper said! Made 'im turn poacher! – Over at the bar Kraeplin is talking to the landlord, a flaccidly saggy fellow in his shirtsleeves who holds fast to the taps and stares out through the mists of tobacco smoke . . . *towards some fatal shore.* You wouldn't guess it from the landlord's distant expression, but it seems that Kraeplin *has a way with him,* because he barges back through the Guardsmen carrying a tray full of liqueur glasses. Slivovitz, he says, mein host, ya, has – you say ziss? Ya, he has been zitting on it zo he haff it for our conquerors ven zey chip up . . . So . . . so . . . for all bodies? He offers the tray round and everyone takes a glass except Annette – Kins bags hers, then shouts, Prost! and Mackeson says *very drily*, Here's how. Kraeplin mutters, Bin gar keine Russin, stamm' aus Litauen . . . The cherry-bomb incendiary in Michael's throat is the bright-red wax droplet on the candle, the flame-shaped bulb of which *flickers* behind a furl of parchment . . . *Fake, fake, fake – all fake.* – They're out in the street . . . *caught in the spotlight.* Kins has manoeuvred to take Annette's arm, but as the pub door swings shut *the scene ends* . . . with her refusing it, and Michael's eyes prickle with . . . *blips and celluloid scratches.* Mackeson says, It helps to be a little pie-eyed if you want to find your way in the blackout – how's about Oddenino's? We could get some more drinks there, and sandwiches on the extension – for my own part, my fire-watching stint don't begin 'til midnight. – They revolve up the road and tumble along an alley. The *big dog of war* has ambled this way, lifting its leg and jetting fluorescent paint at lintels, door-jambs and kerbstones. They stagger and trip, colliding with . . . *the darkness itself made flesh and bone.* Someone remarks, They've salami and potato salad there – French bread too, all off the ration. – In what Michael surmises is the Tottenham Court Road, his companions' faces acquire an odd luminescence as they sop up the blue emanations of buses grumbling along the carriageway, and the silvery ones from the bashful moon . . . *grabbing at clouds to hide her nakedness – it's a peek-a-boo night.* Only a few minutes can have passed, but already the blackout has jumbled up time, so he can no longer remember if the proposal to provision at an Italian delicates-sen, then hold an informal supper party at Kraeplin's digs, came before they left the pub or only now – in response to the sirens and the steady rumbling of approaching bombers . . . *coming to drop salami and potato salad on us.* The lights of a nearby battery shoot up – the 20th Century blood drums in his ears, Brrrum-bum! Brrrum-bum! The Foxfare blares, Baa-b'-b'-baaaaa! and Michael thinks, This is utterly thrilling! He can hear Kins some way ahead, refusing to *let go of his yarn:* Told me the whole sorry tale over a breakfast of roasted pheasant – with bacon! Best damn meal I've had since the beginning of hostilities –. Pack it in! An ARP man has fallen in the middle of them at precisely the moment they register the first detonations – dull crumps that sound . . . *rather ineffectual.* He pushes them bodily down the road, and Michael breaks into a trot, his gas mask *banging on* at his hip . . . *put-me-on, put-me-on, put-me-on* . . . the sharp smack of footsteps on paving goes hollow and the Guinness Clock disappears overhead into a flickering sky. On the long trudge down the stopped escalator, he gradually identifies the young woman in front who's sinking by the dim fizzle of declining bulbs, her high hips rising, her reddy-auburn hair swishing between her shoulder blades . . . *Seven we were, and five are gone: five! What are those remaining? Ghosts of the past, with cloud o'ercast, Cloud that is always raining! Put-me-on, put-me-on, put-me-on.* At the bottom people are milling about trying to decide . . . *if Herman has it in for the Northern or the Central Line.* Spotting him, Annette elbows her way through and, *rather unexpected, this,* takes Michael by the hand and leads him down a second stalled escalator . . . *We're all for QUAKER CORN FLAKES – they're MALTED and we find they need less sugar* . . . She flings back, I know a spot behind the platform guard's box . . . then laughs gaily: I left two old blankets there last week on my way to work, I've high hopes they'll still be there! – They are, and together they spread them out . . . *Sleeping when it's raining, And sleeping when it's fine . . . Pavement is my pillow* . . . and one or two trains do indeed come . . . *rattling by.* Annette, seeing a few bona fide passengers who look *frightfully put out* as they pick their way between the supine bodies, says, There's really no point – if it's a big raid they'll stop the train at Mornington Crescent, which isn't nearly so deep down. Then she lies straight out in their private nook, her head against the curve of the tiles, her hair fanned out on the yellow blanket, her stockinged feet aligned with its satin hem. She smoothes her skirt with both palms and laces her fingers beneath her breasts. You may as well settle down, she says, we could well be here all night . . . But Michael can't – he keeps craning round the guard's box to see what his fellow tramps are up to. At first they're strung out along the platform in a disordered mass, though soon enough they begin organising themselves into . . . *a community.* Pitches are speedily demarcated with rolled-up macs and beer bottles – pipes are lit and evening papers spread wide to catch the ebb and flow of the electrical current . . . *A nucleus of enlightened, sane and intelligent men and women who shall keep events in their right perspective* . . . and Michael muses, Perhaps these are they? A wholly arbitrary group who'll stump up the stairs at dawn, smelling of soiled linen and soured beer, to find a smoking shattered plain where London once stood, and who'll have to pick through the rubble, not for survivors – there'll be no survivors – but solely for the wherewithal to rebuild socie–. They're almost all Jews, y'know,

Annette pipes up, propping herself up on her big elbow. – I'm sorry? – The trogs – that's what we call them – they're almost all Jews. They get down at Liverpool Street and find the platforms already full up, so they head west. It's a sort of exodus, I s'pose. Michael looks at her mouth – it has the precise corners and sharp red flanges *of a posting box*. He wonders if she's trying to be witty. But on the contrary . . . *she's being pi*, and is also rather thrilled by her own proximity to these aliens. – Sirbert says the Jews –. He stops short, not wishing to explain who Sirbert is or what he says. Instead he considers whether she may be expecting him to make love to her. She's N.B.G. – that's plain, yet in his experience it's often the N.B.G. ones who expect you to try, rubbing up against their own tightly belted chastity . . . *excites them*. She doesn't excite him – however, smoothing his eyes over her sensible fawn skirt, he's aroused by the idea of . . . *betrayal – it would jolly well serve Kins right*. EDGWARE, HIGH BARNET, MILL HILL EAST – the indicator creaks and the wind from the tunnel-shaped nowhere pushes smut and an excremental smell into the nostrils pressed against the platform. Michael wads his gas-mask bag behind his head and pulls his cap down low on his brow. It seems to him that it's deep below the detonations rumble on – of no more account than the underground trains he heard rumbling beneath the cinema when Chips's boys were sobbing their goodbyes. Good idea, Annette says, I'm 'fraid I hardly ever wear a hat . . . Michael blanks her – lying prone he's become *a fuselage* . . . and the tunnel his . . . *long hollow wing*. He pulls back on the stick *rather abruptly* and forces him, her, the trogs – *all of them* – to loop-the-loops fastening her brassiere. Give over! Moira cries. You'll bend 'em. Kins lets his heavy head fall back against the day-bed's hard padding. His liquefied brains slosh against his eyes, before which her bare back curves . . . *mailed by the light from yonder window* – her *breast-plate* slides into her lap, and she turns to show him . . . *her perfections!* Careful now, she chides him, don't paw at me – you'll rip me knicks, an' they're crêpe-de-Chine – not likely to see any more this side of Christmas, not at eight-and-six the yard. Then *with holy grace* . . . she wriggles her bottom from side to side, bends to remove the undergarments from her toes and, sitting upright, carefully folds, then puts them on a portion of empty shelf inside a bookcase, the shattered glass of which lies all about them on the Persian rug . . . *mingling promiscuously* with common window glass. – The few sticks dropped on Bloomsbury were, Kins thinks, only incontinence on the Luftwaffe's part, hurrying *comme d'habitude* to relieve themselves *in their favourite pissoir*: the docks. When he and Moira found themselves separated from the others and clattering along the austere terrace as the bombers grumbled away south, she'd stopped, pulled at her garments, squatted in the gutter. The *babbling of her brook* was more shocking to him than any explosion. Whassermatter, she'd said, ain'tcher seen no one takin' a whizz before? Now she rears before him, smelling of boracic, cold cream and Guinness – and subsides to snuggle beside him. The net curtains flick up in the breeze, fingering the underside of the sash. – Exhilarated to a frightening pitch . . . *we'll be caught!* . . . he'd followed her in through the crippled door, along the dirtied passage and into this study, where, by intermittent flashes, he snatched quotes from the blasted books:

Sir Peverel from the castle rode out, his puissant steed . . . functions in inverse association to the anima or tribal sex-instinct . . . heard, yet declined to give any further account of these monstrous occurrences . . . I say, Kins says, sitting up, don'tcha think the people'll be up from the shelter pretty soon? He presses his lips together, *mangling out the booze* from phrases he hopes sound . . . *calm and sober.* She's so very close – he daren't touch her . . . *lest I explode!* Give over, Moira says, there weren't any lights in the square – an' that ain't because they're so bloomin' careful, it's 'cause they've all sodded off for the duration – packed their kiddies off to Canada, while they're all down in the country noshing on snob's duck . . . She folds her arms *wantonly* behind her head and says, looking at him appraisingly, Arn'tcha gonna do nothing, then? You want I should give your thingummy a rub or sumfing? I'm getting bloody parky – there's a hell of a draft in 'ere. He shrugs off his sports jacket and enfolds her in it. She giggles: Ooh! that tickles, and he stifles her giggles with his lips, seeking *against Sirbertian odds* sobriety in her sharp little tongue's staccato. Withdrawing, he affects pomposity: I'm a man seeking a position . . . Which he does, disposing his long legs carefully so *my thingummy* is pressed hard against the upholstery. Kins feels himself subsiding, so, to buy himself a little time, he tells her . . . *a chaise-longue story.* They were a day and a night on that breakwater, don'tcha know. They hung to the ironwork, but when the tide came in some of 'em were washed off – others were machine-gunned by the dive bombers. Plenty lost their nerve – cracked up. Apparently some of them screamed so much they . . . they threw up their own blood. My poacher got taken off by a pleasure boat on the second morning and was brought back to Worthing – they set him up in the little bar on a pile of old bunting, and gave him dandelion and burdock laced with brandy . . . As Kins speaks Moira touches his face, splaying her fingers against his sunburnt forehead, his ruddy cheeks, his soft chin. Gotta gasper? she says, and, as he gropes in his jacket pocket, she giggles. He strikes a match . . . *and we meet and are consumed in the flame.* Two days later, Kins puffs, my chap was skulking on the platform at Peterborough – they'd scattered to the four winds, y'see, chucked away their warrant cards, torn up their pass books. A few had even smashed their rifles – naturally none of that made it into the papers. Anyway, my chap's skulking because he's no warrant or ticket, when he sees one of the officers from his company. What're the odds on that! My chap's taken with an ice-cold rage – and he's no hothead, he's a sensitive type. Waits until this officer goes into the gents, follows him in there and barges him into one of the stalls. – Kins takes a long pull on his cigarette, and carefully tips the ash on to the shelf below Moira's underthings. – Well, I should imagine you can guess what came next! – Moira touches his chin, her own tongue, his chin again – she rubs the saliva between her fingertips. When they begin to make love he's taken aback but *profoundly grateful* . . . for her skilful . . . *finessing*: she draws out from him the caresses he wishes to bestow but doesn't know how. How, he wonders in the mess of her hair, can it be that this chit of a girl – a common slut, apparently – understands my body with *such thoroughness?* Moira's fingers beckon him forth, then . . . *choke me off!* First time I done that, she husks, was to the tallyman, stopped him dead in 'is tracks . . . This further bromide comes to Kins, unbidden: *Sirbert* . . . diving down over the cards . . . *a bluff, of course* . . . for he's only to glance at his hand to know what he has . . . and, by extrapolation, what *everyone else has as well*. Sirbert, his dorsal nose beginning to marble with veins – though he drinks far less as a rule *than the rest of us*: only the stout in his morning messery, a glass of wine at supper, and perhaps two or three Bombshells when the cards are dealt . . . *under the table*. Moira pulls his sweat-encrusted shirt from his shoulders. Kins says, I'm 'fraid I haven't bathed in a while. She chuckles. He supposes she's pretty enough – but that's not what grips him. When she leans forward and his sports jacket falls away, he's overwhelmed by . . . *Brockleby's Friesians lowing and swaying their way into the parlour*. There's her *teat* . . . stiffening between his lips, her other breast pressing against his cheek – there's her skin, smooth beneath his fingers as he *forages* from hip to thigh . . . *and into the thicket*. After that matters take *their natural course* . . . although the girl manifests some strange behaviour: scratching Kins's bum . . . *KENBAR toilet paper in the gents at Victoria* as she shows him . . . *entirely matter-of-factly* how to put on the French letter. – C'mon, it's just like puttin' on a sock – you rolls it up, an' rolls it down. But how did you get hold of it? Kins asks – he'd visited a rubber-goods shop some Wheatsheaf regulars spoke of, but run away when he saw the old woman behind the counter . . . *a withered procuress*. You aren't – his cracked diction falls on to the broken glass – a, um, lady of the night? She slaps his member, lightly, and it twangs back and forth. The bloody cheek of it! she says, I oughta turn you out! She does it for him, the rubbery smell and the tickle of the French chalk is . . . *sobering as the schoolroom.* All right, she says, all right, luvvie . . . All right, she grunts, all . . . right . . . now . . . luv-vie . . . Lying on top of her, he's too terrified to move: for years he's carried this fuse between his legs *primed – and ready to go off!* should it get anywhere within a few inches of its target. Here it is, after some awkward bumping and boring – *deep inside!* Moira bucks a little and Kins smells *gas rings* . . . tastes *burnt milk* . . . and sees *kipper scraps congealing on a greasy plate* . . . She bucks a bit more, and the small movement turns a crank that pulls a chain that opens a trap that releases a ball-bearing that scours round a spiralling groove and drops through a hole on to a pressure-sensitive plate that tilts a lever that withdraws a cork unleashing water down on to a wheel connected by rods to the two tiny figures deep in the brick-lined shaft of Gordon Square, Heath Robinson marionettes that all at once begin . . . *to go like the clappers* . . . Suddenly there it was: *THE END* of his boyhood, the titles rolling up on the screen and the seats banging as their occupants rose to the first organ chords of God Save the King. – Into this *interlude* Moira intrudes: Get that slimy fing off yer todger, there's a good boy. Kins happily fuddles: *There can be no posture less dignified* . . . then quotes to himself: *The greatest fault of penetration is not that it goes to the bottom of a matter – but beyond it* . . . Moira, watching him fold the deflation into a page taken from one of the broken books, says, I started out doing HP ledger work for a timber merchant in Poplar, y'know – same time I was doing evening courses at Pitman's to get typing and shorthand . . . Kins catches her drift: she wishes it known – as if he didn't know well

235

enough already – that *I'm in capable hands.* He falls sideways . . . *a dray horse, dead in the shafts . . . killed by the drink he dragged . . .* She draws him into her lap so they lie . . . *chair-o-planing* through the onrush of time and the night — That day, ranging along the banks of the Lincolnshire eau, Williams gave Kins a course in practical botany. A charm the young conchie had never known he possessed gained him the angry deserter's support for what had become . . . *a quest*: I cannot account for it, Kins confessed, I feel unclean, though – shrink from any contact with our fellow men . . . and their machines. I s'pose rationally I know I shan't be shunned by all . . . For now . . . I don't want to be melodramatic, but I'd sooner be dead meat than press their flesh . . . Williams was pragmatic: Missus'll give yer a can or two of Spam, an' we've home-baked bread – but game'll spoil quick, cheese'll sweat to buggery in this heat, an' there's nowt to spare off the ration. Kins said, I understand, really, Mister Williams – it's terribly decent of you to bother with me at all. To begin with Kins had floundered about in the woodland spreading out behind their cottage – he was unused to daytime's pitiless visibility, or to the thickness of its information. When he told Williams the leafy green carpet between the trees put him in mind of a cheap Bible's typography, the poacher snorted: Wood sorrel? Oh, yes, it's good news if you've an empty belly – it'll make a serviceable salad stuff, and this – he strained ferny leaves between his fingers – is tansy, if you steep it you can get a potable tea. – On they went, Williams pulling up long sticky tendrils of goose grass and hauling down thorny stalks clustered with . . . *Haw-Haws.* When they reached the woodland's edge, there was a stiff fringe of bracken, beyond this another eau, and on its far side golfers were breezily teeing off. Williams motioned to him to take cover. Outstretched, pollen tickling his nose, Kins thought first of Belgian nuns being ... *ravaged in bunkers*, then began to analyse the golfers' swings. Williams spat, Mister-bloody-Barnes with his private-bloody-army! Only then did Kins see that half the cumbersome eight were gamekeepers in rough tweeds and gaiters, who, instead of drivers, had shotguns cradled in their arms. What a laugh, Williams said unsmilingly, if the Nazzie parachutists were to land here he'd invite 'em up to the big house and serve 'em a fine bloody luncheon. – They retreated back into the covert and Williams coaxed his pupil's clumsy fingers through the fine work of rigging a snare. Kins said, I'm 'fraid I shall forget how to do it more or less pronto – I doubt I'd have the patience to wait for the birdies anyway, or ... frankly, the gumption necessary to dispatch and prepare them. Williams wasn't interested in such defeatism – he grasped Kins's arm, saying: You've a choice, man, more 'n I do. They'll be coming for me any day now and it's the fucking glass-house for me – how d'you think I'll stomach that, eh? Least you can do is be free for the both of us. – Missus Williams had a sickly yellowish tint – Kins wondered if she might be jaundiced. Looking at her, listless as she took the baking tin from the range, a smudge of flour on the puffed sleeves of her homemade frock, another stain on its pie-crust collar, he felt her sadness. They saw him off at sunset, standing in the porch, its fretwork coping throwing shining hearts on them. Williams's arm was around his wife's resisting hips, his lantern jaw was in her hair, and as Kins walked away he looked back once to see the ivy slowly tearing the tiles from the cottage roof . . . *and falling in tresses.* – He kept doughtily on, the Milky Way sparkling underfoot as he maintained his southerly course, night after night – Kins put it down to Williams's stiffening influence. On the fifth, he rose up out of the fenlands and gave Peterborough a wide berth. The following evening he rolled from beneath a hedge and, picking up the Great North Road's course, he followed it on towards . . . *the immense and stagnant lagoon.* He'd scrumped apples and pinched eggs to boil in his spam tin – a tramp he ran up against on the banks of the Ouse shared tea from a screw of newspaper and half a good white loaf. In return Kins gave him a half-crown – and the tramp tried to embrace him. They'd dozed away that day together, in fitful ignorance of whether a gauleiter was banging his Luger's butt on the arm of the Speaker's chair . . . *until it broke.* – A bold white sun with bold white rays rose up . . . *Brasso* . . . on the stuccoed gable end of a general provisioner's Kins sloped by in the unearthly hour before dawn. Laying up for the day, he heard the traction engines' steady chuffering and the tractors' rapacious roar – all of it, he thought, components of a production line designed to whirl the grain away in a sulphurous cloud: the soldiers' bellies needed bread – the guns fired fresh-baked rolls and loaves, the brimstone mills went on grinding out . . . *lead and steel.* Contra the hopes of Feydeau, Cornwallis and Brockleby, the very land itself was being transformed into *an extension of the battlefield.* He slept uneasily, and in his dreams ears of corn burst into flame, while vaporised ducks left their flying shadows imprinted on the sides of barns. –

So at last he came to Epping, where a tricky uphill Par 3 took him to the crest of a hill. Crawling through the rough on his hands and knees, he reached the pockling of a rabbit warren and decided . . . *entirely arbitrarily* . . . that this was the end. He made his final calculations: the extraordinarily long course, its holes succeeding one another unflaggingly, had stretched for 218,470 yards from Holton-cum-Beckering to here, and he had played it with 4,853 strokes – including 74 penalty ones for lost imaginary balls. These were, he conceded, only approximate figures – he was no cold calculating machine. Spread out on the cooling ground, listening to an owl's subdued wisdom, Kins speculated: had his strange walk been *some form of pilgrimage*, and, if so, *have I done sufficient penance?* Rising, going on he saw that the hill was a vast and . . . *Sibertian dome*, the far side of which was . . . *crinkled up into ridges by disapproval.* Beyond the last clumps of gorse the ground fell away and the city's still vaster face confronted him, its Stygian complexion pin-pricked here and there by the slitted feline eyes of 'buses and motor-cars padding silently through the blackout. For a long time, as he stared away to the south, Kins could make no sense of what he saw, lit up by bright flashes reflected by the clouds. Had some sort of *giant chair-o-plane* . . . been set up above the East End? It was only when several of the shapes detached from the vortex that he realised: this was no fairground – it was . . . *the United Airmen!* They'd got here first and *because they don't approve of independent sovereign states* . . . they were . . . *bonking London to smithereens!* – Everyfing tickety-boo, cock? This from a stalwart fellow sealed into manila-coloured overalls, who'd been delivered early to the late-summer morning. The young collie dog that ran out in front of the man, set then rounded Kins up — *was perfectly instinctual* . . . he thinks as he lies in Moira's arms, admiring the shattered composition of the broken glass scattered about the day-bed . . . *deceptive as memory.* — The dog must've smelt him from a long way off: for eight days he'd swopped one dirty shirt for the other, his cricketing pullover was in shreds, only his sports jacket . . . *holding it in together.* The man – who, Kins supposed, was a fitter or printer come off night shift – showed no dismay, only stood below Kins on the hillside, the sun-smitten reservoir *burning behind him* . . . and warned: There's an unexploded whizz-bang jammed under a bakery on the 'igh road. Bunch of ARP prats doing the fan-bloody-dango – nothing doing for a gentleman of the road such as yourself, so I'd give the area a miss if I was you . . . As the man spoke his collie had come forward to thrust its warm wet muzzle into Kins's groin, and he'd pictured it wolfing down . . . *macaroons and Eccles cakes . . . How much is that bombie in the window, the one with the wagg-er-lee fuse . . . How much is that bombie in the window, I do hope* you realise, Annette says to Michael *out of the blue*, when they've tunnelled far into the night and the only light along the platform comes from the *glow-worming* of a cigarette, your brother is already a dipsomaniacal behaviour, making awful choking noises as he strains at the leash. Oscar has spotted the tabby from two doors down . . . *stupid as a fly – maddeningly narcissistic with it* . . . as it comes smarming along the top of the wall, plops! soundlessly to the pavement, and smarms on up the road, its tail dabbing at the air, its swivelling hips retracting all sight lines *into its anus.* What was it Ronnie had said? He'd been, as usual, drunk as a Gorbals laird: *Have you everr considerred putting yourr fingerr inside the anus of the family dog?* Oh, Ronnie, Ronnie! Busner sighs aloud, seeing the white hemispheres of his former mentor's eyelids, below these the *placental mess* of his eyes, and depending from them heavy bags . . . *already packed for another world* . . . Oh, Ronnie – Ronnie, you've abandoned your noble gift! *La donna è mobile . . . Arseholes are cheap to-daay! Cheaper than yes-ter-daay! Buy one for two-and-six, Big ones take lots of –.* Although, as they follow the cat, Oscar's frenzied belly grinding at the paving stones, Busner is dragged to this conclusion: Now would be as good a time as any to do exactly that: now, in the lull of mid-morning, with the net curtains of Chapter Road knotted up *in bondage* to cleaning, and door mats slung over front gates *for flogging.* Hearing the lascivious groan and whistling suck of hoovers in front rooms, Busner meditates using a mantra every transcendentalist knows: *Dust is skin – skin is dust . . .* His attachment is to the last thing he saw before he swung shut the door of 117: an envelope stuck by its gummed flap to the wallpaper's one-dimensional blizzard, written on it in blue crayon FAITHFUL YET WITH BEAST. The telegraphese of the psychotic, he concedes, lends itself to such statements, ones that are simultaneously smirking gnosis – *I'm faithful yet with beast, but I'm not going to tell you which one* – and chummily phatic: *How's it going, man, faithful yet with beast?* The stop-go of such communication is, Busner thinks, not unlike walking the dog – for Oscar has stopped abruptly to cock his leg and scatter a few *emeralds* in the budding privet. He strains on – and so does his master: It's also of a piece with the residents' tedious magical thinking, the I-Ching-bloody-Ching thrown using coins needed for the gas and electricity meters, the doleful allusions to unseen spirits . . . *yanking their chains.* During the last rainy month the tobacco smoke tangles, the gas fire fumes, and the condensation fuzzily felting the windows have all combined into . . . *a thick miasma.* It's no surprise, Zack thinks, I was taken in by that idiotic pair, because in the clear light of day it's patently absurd – they wouldn't dare spike me with LSD. – Ronnie is it, now? says the postman, who's squatted down to rub Oscar's head with his knuckles . . . *faithful yet with beast.* He's capless and tieless, his grey suit and bandolier of empty canvas sack give him a timeless feel – Zack can see him pushing a pram piled high with salvaged household effects *through the remains of a bomb-shattered city.* No, no, he says, I was thinking out loud about a friend who's in a spot of bother – he's still Oscar, I s'pose he always will be. The postman, who's also balding and ageing . . . *should I rub his liver-spotted scalp with my knuckles?* . . . looks up with *hanghuman* eyes, and Zack's impelled to: I hope he – or anyone else at 117 or 119 for that matter – hasn't been bothering you? But the postman continues entreating, and Zack thinks, This is bloody futile – because, of course, the residents are *nothing but a bother*: constantly in receipt of post lacking sufficient postage, or railing against the poor man because they imagine his badge marks him out as an Imperialist lackey or an alien invader. – Straightening, the postman says, I've no quarrel with your tenants, Doctor Busner. I've a sister got the mentals, bin in Hanwell for five years off an' on now –'ad electrics 'an all sorts. Shocking business. No, it's that lot opposite I can't be doing with – nig-nogs and religious nutters to boot . . . Oscar is left leaning disconsolately against the hedge as the postman clicks away on new Blakeys. Probably changes them more than his underwear, Zack thinks, so's to be ready to *put the boot in* . . . The dog tugs Zack's mind on along the coastline of Chapter Road, with its inlet porches and bay-window promontories, its *foreshore of privet and tiling.* Why do people do that? Is the associative faculty merely a matter of neurons randomly zapping together, so that . . . *electrics sparks shocking?* Or is this activated by . . . *latent psychic content?* If it's the latter, why should it require any further investigation – after all, it's a perfectly clear example of a circular diallelus: that the postman's sister has had ECT is indeed shocking to him . . . *we need dig no further.* – Deacon Road, Sandringham Road, Churchill Road – *all file by.* To parade through English suburbia is, Zack thinks, to have Church and State . . . *passing in review.* He would've turned right out of the gate . . . *Muß es sein?* . . . were it not that he'd then have had to pass by Westminster Wine and Walter E. Tucker, Newsagent. Both shopkeepers had been known to come barrelling out from their premises in order to haul Zack up over one or another transgression: the Kid trying to buy gin, or Eileen presenting an appalled customer with a big wad of moistened toilet paper she said was her dead baby – or the Creep building a little pagoda with all the tubes of Rollos as he *talked the most filthy smut imaginable.* It needed no imagining for Zack, who'd to listen to it day in and day out . . . *a fish-hook caught in whatever's salient . . . Throw de darkie in de coal hole wid de muff-tash on he face* . . . On the same side of the road there was the So-White

Laundry, another *DMZ* for the Concept House residents . . . *although nig-nogs're welcome*, and Rodgers's Garage, where Zack had the Hillman serviced until the small matter arose of an unpaid bill . . . *smells can burrrn your eyes but on-ly peep-pul make you cry.* Why, he thinks, fingering his own none-too-white collar, did I bother putting on a tie today? Why, come to think of it, did I put on any clothes at all? It would've been better to have stayed under the sleep-tossed covers – after Chappaquiddick, what do anyone's nine missing hours matter? Instead, as he follows Oscar's *podgehole* up the road, there's this weary acknowledgement: *Es muß sein!* For there isn't a business in the neighbourhood with which some petty debt or minor outrage isn't associated: Snook, the fishmonger, and MUSICLAND RECORDS – the Segovia Café and LORETTE Ladies' Hairdresser, outside of which stands the *hollow boy* . . . in his orthopaedic leg-iron, with a slot in his painted hair, waiting to be *filled up by suburban beneficence – I wish me was he.* On one especially miserable malicious April morning, Zack had been walking Oscar under rusty, guttering skies when he was accosted by *an excitable little nebbish* called Mister Green, who, with his koppel slipped sideways to expose a bald patch . . . *exactly the same size!* . . . came scuttling out from DOUBLE GEE WIGMAKERS, a bill in his hand . . . *for a sheitel!* – Irene had no money to pay for the ghastly thing, so screamed horribly until Maggie wrapped a scarf around her butchered locks . . . *hiding them from His all-seeing eyes.* How Irene had acquired the rudiments of her newfound orthodoxy was . . . *mysterious.* Certainly not from her usual Holy Writ, Flying Saucer Review, which was posted to her twice-monthly from an address in Leytonstone. But, now he considers it, Zack supposes she might have picked up bits and pieces of doctrine from Maurice – after all, together with the Creep, Irene had been one of the founding residents, present during the three weeks Maurice spent at Chapter Road, sleeping in the back bedroom of 117. Zack's uncle had come to see for himself whether the community would be suitable for Henry, should they be able to secure his discharge from hospital. And Miriam, seeking in her *intuitive, thoughtful – highly prescriptive* way to help him join the group, had made it her business to cook a Shabbat supper for them all, bringing sweet-glazed challas from Grodzinski's on the High Road, and fetching schmaltz from Bloom's in Golders Green. She'd boiled up brisket on the cooker, and standing nearby . . . *in one of his occasional patches of lucidity* . . . Claude sniffed theatrically, then said, Gosh, Miriam, that sure does smell like somebody's childhood . . . before rounding on Zack and snarling: But not yours! – Oscar halts in front of the bland brick façade of Churchill Court, and, carefully arranging his twitching rear over the kerb, he quivers out . . . *one . . . two . . . three* dollops of . . . *chopped liver*. The old man has been gone these five years, dragged off-stage on his gun-carriage to . . . *some brandy-soaked Valhalla.* Really, though, he'd never leave – he was *too solid* . . . for any other world, so had been . . . *reincarnated* into a road and a block of flats. Zack feels a swirl in his belly – not precisely . . . *butterflies,* and not altogether . . . *dyspepsia,* but something which alerts him to . . . *the chopped liver of my own experience* ceaselessly . . . *quivering out.* It was the Creep *of course!* The Creep who'd written on that envelope *Faithful yet with beast* . . . Then came the postman with his sad circularities . . . *for me, the kikel* . . . his knuckles on Oscar's head, his *bin in Hanwell* . . . his *shocking 'lectric* . . . *Never seen a sight that didn't look better looking back!* Zack shudders: *Someone's rubbed a balloon on my woolly thinking – sparks are beginning to fly out from* . . . Claude . . . *in concentric rings of coincidence!* When Zack opened the curtains that morning, the sky had been blissfully clear – now, *chicken clouds* . . . are . . . *fleeing* overhead, and from minute to minute the atmosphere thickens with premonition, as, no longer content with announcing his own presence in advance, *the shaman* has begun to throw out harbingers of a more . . . *general disaster!* – Man and dog move on – or, rather, dog uses lead to *sling man on* . . . *Fort – Da!* At once they're at the end of the road, where a much larger block of flats . . . *forms a prow.* Busner looks up at the seven storeys of brick-and-concrete striping and thinks, In there are all sorts of peculiar passengers . . . Frantic old maids amassing jam jars full of cat fur . . . Punctilious drunks who only spittle at Richard Baker . . . KINGSLEY COURT! Its rubber-block nameplate stamps down on him, just as the block itself stamps down on the white sheet of the street, and up above there's a twig-fractured *pain of* . . . sky . . . *They wouldn't dare, would they?* He bends down to seek reassurance in Oscar's broad thick skull, searching the dog's fur for . . . *my soul – or his?* Looking up at the block again, he sees tiny agitated suicides . . . *all the schizophrenics we've failed to help* hurling themselves from the balconies and flapping into . . . *pigeons!* Relieved, he straightens up and chides himself: Kingsley Court has always been here. However handy he may be, Claude wasn't up the end of the road all night . . . *a fairytale goblin* . . . laying bricks

246

and pouring concrete. – On Oscar pulls: up the Avenue, past the enormous Edwardian villas built for . . . *pre-pill-sized-families*, their turrets and garrets now full of . . . *childlike hippies on the dole.* They reach the High Street, and Busner does his best to appear exactly what he is: a middle-class professional man, on the cusp of middle age, walking his dog – but the real mantra is unceasing: *Those bastards, they wouldn't dare, would they? . . . Those bastards, they wouldn't dare, would they?* But of course they would . . . *and they have!* In the window of Thomas Cook's a V-shaped stand bears a Tunisia-bound Boeing over a rumpled blue Rayon Med'. He rattles the change in the pocket of his trousers: *It's one-and-nine into Holborn, where I can prevail upon Mister Wentworth to increase my overdraft by fifty-nine guineas . . .* Everything, Busner considers, might seem a bit more bearable after fifteen nights away. He sees himself changing trains at King's Cross: the worn ribbing of advertisements on the tunnel walls, the escalator carrying him down as the familiar warm smelliness rises up to encompass him . . . *a rollneck worn by a multitude.* No! That would be the coward's way: *I will return! Es muß sein!* There's Miriam and the boys – there's Maurice, who made the whole *ghastly wrong-headed failed stupid* experiment possible — and who, when he came to stay at Chapter Road, brought his Meissen figurines of Napoleonic marshals. Silly, really, he'd said as he arranged them on the windowsill in the back bedroom and a passing tube *tinkled Ney.* I s'pose they're rather like my teddy bears. – Maurice did his best to fit in with all the others' infantilism: He joined Irene in batiking sessions, his shirtsleeves rolled up and secured with gold-plated protectors. They laid out the cloth on the kitchen table while Claude commented: Ooh, what a swish-dish, ain't he, this fella – a tutti-fruity-galootie too good to shootie – as ofay as All-Day's. Y'know, I once calibrated the degrees of the pyramid of the moon and the parhelion of the sun and the fanny of Tallulah, and it all told me WHAT I SHOULD DO, which was take out the earthenware heads, take out the planters and HANG THREE FAGS! He thrust a copy of the Chronicle in Maurice's gentle and wounded face and . . . *went relentlessly on*: Acts of gross indecency, see! Between men in Roundwood Park, see! A fifteen-pound fine – but you can afford that with your skin wallet and your skin money –. Only then – *then!* did Zack have the guts to intervene, crying out *like some minor Shakespearean character*: Still! Be still, Claude! — And although Maurice has long since fled back to Redington Road, Zack continues to see his uncle . . . *everywhere*: nailed up on the cross outside the gloomy hulk of St Andrew's, or in bas-relief on a memorial plaque stuck to the bus garage's wall. And where Zack stands now, in front of Edward's the baker's, revolted all over again by the EGGLESS CAKES stencilled on the window. He also spots an uncle-alike heading into the Dickensian Crown, with its *peggottywork* of crazy timbering, and only dispels this vision by checking his watch. The watch – a fancy Omega automatic wristed down by Maurice – has never kept good time, but still has the effrontery to point out it's only *10.15*. Zack feels seconds stretching out before him – a sticky temporality . . . *chewing gum or possibly Bovril* – adhering moment to moment, forestalling the possibility of anything so prosaic as the Crown opening . . . *at all*. He sees himself loitering interminably for a restorative whisky and soda, and for once is grateful when Oscar strains at the lead: *We can simply go on* . . . ticking up Normanby Road, left into Mulgrave Road, left again on to the Parade, back once more into Normanby Road, *round annaround* . . . for however many hours it'll take before he's no longer troubled by this diagnosis: the city is an ugly and ever-expanding haematoma . . . *bleeding beneath the earth's scabby surface.* – It had happened before: Zack had *nibbled the wrong side of the mushroom* . . . and . . . *got trapped* in the suburban wall of death: his Hush Puppies snuffling the screaming semis, his face battered by fence-post and privet as he went *round annaround*, his perpendicular body prevented from crashing to the ground solely by his own centrifugal effort . . . *Round annaround* and bedevilled – as he'd then seen it with hallucinogenic clarity – by his *Great Task*, which was to develop a *Grand Unified Spiral of expanding and contracting schemata*, making it possible for him to swim freely between the most abstract ideas and the most concrete situations. On that occasion there'd been . . . *no Laika at the controls*, and it'd taken him hours to summon the necessary impetus to break from this orbit. But, instead of returning to the house, his *ballistic arc* had shot him out through the asteroid rings of Wembley and Harrow, until at dusk he discovered himself in the outer space of Ruislip, standing in front of the bungalow where the Krogers used to live, and puzzling over all the schemas that might still be inside *expanding and contracting*, despite the searchers' rigorousness and the new owners' imposition of their *fresh design for living*. He peeked through half-open curtains at reproduction Sunflowers, curious as to whether there was *microdottal blight* on their petals, or *encrypted crumbs* behind the bread bin, or a powerful transmitter *rotting away beneath the compost heap.* – Zack had met Helen and Peter at a book launch an arty friend of Miriam's held at Zwemmer's. It hadn't, so far as he remembered, been a particularly bohemian crowd: the men drably suited, the women *on the dumpy side*, but squeezed into Dior dresses *too little and too black for them.* Everyone had been talking very loudly, tossing back the usual *got-rut* . . . and rubbing up against the bookshelves . . . *presumably hoping to absorb culture by osmosis.* He'd exchanged a few inconsequential remarks with Peter Kroger . . . *about Modigliani's sexual pathology, as I recall* . . . When they were unmasked . . . *I'd felt personally affronted* . . . although also . . . *rather impressed.* After all, if the adult world was always *rather bogus*, their impersonation-in-triplicate allowed this truth to show through: *We're all carbon copies* . . . — Putting the newspaper report of their arrest to one side, smelling the newsprint smudged on his fingers, Zack had remembered the stench of candyfloss and the stridency of gulls — *the three of us* clambering stiff and blinking from the Bristol. While Maurice went to park it somewhere safe, they'd wandered *hand-in-hand-in-hand* . . . into Dreamland's lurid mêlée. Bubbles had been another of Maurice's *artistes* . . . She wore a cape chased with gold embroidery and smoked gold-ringed Egyptian cigarettes in an onyx holder. Bubbles thought it'd be *frightfully jolly* to motor down to Margate and take their pleasure . . . *with the common sort. Which was what she most certainly was too.* Bubbles had a *ghostly* powdered face, and with her gory lips and her pencilled arcs for eyebrows she *surely belonged in a glass cabinet* . . . jerking into life and . . . *pulling down the brim of her highwayman hat* when someone dropped a thru'ppence in the slot. Zack, confused by the rattling glare and jostled by scabby and dwarfish *Clitheroe kids*, got lost in the funfair. – They found him much later, standing in front of just such a glass cabinet, transfixed as much by the recorded voice – *See here the representation of the assassination of Trotsky* – as by the small-minded Guignol itself: the little *Jewikin* – obviously so, with its hook-nose, professorial specs and wire hair – that each time the pennies dropped *jerked into death for the proles' amusement*. – Sometimes, Zack awakes silently screaming, the distinct tangs of Brilliantined hair and caramelised sugar only slowly blending back into the commonplace stink of his own sweat. — On the corner of Chapter Road Busner pats down all his pockets: four in the jacket and the three trouser ones – it's futile: *No one takes his prescription pad out with him when he's exercising the dog.* He's condemned to walk the plank pavement, past the recently pollarded plains . . . *amputrees* with green shoots already thrusting from their . . . *pitted patellar surfaces.* Back at the house, he'll be submerged in the ugly ocean swirling around *everything and every-bloody-body* – then there'll be the long paddle back to the chemist, then the final length . . . *gasping, arms windmilling* . . . before he reaches the tranquillising life-raft and *tarries there a kaleidoscopic while* . . . watching rainbows *being sucked back into the chimney pots* and garden gnomes *reeling in their hooks.* Struggling by the entrance to Dollis Hill station, Busner glances along the foot tunnel to where it becomes *a gantry* over the line. He fights to remain . . . *earthbound*, jamming each toe into the cracks between the paving stones, thankful for Oscar's anchoring – he's sufficient clarity to think: Tomorrow I'll convene an emergency house meeting – I'll shut Claude up if I have to bind and gag him. Rodge and Lesley as well – they want to shake things up! They want to kick out the jams – I'LL KICK THEM OUT! And if they won't go? Well, it's over, isn't it – that Nazi metaphysician is right: the dreadful has already happened and therefore: there's nothing to fear . . . He would, he decided, *go on bended knee* to his uncle and admit the failure – then he'd release the other residents: *Fly, my pretties, fly!* Irene, Eileen, Clive, Maggie and the Kid . . . *My pigeons' house I o-pen wi-ide, and I set my podgeons free* . . . scattering to the four winds, then homing back in on King's Cross squats and the Centrepoint Project. – Oscar has got them home: he tugs his master into dock with the front gate – and they're in the porch, panting. *It's zero minus something-or-other* . . . and . . . *the light from ten thousand suns* flashes off the Meehans' front windows. For several days they pause in the porch: Busner gets lost in the tiles fixed on either side: roving from boats with lateen sails to blue remembered hills, between tiny sheep and on to still tinier farmhouses . . . *the long trek ends here – in Delft.* At last the key is in the lock, the latch spasms, and the Concept House *wraps around my anamorphic head* . . . Kneeling to let the dog off its lead, Busner thinks: No one will recognise me unless they lie on the floor and look up at the right angle . . . The dog disappears – and Roger Gourevitch appears at the end of the hall looking wan, furtive and resolute. Hi, Zack, he says . . . *hell is in hello* . . . I think it'd be a swell idea if you joined us in the kitchen – Kit's guardian has shown up, and he wants to take Kit away with him. And . . . well, for pretty obvious reasons, I don't think it's such a swell idea . . . Busner is carried *by the swells* into the kitchen, where the Creep is saying, I was in Bellevue, for a fact – that's how it is, feller, some snobs boast about their lousy vacations, I boast about my nut houses. – They are in, Zack realises, one of Claude's rare patches of lucidity, smooth water he'll skim across only to sink once more into *the dark and oily swell*. F'tung-chung, f'tung-chung, f'tung-chung . . . *No, the trek ends here beside the railway line* . . . each f'tung-chung thrusting into Zack's famished eyes a blue-and-white-striped egg cup sitting on the draining board, the palindromic OMO, and the legend DROITWICH that stands out *proud* from the AA road map someone has pinned to the wall. Why is it . . . he thrills to this inconsequence . . . that the residents so favour maps as a form of wall decoration, rather than Aristide Bruant dans son cabaret? – Thinks this even as egg cup, OMO and DROITWICH simultaneously swell and outflank him, while the man rising from the table and holding out his hand remains resolutely . . . *the same size!* Sharply delineated by his bright white shirt collar, by his red-and-maroon-striped tie, by the short back, longer sides and exacting parting of his greying blond hair, by the deep creases in his gaunt cheeks tending *at precisely the same angles* as the lapels of his conservatively dark suit jacket – by *respectability* itself, which is etched by every thread of the smoke *slip-streaming* from his pipe as he removes it from his haggard mouth and carefully places it on a dirty plate that has *by common usage* become an ashtray. He extends his hand further – and Zack is overcome by a sense of the man's vulnerability . . . *he yearns to be bitten* – and says, I'm Michael Lincoln, you must be Doctor for an ultrasound seems fucked up – fucked up. Last time there was only a techie woman who tucked the paper towel down the front of her jeans an' sorta said, Eeeuuu! but hiddit 'cause Cutty was there an' you don't try it on when Cutty's around. *Then – then!* How Genie now wishes it was *then* . . . When the techie woman spread the goo on Genie's tummy, smeared it and said, You're awfully thin – according to your notes you've a history of substance abuse . . . But that was all she said – then she swiped the racket thingie over Genie's tummy a couple of times . . . *a dykey-looking old Billie-Jean she was*, handed her more paper towels, said, OK, clean yourself up now, and went out, leaving Genie to struggle up from the examination couch on her own, and sit there staring down past the *fat white dumpling* to where her *crab stick* toes wiggled from her torn socks, wondering how the fuck she was gonna get her trainers on, 'cause Cutty had gouched out with his head on the sharps bin. – It'd seemed pretty grim at the time, but this is . . . *much worse*: there's a doctor with brown mullet and weird sticky-out paper-thin ears, who's going to work on Genie, his big square hand digging into her belly, making room for the probe that he pushes in hard *here!* and then *there!* So hard Genie thinks it's gonna break the skin and poke through into her womb. From some neglected celluloid strip of her memory a Yank steps into the frame saying: *Start in the alimentary canal – open the digestive tract* . . . The doctor's fingernails scratch . . . *the blackboard, 'orrid racket – goes right through me* . . . and catch *in me short an' curlies*. Genie so wishes Cutty were there . . . *'cause Cutty by name* . . . he'd cut through this crap and make the mullet tell her *what the fuck's going on*, instead of hunching silently over the glowing screen while *'e gives me the dig*. The first time the techie lezzer had encouraged Genie to look as the probe swept over her undersea world and woo-wooed ultrasounds into this sight: two fishy things, curled up round each other . . . *turds inna khazi!* My, my, she'd said, it's twins, you're going to be a very big girl indeed before you're through. Genie would've spat in her face if she hadn't just had a hit. The second time Cutty was there, and 'though he'd done his best to look . . . *presentable*, the techie still shrank back when he came forward and the screen lit up the razor scars on his cheeks . . . *bright white*. Can ye tell me what sex they are yet, hen? he'd asked – but the techie said she couldn't 'cause of the way they were positioned. Cutty squeezed Genie's hand and said, Spoonin', and her heart *overflowed wiv love for 'im*, even though she knew he only wanted to find out if they were identical. Back at the flat, doing his home chemistry – freezing the wax out of a methadone suppository – Cutty'd cackled: If they're idents we can perrforrm unnaturrral psycho-logi-cal experrriments on them, eh, girl? Then there was the last time, when Genie was already so huge, *a fucking whale*, she could scarcely haul herself up to the clinic. She'd been by the needle-exchange caravan on South Wharf Road before, and she'd a paper bag full of fresh works in one hand and a 500 mil' bottle of linctus in the other . . . *I couldn't be bovvered with 'iding.* Right away the nurse started getting on her case about treatment plans *that have been agreed with your team!* and dogged her all the way into the ultrasound suite, and would've taken the works *offa me* . . . if Genie hadn't snarled and *given 'er me dead eyes.* – All this seemed bad enough at the time, especially when the lezzer said, Eeeuu! *as if I was a common tart*, but now it's *bathed in golden light* . . .

and the lezzer techie *'as a fucking halo round her curly nut*. It'd been back round March time, Genie thinks – 'cause Cutty'd gone up West the day before her appointment *to serve one of 'is getters who was 'aving 'is'air layered at fucking Trumper's*. When Cutty came out of the tube at Tottenham Court Road *it was all kicking off*: a load of filth all bunched up under riot shields, and there were Class War types and bog-ordinary yobs chucking bottles and scaffolding poles at 'em . . . *or so 'e said*. Cutty turned tail and went back down the rabbit hole – with his form, and holding too, *'e couldn't be doing wivvit*. Now it's May, and *the flowerpot men* are due to pop out in a week or two, but the Mullet's saying, May I call you . . . He looks at the notes rattling in his hand to see *what the fuck he should call me*, and Genie says, Call me whatever you like, but tell me what the fuck's going on. — The great white shark comes nosing upriver, its tail lashing from side to side as it swims round the exploding . . . *disco ball* of the Isle of Dogs. In its visual field there's . . . *mud – and more mud* . . . an old car tyre bounces up from the riverbed and is *driven over*. Then at Bankside the keel of the Marchioness *scrrrapes past* . . . — The Mullet's face is drowned-grey and stupid, and he says, I'm afraid I've got some bad news for you, Ms Gruber, one of the foetuses is dead in utero – in your womb. The other's still, um, viable . . . I think, but we'll have to perform an emergency caesarean. Even then I'm afraid the odds – the chances . . . aren't that good. – Genie, lying flat out on the *slimy wooden decking* with a dead baby inside her, realises *inna gush*: I never was pregnant at all – how could I be when I never had much of a period, an' if you don't get your period you don't get done by the shark, 'cause the

shark smells the blood in the water – every tosser knows that . . .
The Yank voice comes again: *You yell shark, we've got a panic on our
hands on the Fourth of July* . . . Mullet and his *lovely assistant* move
fast – they push her down when she tries to struggle up and slam!
up the rails so that *Hey Presto!* the examination couch turns into a
trolley. What about my gear! Genie yells – the nurse who's pushing
her snarls, It's almost certainly your gear that's killed your baby! –
Genie can't see past her belly, while walls hung with prints of
old-fashioned balloons taking goats and sheep for a gentle float . . .
fly by . . . Bang! The trolley slams through double doors, crash!
some more – Genie wants to hide in a hut somewhere . . . *in London*.
She sees herself pelting along brambly Charing Cross Road and
dodging through Leicester Square, the grass swishing at her stinging calves. But it doesn't matter how fast she runs . . . *'cause the sea's
inside me*, and, despite *me runny ears*, she can still hear the *thrum-
thrumm, thrum-thrumm, thrrrum-thrum* of the shark's approach.
The Mullet is on the phone, the pocket of his white coat is . . .
pregnant with his beeper and a row of biros – one of which must
be . . . *still viable*, because yakking he hunches up so he can scribble
on Genie's notes, then calls to the nurse, who's faffing about with
stuff . . . *the way people do when they ain't got a fucking clue.* – There's
a vacancy in theatre in fifteen minutes so prep' her right away,
please. My gear, Genie protests again, and Mullet comes over and
gets *right in my face*. What've you taken today? he interrogates. It's
essential that you tell me the truth or the anaesthetist can't do
her job safely. Genie thinks: Safely, that's a fucking joke – can't 'e
hear it? — It's smashing against the grey granite blocks of the

embankment so hard fat tourists lurching through the rain lean over the wall and peer down to where, among all the old squeezy bottles, fag butts and *pukey scum*, the curved head batters and batters *anbatters* . . . while the huge body arches and plunges. The shark batters until a block's loose enough to be taken in its open jaws, then it worries this out. – Once one's gone the second, third and fourth are . . . *easy-peasy*: before the tourists have time to get out their Instamatics, the shark is chomping its way into the heart of London, *thrum-thrumm, thrum-thrumm, thrrrum-thrum* . . . its slip-sliding teeth sawing away through gas pipes while its tail smashes souvenir stalls *to smithereens.* — I ain't 'ad nuffink today, Genie says. Nuffink – juss 20 mils when I got up to come 'ere, 'cause I was gonna pick up me scrip' as well, weren't I. The Mullet says, You're absolutely sure about that, are you? You've had no heroin, or pills, or anything else at all? She spits back: I'm sick, you wanker, I'm sick! – Ooh, what a bloody meal they're making of it, she thinks, pinching me, slapping me, velcroing on the tourniquet, then rrripping it off again, slapping and pinching . . . *againann- again, stupid Jeanie's got no vei-ns, Now she ain't got no brai-ns* . . . BP one-over-eighty, one of them says, and Genie thinks: What a bunch of stupid cunts bothering with this – they should shape up and ship out, 'cause here it comes! — Humping up the stairs to the fifth floor, its dorsal fin whacking the lights so they swing wildly on their chains . . . — OK, Genie, says the anaesthetist, who has a thick German accent and a pink blancmange mole on her Tupperware lip, I vaant you to count backvards from ten for me, ya? You can do that? Backvards, zo . . . Ten, nine, eight, zo . . . – Ten, Genie wearies, Nine . . . she declines, because there's no point fighting it any more: the big fish has its head rammed inside the double doors, and, try as they might – and they do, heaving oxygen cylinders into its gaping jaws – they can't fend the brute off. Hooper is ventriloquising the anaesthetist: *I think I can pump* 20*cc's of strychnine nitrate into it if I can get close enough* . . . – It don't matter, though, Genie realises, if you got kids or you ain't got kids – either way your life gets bitten in 'alf. – Slopping about on the sopping tiles, the shark turns one piggy little eye on her, then the other . . . *screwing me out*. It humps and bumps, the floor tilts, the trolley rolls, Genie wallows waist-deep in its mouth . . . Ate, she giggles as the toothy chain tightens around her tail end. Ssseven, she hisses as she's winched above the jetty. Sick! she grunts as Hooper plunges his rubber-handled knife up underneath her ribs. F-Five! she gasps as he wrenches it down and her milky waters splash on to the planking, followed by a Florida licence plate that hits the planks with a clank! Four, Genie giggles – 'cause po-faced Chief Brody looks . . . *like he's gonna puke his guts out.* Th-Three, she gasps, appalled by the thing the marine biologist has pulled out of her, its battleship-grey skin smeared with . . . *smeg*. T-Two? she implores him, but Hooper shakes his curly head: Only the one, he says, but it's a fine squalus. Take a look at its belly, here – see how swole up it is? That's 'cause it's eaten its own sibling – they do that, sharks, feed on each other in the womb. Why, I've opened some pregnant nurse sharks and found the one pup, but when I've cut it open I've discovered the remains of eight more inside — she says, You took me to see the Sound of Music, mind you that was in Hemel. Mumsie doesn't reply – she's in the old Chesterfield wing armchair with a book in her lap and a drinky-pooh on the stool beside it that looks suspiciously *like water*. You took me to Half a Sixpence and Doctor Dolittle at the Odeon, didn'tcha. Still Mumsie says nothing. She seems smaller, hunched in a blue cardie, her legs tucked up under her, and her hair scraped back in a leatherwork grip that Genie remembers Debbie making years ago, but which she's never seen her mother wear before. Genie stands by the front door, her rucksack at her feet, her long gypsy skirt is patterned with tiny bits of mirror and blobbed with dried mud. She tries another tack: Bloody everyone's seen it, Mumsie, an' they all say it's fucking brilliant, a right bloody laugh – an' we all need a laugh, eh? – Genie certainly does. — That morning she'd woken underneath a tarp' stretched over a tree trunk felled across a hollow deep in the woods outside of Newbury. Before she'd sat up and felt the buckler of frozen rime down the front of her sleeping bag . . . *crackle* . . . Genie was intent on going back to Berko: *'nuff's enough – my muff's matted . . . my toes are black . . . All around my prat, I will wear the green willow* . . . Benjie the horse stood still and miserable in his botched-up coat: a crocheted blanket and a nylon quilt held round him with clothes pegs. They'd bought him from a knacker's for twenty quid, and he'd been their companion these last few months as they clopped up and down Middle Earth, from tepee hamlets to free festivals. – Ahem! It had been this stagey throat-clearing that had awoken her – the others were all still crashed out. Ahem! *came again* as she struggled to her feet and hopped . . . *clumsy Kanga* . . . towards shiny black boots and knife-edge creases running vertically from them to the pink cheeks of . . . *a piglet*, who stood there, his breath dramatically smoking in the morning sunlight. Shining around him was the bright-white spun-sugariness of frosted bracken, and, as Genie stared, he raised his gloved hand to knock on the mossy bark of a tree . . . *like it was our front door, the prannet!* She laughed delightedly – went on laughing as he explained: Sorry to bother you, miss, but there's been some, ah . . . well, some concern in the neighbourhood about this horse. People're worried that he might not be getting fed properly. He should really be, ah . . . stabled for the winter now. Genie let go of the sleeping bag and was disgorged . . . *from me own pouch*: a tousle-headed Roo who deliberately pulled at the damp bunching of her skirt, tights and pullovers so he got a good look at her tits . . . *old 'abits die hard*. She laughed again, but bitterly: Lissen, if it hadn't've been for us, mate, this horse'd be glue by now and some dumb Mick'd probably be sniffing 'im. – Genie needed stabling as well: it was cold and wet out in the woods – besides, now the Old Bill knew they were there, it'd only be a matter of time before trouble started. – She was gone before the others had rubbed the fungus dust from their eyes: standing on the M4 slip road, thumb and hip stuck out . . . *jaunty, like*. The first lift was a Cavalier stinking of Victory V Lozenges, and with his free hand its driver got at her through her clothes – but he took her all the way to Shepherd's Bush, where she begged for the bus fare. She sat on the top deck sipping one . . . *with Limeade*, and looking down at the piles of rubbish lining the streets: black bags, rotten cardboard boxes, all sorts of stuff – the city . . . *shitting itself*. She'd stood most of that afternoon on the wedge of pavement between

Ballards Lane and the High Road – getting more and more narked as delivery drivers holding number plates were picked up by others of their kind . . . *fucking sexist bastards*. Genie spent the time embellishing the BERKO she'd written on a bit of cardboard with more and more flowers and rainbows. The old codger who finally gave her a lift said he'd only stopped to find out, What it says on your sign there, love. He turned out to be *solid gold*, passing her Navy Cuts on the outskirts of Watford and standing her egg and chips in a café. The fat bint who ran it kept the tea refills coming while Genie and the codger – whose name was George – had a bit of a set-to about this and that, and finally Balcombe Street, 'cause Genie said that it wouldn't've been so bloody dreadful if things had gone the other way. Uncle Georgie said, Such anger – wishing innocent people dead. I thought you hippies were meant to be all about peace . . . and love. Genie said, Love don't enter inter fings when you been done over by the State, 'sides, that couple, watching the telly in their nice flat – you tootling about in your Grenada, you're all com . . . com . . . Complicit? George offered, and Genie said, Yeah, that's right: you're all complicit, the only way not to be complicit is to strike back any way you can – or else fuck off on the road like I done . . . Then she shed a tear or two for Benjie left behind in the woods, and George gave her his hanky – *which was civil of him*. He said, We'll just have to agree to differ, and after that he drove her back to Berkhamsted . . . *which was miles out of his way*. – He let her out by the Odeon, where she saw the posters and a thrill went through her. That's me, she thought, I'm a minnowy thing swimmin' along on the surface kicking me tootsies, but down below

there's this fucking big monster that's gonna bite me in half . . .
Genie recognised one or two old Ashlyns girls among the queuing
couples who were already *feeding on each other's faces.* Then she
hurried home to the little terraced house four streets away with
this jolly idea: Genie and Mumsie enjoying a reunion night out
together at the cinema, the pair of them munching on popcorn,
knocking back Cokes and chuckling away as the Berko berks
oohed and aahed because this was . . . *the closest they're ever likely to
get to real life.* — But Mumsie sits there . . . *the hatchet-faced old
cow* . . . not saying nuffink – which is worse than when she's angry,
'cause you know where you are with Mumsie's anger: it's . . . *relentless,* always moving forward, always looking for more to . . . *eat.*
Mumsie without her anger – well, she's . . . *dead in the water.* Not
that there was much in the way of actual fisticuffs any more – not
since Genie landed one on the old bag that *near laid 'er out cold.* And
not – more to the point – since Debbie and Genie had *fucked right
off out of it altogether,* leaving Hughie to take the crap – not that he
got any: Mumsie's wistful little boysie, plinkety-plunketing on his
acoustic guitar, My hair's a-risin', my flesh begin to crawl, My hair's
a-risin', my flesh begin to crawl, I had a dream last night, babe, saw
another mule in in my doggone stall . . . But he wasn't indoors . . .
prob'ly taken 'is crown jewels to some fifty-pee kiddie stomp. Come
ooon, Genie wheedles, it'll be a right laugh – you can't tell me you
don't fancy seeing a bunch of Yank wankers getting eaten up by a
dirty-great shark – yummy-yummy, munch-munch, all gone 'cept
for a few denim shreds it can't get outta its teef. – Nothing. Mumsie
says nothing – only stares hard at Genie, her green eyes burning,

her lips all puckered up, her nails digging into the chair's arm –
there's not even an Embassy to be seen, and the poky front room
is all spraunced up and stinking of . . . *Glade*. Comesie-onsie,
Mumsie, Genie baby-talks, puh-lease, pwitty puh-lease, Genie
wants Jawsie, Mumsie, Genie wants Jawsie! – When the answer
comes it's a spray of blood and gob, and Genie realises: I wanted
this – I pushed her to this 'cause she's weak, and I don't 'ave to run
to the nooky shop any more, or London – I've crumpled up the
dumb fucking letter, I ain't afraid of breaking the chain. – Mumsie
somehow manages to lisp and scream *at the same time*: YOU
THAKING THE PITH! YOU THAKING THE PITH!
Her trap's flapping, her gums are all bloody and broken, her torn
tongue curls into her raw gullet . . . *and there're no teeth – she's got no
fucking teeth!* – They go all the same: Genie holds Mumsie's severed
hand in the padded and acrid murk of the Odeon. A cone of light
expands above their heads into Hooper's bearded face, which
says: This is what happens – the enormous amount of tissue loss
prevents any detailed analysis . . . Mumsie winces, her severed hand
squeezes tighter. Hooper snaps at Chief Brody, I wanna be sure.
You wanna be sure. We all wanna be sure . . . Then he chats into his
natty little tape recorder: Partially denuded bone . . . Massive tissue
loss . . . With her free hand Genie *grabbers-up* more salty popcorn.
She dumps it into her stinging mouth and chews methodically,
savouring her own . . . *teeth*. If she sticks around in Berko, what
sort of Christmas will it be? *A shitty one, like all the rest* . . . the four
of them . . . *at each other's throats* on the day itself, eating and eating solely for something to do. Eating and eating . . . *'til you'd be*

grateful to be hauled up by your tail an' gutted by Hooper: all that
turkey – all those roasties, sprouts and that plum-fucking-pudding –
all of it plummeting down in a . . . *saucy white whoosh!* Then, come
Boxing Day, Mumsie's pals'll pitch up – the Deacon, Jeffers, the
Duchess, Miss-fucking-Marple, and that ultimate twat, Kins –
all of 'em getting veinier and fatter by the year, and clinking with
them the crap booze left over from their own miserable festivities:
Sandeman's port, Emva Cream sherry . . . *and Bols bottled vom'.*
They'll float in the telly's searchlight on the greenish surface of their
own *rank piss-artistry.* Kins'd probably bring presents for Moira's
kids as well. He tried to be fair . . . But it's stark-raving obvious,
Hughie said, you're his favourite. – Which made no sense, 'cause it
was Hughie who was at the Grammar – Hughie who could have
proper conversations with Kins about free collective bargaining . . .
and all that bollocks. Last Christmas Kins had given her a pair of
Snoopy earrings . . . *solid silver, granted* – but fucking Snoopy!
It took all she had not to fling 'em back in his stupid red face – a
face that balloons out of the hole in the hull . . . *right now! Worms
in its eyes!* Hooper rears back, his flippers cycling in the bubbling
turmoil. – Genie lights her roll-up and angles the smoke towards
Mumsie *out of sheer spite.* She remembers how she pawned the
earrings in Hemel on New Year's Eve . . . *got a fiver, spent it on five
blues and five tabs.* – What we're dealing with here, Hooper says, is a
perfect engine, an eating machine. All this machine does is swim
and eat and make little sharks . . . Genie thinks: Little sharks is
fair enough – little sharks ain't too much trouble, specially little
sharks with a future . . . Not the sort who get stuck behind the bus

shelter with their liquorice bootlaces – but this kind: who hang out at lovely parties in the sand dunes, strumming guitars, painting flowers on their cheeks . . . smelling the woodsmoke, lying back in the reedy grass wearing Val Doonican woollies, getting up only to . . . *drop their knickers – luvverly.* – Genie pokes her rollie right at Mumsie's eye and hisspers, Who'ss my dad? Their faces are lit up by the bright doomed summer of Amity Island, and Mumsie lisspers back, Whoever 'e ith e'th a creepy cunt. — The tarmac bakes Jeanie's feet as she crosses the road from the cottage to the canalside. There are red poppies in the grass and she has flowers drawn with felt-tip on her cheeks, flowery inserts in her jeans and a complicated flowery pattern all the way up the calves they cover. She's a flower child . . . *Jeaniefer – Juniper rides a dappled mare* . . . Some days she'll step straight on to the deck of a passing narrowboat and ride it as far as she feels. It doesn't matter if it's one of the Lime Juice-run boats, a BCA dredger or day-trippers who've to wrestle their way through every lock – nobody minds. Grizzled old bargees chuck her under her butter-loving chin – bobble-hatted Fionas make her milky tea in their busy-lizzy galleys. When they pass through the towns and villages, they all peer in the back windows of the tip-tilted houses propped up by drain-piping – out in the country they all listen to the fat coils of electricity substations humming in the meadow grass. The boats go slower than you can walk – your thoughts go slower than your senses. Bye-bye . . . Whenever she feels like it, Jeanie steps off and waits for a boat going back the other way. — One time Jeanie had a scrap with Mumsie and ran away to real London on a cement barge coming back empty from Birmingham. The decks were thick with powder, and clouds of it blew back behind them in the breeze . . . Dudswell . . . *disappeared into dust*. The bargee talked about the Big Freezes, how they'd done for his sort. He sang out the names of the locks as they came upon them: Old Ned's Two Locks, Wider Water Lock, Berko Two Locks, Broadway Lock, Winkwell Three Locks, Slaughter Lock, Fishery Lock. Jeanie had hopped on board straight after breakfast, and the whiter her school pinafore dress grew with dust the happier she became. It was mid-afternoon when she picked up her satchel and skipped away along the overgrown and collapsing tow path. The bargee asked if she knew where she was, or where she was going – and Jeanie said she was off to see her nan, 'cause that's the sort of thing she knew proper kids did. She'd no idea where she was – only that this was the city and she was overawed by the huge squat chimneys hunching over the hundreds and hundreds of rooftops she saw from the canal bridge. She stopped a man in the road and asked him what the chimneys were for, and she thought he said they were cool towers – but she couldn't be sure 'cause it was a busy road and the traffic was roaring past. She walked up the road towards the cool towers – on either side there was a waste land of shrubbery, gravelly piles, big puddles and broken old train carriages. It didn't seem very cool. People looked at her funny 'cause she was still all dusty – dusty and hungry. Past the cool towers she reached a busy high street, and she looked in the shop windows for a while, but there was only the same sort of stuff as in the Berko shops, besides she didn't have any money. She walked on, tiring now, her socks slipping sweatily down to her ankles . . . *againannagain*.

It was boring, London, with street after street of houses all the same, all looking dead and lifeless. She began to feel scared – maybe there was no one here? Maybe it was a city of the dead, and the zombies were massing in the back gardens, waiting to come out and get her? In a long road somehow duller than all the rest Jeanie couldn't stand it any more – she had to know if there was anyone real here, anyone alive. She blundered through a gate and pressed her face against a front window. There were one, two, three, four men in the room and a boy lying face down on a mattress. Jeanie was so shocked – 'cause they were definitely alive – she stood there, breathing on the window. What were the men doing? Had they murdered the boy on the mattress? One of the men, who was sitting on a sofa, looked at her and his face was all mad and scared – like he'd seen a ghost . . . *like I'm a ghost!* Then he shot forward off the sofa, and Jeanie tore herself away from the window and ran, and ran, 'til she couldn't run any more. Then she asked someone the way back to the canal. — Another time there were real proper hippies on a beaten-up old motor-cruiser. They'd hair down to their arses and Afghan coats smelling sweetly of . . . *goat's piss*. They made a big fuss of Jeanie, delighted by her hand-drawn trellises, rubbing their grubby fingers up her brown ankles, her paler calves, her white thighs. They tied up and took Jeanie and rugs up into one of the dry botttoms. Two . . . three . . . four . . . She nested blue and buff egg-pebbles in twists of straw while they hooked their hair behind their ears and cooked up 'shroom tea in a sooty pot and gave it to her in a plastic cup off the top of a thermos. This . . . *I re-mem-ber-member*: getting home long after dark, although it was broad daylight in her head, which was full of the wind-strummed contrails of Luton-bound jets. Mumsie was sitting in the Chesterfield armchair reading out suicides to Hughie from the Gazette: Missus Jeanette Little, aged twenty-seven of Fantail Lane, Tring, was found dead by firemen in her gas-filled kitchen – kitchen towels had been used to plug up the gaps in the door . . . They were *so much in love* . . . Mumsie and Hughie, that they didn't notice her come in and slump down on the rug: elves, roped together with golden thread, were climbing up the inglenook. Jeanie wondered at . . . *little Jeanette Little* . . . and also: if Mumsie could smell her fanny on the hippy's dirty fingers . . .*'e's gotta be miles away by now* . . . — A maroon Ford Zephyr is pulled over by the canal, its radiator nibbles at the stringy daisies and the stopped clocks of dried-out dandelions. A man leans out from the rolled-down window – his hair is Brylcreemed into an ill-fitting helmet, he wears . . . *an iron grin*. He calls to her, Hey, girlie, how'd you like to go for a ride? It's the first time Jeanie's heard someone speak with an American accent who's not on the telly – it's . . . *tasty*. She minces through the flowers and places her hands on the car's hot roof – there's a swan on the canal with three cygnets . . . *they don't care*. The man has on a sharkskin suit with a peace badge on it, a whiter-than-white shirt with a thin death-black tie clipped to it by an ace of spades tie-pin. His knee is pumping up and down, and Jeanie can see a polished shoe dancing on the floor of the car: tippety-tap-tap, tippety-tap-tap –. Hey, girlie, he says again, how's about it – you, me, the open road? He pats the bench seat beside him, running his hand over the oxblood vinyl, gathering up . . . *nothing*. His eyes are Pink Paraffin and there's a big cold sore on his lip, his breath is . . . *VAT 69*, and there's a simmering saucepan of words in his head . . . *about to boil over*. Jeanie says, You must fink I'm mental, I wouldn't get in your car for all the tea in China. My mum's told me about pervs like what you are – you'll drive me off somewhere an' rape me. Yeah, the man says, your mom, she's a smart cookie – she knows the score, does Mumsie. Okey-dokey – he leans forward and turns the key, the engine snorts, then trots into life, the radio singing, Jennifer . . . Juniper . . . rides a dappled mare . . . Y'know Mumsie, do you? Jeanie slips her hands into her jeans pockets, thumbs out. She blows the thick curls of her fringe. Sure do, the creepy Yank says, met her at a CND meeting – you know what that is, right? Genie withers at him and he grins still more and holds out his hand, the wrist cocked. Claude, he says, Claude Evenrude – and you're Debbie, have I got that right? No, Jeanie says, shaking the man's hand, I'm Jeanie, Debbie's two years bigger than me. The Yank's hand is a bit sweaty – but it's cool, which is strange. Jeanie wonders if he might have a fridge in his car – she's read in Look and Learn that some Yanks had crazy stuff like that in their cars . . .*'cause they live in their cars*. Oh, OK, my apologies, young lady, forgive me, please – Jeanie, right, Jeanie. Moira's told me ever such a lot about you – she's real proud of you. – Claude puts on Secret Squirrel sunglasses to drive the Zephyr, one hand flops over the steering wheel, the other fiddles with his tie-pin – but they haven't gone very far when he pulls over on a bend from where they can see the railway line cutting across the big field, and floating beside it in the heat-haze the big glossy-green teardrop of London. A goods train comes up the line, its triple-decker coaches carrying new cars . . . *bonnets sucking off boots, boots bumming bonnets.* Claude passes Jeanie a bottle of Cherry Corona with a . . . *leetle* drop of whisky in it. We went out West when I was a kid, he says. That was before the war – long time before the war . . . My pa an' me, we spent hours standing on the balcony of the caboose, watching the desert runnin' out behind. I'd pick out an itty-bitty bit of sagebrush, or a cactus, or any fool thing, and I'd hang on to it with my eyes, burnin' it inside here for-ever – he holds up Devil's horns fingers and stabs them at his forehead, his knee pumps, his shoe taps, he lights another Chesterfield from the end of the last one and Jeanie puzzles . . . *Is it the same firm what made the chair?* – Up through Royal Gorge, Claude says, then come the Rockies. The fruit cars heading East were so long it took mebbe half an hour for 'em to pass by. We'd stop at the foot of each pass and they'd double-team the locos to get us up the grade – some places they'd triple-team 'em. – Now the Zephyr's fifty yards off the road, flattening the tall bracken on the edge of the common. Claude kneels backwards on the front seat, his arse on the dashboard, and takes off his shiny jacket. He's wound up all the windows and the air is smoke and booze and rubberiness. They aren't on a train any more but in a plane: You gotta 'preciate, Claude slurs to tipsy Jeanie, they were working in conditions near as cramped as these. Sure, a Super Bee is a big ship, but there's only an itty-bitty nar-row tunnel connecting the fore and aft sections . . . He swarms over the back of the seat, his shirt-tails pull free, and Jeanie glimpses the pale pucker of his belly hanging down . . . *yucky.* 'Course, being the target-spotters, we didn't have much of anything in the bomb bay – juss some gizmos for measuring the blast and the radiation and stuff – but if you were flying with Tibbets every time you crawled along that companionway you were crawling right over the bomb itself. I tellya, little Jeanie – hands on the back of the pew, he preaches smoke at her – I knew he was a fellow whose imagination wasn't worth a damn when I saw what he'd had 'em paint on the nose of his ship. I mean, how'd he figure it? If the ship was his mumsie, what the hell did she have in her belly? A nine-thousand-pound friggin' atom bomb baby, that's what – right? An A-bomb that had to be his own half-brother or half-sis', right? The radar man on the Enola Gay, Beser, he told me how Parsons – good ol' Deak – he snuggled up right beside that bomb-baby all the way there – cuddling with it. A cold hard de-termined man, Parsons – screwdrivers were his forceps. It didn't matter how the ship bucked about, he kept right on screwing in those charges . . . – Claude isn't bothering with the Corona any more, instead he swigs straight from the whisky bottle and lights another Chester-field with a click-clack-rasp of his big steely lighter. The green ears of *little ear-wigging weeds* press against the car windows. But I ask you, hon, Claude goes on, who's the worser guy? Man who pulls the trigger, or the one who points it at a whole goddamn row of slanty-eyed folks, all of 'em stood there in their jimmy-jammies with their pitiful empty rice bowls held out, and says: That one – that Hee-ro-sheema. He's blindfolded, his goddamn hands're tied – it's a sure-fire bet you guys can shoot him dead with no trou-ble at all! – Later on, when Jeanie's tipsy, they fly the ship together. Claude sits on the co-pilot's side of the bench and explains a bit about take-off torque, rudder control and advancing throttles. Jeanie wrenches the steering wheel from side to side as she fiddles with the indicator stalk and gear stick. Then they get ready to deliver the bomb-baby: Claude explains to Jeanie how the bomb-sight works and they crouch together in the glass blister of the Zephyr's windscreen, Claude twisting the knobs on the radio until the static tunes into a whistle and the hairs of their tangled heads cross. Leaning down, their fingers entwined, they yank up the handbrake and the car rolls forward a few yards before it grounds on a molehill. I see skin angels, Claude says rapturously as his fingers squeak out a little porthole on the misty glass. A great host of 'em flying round an' around the mushroom cloud. I see 'em – he hisses into her scaredy face – and they're the people we've just this second incinerated . . . They're like . . . They're like – his fingers wiggle expressively – the burning leaves floatin' up from the hobos' fires in the Hooverville on the other side of the streetcar tracks – you remember that, right? Sure, they look pretty enough from a way off, but when you get close you can see the skin scorched off their backs and arms flapping in the terrible heat, the terrible heat that bears them spiralling up and up to heaven . . . Skin angels! – Jeanie sees . . . *snow angels*: the Fab Four stretching out their capes and toppling over into the whiteness . . . *no, not just any-body* . . . To Claude, she's drunkenly earnest: You couldn't 'elp it, you wasn't to know – you said that man, Parkinson –. Parsons, he corrects her. Yeah, him, Parsons – you said Parsons only told you what bomb it was that night – you didn't know what it was gonna do, how it was gonna kill all those Japs. We knew, he says leadenly. It was in the comics ferchrissakes – the movies too. Everyone knew what kryptonite did . . . But it weren't you, she insists, you didn't drop it – you were in the spotter plane, you said that! He shakes his head vigorously and spikes of his Brylcreemed hair stand up . . . *Statue of Liberty*. He says: When we weren't takin' a dump on Hiroshima, it was other cities – we were all that bastard LeMay's faithful worker bees, packin' bombs into our bellies, then shitting down fire on the Japs. They pinned a medal on us, Jeanie, when we were through making skin angels – but there wasn't any bravery in what we done, bravery's takin' on a fuckin' Marine when he's gonna stick his Ka-Bar in you! Awww! Claude suddenly sings, I wanna go down to Tom Anderson's ca-fé, I wanna hear that Creole jazz band play! The Cadillac, the Red Onion too, the Boogie-Woogie an' the Parc Sans Sou', You can enjoy your-seelf down on Rampart Streeeet! He goes on like this for a while, strumming his banjo belly, his cold sore growing bigger and hotter and angrier in the smelly Zephyr – and Jeanie doesn't know what she should feel. – Later still, Claude's fallen asleep, his head stuck down between the seat and the misted window, his legs spread. His socks have clocks, and there's no hair on his ankles. She leaves the car door ajar, taking care not to wake Claude, because she both fears and pities him. Jeanie's legs run away with her down the steep hill to Aldbury: a few staggery steps . . . a hiccupping halt, a few staggery steps . . . a hiccupping halt. She's proud of herself . . . *I ain't puked*. A crow spies on her as she limps out on to the lane that runs away from her to jump over the railway line to the canal. As she stumps along the overgrown tow path, one of his crazy songs rises up Jeanie's throat – this she does spew: Oi, blackies, 'ave you

seen your master, wiv a moustache on 'is lip! Oi, blackies, frow 'im
inna coal 'ole, wiv de moustache on 'is face ... When she reaches
the cottage Mumsie's sitting in the armchair – Jeanie sees her hang-
over, a fireball round her head, tongues flaming out from it to *lick*
Jeanie's own burning brow. Faithful Hughie is lying at Mumsie's
feet, watching the telly smoulder in the Inglenook fireplace, slowly
roasting Fanny and Johnnie. Mumsie doesn't ask where Jeanie's
been — so Jeanie doesn't tell her about the whoring – she should tell
'em about the whoring 'cause thass what's done it: one of the babies
is a whoring baby, and thass why it's eaten the other one right
up! In the darkness there's a lit-up lime-green stick man who's
escaping ... and Genie feels the gentle burring of ... *sick breff*
on her face and her arms, which lie on top of the tight covers. If she
wasn't paralysed she'd reach for the buzzer and p'raps one of
the nurses would come, her torch beam poking into the weedy crack
the shark baby ... *chewed froo me.* But Genie's tied down by tubes
and crucified by the spike they've hammered through the back of
her hand ... *always take a claw one if you're gonna open a squat* ...
Cutty's not coming ... *no one's coming*, except for Genie's own cold
white conscience, which has already arrived – and at first circles her,
keeping its distance, held in check by curiosity and fear, before
moving in closer ... and closer, until its slickly rough skin rasps her
face, and its *cherrywhisky* breath fills her nostrils ... It veers away
and swims out through the fifth-floor windows. – As Genie floats
in the cold remote middle of the Paddington night, a doctor comes
to plummily abuse her: *Dipper-dipper-dation, your op-er-ation, how
many junkies at Padding-ton Sta-tion* ... His eyes are clock-radio

digits, he whispers: It's a nice irony, young lady, that you're a heroin addict — since this hospital is the very place where diamorphine was first synthesised. What goes around . . . he sniggers . . . comes around. — They do come around, the punters: the blunt snouts of their Vauxhall Cavaliers and Ford Sierras push into the mouth of Queen's Drive, and their headlights cut holes in the drizzly netting draped over the slick rooftops. Down the punters come, licking spittle on to their flaking lips, their fingers fidgeting with the flip-tops of their fag packets, their feet faffing with brake and accelerator so they keep the slow speed they need to scan the meat rack: kebabbed womanflesh rotating in the streetlamps' sodium light and the washed-out neon signs for the COUNTY HOTEL and the BELLAVISTA GUESTHOUSE. Genie's never been inside these particular . . . *knocking shops*, but she remembers what they're like from more affluent times: full-flounced and thickly carpeted interiors, the small rooms bursting with H&C, TV and other stuffed mod cons *these sad mingers* . . . in their torn fishnets and red plastic miniskirts . . . *can only fucking dream of.* – The punters go round *annaround* . . . *but that's shopping for you*: from Queen's Drive they turn right into Somerfield Road, and from Somerfield Road they take another right into Wilberforce, a tomcat's yowl . . . *screwin' froo* their engines' receding drone. At the junction with the Seven Sisters they wait, sweaty, suckered to their steering wheels, before leaping into the traffic stream and for a few seconds going with the flow of lorries heading for Green Lanes and . . . *all points north*. Then they take the first right back into Queen's Drive . . . *and down they come again.* Sometimes, angered by their protracted browsing, one of the girls advances out between the parked cars into the road and, lifting up her skirt, bumps and grinds in the punters' headlights: You wannit? she'll screech above the long, drawn-out moan of the city. Then fer fuck's sake pull over and geddit! – The punters the girls all long for are the frummers from Stokie and Clapton – always driving Volvos, always polite. The Yids don't go round . . . *annaround.* Whatever people say, they . . . *ain't nosing for a discount or extras such as up-the-gary wiv no rubber.* They come straight down the Drive and stop at the first brass to tickle their fancy – usually the plumpest, mumsiest-looking one, so if you want to catch yourself a frummer, it's best not to bother with heels, a push-up or . . . *any of that malarkey.* So they're a little fishy-smelling, what of it? Spunk's fishy-smelling anyway . . . *so it's only double-fish.* The important thing is: *all they want is a little TLC* . . . to have their beards stroked, bury their heads in a pair of titties, and be told they're *Mumsie's dearest, sweetest, cleverest, icklest boy* . . . after that it's a couple of pulls on their plonkers . . . *anna happy ending inna Andrex.* But if they do want sucking, there's plenty of room in the front of a Volvo – no need for the back . . . *which is where the trouble usually starts.* They call you Miss . . . *wouldya b'lieve it!* Miss, would you mind? Miss, if it isn't too much bother? Cough up on the nail an' ask after your health . . . *way their Mumsies taught 'em to.* – Business, Genie says, sticking a hip out and staggering on her broken heel. From inside a Merc' a Yank 's voice says, Sure, hop in. But as soon as Genie does she knows she's made . . . *a big fucking mistake,* because he pushes a button and chonk! all the doors are locked. The big car stinks of . . . *Jennifer, Juniper . . . rides a bottle of . . .*

gin – and the Yank, who's wearing a camel-hair overcoat, puts his foot down hard. Through the back window Genie sees the Bellavista disappearing fast, and Gloria out in the road waving her hands – which means she hasn't been able to get his number plate. *Good old Gloria* . . . who shoved all her mortgage payments up her snooty nose, posted her keys back through the letterbox and clip-clopped down here from Hampstead. Funboy Three, the dealer she owes, turned out to be a pimp who stopped grinning his gold crowns at Gloria and fed it to her hard and fast . . . *Arseholes are cheap to-day, Cheaper than yes-ter-day, Buy one for two-an'-six, Big ones take lotsa pricks* –. So, the Yank interrupts, I thought it'd be cool if we went somewhere quiet – so we can get properly acquainted, yeah, far away from the madding crowd. No busy-buzzy-bodies flyin' up in our faces, right? Genie doesn't really hear what the man's saying – only registers a palpable threat: the curls ungum from the back of her neck, the scabs in the pits of her elbows scratch the sleeves of her sparkly Lycra dress. Lazily, with one hand, the man circles the Merc's steering wheel, so the big car rears up on to the main road. *Saw-toothed* shadows snag on the *knots* of his face and Genie's terrified because . . .*'e's old!* and old men can get very, very angry *when they can't perform*. The Yank has gnarled hands, his nose is a *grater made of cheese* – what's left of his hair has been scraped back into *My-Little-Pony-tail* . . . His speech is clear and level, his accent nasal . . . *the way posh Yanks' are – why didn't 'e call a proper escort, he's obviously got the readies* . . . Genie's hours away from her last hit – if her judgement had been clearer *I'd never've got in*. There's a charged malevolence about the Yank – it's in his

278

lip-chewing and the blinking of his eyes, his fingers tapping and the jiggling of his knee as he forces a petrol tanker to slow down and admit him. The Yank turns left at Manor House – Genie looks at the clock on the dashboard. It reads 8.15, and she acknowledges the truth: I'm back with the heavy mob — *'cause that's the time it's always bloody been.* Back knocking out hand-jobs in Delilah's, a massage parlour off Maid's Causeway in Cambridge . . . *way off it – carefree days, though* . . . Candles stuck in Chianti bottles and beef buggered-up – which was what they called their five-day stews, eaten on check tablecloths they spread out on the damp floor of the squat in James Road. Carefree days, all arty-farty types together: naive students – innocent whores: *I was exploring my sex-u-ality* and drinking a lot of Abbot Ale after evenings *beating the bishop,* her arm cranking that hot piston *innanout, innanout* . . . until it ached fit-to-buggery. But it weren't too much bovver – the punters were mostly wimpy geezers, some of 'em profs from the univer-sity . . . *rub 'em up, flip 'em over, flash yer tits, finish 'em off, bish-bosh, another happy ending, another fiver.* — One summer evening, *just after eight, 'cause that's when I knocked off,* the two ginger apes who own Delilah's pitch up, they're Seth Effricans – twins, Genie assumes . . . *they've identical shaving rashes* . . . who force out their hard shitty words between tightly squeezed lips: Git in – they've pulled their old Jag over so it blocks the back door . . . *poor little Genie.* They give her a slap, bundle her in and drive her to a town . . . *a stew later* she finds out is Newmarket. There's a bandy-legged gnome waiting for them in a flat smelling of fresh paint, new carpet underlay, ammonia and cigarette smoke. The cigarette is poised on the edge of a hefty cut-glass ashtray on a glass-topped coffee table – everything in the flat is brand-spanking new except for the gnome. Genie thinks, A girl could get 'erself cut to pieces in 'ere . . . Danger UXB is on the telly, and as he watches a brave bomb-disposal expert crawl towards the Nazi blockbuster, the gnome – who wears a zip-up cardigan with suede facings – draws heavily on his Embassy . . . *my new Mumsie*. PeeOay, one of the apes squeezes out, as fuckin' egreed. And the gnome, whose name is Terry, picks up a car key on a leather fob and tosses it at them, saying, It's down by the garages. – When the gingers have gone, Genie says, What's the big-fucking-idea here, then – you just buy me, didja, for a fucking motor? Terry says, An XJS – but it's second-hand. – He requires her to wear a maid's uniform: a shortie black nylon dress with white collar and cuffs, a frilly white apron and a frilly white cap that she fiddles into her thick curls with pins *'e foughtfully provides*. Genie flicks the Venetian blinds with a purple feather duster – she flicks it at his purple cock and he spunks on the fitted carpet. Ooh, she says, what's this dreadful mess we have here . . . and goes to fetch kitchen roll from a kitchen smelling of Lemon Jif. There are jars on the shelves labelled SUGAR, FLOUR, SALT – all empty. Genie is the empty vessel of a woman in a maid's uniform – she thinks often of latex blow-up sex dolls that're . . . *forty-two inches plus*. He likes to wear her knickers while she dusts him . . . *We free kings of orient are, selling ladies' underwear, 'ow fan-tastic, no elas-tic!* Terry tells her he's a top racehorse trainer, but it ain't all it's cracked up to be – the stable lads are always giving him grief: they won't keep the yard clean, they think it's enough to hose the stalls down.

His wife's a slut innall – which is why he got the flat with the BREAD BIN what's never known crumbs. On the telly – which is a fancy colour one – orange-faced Ken Barlow breathes down the necks of his machinists. On the black leather sofa Terry sits with his corduroy breeches and Genie's knickers down round his ankles. Every time Genie makes him come he goes and washes his hands – he never lays one on her. Each afternoon he brings her a portion of cold chow mein and some gelid sweet-and-sour pork balls, and each evening when he leaves with the carefully crushed foil containers double-wrapped in plastic bags he carefully double-locks the door. All the windows are barred and locked. Appearances can be deceptive, Terry says . . . *the fucking loony*: this is a high-crime area, lotta break-ins. At night Genie sweats out the dregs of the Abbot ale and that day's MSG on to pale-yellow Terylene sheets that she changes every morning. From the window she sees small children throwing a beachball at a cat on top of the garages – beyond a clapboard fence there's a twenty-foot-high shock of pampas grass. On the fourth day she curtseys the way he likes her to and says, I'm so sorry, sir, but I've run out of Domestos to do the lavvy and it's a bit mucky in there . . . He panics and runs out of the flat, forgetting the mortice. – Wandering barefoot down the road, Genie sees nets twitching and marvels at this: the maid's uniform, which served its purpose perfectly well back in the flat, now seems . . . *like nothing at all*. She marvels – and she understands this: from Berkhamsted to Cambridge, clip-clopping . . . *round annaround* the country with Benjie, then back to Berko again – now back to Cambridge. All the time chucking down booze, sniffing up sulphate, slobbering on cock, sucking up beef-buggered-up – always getting *stuff inside me*, but none of it – *none of it* – ever so much as *touches the sides* — as the Merc' turns left the Yank's face turns towards Genie and . . .*'e screws me out*. Words start pouring from his dry lips, Amity, y'know, means friendship, and he not busy bein' born is already fly-in' – you dig that point, right? Fly-in' on a Fudgesicle through the sky to land, oh . . . I dunno, mebbe up in the Smoke or down in the borderlands . . . I dunno either, Genie says, I mean, I s'pose so. – He accelerates, choking her with the inertia of her own tongue – his spiel bubbles in her ears: We could fly there, oooh takes 'bout half a day if we go by my dragonfly here – sure, it ain't Spain, but, as dead-headed roses say, what's inna name? 'Sides – he pokes another button so that hot breath pants against her tights – the wind's in the right quarter, who knows you might even be my . . . – Genie knows she needs to . . . *get a fucking grip*, but she can't – she keeps sliding down deeper into shocked numbness. All she can see is the Yank's dingy teeth eating the past, *chewing it all up*. But, like any food eaten when you're on smack, *it don't digest*, only lies there in the stomach: crisp and hard and stuck together with chocolatey sentiment. — Genie sees Jeanie standing outside the cottage with Hughie and Debbie, all three of them have their little suitcases packed and Gregor Gruber drives up in a Merc' . . . *what's only got two doors* – strange for such a big, flash car. Here he is, the man that's meant to be their father, come to drive them across Europe to visit with his mutti in Vienna for their summer hols . . . *as he always does*. Only this time it's different: Mumsie takes the Tupperware box full of cornflake crispies Jeanie's made for the journey and hands it to Debbie. Not you, she says, you're not going this time, you're staying here with me – I want the company. She puts her hand on Jeanie's head and her nails are . . . *thorns*. The others get in, Gregor slams the boot, and they drive off. A bit of gravel pings Jeanie in the thigh . . . *they didn't so much as wave or look back* . . . — Hand job's a tenner, she gasps, blow one twenny – straight sex is fifteen, no rubber's twenny-five. Circling his hand again so the Merc' noses into Endymion Road, the Yank says, I've done with all the lies, and Genie realises he must've picked girls up off the Drive before – because this is one of the spots where the punters often bring them. He takes the slip road into the park, then turns off this into the dead end leading to the dead railway line. The Yank stops the car and says, It's kinda like I've woken from a long sleep filled with crazy dreams – y'unnerstand, hon? You get me? He turns towards her, his hands kneading his features. You get me, he groans, the moon she flew down to me through cloudy battle grounds of red and brown, and she did it to me, ooh-ooh! But it was all in my mind, see? I'm awake now and everything's copacetic – 'cept for this – he grinds his fists into his eyes – I'm an old man now and I don't want your filthy cunt or any other whore's. – The door catch flaps uselessly in her hand – she'd lunge across him if she had the strength. The Yank kills the engine and looks at Genie – she looks back, her knickers . . . *are wringin'* – *I so know 'is type* . . . She puts a blonde wig on the Yank's balding head, she places a long slim-barrelled gun in his hand, and she remembers David's precise words: *I always think things get a lot realer when the shooters come out* . . . Yeah, yeah – *right* . . . and what became of David? Genie has heard shady gossip loitering on crim' lips: he'd been banged up on remand in Brixton – then so-and-so sat behind him when he was ghosted. He'd ended up in Parkhurst – either taking it in the shitter or giving it to Nilsen, the serial killer. Then he hanged himself. Genie sees the crap prison slip-on shoes – sees the shadow-hands they cast on the floor slowly revolving one way, then the other. When they stop . . . *it's the hour of 'is death.* Genie sees the brave little spider, sent to inspire him . . . *drowned in 'is piss-pot.* David was only the first, already there've been others – and there'll be many more who'll die. But not Genie – Genie won't ever die, because if she did . . . *that'd be the end of* everything. That's what the heavy mob understand – that's how they . . . *pull one over on the rest of us.* She stutters, P-Please d-don't hurt me, I'll do anyfing – anyfing you want. – The Yank pulls a pack of JPS from his overcoat pocket and offers her one. He lights both cigarettes with a stream-lined Ronson: hers *dowses* furiously, *seeking a way out* – his is *a bung*, his words . . . *leak from it*: Sheesh! Ssso very sssorry, kiddo – I kinda forgot myself there. Y'see I'm a traumatised guy, yeah? I got this, uh, sssyndrome, yeah? I'm mostly cool – got my itty-bitty apartment down in Covent Garden . . . Cool place . . . All set up for me by my good buddy – 'ceptin' he's gone now . . . Anways, it's all cool – I go up to the Whittington, talk to the shrinks there . . . I get my medication – I eat my medication. It's all cool so long as I eat my medication – chew it up, yummy-yummy in my tummy . . . Sometimes . . . well, I kinda forget it. You scared me, Genie says, why'd you lock all the doors? Did I, the Yank says, did I really? I'm so sorry – see, this ain't my auto, it's a rental – the money comes in and the money don't come in. Pop, y'see, he put it all in trust for me, and my brother, Gertie – that's Gerhard – he's a kinda capricious fellow, manages the trust: sits on it, then he lets a piece go – sits on it, then lets it go. – The Yank shakes his head wearily, and, crumpling his cigarette in the ashtray, he pushes his head up against the windscreen. – It's like Gertie can't forgive me for . . . oh, I dunno what he can't forgive me for. The Yank sings: Wehe dem Fliehenden, Welt hinaus ziehenden! Fremde durchmessenden . . . His voice is warm . . . *and beautiful* – but then he switches abruptly to a creepily babyish . . . *Shirley Temple*: No, no, don't take me down in the root cellar, Johnny! I don't want my clean dress to get ALL MUSHED UP! Then switches again to a worryingly ordinary voice: Busner, his name is Busner – he's the man hereabouts. I mean, he don't wear no white coat, he don't give you a sneaky rabbit-punch like a state orderly – he don't put no 'lectrodes on you, but he still CON-TROLS THE JUICE, he still got the POWER, don'tcha, Zack? Doctor Busner, who's plumpish, in his mid-thirties, and has a baffled expression spread across his sallow features, says, Well . . . I really don't know about that, Claude, I don't know about that at all. Releasing Busner's hand Michael says, I've been having a pow-wow with your colleague here about the situation with young Christopher, who's my ward. Listen, his father and I certainly appreciate your taking him in here, but we can't help wondering if this is the best, ah, environment for him –. He stops: a bed spring has broken deep in the fundament of the world – or at least . . . *that's what it sounds like*. More disturbingly the reverberating boing-oing-oing is followed by *a flock of mechanical seagulls* and a banshee in the next room wrong-headedly crying, It is not dy-inggg! Busner, who looks *a bit green about the gills*, pulls out a chair and sits down at the table. He wears a houndstooth jacket and has a brown knitted-wool tie fastened none too efficiently around his grubby collar. To all intents and purposes he seems . . . *a typical specimen of the breed* and Michael is wary: he's watched psychiatrists this past decade or so as they've grown hairier and more wayward – begun bandying about terms such as existentialism and phenomenology, speaking in hushed, priestly tones or hectoring and rabble-rousing ones – in either case . . . *hardly helping matters*. D'you mind? Busner says, taking out a packet of Gold Leaf, and Michael, picking up his pipe, says, Of course not. Scratching a match, leaning into its . . . *flare path*, Busner's . . . *Whitley nose* zooms over the dirty breakfast crocks. You must, he puffs, forgive the mess . . . Appearances can be, um, deceptive – we try to alleviate distress here with mutual assistance, we're seeking new ways of living, and if it seems we aren't running a very, um, tight ship, it's only because the residents expend most of their energies on mutual –. Gourevitch, the American psychiatrist with curly red hair and apish sideboards, who'd welcomed Michael with similarly nervy platitudes, now interrupts: I think Mister Lincoln is pretty up to speed on our kinda ethos, Zack – he's set up several communes of his own, you've heard of the Lincoln Homes, right? Busner puffs, Ah, yes . . . of course – for disabled ex-servicemen, aren't they? Michael thinks: I'd like to drill these bloody hippies in short-sleeve order, then give this Busner chap a two-five-two and slap him in the glass-house . . . But he only says, meekly: That's right, I try to do my bit. Rather than

286

responding, Busner turns to Gourevitch and asks, Where's Podge? Giving him a *shifty look*, Gourevitch replies, Chill out, Zack, Lesley's babysitting her. Busner doesn't seem at all reassured – he fidgets with his matches, scratching open and scritching closed the tray, before, with a heavy sigh, beginning one-handed to roll and unroll the end of his tie, a tic Michael at once realises . . . *is his habitual comforter.* There's a heightened pressurised atmosphere in the poky kitchen that Michael can't identify the cause of – clearly he's walked in on something . . . *I hope there's nothing wrong with the boy* . . . I shall, he says, have to insist on seeing Christopher at the very least. I need to make sure he's all right – I'll want to interview him . . . in private. – Abruptly the older mentally ill American, who's been slouching by the gas cooker, talking the whole time in a barely audible monotone . . . *Lakeland stream tumbling over stones* . . . pulls himself to attention, snapping his heels, crack! and exposing the map on the wall behind him. Michael remembers . . . *that intel' officer, Phelps.* – He was given to such dramatics: whipping the sheet off the map-stand as he announced the target for that night's op': *Gentlemen, you will proceed to Bremen, and with the blessings of Jove – annihilate it!* The American is certainly old enough to have served, but his military bearing is . . . *preposterous* given his bare, hairless and hollow chest is hung with . . . *mad medals*: a tin opener-cum-corkscrew, a Japanese transistor radio, amulets of some sort, all of them tangled up with chains and thongs in a lurid cravat. He snaps: Yes, sir, yes! Lieutenant Claude Evenrude reporting, sir! I will fetch the prisoner from the stockade right away, sir! He stamps about-turn and marches out. Gourevitch tips back on his chair, his leather jacket squeaks as he passes his hands over his glistening forehead . . . *Why the blazes is he sweating?* and, stifling a yawn, says, Claude Evenrude is a very damaged individual, Mister Lincoln – he witnessed terrible things during the war, maybe the most terrible thing there is. Michael says nothing – he has his pipe to attend to . . . *it's an alibi, really.* Gourevitch goes on: Things that made Claude so very angry he took up the only arms he had in the cause of justice – his pen, his voice, his spirit. He became determined, Mister Lincoln, to expose the power-mongering lies of the warmongers –. Rodge, Busner breaks in, really – I think that's quite enough, um, mongering. Mister Lincoln isn't here to hear about Claude – or hear from Claude for that matter. Gourevitch says, I was only explaining, Zack, I truly believe Mister Lincoln should hear about these things, after all it's men of his generation who dropped the bombs, who perpetrated the real madness –. Rodge! Busner is more than simply exasperated: Mister Lincoln has had plenty of experience with those damaged by the war – you said so yourself. I think it's fair to assume he's on the side of the angels, and I'm bloody well certain the last thing he needs is a potted lecture from you. – The instant coffee Gourevitch made him really was stirred with *pathetic inadequacy.* The bitter film coating Michael's tongue and the roof of his mouth is in some obscure way *of a piece* with the phantom skiffle-boys, whose t-tinking of spoons on cups and plates . . . *Well-if-you-ride-it-you-gotta-ride-it-like-you-find-it* . . . it takes him several confusing seconds to realise, is actually being produced by a tube train drumming past along the embankment behind the house, a juggernaut that although invisible is nonetheless of this world . . . *while I'm on the side of the angels.* He finds the posturing of these men both absurd and contemptible, yet the habit of conciliation is so ingrained that he says, Please . . . gentlemen, I don't think anyone can pull rank in these matters – there's no high moral ground to be found on others' sufferings. I'm also sure what we all want is the best for Christopher. Absolutely, Gourevitch says, he's a great kid. Busner nods sagely. Michael takes a deep breath and *pushes on*, although it's proving increasingly *heavy going*: the . . . *props of my mind* are *feathering* . . . and glancing to either side he sees not the disturbed psychiatrists but . . . *skin angels!* flying in a bee hive formation, wind humming through their shredded wings as they *shepherd me towards the target* . . . Michael continues *smoothly enough*, albeit through gritted teeth: Knowing him as I do I often think what Chris would really benefit from is some carefree sexual experience . . . At this Busner and Gourevitch come . . . *back into focus*: as he suspected, this faintly outrageous remark has grabbed their prurient attention. Yes, some carefree sexual experience – he's basically a good chap and a sound one, but he's socially isolated and he doesn't think much of himself. He needs some self-worth – more to the point, some vim. Now, there's a very nice girl whom he knows – she works for a solicitor in Worthing, and Chris has met her several times when he's come down to visit his father, who – as he's probably told you – stays at my place there. Well, this girl's very interested in Christopher . . . and I'm sure she would – if only he'd . . . ask . . . Michael stops. His smoothness has deposited him . . . *in the rough!* He's said *too much!* and *too loudly!* Because the tube has sailed away and in its wake the silence has surged back, bringing with it . . . *this shipwrecked soul*: the Kid, who stands in the doorway. The creepy American looms over Kit's hunched shoulder, his mouth open . . . *He's always hungry – he feeds on discord* . . . and shouts, Hup! Twoop! Threep! Four! First squad to the rear – march! Second squad to the rear – march! Then, as Kit shuffles into the kitchen, the American sings: With a step that is stead-y and strong, the Campfire Girls march a-loong! Kit's fringe fills his sunken eyes, his bitten fingers are bandaged in his muslin shirt cuffs. He says, Hullo, Uncle Mike – but he's scarcely audible because the deranged American's in full swing, marching on the spot and turning ninety degrees at a time, and, as he dizzyingly revolves, his barked self-commands – Rrrright turn! – punctuating his usual dirge: Well, if'n they told us six was nine, why, we didn't mind, Rrrright turn! And if they backed us up against the wall and spat in our faces, we took it – by golly, yes we did, Rrrright turn! It was a sight better than the bullshit at Wright-Patterson, where those good 'ol boys lay 'round drinking greasy dick, Rrrright turn! They cut off all of our hair but I didn't care – put us in the Eden Roc, six to a suite, Rrrright turn! So humid in between kit inspections I'd put my goddamn undies in the icebox, Rrrright turn! – Lesley appears, furtively licking his lips, and says, Hey, Claude, best you come back to the cool vibes room, man – this is the hot vibes room . . . Michael stands up and says, Now, come along Christopher, it's high time you and I had a proper confab'. Busner sits staring at his cigarette, which has burnt down to its filter. The American runs on: I didn't care, I weren't no Willie-the-Weeper – I'd graduated Phi-Beta-Kappa while these bohunks were beating their meat in the barracks, Rrrright turn! – Busner snaps out of it, stubs out the butt and, getting up, says, Yes, yes, so sorry, Mister Lincoln . . . He leads them from the kitchen into the living room, where Clive is still huddling on the floor among the detritus of last night's fish supper. Busner says, Look here, Clive, Kit needs to have a private chat with his . . . ah, friend – would you terribly mind giving them some privacy? Clive says, Oompah-lumpah, stick it up yer jumpah, then picks up a couple of the empty Worthington tins and does exactly that before getting to his feet and obediently clankling out the door. – Back in the kitchen Lesley has taken Busner's seat at the table – he and a cowed Gourevitch are corralled by the Creep, who's singing, I wanna have my coffee! I wanna have my biscuits hot an' eight inches long! as he marches round them. Seeing Busner, he cries, Hup! Twoop! Threep! Four! but continues his circuit, shoving past the chair backs, his fists swinging. Zack places one . . . *Benedictine* hand on Lesley's head, one on Gourevitch's and stutters out, I-I f-felt I was r-running to get on the bus, y'know – and . . . and I was going to miss it, and . . . and as I was p-pelting along the pavement the conductor was sort of grinning at me the way they do . . . You . . . two . . . you were next to him on the platform – he gives each *hairball* . . . a stroke – Th-Thing is . . . I couldn't decide whether you wanted me to catch the bus, or if you wanted me to t-trip and f-fall and h-hurt myself – p'raps fall under the wheels of the bus and . . . d-die. Then – then I managed to grab the pole, and for a few s-seconds there I was filled by the wind . . . I was a sort of windsock full of air and thoughts. But here's the strangest thing: the bus kept on getting bigger and bigger, while you two . . . you two stayed exactly the same size! At last you . . . you reached out your hands and pulled me on board – hauled me into this –. Hup! Twoop! Threep! Four! the Creep barks, and Zack cries above him: AND I LOVE YOU FOR THAT, RODGE – I LOVE YOU TOO, JOHN. Gourevitch says, Oh, man, I think I get . . . yeah, I get it: bus as in Bus-ner, yeah, Bus-ner. It's so beautiful, man – you were climbing ON BOARD YOURSELF. Wow, Zack, that's so way out! I love you too, man – don'tcha love him, John? Lesley says, He's cool, I s'pose . . . shall we do the washing-up? And Zack says: What a tremendous idea! The three of us'll do the washing-up – we'll do it all up, every last teaspoon, and the cheese grater – we'll pick all that rotten stuff out of the cheese grater from when you grated that nutmeg, John . . . and . . . and then we'll straighten out the pantry as well, 'cause there's a lot of stuff in there that's pretty off, and . . . and . . . while we're at it we could wash the kitchen floor – wouldn't that be splendid, would that be, um, communal? Gourevitch gets up: If you're not gonna help us, Claude, p'raps you'd better hang in the cool vibes room, like John said, or, if you wanna march go march in the garden where there's PLENTY OF ROOM. Claude continues to bellow, Hup! Twoop! Threep! Four! as he goose-steps round the kitchen table, his fists swinging into the psychiatrists, and Busner cries, Open the bloody door, John! . . . *Wild fresh air, long steely scrape of steel wheels chopping the butterflies in my tummy into . . . confetti . . .* Clive clankles in, saying, Oompah-lumpah, stick it up yer jumpah! Picks up the salt, yanks up his pullover, sticks the salt up there and tucks it in again. Lesley cackles, Look at

Clive with his big boobies! Gourevitch titters, He's s-sittin' on a c-cornflake! Accompanying himself with a cereal-box maraca. Zack and Lesley . . . *convulse, tee-hee, tee-hee*, tee-hee, TEE-HEE-HEE! Shoulders heaving . . . *wind-up teeth clickety-clacking* as Claude finally marches out: Hup! Twoop! Threep! Four! Clive shuffling behind him, and Oscar bringing up the rear, tail a whirling blur in which Zack yet sees . . . *every single hair!* Zack says, I wonder some-times where that dog goes to – and Roger says, D'you wanna look inside his head, Doctor? Giggling, they take off their jackets and roll up their sleeves – Zack pushes *my furry tongue* between his shirt buttons and says, I'll brainwash, Rodge, you brain-dry, and Lesley complains, Hey, what about me? Zack admonishes him: John, you stack the dirty crocks up here on the side – observe us, but you mustn't intervene in any way, 'cause that wouldn't be scientifical . . . scientifi-cacious . . . scientif . . . scientif –. Scientific! Roger throws up. Science! It wouldn't be science! The three of them stand by the sink, their bellies squeezing out hilarious bubbles that pop *hee-green, ha-red, ho-blue!* from their mouths. Through the misty window Zack sees the Creep and Clive . . . *teddy-bear shapes* . . . they are indeed marching . . . *round and round the garden*, keeping to a precise circle, one that forces them to clamber over the bloated corpses of two defunct armchairs that have been dumped out there, kick through forgotten raspberry canes, crunch broken cucumber frames and climb through the wreck of the old garden shed. As Zack watches the Creep turns back to help Clive, who's stuck in the splintering window frame, while Oscar barks soundlessly at the tube train driving over their heads. Zack stops laughing, turns the hot tap and the geyser rattleroars into life. Gentlemen, he says, we have lift-off, and Roger, holding up a saucer *virulent* with congealed egg yolk, says, I think this is badly contaminated. Zack takes it from him, thinking, You thought you were high when your heart hammered and you added up all the telephone numbers in the Classifieds . . . You thought you were drunk when woozy-headed you embraced Clive and told him he was your best friend – but that wasn't intoxication, this . . . this is intoxication! Decisively, he puts the *radioactive* saucer in the sink with all the other *twisted wreckage*, and his *remote-control hand* locates the plug, puts it in, then squirts the *decontaminant*. Prismatic bubbles *fission* into the steam, and, as his robot claws manipulate a saucepan and a greasy dishcloth, he hears the Creep yelling at Clive: Call off your kit items, you fat-fuckin'-jerk-off! Sing it! And call off the pro-ce-dures – sing 'em out! Clive, his arms waving, bellows back, Oompah-lumpah, I'm stuck up me jumpah! In the living room . . . *the poor kid is dying*. He lies flat on a bare mattress . . . *sobbing without surcease*. Michael yearns to comfort him but cannot bear to touch his shirt's *blistering skin*. Moreover, the top gunner . . . *rolls so*, back and forth in the crawlspace beneath the astrodome, as he futilely attempts to relieve the pain of his smouldering Sidcot, while the flak bursts keep right on . . . *rocking the bus*. Michael's mouth is full of . . . *instant bile*. He looks about frantically for an extinguisher or a safety blanket – but can see only dusty swathes of Indian cloth and pillows . . . *spitting feathers* through their worn ticking. When they'd been hit, Michael was up front and he watched, appalled, as the twisted blades of the port prop whisked to a standstill . . . *Angel's bloody delight.* He was conscious of *dullness . . . dampness . . . a bitter throb . . .* in his shoulder – but more pressing were the Kid's howls in his headset. He handed over the controls to Marwick and went back. – It was his first op' after ten days' survivor's leave, during which there'd been a long evening with Sirbert on the public course at Carshalton. His father – and this was *unprecedented* – had laid his hand on that selfsame shoulder . . . *as I dug and dug again at a bad lie,* saying, Have a care, old boy, you'll give yourself the yips if you persist like that . . . For a sec' Michael had been on the brink of . . . *letting it all out* – but he hadn't: it wasn't what either of them wanted or needed. Besides, Michael knew Sirbert was well aware of what had happened to Tufty, Claus, Jimmy, Jacko and Jimp – aware also there'd been five casualties, because this was *a verified statistical report.* Not aware, of course, that Jimp had turned eighteen two days before – nor that he'd spent his last night on earth being viciously teased in the mess: served up with a po filled with bitter in which floated *a highly realistic turd crafted from parkin . . .* and believing this to be part of his initiation he'd gamely choked it all down . . . *but that was then, YOU BLOODY FOOL!* The top gunner was hit over *Wilhelmshaven, not . . . Willesden!* To steady himself Michael does *a cockpit drill.* Empty beer tins – *check.* Overflowing ashtray – *check.* London tube map pinned to the wall behind the television set – *check.* But it's no use – no matter how hard he tries to *keep things rational!* the subsurface arteries – boldly coloured purple, green, maroon, black – infiltrate his eyes, as the intel' officer smacks the map with his pointer, self-satisfaction oozing through his barathea uniform. . . *of impeccable cut.* Pay attention, gentlemen, he says. Herr

Hitler's flunkeys have dug their rocket factories in deep underground, here at Tottenheimstraße, and our boffins think it'll take a direct hit to winkle 'em out. Not much in the ack-ack department, but we've it on good authority from our friends in the resistance there are night-fighter squadrons here – *tap!* Here – *tap!* And here – *tap!* at Green Park. – Michael suspects this: the terrible strain required to knit together his worlds has begun to show . . . *I'm fraying as I go round annaround* . . . Bexhill, Banstead, Royston, Shoreham . . . *round again.* Show as the profound seediness of a man not simply without a woman, but *without womankind* . . . As the leprechaun cabby piloted him up the Edgware Road, and then along the avenues towards Willesden, Michael's hurting eyes alighted on bright sprays of buddleia and the dried stems of last summer's willow herb. The bomb sites, he thought, have been left for so long they're invading the neat suburban gardens. His own *seediness* . . . was vegetative: the bristles of his toothbrush . . . *engrafting*, his underwear . . . *fungal*, and no matter how many circuits he did there were always . . . *these bumps*: I cannot abide these bloody cripples! she'd screamed – but, truth to tell . . . *I can't stand them any more either*, especially the one inside, *the fifth columnist* who wears Michael's own skin *for his Sidcot*, and who now stretches his arms and legs so Michael's compelled to bow his head, lean heavily against the wall, then slide down it, the blizzard of snowflakes frozen on the wallpaper *scccrrraping* against his back. Each and every one of my cells, Michael thinks, is engorged by eating another: *No wonder I'm not feeling that chipper* . . . and still poor Kit keeps on: I'm. Being. Swallowed. Up. By. Ancient. Cell. Wisdom. It'd

been, Michael thinks, utterly pointless synchronising watches . . .
*40 seconds . . . 30 seconds . . . 20 seconds . . . 10 seconds . . . 5, 4, 3, 2, 1,
8.15, gentlemen* . . . because time refuses to be commanded in this
fashion: formed up, *drilled in short-sleeve order*, then sent forward
double-quick. Instead time keeps on *betraying me*, by planting
memories in the future *that explode in my face*. Kins is closer to
Michael now than Hobbles, the Scamp, Smalls, Dotty, Tommo,
Taffy and the Barrel. — *Un-der-neath the arrr-ches* . . . of the Opera
House they lounge, watching the thick broth of young men and
women being sluggishly stirred by the clarinets and trumpets of
Billy Cotton's band. Had it been that night or another Kins ended
up, *or so he claimed*, tasting *all the delights known to man*, while
his younger brother lay rigid on the station platform, Annette's
ungovernable elbows digging into his side . . . *sharp . . . unyielding . . . N.B.G.* It was hard to say, because on every leave he'd had
throughout the war, Michael sought Kins out. – Fewer and fewer
had rallied to his white standard, and by '44 the conchie was a
bearded and filthy anomaly: a non-combatant corps . . . *of one*. Kins
told Michael he only went home to the Paragon every fortnight or
so for a feed, a wash and to change his togs. Mostly . . . *the bloody
irony of it!* . . . he ate in British Empire restaurants and slept in the
bombed-out terrace on the north side of Fitzroy Square, together
with a motley bunch of would-be Bohemians . . . *some of who were
indeed Czechs*. When he met up with Michael in the Wheatsheaf,
Kins castigated him: I tell you what you are, man, a bloody Soho
non-Blitzer. Some of us stuck it out here on the receiving end, while
you were over there dishing it out – and now we've these bloody

doodlebugs to contend with! Kins had his old varsity scarf wrapped twice round his hairy neck – his jacket pockets were stuffed with the peculiar little toys one of his Czechs twisted into being out of pipe-cleaners. Kins peddled these for pints once his paltry lecturer's fees from the WEA had been drunk up. *I should've popped the lucky bugger on his snoot for his bloody cheek!* But by then Michael too was . . . *a lucky bugger.* After Willemshaven his nerves were shot – they tried letting him fly milk runs, and when he protested he was seconded to the chair-borne division at High Wycombe, where he flew at ground level, covered in plenty of scrambled egg – the DFC and bar: a heroic bureaucrat, all of whose green metal office furniture was *bolted together out of the young men's bones.* There he'd sat, shuffling papers, his feet resting in a pool of *cooling guts.* Having completed fifty-three ops, he was – statistically speaking, as Sirbert would say – dead four times over, *a zombie with beautiful shoe leather,* resurrected again *annagain* by the higher-ups to *do as I was told and look where they pointed.* — Face down, the Kid goes on sobbing – and Michael calls to him across the devastated landscapes of . . . *Hamburg and Dresden, Eniwetok . . . and the Montebello Islands:* What is it, my child? What's troubling you – I'm sure if you tell me I'll be able to help. Kit sniffles, I-I-I don't mean anything, Uncle Mike, I don't mean anything! – Michael's repulsed by the beer tins and the crumpled fish-and-chip wrappings strewn across the floor. Each vilely insignificant object is, he notices, lit up by the spring sunshine *so very brightly* . . . and precisely because of this *has its utterly dark side.* He rouses himself enough to say, Come along now, Chris, you're a thoroughly decent chap – and that's the tip-top thing to be. But Kit goes on sobbing: I-I d-don't mean that, Uncle Mike, I mean I – I doesn't mean anything . . . I've got no I . . . – It's the American, Michael thinks, the creepy chap they call Claude – he's the one who's dancing me back to the hula-hula night-time of Tinian, back into the hot metallic fug of the Quonset, where the cockroaches chirr up into the projector's beam – back to the yelps and catcalls of the men who tread water in their smoky lagoon, watching as Sonja Henie twirls on the icy spot, her white tulle skirt . . . *frothing*, her golden girdle . . . *flashing*. — Luckies had been four bucks a carton from the PX, and the 509th Composite had first dibs, which explained why . . . *they were all toasted*. Liquor was officially prohibited on the base, but everyone seemed to be chasing the watery beer with nips from flasks and pint bottles. They gotta let off some steam, said Sergeant Duzenbury, who was sitting beside him – and, so saying, *added his own vapour to the slipstream above our heads*. But Michael couldn't let off any steam: it went on building up inside him, exerting more and more pressure, until he felt his innards . . . *condense*, because *I realised then* that the monstrous and unearthly flash that had irradiated the cockpit of the B-29, so every switch and lever had its utterly dark side, *would never leave me*. On the six-hour flight to the target there'd been scarcely any chitchat. Tibbets kept the intercom off, but Michael had gathered at least this much: back in Utah they'd practised radar and visual bombing, but the manoeuvre they'd worked obsessively to perfect was a 155-degree diving turn . . . *so we could keep our nose down and get the hell out of there*. For long undulating seconds Tibbets rode out the shockwave – then this man, who, in his monstrous American innocence, had named the airplane after his mother, *took us circling back*. Through his thick, smoked-glass goggles Michael saw what the little boy Missus Tibbets gave birth to *had done*: a hemisphere wobbled up into being, its surface *slick and obscenely glossy* . . . A quarter-century later Michael cannot credit that he really witnessed this – perhaps it'd only been the hypnotic pomp of his early-morning imagination that *at 8.15* . . . spawned death . . . *sunny side up*, swelling and then cracking open the heavens. Cosseted in their padded seats, the air circulating them pressurised, filtered and warmed, they'd gazed down to where, moments before, there had been the five peninsulas of Hiroshima . . . *a trusting hand open to receive a gift*. The United Airmen looked down and saw *the shape of things to come*: black oil boiling in the green crucible of the surrounding hills – and the filthy geyser of the earth's innards *spurting into the sky*. Michael had estimated *one angel, two angels, three* . . . before Tibbets took his mother-ship into another sharp turn and they set course *home to Henie*. — T-minus seven hours. The Superfortress was towed over from the tech' area, where the weapon they coyly referred to as the Gadget had been loaded using a super-heavy hoist. Meanwhile, in the Quonset, immediately after their final briefing, the twelve-man crew and their Royal Air Force *Judas* had stood heads bent to receive the blessing bestowed by a sandy young chaplain with keen blue eyes. Michael was distracted by the steady pitter-pattering of night bugs against the screen door. Ever since arriving on Tinian, he had felt the oddity of the American war effort bearing down on him: a great weight of carefully inventoried ordinance. He didn't doubt the gravity of the situation, or the estimated casualties involved in taking the home islands, but his USAAF colleagues conceded that, now air supremacy had been achieved, the main threat they faced came as their overloaded aircraft rumbled to the end of the landing strip and failed to get aloft. Twilight's last gleaming was a Technicolor extravaganza everyone ignored. Each evening they stood in the chow line or lay on their bunks listening as engines caught, then roared, propellers smote the dusk and the fat-bellied bombers took off – one after another, until they could be seen from the 509th's compound: *Phaetons* strung out across the sky, while down below was the one that had crashed . . . *and burned.* — Michael stares at the chaplain's surplice, which, as he warms to his theme, rides up to reveal high-topped flight boots. Ferebee, the Group Bombardier, drawls in Michael's ear: He don't put on no dog, stateside Chappie flew with us whenever he could – hell, he'd come with us now if they'd let him. – Michael expects the blessing to be pro forma: Blah, blah, God . . . Blah, blah, Country Before Self . . . Blah, blah, Merciful . . . Instead, killing his cigarette in a tin ashtray on the lectern, Chappie brandishes the Bible he holds and extemporises a lengthy homily on Matthew 8: He came down from the mountain and he healed the leper, and he relieved the centurion's servant of the palsy, and Peter's wife's mother of the fever – and He cast out devils. All this He did, yet still solemnly He adjured them: the children of the kingdom shall be cast out into outer darkness, where there shall be weeping and gnashing of teeth . . . — There's still weeping and gnashing of teeth . . . *there's still darkness,* Michael thinks, his fifty-year-old face held in his shaking hands, Kit's whimpering negations filling his ears: No I . . .

No I . . . No I . . . There were, Michael thinks, multitudes about me at that time — not only the crews of the three B-29s assigned to fly the mission, but all the other personnel on Tinian – and beyond their orderly piquets of tents and Quonsets, up in the caves pitting Mount Lasso's jungle-covered cone were the Japanese troops who continued to hold out nine months after the first marines came ashore. Smelling of their own faeces and the rubbish they scavenged by night from their conquerors' bins . . . *the free economy of a democratic capitalism*, these *poor, emaciated devils* . . . slipped in through the screen door to fill in the gaps between the men of the 509th Composite – some of whom, gorged on fresh fruit, vegetables and meat flown in from the east and the south . . . *were actually plump*, their throats bull-frogging from the elasticated collars of their freshly laundered T-shirts as they Aaaa-mened. Big kids, Michael had thought, remembering the wizened figures who sat beside him in the sickly green glow of the cockpit lights when the Lanc' fought its way up from the Lincolnshire flatland into the dimensionless sky above *the German Ocean* . . . which was what Sirbert still calls it, quite possibly . . . *his idea of a joke*. Chappie rises on the toes of his boots as he nears the crux, and the snowy hem of his surplice . . . *rises yet higher*. He says what Jesus saith: *The foxes have holes, and the birds of the air have nests, but the Son of man hath nowhere to lay his head* . . . A pompous attitude, Michael thinks, coming from the junior arm of the Trinity. But Chappie continues: So, one of the disciples asks Jesus, is it OK if I go bury my dad? Well, this is what Our Lord said to that guy – and this is what I say to all of you brave men here tonight, one thousand, nine hundred and some years later, many thousand of miles from the Holy Land, as you make ready to depart for the other side: Follow Jesus! Follow Jesus – and let the dead bury their dead! — In Washington, where the British observers stopped off en route, Michael had been one among a number of *very important murderers* . . . who'd attended a cocktail party at the Embassy. As quickly as he could he jettisoned Cranfield, the Scientific Adviser . . . *a spectacularly boring man*, with the tall, crooked gait of a wader, for whom there were no minutiae so infinitesimally small he wouldn't *stoop to peck at them*. The ambassador had commiserated: I flew by Mosquito over to Bermuda a few weeks ago, bloody bumpy ride – cold and cramped as well. Saw your pater there – probably shouldn't say so, but what the hell. He was on good form, we got in a round of golf between meetings – incidentally, this might amuse you, it's all true what they say about the PM . . . What's true? Michael obliged, and the ambassador delivered this: He's had a special oxygen mask made so he can smoke his cigars in flight! Michael feigned amusement, but thought: I knew that already. – The ambassador's lady, her head encased in lavender-coloured daisy-shapes, bade Michael to admire the flower arrangements. She said, One of the Negro pages shows a genuine sensitivity – at least in this regard. – Later, when everyone was blotto from the Martinis, a heavy-weight USAAF general backed Michael into the red velvet drapes: Not that we don't 'preciate what you fellows have done to the goddamn Fatherland, but by the time we're through the Japs'll be performin' their tea ceremonies with ditch water! The ambassador's wife came sailing in to relieve Michael: Oh, General Stokely! she laughed gaily. You mustn't upset the Group Captain with talk of tea when it's impossible for an Englishman to find a decent cup the length and breadth of your otherwise splendid nation! – No, no tea – and only insipid coffee, little better than ersatz. There were fruit juices and sickly varieties of pop – and of course plenty of liquor with which Michael could stun himself to sleep each night, the alcohol dissolving together the faces . . . *of the living and the dead*. – Sonja had her troubles with liquor: her icy fantasia rattled around in a highball glass. She wanted to keep her brawling ex-hockey-star husband with her whatever way she could, and she implored him over the raucous heads of the A-bombers to . . . *quit drinking*. The cockroaches *wouldn't quit* . . . chirring up into the projector beam, the sweat wouldn't *quit dripping* from Michael's armpits into the sodden sleeves of his shirt – and he *couldn't quit* thinking about dirty bearded drunken Kins, dodging . . . *un-der-neath the ar-ches* while the doodlebugs were *rattling above!* As for their night's work, had it all been worth it for this: the chorus line's lime-green elbow-length gloves whirling as they twirled across the glass pool, wending between the weepy willows, where light spangled their flesh-coloured tights. *A feeble melodramatic vehicle barely supported by Miss Henie's double-axels . . .* was how the De'Ath Watch would probably have dismissed It's a Pleasure, starring Sonja Henie and Michael O'Shea – nevertheless, despite his beer-brown studiousness, Kins would've acknowledged that . . . *the Technicolor was superb*. — During the mission briefing the balding and thick-set intel' officer who had introduced them to Little Boy also tried to show them a flick, but when the projectionist pushed the buttons the film mangled in the sprockets and odd globules fissioned on the screen. They never got to see the film of the test – only witness at first-hand of the first use of the A-bomb in war. *If you could call it war*: a camera-flash so hotly bright it transformed an entire city into . . . *a photograph of itself* – the outlines of women, children and men left on the few remaining walls, the shadow of an incinerated hand marking the face it tried to shield. *One angel . . . Two angels . . . Three . . .* an entire host had straddled the dizzying dark thermals that mounted towards the B-29. At first it was impossible to see them as anything but . . . *flung confetti at the wedding of nightmare to reason*, but, as they gained altitude and came within range, Michael distinguished them from the swarming phosphenes by their curious morphology: the skin the great heat had flayed from their backs, legs and arms remained attached to wrists and ankles, so each damned creature was lifted heavenwards . . . *on wings of itself.* The skin angels had this in common with ME-109s: having appeared to be at a safe remove well below . . . *they were suddenly upon us*: their smoking eye sockets pressed against the Perspex nose-cone of the Superfortress, inside of which sat Tibbets, his co-pilot, Lewis, and Parsons, the intel' officer, studiedly ignoring them. — It was Ferebee, the Group Bombardier, who'd beckoned to Michael as they sailed through the cloudless blue, led him aft, encouraged him to take up position on the jump seat, dip his head down . . . *for apples* and stare into the crystal ball of his Norden bombsight. See there, Ferebee drawled, see the T-shape? That's where two bridges meet at right angles, that's our aiming point . . . *I saw the future – and it works: the bridge is gone, the outstretched hand is gone, everywhere great finned cars nose forward like fish, a savage servility slides by on grease* . . . — It had also been Ferebee, who, before the mission briefing, took Michael to the hangar where Little Boy lay beneath a grey rubberised tarpaulin . . . *completing his last few hours of gestation.* When Ferebee had one of the ground crew remove this *militarised swaddling*, Michael saw a stubby and malformed infant. He found it impossible to join in the bombardier's amusement as he pointed out the graffiti on the A-bomb's flanks and fins: Greetings to the People of Japan from the Men of the Indianapolis, Kilroy's phallic snout and flipper hands, and other, cruder messages – Take this up your Keister! — The Thirteen sat on the horizontal upright of the *flying crucifix*, its four massive Wright Cyclone engines screwing them through the sky. Tibbets had told Michael the fuel-injected units were electronically calibrated so their drive shafts . . . *could be reversed.* – Michael hypothesised: might it be possible for the whole business to be . . . *undone*, for them to circle anti-clockwise over the target, suck up Little Boy and return tail-first to Tinian, reversing in over the lava cliffs to make a perfect landing, while back in the Heavenly Kingdom the monstrous cloud that had risen over Hiroshima shrank down into the fertile ground . . . *with mushroom alacrity.* But it was *no bloody use* . . . towards the stern the *noncompoops* were whooping it up, their cries echoing in Missus Tibbets's empty womb, while the steering column kicked against the autopilot and the Apostle Paul scratched, yawned and relaxed safe in the knowledge of a gospel well transmitted . . . *the resurrection of the American Dream.* — He's still preaching, Michael thinks, giving the sales patter for some corporation or other . . . *GOD IS WITHIN ME AND*

THEREFORE I AM MY OWN MASTER . . . Ho! the noncoms cry, and Hee! and Ho! again. – Squirming round on the mattress, Kit manages a vintage ejaculation: The bloody swine! – The door crashes open and Claude marches in chanting, Ho, darkies hab you seen de massa, Wid de MUFF-TASH ON HE FACE! Followed by Clive, the two manage one circuit of the room – kicking tins, whipping up feathers – before Busner appears in the doorway, sporting an elaborately embroidered Victorian-style apron, and directs them both out again with a dripping dishcloth. Awfully sorry about that, he says, his polite tone wildly at odds with his eccentric attire, mussed hair and dinner-plate eyes. He then backs out, gently shutting the door behind him. The stamping retreats: Hup! Twoop! Threep! and Michael asks – as much of himself as of the boy – Why is he so very . . . well, so very disturbed? Kit, up on one elbow, stretches to pull each word from the crowd of them swirling about in his head: It's . . . a . . . fact, Uncle Mike – Claude . . . Claude was the target-spotter for the Hiroshima bomb . . . He flew ahead – ahead he flew . . . I thought you knew: he murdered a million babies . . . When the starship comes they won't take him with them to Sector 6, and they won't take me either because . . . because I'm not an I any more –. Poppycock, Michael snaps. You know fine well, Chris, I was the British observer on the A-bomb mission – that's why I set up the Lincoln Homes . . . He pauses, listening to the shuffling of the Kid's flares as his legs feebly bicycle, then, *for want of anything better*, resumes: And I can absolutely assure you there was no one called Evenrude serving with the 509th Composite – not that I knew all their names at the time, but I jolly

307

well found them out later, when the true enormity of what they – of what we – had done became clear. – *The true enormity* . . . of the pillow has overwhelmed Michael's ward: he clutches it to his ears and moans – more feathers leak from its seams to twist in the stale air, a miserable allusion to . . . *the possibility of flight.* Michael relights his pipe and listens as the extinguished match creaks into charcoal. *A by-product, Ape* . . . Pouting a small cloud, Michael thinks, The most substantial thing about me is this smoke . . . And then: It doesn't matter whether the lunatic American was on the A-bomb mission or not, the coincidence of the two of us, here, now, is . . . paralysing. *Skin angels are roosting on the peak of the suburban roof.* He sees them hanging on to the wonky television aerial with their squamous hands. Chris whispers: Please don't look at me, Uncle Mike, the aerials coming out of your eyes are spearing through the back of my head and out of my eyes, and I haven't got an I – I said that already, didn't I? You said that already, Michael confirms. We are, he thinks, lost in the outer space of our own traumas. He squints at the anaglypta snowflakes and the flittering feathers and sees them as . . . *meteorites.* He's no idea what's wrong with Christopher, only that it's absolutely plain: *This is no place for him* . . . although the business of getting up, getting him up, gathering his things together, ordering them a cab, piloting the psychotic child through the city . . . *is beyond me.* Instead, this prosaic concern settles on Michael's stomach: *I'm hungry* . . . He recalls the kipper, *swimming in butter,* left on the Pullman's heavy monogrammed plate and supposes . . . *there might at least be the makings of a sandwich* in the madhouse's kitchen, where Busner cracks! open the window above the sink. The door of perception, he remarks conversationally, if only it were clean everything would appear to us as it is: infinite. Gourevitch says, Infinitely warped – it's totally fuckin' warped, been sopping up the rain all winter. Lesley offers, I'll strip off that old paint, bung some turps on it and repaint it when –. You die, Busner interjects, and are reincarnated as a useful member of society! – All three guffaw draughts of privet-smelling air into their creaking lungs. *The warped windowframe frames the broken window-frame of the garden shed* . . . Clive's stuck in it again, chanting, Round and round the garden like a teddy bear . . . while Claude pulls at his arms, saying, Damn right, my man, round and round the exercise yard with some goon up in the tower pointing his Remington's goddamn peter-hole at you. I tellya, you think your loony bins are hard time, they're a fuckin' teddy bear's picnic compared with the secure state hospitals stateside . . . – Trapped Clive is running on, his words clambering through Claude's: One step, two step, tickle you under there! Overhearing all this from the kitchen, Busner sees Claude, shrunken and furry in the guise of a pyjama case lying on a child's bed, and the child – with her hand *stuck up inside him* – screaming hysterically because . . . *no teddy bear, he!* Then, hitting a patch of lucidity . . . *a savage servility slides by on grease* . . . he intuits: *Claude's untouched!* The acid has somehow *integrated him* . . . he isn't all over the place, but has entered his own – perhaps much larger – lucid patch, a *Sargasso of sanity* . . . where he's . . . *becalmed* while all around him *the ocean roars!* Gourevitch scoops up a handful of foam from the sink, its myriad tiny spectroscopic bubbles . . . *winking in and out of being.* He blows into it and speaks through . . . *the destruction of whole universes*: Ma-an, that cat Alpert – Leary's stooge when they were in Cambridge – when I ran into him he told me, man, when he blew to India he took with him half a fuckin' mason jar of Sandoz's finest . . . An' each time he'd track down some naked fuckin' sadhu standing on one leg in a mountain stream with his other foot shoved up his dhoti . . . Well, he'd offer it up an' it'd make no difference if'n they took a hit or not . . . They were just the same . . . Kinda blissed out for sure, but holding it together: boiling up their rice or their tea, yakking their holy stuff . . . totally unaffected – like we are . . . – Zack passes Rodge a beautifully clean plate, and Rodge swipes it with a deft flick of his dishcloth before handing it off to Lesley, who flips it equally efficiently into the wall-mounted cabinet. Scrub–rinse–swipe–flip – *annagain*. Working with the jaunty assurance of dwarves, Zack begins the humming – soon enough they're all singing the refrain, Hi-ho, hi-ho, it's off to work we go! and tum-tumming the verse, since none of them know the words: Tum-tum-tum-tum, Tum-tum-tum-tum, hi-ho, hi-ho, hi-ho! – Out in the garden they've stopped marching round *annaround*: Claude sits on an upright kitchen chair while Clive is flat out in a deckchair. Claude is indeed perfectly lucid. You've no idea, he says to Clive conspiratorially, quite how vicious the regime is in those big funny farms – I'd got desperate, Dad was still alive then and he thought he'd do the decent paternal thing and cut off my funds – well, what with the sauce, the hop and the bennies, I wound up holding up a liquor store in the Loop with an eggplant in my coat pocket. I know . . . I know . . . Claude waves away the exclamation Clive hasn't made – he only sits, inky-pinky-spidering his fingers up the wall of his belly . . . it was ridiculously stupid – specially since I'd hung a little paper in the same store the week before . . . Anyhoo, with my sheet – VA joints, county lock-ups, private clinics – they ship me off to the state asylum, where, this bein' the Midwest, all the guards are fat and the inmates are thin, brother, you best b'lieve it – how so? 'Cause Admin. are riding that gravy train for all it's worth – siphoning off the food-fuckin'-budget and selling off the meds to whomever, whenever. How'd Curious George here figure it out? I'll tellya: first day in the can THEY PUT ME THROUGH INDUCTION – SAME OLD, SAME OLD, SCATTY CATS SHUFF-LIN' 'BOUT IN THEIR BVDs, SCRATCHIN' THEIR PITS, BUMMING SMOKES, GETTIN' SHAVED AND BUZZ-CUT – SEE, THAT'S THE PUREST FORM OF CONTROL THERE IS, RIGHT? STRIP A MAN OF HIS CLOTHES AND HIS HAIR AND YOU STRIP HIM OF HIS DIGNITY – SPECIALLY IF YOU STAND OVER HIM IN A FUCKIN' UNIFORM. THEN THEY TURN ME OUT IN THE YARD AND I START DOING WHAT I ALWAYS DO IF I'M DE-PRIVED OF MY LIB-ER-TY: CIRCUITS BOODLIE-BAR, BOODLIE-BEE, I BUZZ OVER HERE AND SIP UP SOME WORDS – I BUZZ OVER THERE AN' DROP A FEW OFF . . . BUT PEOPLE AIN'T SAYING TOO MUCH . . . LOTTA 'VOIDANCE. BLUE SKY'S BLACK WITH CHAINLINK AND BARBED WIRE – THOSE CATS, MAN – HEAVIEST I BEEN IN WITH. SURE,

SOME OF 'EM ARE COPPING A PLEA, I GUESS ... BUT I GET FEARED UP, BOODLIE-BAR, BOODLIE-BEE ... LUCKY I KNOW HOW TO KEEP IT WITH MINE – KEEP MOVING, HEAD DOWN. I TELLYA, TIMES LIKE THAT I'M GLAD THERE'S SOMEONE RIDING SHOTGUN ... ANYHOO, THEN I SEE HIM, WHITE AS CASPAR, BACK AGAINST THE WALL, ASS IN THE CRAB GRASS –. Claude stops. The tube train has gone, replaced by Gourevitch, Busner and Lesley, who're ranged by the back door of the house, aghast as they survey the scene. Zack says, I've never heard you so ... well, so lucid, Claude –. Then he stops, because he doesn't wish to antagonise him, and also because ... *all those hours spent on the couch!* return to him, together with the overpowering intimation that sitting behind him was no dispassionate analyst, but ... *the Creep!* nodding and note-taking, with his Japanese trannie *gibbering a tinny commentary.* Join us, why don'tcha, Claude says, pointing to the balding patch at his feet where straggly dandelions and buttercups have been ... *combed over.* I was tellin' Clive here how I met up with my near-namesake, my des-ti-ny – you'd be innerested in that, wouldn'tcha, Roger? I mean, you and I go ways back – but not that far. Wouldn'tcha like to know the truth for once in your cockamamie life, huh? Or p'raps it's more important to you that two doors down is being built right this instant from the smoke it's SUCKIN' OUTTA THE SKY! Gourevitch yelps – and, turning to see what his spongy eyes have sopped up, Busner's also overwhelmed by the squat chimney pot inhaling the blue sky. He stares at the blackened lip of the pot, amazed by the clear air mysteriously condensing into thick, yellowy-grey smoke that instantaneously solidifies to become the stack's brickwork. Crushed by this . . . *weightiness*, Zack throws his eyes back up into the heavens, where they intersect with a . . . *scission of starlings cutting a cirrus ribbon*. Clive says, Oompah-lumpah, stick it up yer jumpah . . . and Claude snaps: Can it! That's enough of that BS – we're done with Hullabaloo-don't-tell-Lulu, we're done with toboggan rides and the surrey-with-the-fuckin'-fringe-on-top! – Roger's fingers grip Zack's arm, his words *blow in my ear*, each hard consonant tickling one of the fine hairs sprouting from . . . *the tragus*: We GoTTa Go To him, man – you GeT iT, righT? Claude . . . he's GoT the ancienT cell wisdom, he's ToTally GroKKing iT Now . . . – Maybe, Zack thinks, but it's so very absurd of Roger to be wearing a cow's skin, sliced up and sewn – 'Sides, Roger stagily whispers, over there . . . and there, and there at the back of the yard by the fence, can't you see them creeping? The iddy things, man, the wild ones? Zack sees next door's . . . *saber-toothed tiger*, smarming around the rusted post propping up the washing line, its fangs bared, its slitted eyes squeezing out . . . *dumb and unknowing hatred*. I think, he says, I get you, Rodge – the iddy things are akin to Jungian archetypes, and they're invading your garden, which is an archetype of safety and . . . normalable-ness . . . Roger titters maniacally and his fingers dig deeper, their pressure synchronised with the tinny emanations from Claude's trannie: Gimme-gimme-gimme dat ding! the pop pops, and Zack thinks: It's referring to the Ding an sich, how profound – and why on earth did I give up using this stuff for analytic sessions? Because it's perfect – taking you to a place where there's almost infinite time with which to contemplate the hidden connections that subsist between every . . . ding! Gimme-gimme-gimme dat –. Lesley swells into view, his face *a van Gogh morass of pus and pore*. He's right, man, he says, the iddy things are . . . like, messengers, man – they've come to tell us that there's no such thing as coincidence . . . That geezer, Hofmann, man, he takes his bike ride, yeah, into the void – 'cause it's all there in the bardo, man, all of it: Switzerland, man, with Heidi and cuckoo clocks and big horns an' shit – all of it free-wheels with him into the void, man . . . And right when this is happening, man, those cats in Arizona or wherever it was, they're cranking up their cyclo-whatsits and pat-a-caking together their big hunk of kryptonite stuff . . . Smart monkeys, yeah – iddy things with their potions and cyclo-motions and bombs . . . But Hofmann, he's the smartest monkey of them all, 'cause he's found the solution, he's got his own cyclo-whatsit, which is a good old bone-shaker, man . . . He's guided by the ancient cell wisdom, man, smeared on his lips: cosmic-fucking-consciousness, man, only a few micro-grammes, man, but they've been sorta fishy-whatsisting ever since –. Your point being? Zack interrupts – not to be cruel, but because he feels dizzy and nauseous, and he needs to *eat more dings!* – My point being, man, that Claude was there, man, he saw the mushroom growing – he saw the people dying, man, and now he's here with us, man, on this merry May morning. He's gotta be here for a reason – I think he's here to tell us something . . . Roger whispers, He's right. – Not knowing if it's they who lead him, or he who guides them, Zack begins edging over the innumerable ridges of the

314

illimitable concrete plain – days later they reach the scraggy lawn and take their places at . . . *the Magus's feet*. Claude says, Shrink cat sat behind a plain metal desk, smokin' away and peckin' at his typewriter, the peckerwood . . . And Claude's trannie says, Gimme-gimme-gimme dat –. I say, Claude, Zack blurts out, be a good chap and turn it off, would you? And to his astonishment Claude obliges, then assumes a German accent: Ach! Are you getting much of ze sex satisfaction? Are you liking of ze big breast or ze small breast? Me sittin' there, nice as in BVDs with the washing instructions printed on the goddamn singlet. I tell the Kraut shrink: If you continue treating me like a child, I just might become strongly attracted to ze very small breast. He says, This is ze typical kind of rrreasoning associated mit your condition. And I say, Doc, you gotta level with me: is it scatziphrenia, scatosis, or the very worst there is, scaphunkiness? Boodlie-bar, boodlie-bee, boodlie-Israel, boodlie-Palestine . . . As Claude scats, Zack's seized by anxiety: Where's Podge? Because if she's feeling anything remotely like this, she'll be in a hell of a state . . . The thought – a *protozoan paisley blob* – floats towards the house, where it metamorphoses into a sway-backed form wrapped up in a tartan rug being manoeuvred through the back door by Eileen, Irene and Maggie. Through the rug's folds a hand emerges to . . . *tuck itself up from within*. The sight is disturbingly reminiscent of *a corpse being carried from a pacified village by General Shoemaker's dog-lovers*, but Zack's pleased the women of the house have *made common cause*. They stagger across on to the grass and dump the bundle, the rug falls open, and there's Podge, curled up in a foetal position, her tartan mini-dress riding up to expose her white-and-pink-polka-dotted knickers. Her eyes are wide open and absorbing the bright sunlight of . . . *this, her first day on earth*. She takes her thumb out of her mouth and says, Goo-goo, ga-ga, I'm a little rainbow baby . . . Claude pokes her in the belly with his steel toecap. Waaa! Waaa! Podge cries, I'm a little rainbow baby and I'm hungry: I want milky! – The other three women have arranged themselves: Maggie seated and already knitting beside Zack on the grass, Eileen next to Lesley, and Irene standing with one hand on the back of Claude's chair, the ends of her velour headscarf trailing . . . *Madame Sosostris*. Well, Rodge drawls, looks like we got us a kinda Déjeuner sur l'herbe scene going here – what say we eat? There's gotta be some of that picnic stuff left over from yesterday . . . It hasn't occurred to Zack before, but now that food has been conceptualised he thinks, Yes! I'm starving – my stomach's a great yawning crystal void screaming out to be filled with ripe fruits and cool draughts of foaming champagne! True, the idea of putting anything in his mouth and chewing it seems . . . *shockingly carnal* . . . but, on the other hand, eating would be normal and natural, eating is *what people do*. Claude says, I tell that Kraut shrink with his Strangelove spectacles: Man, if the gov'ment keeps on stockpiling all those nukes, sooner or later they're gonna use 'em – 'cause that's what kiddies do: they gotta a heap of candy, they eat that candy. – Caught up in the mandibles and the *viridian Cézannery* of a grasshopper clinging to the blades crumpled between his grey-flannel knees, Zack ruminates, How very absurd . . . – not Claude, who for once is making perfect sense – . . . but this jacket makes none! It was sheep's clothing and

316

now's mine, together with the dag-tail round my neck, which has also got away from the flock. He shrugs off the jacket, loosens his tie and reverently addresses the grasshopper: Bertrand Russell, recently deceased, did you know him by any chance? The grasshopper, his tiny pyramidal head vibrating, seems to take this conversational sally in good part . . . *he's thinking about it* . . . but then he's gone . . . *to be in with the in-swarm.* Rodge says, How 'bout it, Claude, you must be hungry too? And Claude says, I wouldn't eat so they put me on suicide watch – nothin' personal. They was waitin' to see me take a shit inna stainless-steel bowl – a shit show, yeah? When the shit comes, after a boodlie-day or boodlie-three, it's so hard I can draw hieroglyphs with it on the cell wall. We-ell, they don't like that one little bit, no siree. They drags me out an' shaves me none too gentle, all the while there's this coloured boy in the corner, he was dancing about and screaming, so I began to sing out too: I wanna go down to Tom Anderson's ca-fé, I wanna hear that Creole jazz band play! The Cadillac, the Red Onion too, the Boogie-Woogie an' the Parc Sans Sou', You can enjoy your-seelf down on Rampart Street! – Irene has returned carrying a tray with tinfoil-wrapped packages on it – Maggie has a rug she flips over their heads so that . . . *We're parachuting!* But everyone lands *right back where they were before*, the rug subsiding between them, one flap re-covering Podge . . . *clever that.* Paper plates are passed round as Claude maintains: I told the Kraut shrink boodlie-Jew, boodlie-A-rab, if it ain't your lot, it'll be the kikes – titty-for-tatty, y'see. The Kraut, he don't wanna know – and he's got the most god-awfulest teeth, don't matter how much he smokes his breath stinks of rot . . . I tell the Kraut shrink: war by '72, you can count on it – but he don't give a shit, and since I'm naked already and not exactly in the mood for any rough stuff from the guards, I lie down on the table and spreadoutski: arms wide like the skinny li'l angel chile I am so's they can fasten the restrai–. Not the tongue! Roger cries, Jesus H. Christ! The last thing you wanna see with a head fulla acid is that ghastly tongue! But Zack looks at the tongue lying on its crinkly tinfoil bed and finds . . . *I don't mind it.* There is, he thinks, an honesty about the tongue – it isn't trying to pretend it's not a body part, unlike the . . . *holy Shippam's beef spread.* Maggie tears a French stick in half and shoves a slice of the tongue into its soft end. Really! she says, passing the roll to Zack, really . . . In the noisy tumult of flesh and crust Zack's still aware of this: Claude's own tongue *flapping on*: They gimme a shot anyway – Stelazine, the Kraut says, only for ze relaxing of your muscles. He's standing right over me, inch of ash on his cigarette, shirt-sleeves rolled up – he gets a square of cloth and lays it kinda gently over my genitals. Haffn't you got ze lubrication? he says, and one of the guards comes up with a big can labelled – get this – Perfection Oil, and the Kraut stands there greasin' up the tube. Man, it's a Rube Goldberg operation this force-feeding, but when he does it – when he puts the tube in – it ain't such a big deal. Actually, it's kinda inneresting feeling: tube worming up my nose, doubling back and slidin' down my gullet. I wanted to say: Hey, why not link up one end of the tube to the other, then you can cut out the middle-madman. Very gutt patientz, the Kraut soothes, ve-ery nize patientz . . . I swear, I woulda cracked up if it weren't for the weirdness of the sensation – the tube kinda throbbing in my nose and my throat, and my belly gettin' all swole, an' me beginning to feel all full up despite the fact that I ain't done no biting or chewing or swallowing . . . Any-hoo, that's all folks – 'cept to say it was that same day I met Eatherly . . . Each is each, Zack thinks, and all is all. The tongue and bread have solidified . . . *You should never get outside anything bigger than your head!* He remembers Mark's milk tooth dangling from a string tied to a doorknob *blood and gristle* . . . He looks up to the starship clouds . . . *boldly going to Harrow-on-the-Hill.* He wishes Lesley would take his multimedia coordinating more seriously . . . *and rig up the record player out here.* They need holy Bach and the sketching blocks and the coloured pencils *I bought so we could make sure set stayed tied to setting.* But it won't stay that way . . . *blood and gristle.* While as for the women – who're all tightly circled around him, *curious and predatory* – he can, he believes, *smell their blood!* All foods associated with popular entertainment smell, he thinks, sexual. He remembers childhood fairgrounds – the pheromone whiffs of candyfloss lusting after frankfurters, beef-burgers horny for popcorn, all of them . . . *smellier than they were tasty.* — He turns to Mark, who's studying the wall-mounted poster intently and says, D'you want some? But his eldest son, who at this stage of his development presents to Busner as a patient *demanding colossal forbearance*, only hums, Nerr-nerr n'n'-nerr-nerr, as his obsessional eyes examine every square inch of the monstrous shark lunging upwards in its bubbly sheath. I said, Busner repeats, d'you want some – some popcorn, or a hotdog? *No response.* According to hidden speakers secreted in the plush-dark recesses of the lobby, Everybody was kung-fu fight-ing! The film, Busner knows, is a big hit – but this Sunday matinee looks to be sparsely attended. And why wouldn't it be? It's four days into the new year and there are smears of snow on the ground. Any family with the slightest cohesion will've soaped the runners on the sleigh dug out from the back of the garage and gone up on the Heath to slither a few yards before going to ground on last autumn's churned leaves . . . *but not mine.* — Standing at the front door of the flats, Busner had kicked the slush from his shoes and waited to be buzzed in. Instead, Miriam came out and said, Mark'll be a few minutes, he's putting on his shoes. They stood there in the visible expir-ation . . . *of all our hopes and dreams.* No Danny or Oscar? Busner had asked, although what he'd really wanted to demand was, Have you got that shloomp Shlomo in there – is that why you're not letting me in? *Shloomp . . . Shlomo . . . Shloompo?* She touched her new hair-do, short and severe to accompany her incisive return to medical practice . . . *that Doctor Busner, she certainly seems to cut through the red tape* . . . and said, No, Zack, it's an A, it'll be far too gory for them. He had cried out: *Unlike this world, with its throat gored by Carlos the Jackal!* – but heard himself saying, Oh, c'mon Miriam, they're only guidelines, the certs, no one pays any attention to them – and our little ones are too smart to be taken in by a rubber shark . . . – She'd lost weight, he supposed, although it was difficult to tell: her baggy brown corduroy dress was so rigid. She appraised him in turn – and Busner understood he was a rubber shark she was no longer taken in by. She'd stopped swimming around in his delusional sea and had headed for dry land . . . *and Shlomo,* the quiet cabinet-maker with his . . . *exquisite joinery*. Could he blame her? It was idiotic, this caveman jealousy – idiotic and it . . . *doesn't add up*: her single lover and his multiple ones. Miriam had sighed: I'd've thought by now, Zack, that you'd've put all this let-it-all-hang-out stuff behind you – you can see the negative effect it's had on Mark . . . — *Well . . . Mark . . . Yes . . .* There is, Zack belatedly concedes, something off-kilter about the boy. Now he's touching the Perspex covering the shark's gaping jaws, and his nerr-nerr-humming sheers away into: Denticleth, Dad, thath what they're called – thath what they're thkin ith, they're like thousandth and thousandth of little teeth, and each of them hath a tharp leading edge so'th to reducth the drag . . . Zack thinks, No wonder he's so shy and unsociable, with that clumsy brace and the acne already blossoming on his cheeks. He asks again: Do you want some popcorn – or some sweets, Opal Fruits, Maltesers? Mark turns to face him and lisps through steely teeth: Tharkthkin thuiths – that'th what they're wearing, Dad, they're own tharkthkin thuiths. Painfully conscious of his own down-at-heel and unseasonable safari one, Zack's propelled towards the refreshments counter, where he buys a box of Maltesers . . . *all for me*. – When they get upstairs the girl who tears their tickets waves her torch beam at the steep stairs down to the front of the circle, then abandons them. A few people are slumped in the gloom, while on screen there's more darkness and a man in shiny black overalls creeping through it to deliver a box of chocolates to a lady who's never seen . . . *presumably because she's obese*. – It's Mark's choice, the film. Zack's time with his sons is circumscribed – by the ward round *annaround* . . . by other obligations, by the hateful fact that . . . *pro tem* he's living back at Redington Road. He'd have preferred to do something . . . *a little more active* – besides, he knows it's no healthy, thrill-seeking urge that's brought them here to the beaches of Amity Island, to the strange lambency of a night-time gathering . . . *shot in broad daylight*. The chugging orchestra rouses his sluggish heartbeat – his fingertips chase the last few melting balls into the corner of the box, his mouth is already coated with the malty putrefaction . . . *of previous victims*. The camera's passionless eye noses over the seabed, sniffing at a scuttling crab, a weed-frilled rock, a slimy tyre – rejecting them in turn with still more frigid indifference. All the while Mark maintains a low monotologue: They don't have no boneth, Dad, juth cartilage tho there'th no fothils – thientithts don't really know that much about tharks, tho I hope the film doethn't make too many thtupid mithtaketh . . . Was it, Zack queries, always thus? He reaches into the tea chest of memory, throwing aside perished leather portfolios and soggy souvenir calendars in search of scallop-edged photographs picturing the truth about his eldest son: *Was he always like this?* . . . Ith meant to be a Great White, Dad, 'though they aren't actually found that far north. Thtill, the man who wrote the book thaid he wath inthpired by thome thark attackth in New Jerthey – two thwimmerth were killed by a Great White, but that wath agetth ago . . . Zack sees Mark *agetth ago*, a quiet little boy preoccupied by arranging things: lining up his toy cars first in order of size, and then by colour. When he was a bit older it was categorising – he would laboriously glue into being Airfix planes and hold them against the silhouettes of

322

the real things on the identification poster he'd put up on his bed-room wall. Zack remembers the perfect skin of his son's nimble fingers scaled with dried rubber cement, remembers thinking *at the time* that this was an occult practice: that the precise alignment of angles and vertices corresponded in the boy's mind with much vaster phenomena over which he was *exerting control* . . . Thark'th have got a thpethial thythtem for thtaying buoyant – ith not like other fith – they've got thpethial oil in their liverth . . . The sea splashing against the surfacing lens is, Zack conjectures, a deliber-ate device intended to remind viewers' *this is only a film*. At the same time a bell in a buoy *tolls for thee and all the others*: the Lebanese, the Angolans – the nameless hordes of brown and black to whom, he thinks, I cannot possibly extend my already flimsy sympathy . . . *not gold but dross leaf.* – The boy and the girl have skinny-dipped into the chilly water, and, although he turns back to the beach after a few strokes, she goes on. Zack is . . . *at one* with the wavelets licking her feet, calves and thighs, he tastes the salt on her breasts and nuzzles at her gritty pubic hair. He knows what'll happen to her . . . *sexy sea-slut* that she is – and when those feet up-end and she dances jerkily – a marionette manipulated by a vast, unseen and cartila-ginous hand. – Mark . . . *Frank Boughs*: They think there'th at leatht five different jaw movementh involved in the Great White'th attack – the top teeth're thmooth, but the bottom oneth're therrated, tho the bottom oneth're the forkth and the top oneth're the kniveth . . . — Miriam had said: We've nobody to compare him with – he's simply a picky eater. But, so far as his father could tell, Mark didn't pick at all . . . *he arranged*: each perfectly knife-shaped dollop of mashed potato punctuated by a sentinel fish finger – carrot discs ranged in order of their circumference. Mark's small face was *contented in its concentration*, while on the other side of the kitchen table his little brother observed *no such protocols* – spearing the fish fingers *with hith fork* . . . slashing them to pieces . . . *with hith knife*. — The deputy stands beneath the blanched sky of an Atlantic dawn, then hunkers down to dabble in the sand. A crab disdains the girl's ravaged corpse – a moralising crustacean, Zack thinks, it smells the intercourse that dismembered her . . . And still Mark persists: They have a nithitating membrane in their eyeth, Dad, like catth, tho they thine – and the Great Whiteth, their eyeth can thwivel inthide their headth. The betht way to think about what it'th like when they attack . . . *Can there be a best way?* . . . ith that ith like a dog thaking a thtick from thide to thide – you remember when Othcar uthed to do that? Is it, Zack muses, in any sense normal for a thirteen-year-old boy to carry on so? Moreover, he wouldn't have put it past his son, who's *well organised*, to've deliberately chosen this cavernous cinema, with only a few goers stuck in its . . . *well-sprung gums*, so he'd be able to go on ladling out this bloody slop of marine biological facts . . . *Othcar?* For a moment he thinks Mark's referring to his littlest brother, but now he realises he means the old family dog he was named for. — It's a perfectly acceptable name, Miriam had said, and if it makes them feel happier about the new arrival then so much the better . . . Zack has an image of her saying this, standing by the sink in the Highgate flat . . . *five years ago!* the *B-bomb of her breasts and belly* . . . taut enough . . . *to be punctured!* by the toothpick fuse she was forcing into the *tharkthkin* of an avocado stone. – Charlie, Chief Brody says, take me out to those kids . . . The tension of the last few years bites into Zack's back and shoulders. The five of us were, he thinks, on the surface of it perfectly happy, messing about with our rubber rings and our beach balls, but all the time there was a predatory dread circling us and circling us again – a dread that homed in accompanied by . . . *a grisly ostinato: thrrrum-thrum, thrrrum-thrum* . . . a dread that was . . . *my own destructiveness*! You're beginning to prune, Missus Brody says to the boy who's been retrieved from the water – and Zack thinks: Yes, I was beginning to prune, so saturated had I become by that unfamiliar element – *nuclear domesticity*. I felt like Patty Hearst: under the gun held by a kidnapper *I couldn't help but love* . . . — Mark says, Great Whiteth prefer to attack blind, y'know, they've all thorts of thpecial thpooky capabilitieth . . . Bar *the lithping* . . . Zack supposes he should take some pride in Mark's own . . . *spooky capabilities* . . . They thenth thingth at a dithtanth by generating their own electrical field – a Great White ith a complicated weaponth thythtem with radar, thonar, buoyanthy control, the only thing they don't have that Polarith thubmarineth do ith torpedoeth, 'cauth they're the torpedo . . . Pipit! Pipit! the distraught mother cries, and Zack is already sickened by her one-piece bathing suit, by the way it *bites off her legs at the groin*. Then: *She's started a heat wave, by makin' her seat wave!* The stampede for the beach is through a densening delirium of shouts and splashes that only seconds before . . . *were antic!* Pipit! Pipit! – The dog's stick floats on the surface, while somewhere down below Pipit's . . . *being thaken from thide to thide* . . . Zack is overwhelmed by all the sweetly cruddy architecture of his own gullet . . . *Crisp-to-Crunch – More to Munch!* as Chief Brody lifts his binoculars and together . . . *we rush down their tunnels*, so that the horizon wraps around . . . *our fearful faces*, and the dorsal fin rears . . . *into our mouths!* Zack Busner watches as the long brassy insets either side of the cinema's screen, the stylised laurels over the proscenium, and all the other faded Deco detailing is . . . *eaten up* by a baby-blue May sky — there's *no way* . . . he'll be able to swallow the mouthful of bread and tongue. Wine? Lesley lifts the Chianti bottle by its plaited straw . . . *noose*, and Zack thinks, What an excellent fellow, anticipating my needs like that. – But the *Tiber* . . . is . . . *bloody*, and he only just manages to choke it down, spluttering. Wiping his *gory mouth* on his sleeve, Zack remarks, Smashing picnic, Maggie. He's delighted to've managed this pleasantry, given that Maggie's answering smile, and Eileen's crazy grin, and Irene's tentative grimace, and Podge's self-indulgent moue are all *wheeling about me* . . . and . . . *moaning* as the wind . . . *sheers through their teeth!* – Roger calls from a long way away: I'm a little worried about Chris, Zack . . . and Zack sees ranged before him *in mid-air!* all the letters Jean-Claude, his French pen-pal, ever sent him – assiduous exercises in schoolboy English: *I am haved the time for to playing rugby now* . . . Letters Zack scanned once before hiding them away in the bottom of his tuck box – letters he never replied to . . . *yet still they kept on coming!* – Claude says, I wrote every day when I was at summer camp, kinda witty letters, I thought, with cartoons of the counsellors on them – when Gertie began running a high fever and they realised it was polio, they packed all the other kids off toot-sweet, paid off the counsellors too. When Ma arrived there was just this one guy who'd been conscientious enough to remain behind – his name was Mister Dalcroze, but we called him Turnip-Head, and I'd drawn him with weedy threads of hair growing outta his big bald white head, and she got down from the cab and said, You must be Mister Dalcroze. After that she nursed Gertie night and day, massaging his legs, while I went swimming and canoeing by myself – best summer camp I ever attended. She pulled him through, though – he had to wear a leg brace, but he never had any of those operations they did back then, which were all phoney-baloney anyway . . . HE CAN READ MY MIND! Zack thinks, looking fearfully at Claude, enthroned on his kitchen chair . . . *with weedy threads of hair growing out of his mad white head! He can read my mind – and very soon now he's going to TELL ME WHAT TO DO!* – I tellya, Claude says, what we should do – we should all go back inside, 'cause I don't b'lieve the Kid oughta be left alone at a time like this – and you, John – he points his bread sceptre at Lesley – you should organise some sounds, man, 'cause I'll need a strong rhythm to accompany the deal of talking I've still to do: how I met my nemesis, I-fifty-eight, and the Godly integral and the Satanic differential. It's time too you found out why de massa had de muff-tash on he face – most of all, why we threw him in de coal hole . . . Zack tears his eyes away from Claude and hurls them straight into Roger's earnest ones. Never, he thinks, have I seen such loving complicity in another's gaze. He knows I know this, and he knows I know he knows, and he knows how I know he knows I know, and yet . . . still . . . this infinite regression is falling

in between us . . . the rug's thick hawsers of rusty wool are parting . . . obscenely fraying . . . As Zack goggles, the magnifying
squares of Stuart tartan ripple away into the seething grass of the
railway embankment, which, incorporating this motion, body it
forth into the all-encompassing geometry of suburbia, its *life-squares*
and *death-roundabouts*, *reverberating triangles* and *hushed cul-de-
sacs* . . . C'mon, man, Rodge says, easy now – he reaches out a hand.
Phantasy, Zack ponders, as he looks deep into Rodge's kindly eyes,
may become a closed enclave – the dissociated unconscious will . . .
fail to develop. But that's not what's happening here – we're drawing
closer and closer to the essence of things . . . to the very Logos of
experience –. Ow! Owowowowow! His cry is loud – the pain searing. His head snaps back – he clutches at his cheek. Whassup?
Rodge asks, and, pointing to the flat roof above the back bedroom, Zack groans, Up there . . . it's Shoemaker! Zack can see the
general perfectly clearly – he's silhouetted against the roof tiles, his
olive-drab legs spread, his cap's leather peak and the silver insignia
on his shoulders catching the sunlight as he rears back, yanking
the fishing rod. – The fish-hook! Zack yowls as Shoemaker reels
him in towards the back door. It's in my bloody mouth! Claude
catches up with them and, putting his arm round Zack's shoulders,
asks, Where is it, kiddo? Show me. Zack points to his grossly . . .
salient cheek, and Claude puts his nimble fingers into Zack's mouth
and, with a neat twist, removes the savage barb . . . *none of us can
see!* You are my friend, Claude, aren't you? Zack demands, and
Claude says, Sure I am, but I ain't so confident about them . . . They
look back at the overgrown garden: Clive has usurped Claude's

throne – Maggie taken the deckchair. Podge lies on the rug, kicking her bare white legs in the air. She sings: I can see a rain-bow, Be a rain-bow, You can be a rain-bow too! *Vacuum abhors a nature* . . . the hilarity hisses into Zack – he feels his *space-hopper head* swelling dangerously. Yeah, well, he says, Podge . . . she's hors de combat, isn't she. Lesley says, Whore's too much, man – she's just a liberated chick . . . And the space-hopper . . . *that's me* is punctured: Zack sees the orange rubber afterbirth lying on the floor of the bathroom in 119 . . . *covered in a fine sifting of talcum powder* – he senses evil gurgling up from the plugholes . . . *slime of soap and shed hair.* – Claude leads the way into the kitchen, *scoping it out* through the triangular slot in his tin opener. The kitchen, Zack realises, is a cave cluttered with objects of a profound uselessness: a white-enamelled cabinet you can light four small fires on, a second one full of stupidly cooled air, and beside this a steely hull that can be . . . *filled from within.* He sees the film of grease on pots and pans – the scuzz pimpling the window and the slop carpeting the lino. The world is *this skin*: a dirty dermis a fraction of an inch thick *puckering about* mere phenomenal things. Revolted, Zack tightens his hold on Claude and Roger, struggling also to hang on to this insight – brought back from previous trips . . . *through the rainbow door* – that: *Love is the fundamental and the primary cosmic fact.* It's hard, though, because ever since Lesley said the bad thing about poor Podge his spots have swelled, leaking a mucous substance, the *love-juice* . . . of all those chicks he's . . . *liberated with his penis.* – Kit's rescue party reaches the hallway. The early-afternoon sun *machine-guns photons* through the transom, hitting dust motes that . . . *explode into a parallel universe*, where jazzy lino and blizzarding wallpaper . . . *are the fabric of space-time.* Awed, Zack whispers to Claude, Each is each, and Claude responds, All is all. Profoundly grateful for this cosmic understanding – although simultaneously aware that the conceptual basis of the language expressing it is wholly redundant – Zack captures a handful of stardust and holds it out . . . *shimmering on my palm* . . . to his new mentor. You see, he emphasises. I see, Claude raps back, that some shit has walked away with my censoring pen – you can't leave anything lying round in this lousy tub for five minutes without some goldbricking louse lifting it! Impetuously he kicks open the door to the living room and shouts at the Kid's prone form, Didja take my pen? Didja? 'Cause the second post might come any sec', and I don't wanna be responsible for some shave-tail getting a green-fuckin'-banana –. He stops. The rescue party have entered the room behind him and now they stand gawping. It isn't the Kid they're fixated on, but the man who's slumped against the wall by the door. His suit trousers have risen up – hairless calves parenthesise a plate *coagulated* . . . with last night's ketchup and . . . *cauterised* by today's cigarette ends. The man's face – which is long, and has fine features *graven by suffering*, is being . . . *held out to us*, cupped in his open hands. All the light pouring through the bow window is concentrated on this man's face, bestowing *an unearthly radiance!* Zack wine-burps, Oh – but Roger says, Mister Lincoln, right? So sorry, we kinda forgot you were here, it's been – he pinches the *foreskin* of his rollneck – quite a morning. – Michael, Michael says, please call me Michael. He looks from one pair of bug-eyes to the next, then continues: I hardly think formalities are called for, given the state you're all in – given the state Christopher is in. – Put like this – calmly and imbued with all his therapeutic experience – Michael's words have an odd effect, at once setting the tripping residents at ease – and galvanising them. We gotta get things mellower in here, Gourevitch says – and Busner echoes him: Mellower, yes, mellower would be good – yellower too. Gourevitch strides to the window and pulls the curtains half shut. Busner, a queer little moue playing about his plump lips, pushes the ugly sofa against the wall, then tink-tonks a pile of dirty crocks and empty beer tins together in the middle of the room. Christopher remains face down on the mattress, his mumbled self-negation . . . I, not-I, I, not-I, I, not-I . . . rumbling around the room. When Busner has assembled his rubbish heap, he stands before it, seemingly believing that . . . *Sufficient unto the day is the evil thereof.* Michael finds the psychiatrist . . . *really rather repellent*, what with his womanish hips, gingerish hair and fleshy Semitic features. Worse is the lank-haired and spotty fellow wearing a leather waistcoat . . . *like Trampas in The Virginian* . . . whom Busner now directs high-handedly to: Be a good chap and sort out some music, will you, John? I think if we can only play the right sort of music, it might sort of . . . bring Kit back . . . Put his feet on the ground. The one called John exits the room and returns a few moments later bearing a single stereo speaker cabinet that he places at Busner's feet. What d'you reckon, Zack, he says, a little Jimi, axis bold as – or p'raps some doors . . . of, y'know, perception? But the psychiatrist mutters distractedly, Oh, a little, um, heavy all that stuff, John – if you look up in my room you'll see a few LPs

331

by the bedside table . . . classical ones – take your pick, they're all pretty . . . classical – my vote's for old J. S. . . . – Michael watches the spider's leg of his second hand tickle the dial. Three minutes pass until the oddwobbly sound globules of Ich ruf' zu Dir, Herr Jesu Christ begin floating up to the fire-resistant ceiling tiles . . . *they burst – showering us in melancholy and . . . mystery* . . . John joins the other two, who are collapsed on the sofa facing him. Michael thinks again of that all-night vigil in Winchester Cathedral – the sharp chill of the stone flags . . . *eating into my vitals* . . . *Bite into my heart, three person'd God! Consume me!* is what he'd wanted to happen – but there'd been none of that . . . *because I'm too unsavoury, even for Him.* Christopher's moaning is now *counterpointed* by thrashing about, as his arms and legs *swim in the elemental prelude.* I must, Michael berates himself, pull myself together and get this man Busner – no matter how intoxicated he may be – to face up to his responsibilities . . . – But Michael remains swamped in the music, staring through its warm coloratura to where, at the back of the room, he notices something, or . . . *someone, bobbing about in it*: Claude, who's been there the entire time, leaning against the Indian wall hanging by the dormant lump of the television. Claude is there, apparently lost in thought, and *NOT SAYING A WORD!* Zack pans from the Creep's narrowed eyes to Roger's enlarged ones, beaming this message: *HAVE YOU NOTICED?* Roger beams back: *I HAVE! I HAVE!* Zack thinks quietly: On the brink of something, we are – a breakthrough of some kind . . . He'd like to pursue this butterfly insight further as it flits from the sofa's arm to the Creep's baggy khaki knee, to the television aerial's *robotic antlers, to* . . . But the Kid's face rises up . . . *dripping* from the blue-and-white ticking and he says *TO ME AND ME ALONE!* I'm inside a spire and it's made of mouths . . . and the mouths're all open, and the mouths're all screaming . . . d'you know what they're screaming? They're screaming nothing – over and over again: nothing, no-thing . . . The Kid's frighteningly blanched face submerges and his whimpering resumes, No-thing, no-thing, no-thing . . . A snick! A yawp! an agonised slide as the needle, having hit some obstruction, *surfs across the vinyl peaks* before dropping into exactly the same trough, compelling Michael to a prayer: *I call to thee* . . . which turns into a curse: *O Lord Christ!* Transfixed, he watches as Claude swats a hole in the misty sound and stretches out his hand: The five peninsular fingers of Hee-ro-sheema! he intones liturgically, Where the T-shaped bridge marked the spot they aimed at. – Michael croaks, Who . . . Who are you? And Claude flings back at him, Who're YOU, the Archangel Michael, p'raps, come to smite us all with your sword of righteousness? Michael winces, but pushes on: No, I'm determined to have an answer from you, my man: who are you? Because I'm bloody well certain you aren't who you claim to be – Doctor Gourevitch here says you were the target-spotter for the Enola Gay, but I was one of the British observers, and I never heard of any Evenrude flying with the 509th. That's what you said, isn't it, Gourevitch, you said Claude here was on the A-bomb mission? – From a long way away, pan-piping over the bluing recession of successive horizons, which are at once those seen during his childhood vacations in Vermont and the fleshy contours of a new and fantastical *organ*, Roger hears the

Englishman's question – however, to answer it is utterly impossible, because he's standing – together with John and Zack – beneath the flying buttresses supporting the roof of the Kid's mouth, looking up at the great arch of his teeth. Their feet are buried in the squishy pile of papillae on the Kid's tongue – a tongue that rises and falls as the annihilating clamour fills their tiny ears: No-thing, no-thing, no-thing . . . Claude says, I'm Lieutenant Claude Evenrude, retired, of the United States Army Air Force. – Evenrude. Michael mulls it over – syllables it out, Ev-en-rude, Claude, then expostulates: I've got it! There was a Claude Ea-ther-ly on the mission, and he was the target-spotter. A Texan chap – a hard-drinker, a gambler – a big, raw-boned fellow, looked nothing like you . . . What you people called a hot-shot pilot, but he went on to become something of an alcoholic, I believe . . . in and out of asylums – I barely spoke to him when we were on Tinian, but he wrote to me later – in the fifties. He'd become a sort of peacenik – speaking out against the bomb. Not altogether advisable, given the climate at the time. He stops, regarding Claude with dismay: You don't mean to say you're . . . you're impersonating him? – A SNICK, a YAWP and an agonised slide as the needle, having hit the obstruction, surfs again across the vinyl peaks before dropping into exactly the same trough. The music wells up and Claude . . . *floats towards me*: I am, he reiterates, Lieutenant Claude Evenrude, retired, of the United States Army Air Force. I met Claude Eatherly in 1957 in the Clearwater Hospital for the criminally insane in Rosemont, Illinois. He wasn't a happy man – his conscience burdened him. I wasn't happy either: the war had dumped an ashcan on me – the Torpex was still burning in my hair . . . on my skin . . . Claude's hands go to his hair, divert to his necklace, he toys with this, gathering bear claw and trannie, Tibetan amulet and tin opener, into the scallop shell as he perseveres: You got it about right there – Eatherly had been writing to peace campaigners. He'd invitations to visit with them here in Europe and in Japan, but he was screwed – he'd been convicted for a stick-up . . . Claude edges forward and kneels – Michael wonders what's going to happen . . . *some violence* he suspects, yet he's power-less to evade it. Close to, Claude's face can be witnessed in all its haggard splendour: lucidity has smoothed the careworn wrinkles. Shorn of his madness he's . . . *a kindly-looking man*, sheep-faced, and with the high colour of *a sherry-tippling vicar*. Claude says, We – and it was a completely mutual decision – thought it might be advantageous to both of us if I were to, uh, avail myself of these opportunities in his stead . . . Claude's diction is professorial and *compelling*. The shrapnel buried in Michael's shoulder . . . *goads me*: That's a hell of a bloody coincidence, isn't it – you and him, with almost identical names, both flyers, both in the same hospital. D'you really expect me to believe any of this balderdash? – A snap, a quack and a despairing wail as the needle, having hit some obstruction, aquaplanes across the soundsea, then tips over into the same evanescent dip. Claude says, Ich ruf' zu Dir, Herr Jesu Christ . . . We went to Germany before the war, y'know, my father and I . . . In many ways Pop was an unspeakable vulgarian, but he knew his music. It was around '31, I guess – we went on the Nord-deutscher Lloyd Line, which sailed from a pier on the North River . . . In Bremen we saw Parsifal – Pop called it a Ludwigian extravaganza . . . The singing was strong, I guess – but to me the thing was interminable, and the staging cheesy beyond belief: the goofy fool scaled the cardboard walls of Klingsor's castle, then shot a cardboard swan with an arrow on a goddamn string – I could see the string. Then, when he opened his fat Kraut mouth to sing about it, there was this one gold tooth in there catching the spotlight and sending these gleams bouncing all over the auditorium . . . Claude falls silent . . . Leastways, that's the way I remember it – 'though the important thing to hold on to is . . . the sea. Pop had weathered the crash just dandy. No perspicacity on his part: the trust had been locked down solid, bolted to the deck . . . Anyway, he splashed out on a stateroom – every morning I opened the blinds and saw the wide Atlantic – all of it in constant motion, and yet . . . at the same time . . . totally still. – Claude's advancement has been imperceptible – minute knee-shuffles, subtle shoulder-hunchings and torso-curlings – but he's now arrived beside Michael, his back to the wall, his legs outstretched, and he inquires – much as any idler would of his fellow – How's about you – you being here . . . and now. I mean, it's a heck of a stretch, ain't it? You being, so to speak, the perpetrator, and me the victim – you flying high, the avenging Archangel Michael, and me down there in the burning water with all the screaming skin angels . . . Wh-What're you saying? Michael chokes out. What d'you know about the sk-skin angels? Claude clears his throat: a sharp glottal pop! followed by a seagull squawk as the needle – having encountered some obstruction – rips through the *euphonious grooviness* . . . and drops, once more, into . . . the Kid's mouth, the saliva-streaked soft palate and softer cheeks of which are lined with gallery upon gallery of more mouths, mouths receding further and further into the dark gullet – mouths opened so wide their jaws dislocate with a vile crepitating sound as they scream this unspeakable repudiation: NO-THING! NO-THING! NO-THING! to no one and . . . *everyone.* Jumbled up together in the *scuppers* behind the Kid's front teeth, Zack somehow un- tangles himself from the flailing of Roger and Lesley. Th-This is abso-so-so-lutely d-dreadful, he manages to splutter. I-I m-must do s-something – I've g-got s-some M-Mogadon upstairs, if I c-can only g-get there! – Such is the mouthy howl and the screechy vibration of all these epiglottises that Zack assumes he must've shouted aloud, but beside him on the sofa, his face corpse-grey and sweaty, Roger gives no indication of . . . *having heard me at all!* The effort of speaking effected this: the Kid has *vomited us out,* and the tempest lulls – the lino, the wallpaper, the ceiling tiles, all still drip and pulse menacingly . . . *but it's recognisably a room,* while the men hunched against the wall opposite him . . . *are men – not gargoyles or griffins.* Zack can even hear one of them say to the other: We-ell, I guess you know all about the U-S-S Indianapolis, then. — Zack likes to believe that they'd been not unlike this family: existing in the warm pools of warm light cast by tabletop lamps, Miriam in the kitchen merrily adding herbs to a toothsome chicken casserole, a bottle of wine opened to breathe, while he and Mark's moment of affecting intimacy is caught in the lens of an all-seeing camera. He does *just about* recall this sort of thing: peek-a-boo, small fingers copying much larger ones as they mesh and part. Zack *thinksalong* with the soundtrack: *This is the church, this is the steeple,*

Open the roof and there are the –. But no – no simple Hollywood juggernaut such as this, set up to travel in one direction *ineluctably* can convey all the myriad complexities of family life, the treacherous crosscurrents of ambivalences within ambiguities – the loving hatefulness and the *hateful love.* Zack chews on his Malteser cud as Chief Brody solicits a kiss from his son: Why is it we were all so taken by the Pushmi-pullyu? But of course he can supply the answer himself: they were being brought up by one – and dragged down at the same time. – On the spot-lit dock, with the harbour waters *smacking their cold lips,* cuddly Hooper chats into his Dictaphone: Start in the alimentary canal . . . He saws down the fish's belly with a large, serrated knife . . . Open the digestive tract –. Out it all falls in a gush of milky bile: *trayf, the rotten flesh torn by our much-trumpeted carnality* . . . Zack sneaks a sideways look at Mark's steel-rimmed overbite – now that the film's gathering pace he has, at last, fallen silent. He's a strange child, no doubt about that – yet I must grant him his autonomy, surely . . . not presume that his strangeness is entirely my responsibility. We all went a little too far in that direction . . . Still . . . Zack maunders on . . . Have I been a Chief Brody to him, running scared, exercising a febrile authority: I can do anything, I'm the Chief of Police? Or have I been a Hooper, a rich-boy scientific hobbyist, whose forensic skills amount to nothing much besides an expensive motor-launch kitted out with a closed-circuit television system and observational cameras fore and aft? Hooper, like me, has what he imagines to be a nice line in deflating witticisms – *It's only an island if you look at it from the sea* – but really, what can he know, this eternal and wispily bearded boy?

Because, by the same token, *It's only a family if you look at it from the great orphanage of the ocean* . . . A sea Hooper slips into in his skin-diving suit. The fish-finder's electronic whistle modulates to a submarine ultrasonic whine. The expensive motor-launch floats on its pool of emerald light – the fishing boat floats some way off . . . *in proletarian gloom.* Strange, Zack thinks, how easy it is to convey there's no one on board: the absence of any lights, the rocking hull, the crazily swinging tiller – the succession of images invites the most passive viewer to conjecture *some sort of cosmic editor integrating space and time.* Hooper floats in his weightless playground, bubbles boiling round his cyclopean head. He spies a jagged hole in the boat's hull, and as he froggles towards it . . . *We know – we just know* . . . something awful is going to happen. *The shark's inside the boat! The killer's inside the house!* — The sickening abruptness with which the Creep's head tumbles into focus – his jaundiced sclera showing, his yellow teeth bared – pushes Zack to the brink: he hears his own death rattle, his arms flail – and there's the Bach . . . *worse than any bite!* The prelude to his own interment, to . . . *no-thing* . . . because every few minutes . . . *or hours* . . . instead of it fading away there're fingernails *scratching the vinyl blackboard,* until, with diabolic accuracy, the needle finds the same vein of sound . . . *again!* – Zack turns to Lesley, who, he's appalled to discover, is sitting beside him, quite blasé, and licking a cigarette paper that he carefully applies to two others that *he stuck together earlier.* I-can't-stand-this, Zack gasps, I think I'm going out of my mind. Lesley's face is *a seething mass of corruption,* riddled with pores out of which hundreds of laughing maggots are . . . *questing* . . . He says:

Youuuuuu're peeeeeaaaaaking, maaaaan, gooooooo towaaaaards the whiiiiite liiiight. But there is no white light, only the mutating face of the Creep, who's channelling another . . . *spirit* . . . although none of the personae Zack has heard before. This is a calm, deliberate entity, whose words *gnaw me to the bone*: I don't find this an especially strange coincidence, Claude tells the Kid's careworn guardian, who's tapping his tired teeth with his pipe stem. 'Cause you gotta 'preciate – my life has been organised by a far bigger and more mysterious coincidence. In point of fact, I believe what we've got here is a deeeeep leeeeeveeeeel asssignaaatioooon –. Enough! Zack believes he's cried – at least he's on his feet, and from this fresh vantage the familiar, shabby surroundings, and the recognisably human forms scattered around them, are sufficient to suspend his all-devouring disbelief: There might be . . . he dares to think . . . a real world out there, with trees and birds and bird-feeders and clouds shaped like . . . bird-feeders . . . *it's no good!* The wonky edifice wobbles, buckles and collapses in the asbestos dust of . . . *implausicosis!* Gasping for breath, he reaches for the end of his tie, only to find that . . . *it's not there!* Claude looks blithely at him and says, I was telling Mister Lincoln here about my war record – you might find it interesting as well, Doc-tor Busner. I know you've always had your doubts about me, now's the right time to set the record straight. *Set the record straight – that's it!* Zack blunders from the room, and follows the twisted flex through the labyrinth of hall and kitchen to the back bedroom, where he surprises the stereo turntable and . . . *twists its arm!* – In the living room Michael is calmly saying, I confess, I didn't know that, I'd always assumed that the fissionable material was flown into Tinian by the 509th Composite itself. Claude answers him, equally pacific: Sure, the main hunk of it was – but remember, Little Boy was a gun-assembly weapon, so there had to be two discrete pieces of 235: the bigger bit sat on top of the block, and the bullet piece was fired down the barrel, so's to achieve the super-critical mass. The Indy brung the bullet – the bomb casing too, which had been semi-assembled back at Los Alamos. You seem – Michael selects his words judiciously – to know an awful lot about it – were you an engineer yourself? Me? Claude laughs. Lord, no! I was in logistics – basically a glorified shipping clerk, making sure stuff was freighted here and there all over the Pacific theatre. Only planes I got to fly in were C-47 transports – closest I got to a Silver B was helping out on a training film when I was stationed at Wright-Patterson. Thing is – Claude opens and closes the tin opener's corkscrew attachment as he speaks – we all played our own small part, didn't we? Me, I was stationed on Guam, getting blasted with torpedo juice and driven crazy by the heat and the roaches. My boss, Colonel Midgely, was an understanding fellow . . . When a wire came requesting a super-heavy bomb hoist for the 509th, I located one on Midway – they were using it to lift diesel turbines. Midgely let me hitch a ride to Tinian to make sure they got it. Sure, I'd no notion what they were gonna use this thing for, but that doesn't alter the reality: I was one of the guys stood in line to feed it to Missus Tibbets, to put Little Boy in his mom's tummy – I helped as much as those poor swabs on the Indy – hell, most of 'em didn't know where they were, let alone what they were doing. When I went aboard they were still shooting the breeze 'bout the record they'd set on the cruise from Frisco to Hawaii – that or sobbing over the green bananas mailed 'em by Little Miss Droopy-drawers back home. Me, I figured I was only along for the short passage to Guam, but when I got there Midgely said, Go on to Leyte, there's some LCTs there I want you to take a look at. That Midgely, he made his own fuckin' weather – been a big-shot corporation lawyer before the war, and he'd already figured the way to get cured. He cleaned up buying all this shit – the LCTs, the planes, the Quonsets, soon as the war was over they started bulldozing this stuff into the sea or blowing it up, but Midgely used his position to find buyers all over – the Philippines, China, Vietnam too . . . In the back bedroom Zack stares at the wall hanging, captivated by row upon row of Bodhisattvas, cross-legged and with seraphic expressions on their baby faces. Oscar, who's lying on his side on top of the wonky pile of mattresses, turns his wounded muzzle towards Zack and says, You're not supposed to mess with their religion . . . Lost in the curdled depths of the Labrador's mild-brown eyes, Zack isn't shocked by this hallucination, instead rather admires the dog's American accent . . . *better than mine* . . . and his up-to-the-minute grasp on what's transpiring along High-way One . . . *and across the Mekong River.* The Bodhisattvas *fly through the prana* as the wall hangings waver, and . . . *jungly modalities shift.* Oscar's head falls back on the pillow. There are voices out in the garden – and presumably bodies associated with them – but to talk with these *earthlings* would be a terrible risk: he fears their jackal mouths and hippo noses . . . *it isn't safe here*, he must get upstairs . . . *to the bathroom*, where he keeps sleepers in his spongebag. – It takes Busner a long time to get there: dynasties of insect people arise and fall on every step of the stairs. He kneels down to observe them as they build their dust-devil pyramids in alignment with the mystical marks left by the carpet tacks and stair rails of earlier civilisations. On the very apex of their fluffy edifices they sacrifice mite captives, sending their scented screams up in smoke . . . *as they sing their savage hymns.* At last he stumbles upon someone he presumes to be himself, standing in the bathroom clutching the sink's *exposed hipbones* . . . and gazing down into its gently glugging *hymenial sump*, which is being continually strengthened by the dripping taps. The *any-old-iron* of dried blood rises up from the waste-paper basket *but that's alright, Mama* . . . so long as he doesn't make the cardinal error of . . . *looking in the mirror.* Problem is the mirror's the cabinet door – and his spongebag . . . *is in the cabinet!* He looks and is appalled: first by his skin's marine-green, next by ever-changing ripples chasing across it and the visible cat's paws of wind doing the chasing. He grips the sink more tightly, trying to extract certainty from its ceramic finish: *Can this really be me?* The answer, when it comes, is hardly reassuring: Busner's dorsal nose detaches from above his lip. Slowly to begin with – soon enough with mounting speed – it travels around his face. Initially the nose-fin does a simple circuit or three, but then whatever buried intelligence motivates it becomes bolder, and it executes a tricky figure-of-eight manoeuvre around Busner's eyes, swerves up towards his hairline, and, as he opens his mouth to scream, heeling over . . . *it dives right in!* — He made me do it, says the younger of the two kids Chief Brody has hauled out of the water. Busner wonders whether it would be too greedy to creep up the popcorny aisle, then hurry downstairs to get a second box of Maltesers. There's something about being subjected to successive shocks – albeit contrived ones – that stimulates the appetite. Not that he was fooled by the kids' fake fin as it ploughed towards the Amity Island bathers. Perversely, once it's beached he's disappointed by how well made it is – no amateur fin this, but the workmanship of the same department that's fashioned the Great White's polypropylene body. This mismatch between common sense and the mechanics of simulation bothers him far more than the shark. Busner's beginning to warm to Hooper. What was it that he said? *You're going to ignore this particular problem until it swims up and bites you on the ass* . . . The rapidity with which sharkish souvenirs, T-shirts and even a Killer Shark videogame have appeared on the Amity boardwalk in time for the Labor Day crowds might be taken, Busner thinks, as confirmation of the relentless vigour of American capitalism – but he remains sceptical: Film, he considers, now dominates our experience of the world purely because of the sheer transparency of its own self-conviction . . . *seeing, after all, is believing*. Yet this too is a throwback: the polypropylene saint paraded before the believers' eyes before sinking beneath the iconic screen – it'll cruise *round annaround*, down there for a time, but eventually it'll *swim up and bite us on our collective ass*. – Quint's Orca heads out into an open sea that leeches the setting sun. The fishing boat's high wheelhouse, with its fish-bony radio antennae, is caught for a moment in the triangular teeth of a shark's jaw hung up in a quayside shack. Busner chews everything over as the three protagonists joust with the big prop and each other. – Mark, he's pleased to note, is on the edge of his seat, his braces bared. It would be a terrible shame, Busner reflects, if all my son were to get out of spending time with his father were further confirmation of the world's penny-pinching with the truth about . . . *these great and terrible objects*. The shark toy toys with them – charging at the boat, only to dive beneath it at the last moment. Brody, the craven landlubber, is sent up to the crow's-nest to rock there, rifle in hand, while the noonday sun scatters solitaires across the worn decking. I don't know, Hooper says, if he's very smart or very dumb – and Zack queries: Couldn't he be both? When Quint smashes the radio transmitter with a base-ball bat Zack's . . . *relieved*, because the outside world now no longer exists for them, and he too is freed of the requirement to believe in it. – All it's about is these . . . *three archetypes* and their . . . *monstrous delusion*. However, when they're all seated at the cabin table, and Quint and Hooper begin to fence using the unusual yet *deeply suggestive* weaponry of their own wounds, Zack finds himself unable to pursue . . . *the Amfortas one*, but instead is gripped by the resemblance between the three shark-hunters and another trio of men, who, preyed-upon by their own *monstrous delusions*, swim out of the aqueous distortion of his own not-so-deep past. His attraction to Hooper is, Zack realises, *narcissistic*: he'd like to think of his own analytic interventions as precisely such a subversion of neurosis's paradoxically brute strength: *The crackling to pieces of a plastic cup – or a paper tiger* . . . As for Quint, Zack hadn't liked him from the off. The way he scratched the blackboard of the com-munity's anxiety with his fingernails was *pettily demonstrative*, and as a *saviour-who's-really-a-sadist* there's plainly nothing he delights in more than placing them in this *classic double-bind*. The fisherman is, Busner diagnoses, undoubtedly the victim of some traumatic experience – a physical one, probably connected to sharks, such being the simplicity of the fabulated. His resemblance to Claude Evenrude is . . . *really rather superficial.* Yes they have the same high forehead and widow's peak of grey hair. The face, seemingly unshaven, 'though it's not . . . *this too they share.* But Quint is a big, deep-chested man, while Claude – who Busner remembers as he last saw him, five years previously, being led handcuffed from the psychic wreckage of 117 Chapter Road, Willesden – was . . . *and presumably still is* . . . a broken man: skinny and knock-kneed, his emphatically narrow chest drummed upon *from within* by his ragtime demons . . . I wanna go down to Tom Anderson's ca-fé, I wanna hear that Creole jazz band play! The Cadillac, the Red Onion too, the Boogie-Woogie an' the Parc Sans Sou' . . . Around the Creep's battered brow Busner now casts a rosy nimbus of reminiscence: Not for Claude this portentous accompaniment, the string section sawing toothily away, the horns honking, the timpani tinkling as the entire orchestra galumphs through the waves . . . But when Quint pulls open his denim shirt, exposing the bluish blodge, and says, Had a tattoo there, it said USS Indianapolis . . . a stretched tether inside of Zack snaps! and he plunges down the steep beach of his recent past, and even as his voracious understanding dramatically widens its aperture, so events that had been firmly relegated to the historic background zoom into the present, while what's currently transpiring – the miserable wreckage of his broken marriage, the subaquattering of his strange son, the very stickiness of his Maltesered fingers – remains defiantly . . . *THE SAME SIZE!* – If Quint is the Creep and I'm Hooper, then, Busner thinks, Chief Brody must be Michael Lincoln – Christopher's guardian, who followed Claude into the Black Maria that May day, calmly assuming a responsibility *that was undoubtedly mine, but I was pathetically unable to cope with.* – The maimed fishing boat creaks, the three men . . . *now and forever more* . . . confront each other across the tabletop. Hooper says, You were on her, June '45? and Busner testily corrects him: *It was the tail-end of July!* although why such minor recall should rectify *my oceanic amnesia*, he's no idea. Quint says, On her and torpedoed right off her into the drink with nine hundred other clowns . . . Started with nine hundred anyway . . . floating in the big warm Pacific. Must've been like a dinner bell in there . . . Explosions, and half the guys bleeding. Soon as the sharks came homing in on us, we went by the Manual, of course . . . Keep trying to float in groups . . . doin' what it said – splash at 'em, yell at 'em, hit 'em on the — *NOSE! I'VE GOT NO NOSE!* It's a soundless scream because . . . *I'VE GOT NO MOUTH EITHER!* He gawps at the watery expanse of his face and thinks, I better do something quick or my eyes'll go under . . . Thinking for themselves, his hands wrench open the cabinet and sort through the spongebag. These pills, he prays, will surely help. – And they do, right away, for as he lifts his palm his mouth is re-created to receive them. Back downstairs he wonders: Have I been gone for seconds – or years? The five men are in the same positions as when he left: the Kid supine on the mattress, Claude and Michael Lincoln on the

347

floor facing Rodge and Lesley on the sofa. Only the last must have moved – how else to explain the half-smoked joint in his hand, and the smoke leaking from his mouth and nostrils? Zack kneels down beside the Kid and lays a hand on his quaking shoulder. There-there, he says, there-there. Lesley drawls, Oh, ma-an, what's happened to the sounds – we gotta have some music. He stands, and Zack thinks: We do need music, for without that all there is are these . . . *sounds*: the Kid's hiccupping negation, the dull rasp of Roger's breathing and the whispered words flitting between Claude and his . . . *co-conspirator – what're they up to?* A line from Ronnie's Politics of Experience comes to Zack: *These arabesques that mysteriously embody mathematical truths only glimpsed by a very few . . . how beautiful, how exquisite, no matter that they were the threshing and thrashing of a drowning man . . .* Claude trills, Ho, darkies, hab you seen de massa, wid de muff-tash on he face, then says: It was a cracker regime down there in Florida – the sergeants treated us like Negroes, had us doing six formations a day, which meant six shaves a day. My face got raw then rawer – but if you missed one of those shaves the whole bunch of 'em would surround you, slam you up against the wall and shout in your face, Ho, darkies, hab you seen de massa, WID DE MUFF-TASH ON HE FACE! Lincoln says, There was a certain amount of barracking – if you made a frivolous complaint you'd be put on a charge and have to do jankers, but, apart from a few goons, the sergeants weren't that abusive. Claude says, I'd done monkey-drill in basic – hell, everything in basic was monkey-drill. Soon as we'd got the creases outta our fatigues they had us standing in chow lines, lining up for mail calls, lining up for the goddamn latrine ... Lincoln muses, Actually, I never got that much mail, and because I'd been up before the tribunal I rather kept myself to myself – there was another chap on the establishment in the same situation, entirely by coincidence I knew him from PPU meetings in Lewisham. However, we were pretty bashful to begin with, then, after he'd been made up to lance-jack, we didn't speak at all – in spite of Hore-Belisha the War House took a pretty dim view of fraternisation between ranks. Claude says, Everywhere you went in Texas you saw these boards set up – in vacant lots, in motor courts, wherever: big wooden cut-out shapes of hands, and painted on 'em, Prepare to Meet Your God. First time we were introduced to the corporal, he said, I hope you are prepared, because from now on I AM YOUR GOD. He was a Missouri mule-skinner that man, loved his bully-pulpit and he could shout the paint off a picket fence. Got us doing standard formations and close-order drills – Hup! Twoop! Threep! Four! Thing was I didn't much mind it – liked it almost. There was a sorta joy in losing yourself in this many-headed marching beast ... Besides, what'd been happening anyway, not much besides a hell of a lot of drinking – I'd already been in the tank a few times, hocked my pants for a pint on more than one occasion ... and I'd seen the fuckin' aery mouse gobbled up by the rat in the wall, oh yes indeedy ... When Pop was in funds he still treated me with a degree of liberality – then I'd hand it off to the other bohemian types who hung round the Village. We used to meet up at this apartment a fellow had on 12th and Fourth and play interminable games of Go while we smoked reefer and called down to the liquor store to send up

349

pints – but I knew it was bunk and I weren't going nowhere . . .
– Lincoln, drawing on his re-lit pipe, watching its dense greige
smoke attack the thin blue lines advancing from Lesley's joint,
says, Funnily enough, thing I remember most from that time are
the American cigarettes we were issued with – came in round tins
of fifty. Once you'd turned your coin in the groove and levered off
the lid, there was this most wonderful aroma of fresh Virginia
tobacco. Inside there'd be a scrap of paper that said, Manufactured
and packaged by the Proprietors of State Express Cigarettes.
Silly, really, but every time I read that I pictured these very portly
American gentlemen wearing broad-brimmed hats and white linen
suits, and perspiring rather heavily as they sorted big piles of cigarettes into bundles of fifty. D'you see? Those were the Proprietors . . .
Claude says, We'd count off into squads of fifty, TENNN-
SHUNNN! then compete. Thing was to figure out how to move
without your head bobbing – I was good at it. Good at voice and
command too. Squaaad, right! Squaaad, left! Round annaround we
went – and this being the Air Force I used to wonder what
we looked like from the sky: all those big simple profane prairie
boys and me, circling and circling, so tight together we musta
seemed like one big tan fish trying to swallow its own tail. Michael
says, I miss touching the clouds – I haven't flown again since the
war, couldn't imagine doing it . . . When I was a boy, in the Corps,
I thought of the clouds as my friends, well –. He laughs abruptly.
More like my mother, I s'pose, big soft presences that asked nothing
of me but to allow them to enfold me in their ample bosom. I daresay if these chaps here – he pokes his pipe-stem at Busner and

Gourevitch – weren't high as bloody kites they'd put some Freudian interpretation on that, but let's spare them the trouble, shall we – because of course it was sexual, as well, and it went on being sexual as hell when I was on active service. A fully loaded Lanc' with ten thousand pounds of HE and God knows how many of fuel on board was a bugger to get airborne – bloody terrifying. At the point when the stick was shuddering one's hand, and the Lanc' was bumping off the runway, one felt gravity squeezing and relaxing, squeezing and relaxing – then we were up, and the grip gave way to the caresses . . . of the clouds. Claude says, Me, I was surviving on a diet of five-cent novels from the Negro Library – classics, mostly – that way I'd enough green for a bottle-or-nine of Greasy Dick. The prairie boys called me a nigger-lover – and I was too: Marian Anderson came to sing at the camp, and the only folks who showed up were me and a coloured contingent. Then I discovered there were booklets you could get told you how to do the aptitude tests and the IQ tests. So I splashed out and mugged up – I was always good at cramming so long as there wasn't a bottle to hand. Next thing I know I'm riding the Fargo Express down to Miami Beach with a couple of other officer-candidate jerk-offs – one was a master ser-geant, porky fellow, boy! didn't he think he was just the big I-am. Other one was a Jew outta Chicago, and he gave himself plenty of airs too. Funny thing was they were both flat-busted inside of three days – couldn't handle the shaving, or the shouting. Air down there was like soup, and they had us all shacked up in these big hotels, four and five to a double room. Naturally the owners – who were either Jews or connected, or both – were rubbing their hands: what occupancy rates! And not just for the season – for the whole fuckin' duration! We weren't allowed to use the elevators, we'd to march up and down Hup! Twoop! Threep! flights at the Eden Roc. Poolside there were still polo-playboys in terrycloth robes and Waikiki shorts . . . Man! at the time I thought those big hotels, with their metal shutters and cream paint-jobs, were some kinda surrealistic joke – but when I was shipped out to the Pacific I began to think it might all've been a calculated part of our induction, 'cause if you took away the tanning debs, the white caps in golf shoes and the whoring showgirls sucking up their contract highballs, the basic surroundings were the same. Michael says, Rotblat's remarked to me on more than one occasion that flying isn't simply like making love – it's the most sexual thing we've ever done. For many of the boys I flew with in the war this was quite literally the case – not that all of them were blushing virgins, but in those days . . . well, most of 'em would have to go on an awful blind before they plucked up the courage to even get off with a girl. I never flew again, and sometimes I think I never properly made love again . . . either . . . He falls silent for a few moments, shudders heavily, then resumes: Well! the atmosphere in the mess before a raid was thick – thick with lustful expectancy – all those inexperienced boys, absolutely riddled with nerves and staring – if you'll forgive the poetry – straight into the naked face of death while they tried awfully hard to swank it: Toast, Jimp? I say, Barrel, ol' man, roll out the jam, will you . . . In the briefing, I'd look around at all those pinched faces and think, how is it you're all so alive? By a year in quite a few of us had completed a tour, had a leave and were starting a second –

we knew the odds, we looked with pity on the sprog crews, thinking, You chaps are like us . . . already dead wood – faggots, who're
about to take a great bundle of kindling and drop it on a fire that's
already been fed with petrol – faggots who're going to be added to
that fire . . . Faggots who're going to . . . burn. Claude says, They'd
back us up against those faux-adobe walls, five or six of those
crackers, bawling in our faces 'til their spittle filled our eyes: HOW
MUCH WOOD WOULD A WOOD CHUCK CHUCK IF
A WOODCHUCK COULD CHUCK WOOD! To which the
instantaneous answer was: A woodchuck would chuck as much
wood as a woodchuck could if a woodchuck could chuck wood,
SIR, YES, SIR! And if one single item of your kit was wrinkled
or grubby when those bastards came to inspect it, they'd get ahold
of your sad little can of Army-issue polish and rub it all over your
raw, six-times-shaved face with a goddamn scrubbing brush – then
they'd pitch you in the closet, singin' out, Throw de tar baby in de
coal hole wid de muff-tash on he face! You'd be in there for a while –
they'd nail the door shut. Plenty of time to get sick from naphthalene
and the schlockenspiel of the coat hangers – then they'd let you
out when you didn't have enough time to shave and clean up before
the next inspection. I tellya, the only way to survive was to learn to
do without sleep, and to learn to do without any belief in the goodness of your fellow men. Michael says, At the same time – and this
was the most peculiar thing – the more I flew, the more oddly
invulnerable I felt. The flying-control officer would drone on about
icing levels, cold fronts and the shortest possible route from Hamburg to Bremen – I'd look around me at another fresh crop of

faggots, and I'd think, oh well, what the hell, because after all, it was always the others that died . . . Michael stops. The greasy-haired one they call John has been gone for a while, but there's no evidence of his stated intention to *sort out the sounds*. For this Michael is grateful. He cannot quite comprehend what's happening here – what is the nature of the exchange he's having with Claude Evenrude? Confessional? Therapeutic? Or perhaps *the beginning of a wonderful friendship*, in which case the Marseillaise should be *bugling about* . . . He senses acutely these disordered minds rubbing up against his own, a curious sort of . . . *contact*, from which the only respite comes when he addresses Claude, so he says, At Withernsea there were mines bobbing off the beach and rusty coils of Danaert wire scraping over the shingle – it made an eerie tinny noise, schlockenspiel might cover it . . . 'though I used to think of skeletons turning over on bare bed springs, trying to get comfortable – never getting comfortable. We went bathing all the same, and larked as best we could in the muddy water. The coastline there's eroding all the time, big chunks of the cliffs falling away. Reminded me of a walking holiday I'd taken in Suffolk with some pals before the war –. Claude interrupts: I thrived on it, man, thrived on it – I'd done without sleep plenty before, when the booze has you in its grip . . . well, it's exactly like being in the Army. See, the Army says it's welding you all into a single disciplined individual, but that's so much crummy BS. It ain't some new hyper-organism on the social scene – I'll tellya what the Army's like, it's like liquor: it's got no agency or consciousness of its own 'cause it's a cup fulla cosmic nothingness – we crawl through the

354

mud for it, and we shed our blood for it, this bloodless presence . . . Michael says, We put up in a pub a few miles from Dunwich, which is an ancient port that went under the waves during a big blow in the twelve hundreds. Really, all south-east England's like that – none of these would-be invaders should trouble themselves . . . simply sit tight, let the sea do their work for them. The locals said you could hear the drowned church bells ringing on stormy nights . . . Well, I'd my doubts, but it was a spooky spot, no mistaking. When we went digging along the cliffs, we turned up a human skeleton. Some of us thought it'd be a terrific wheeze to smuggle the thing into this chap Folger's bed back at the pub. Thing was, he was a perfectly decent chap and we all liked him very much, but he suffered from a nervous disposition – which was why I s'pose we did it. When he went up to his room that night after rather too many pints, put on the light and saw this skull on his pillow –. Claude sings, Oh roister-doister li'l oyster, Down in the slimy sea, You ain't so diff'rent lyin' on your shell bed, To the likes of l'il old me, But roister-doister you're somewhat moister, Than I would like to be . . . Then he says: Number one in your Lucky Strike Hit Parade . . . and continues: She sailed from Frisco on the same day as the Trinity Test and no one's gonna tell me that was a coincidence. Michael comments, It was bruited about that Oppenheimer made a little speech when the fireball went up – some stuff about being a destroyer of worlds he'd got from a Hindu holy book. For myself, I always thought this sounded like the most dreadful rubbish – I mean he called the test Trinity, for heaven's sake, so he must have felt it . . . the battering of the three-person'd God. And Claude says,

She was torpedoed by a Japanese sub, the I-58, at twenty-four minutes before midnight on the twenty-ninth of July 1945, sailing from Guam to Leyte in the Philippines. There were 1,196 naval personnel on board – there were green-hands and gunneys, gyrenes, swabbies, snipes, skivvy-wavers and shave-tails, and every one of 'em had played his little part in the solution of the Godly integral and the fulfilment of Satan's differential. They'd all kinds of shit on board the Indy when she sailed from Tinian – I knew, 'cause, being a logistics man myself, I took an interest. But there wasn't truly anything of interest 'less you count pogey bait or two-hundred-and-five pounds of fuckin' celery, or all the extra vests and life-rafts they had on board that tub – which turned out to be useless in the event, 'cause there was hardly any time to deploy them between the torpedoes hitting and the whole kit and caboodle going down – including all the ice cream they'd churned up for their dumb gedunk stand. Quartermaster showed it to me with tremendous pride: all the flavours they could make, pineapple, strawberry, tutti-fuckin'-frutti . . . I told him: knock it off, willya, all this makes me think about is making ice cream with my old man, cranking that handle round annaround out on the back porch 'til our arms were aching and our noggins were dripping with sweat . . . Anyways, I swear, when she was going down . . . and the skin angels were flapping across the red-hot deck . . . and there were still more of 'em trying to get airborne from the fantail, I saw him rooted there, not a scratch or a smut on him, but he was bawling like a little kid 'cause there was all this molten ice cream flowing round his ankles . . . You'd not've thought it possible, Michael says, to smell human flesh burning at sixteen thousand feet, but I swear by all that's sacred, it is. Once the TIs had been dropped and the whole target area had been ringed with incendiaries, and we came bucketing in, well . . . first you could smell benzol and burning rubber, and then . . . well, closest thing's frying bacon, I s'pose – never had any stomach for it since. Bucketing in we'd go – Jerry'd have his three-ring circus set up: one of ack-ack, then the searchlights, then more ack-ack . . . The bomb aimer'd be making love to me, guiding my shaking hands: Left . . . Left . . . Steady . . . Steady . . . That was the worst time on any run, obviously – formation falling apart as planes were hit and spiralled away, flak bursts everywhere. Steady . . . Steady . . . they'd keep it up like that, mostly because we all knew pilots went to pieces over the target, got frozen on the stick – and I was never much of a flyer anyway, certainly not a natural. Those big firestorms, they sucked the oxygen out of the atmosphere – you'd be struggling to keep the kite level, stopping the heat from the fires pushing you up, when suddenly you'd hit a queer air pocket and you'd be fighting to prevent her dropping. All the time the spooning'd continue: Steady . . . Steady . . . Left . . . Left . . . Funny thing was, last tour I flew – my nerves were utterly shot by then, had the shakes so bad I couldn't fill my pipe for hours after we got down. But when we were up there, coming into the target area, the nervous system I'd so abused sort of . . . befriended me, and in a very Christian manner turned off the sound altogether, so there was radio silence – Michael taps his forehead with his pipe – in my bonce and the flak bursts became these cotton-wool puffs lit up from within – rather beautiful, really. And the Lancs looked like so many soft-winged moths

drawn irresistibly to the light ... the smoke down below like a
sheet ... thrown over a lit-up bush ... Only thing I could hear
was the spooning: Steady ... Steady ... then, Bombs gone! And
he'd be shouting, Corkscrew! Corkscrew! Hard left! Hard left!
and, as I'd drag the bus round, it'd all come back in a rush: the roar
of the engines, the crash of the flak, and the whooshing headwind
that rose and rose until it became a scream ... Claude says, The
ocean was rough enough, I guess – a long heavy swell that came
whooshing along her sides. The cloud was low – dense but broken in
places, I could see a hangnail of a moon. But, like I said, I always
loved the sea. Oh, Lordy, Lordy! – Claude claps his hands to his
face and *his drowned features trickle between his fingers* – Here's me
forgetting to properly explain: when the Indy left Tinian she had
one supernumerary officer on board, Lieutenant Claude Evenrude
of the Army Air Force Materiel Command. As I came up the
companionway, Captain McVay saluted me from his bridge – he
was an uptight asshole if ever I saw one, full of his own scrambled
eggs – they were all like that, full up with the stupid battle stars
they'd won withstanding the Divine Wind offa Okinawa, and
mighty impressed by the turn of speed they'd put on crossing the
Pacific so's to deliver their precious plywood crate and the canister
that had been welded to the bulkhead in the magazine officer's
cabin. The Los Alamos boys who rode shotgun on that canister
sat in there the whole time and the dumb swabs would swirl their
mops along the decks outside and speculate, Gee, I wonder what's
so special, maybe it's gold bullion, or Rita Hayworth's scented
panties ... Me, I coulda used a dead horse so's I coulda scored some

liquor before I went aboard, but there was nothing doing so I had the sweats. I latched on to this doctor, and he gave me sack room, but the Chief said I'd to work my passage by weeding out green bananas and otherwise censoring the crew's letters ... I was right, Busner thinks, about the compulsion to write everything down: it's inevitably a form of censorship. Without it I can finally hear what people are actually saying – hear every single unvarnished word. He looks at Roger, whose face is *lacquered* with the realisation of ... *his own insignificance – a gone spade.* But Lesley, Zack acknowledges, Lesley was right as well: Hofmann must have been God-inspired when he synthesised Lysergic acid ... *The bomb goes boom – the babies go boomier ... And so we see in-fin-ity in a dried cornflake stuck to the lino ... Wrongie was Ronnie when he burred, Atoms don't explode out of hatrrred – but they da-doo-ron-Ronnie, 'cause atoms are us, and we're hatred* ... The hundredth train of the day *stamps down on the worn striped ticking of suburbia* and the house *rocks and rolls*, alerting Zack to a fact: *Hardly any time must've passed at all!* because when the last one went by *I was in the bathroom* ... A slow wave passes through the linoleum, elongating the linked shit-brown rhomboids and the bilious ovoids, then drawing them back together into *a relatively perrrmanent space-time patterrrn – that's what Wrongie said men must live and die for* ... In the train's wake the workaday reasserts itself: indistinct chirruping, the small bomb-blast of a car door being slammed. – From the garden Zack hears the rise and fall of the women's voices and Clive's Oompah-lumpahing. Suddenly he lunges forward, snatches the cornflake stuck upright by Michael Lincoln's shoe and, *purely in the spirit of experimentation*, pops it in his mouth, where it dissolves into a *malty . . . chocolatey . . . crud*, coating his tongue, teeth and the roof of his mouth. — Thick, empurpled smoke plumes up from the stricken Orca into the bare sky. Silence, except for the waves' *tippling*, waves that climb up on deck through its ruptured planking. Zack looks sideways at Mark, whose concentrating face looms bluely in the mutating gloom. Lucky old him, Zack thinks, the drama compels his attention – I, on the other hand, know only too well how it'll all end . . . how it did all end. Hooper says, He can't stay down with three barrels in him, not with three he can't, and Zack thinks, I rather wish he would stay down there – stay down there, then skulk back the way he came, along the seabed, nosing past weedy outcrops, until he gains the deep ocean, and the surprising freedom such a godlike machine must enjoy . . . *once it's no longer shackled to a plot.* Hooper says, I think I can pump 20cc's of strychnine nitrate into him. If I can get close enough. And Chief Brody says, You can get this little needle through his skin? – Oh, yes, Zack thinks, I could've got a very little needle into his skin – into her skin as well . . . into all of their skins. If I'd've managed that, things might've turned out very differently indeed, because there's no three-act problem in life, only crises waiting to happen . . . *in every bloody scene.* The epiphany, which he holds poised between his teeth, is *candy-coated*, a super-critical mass of *brain-rot*. The urge to bite down on it is *overpowering* . . . yet he knows soon enough, *probably before the credits roll*, it will have dissolved into . . . *the sickly shapelessness of things to come.* Pausing in the foyer of the ABC Muswell Hill, smelling the petrol-tinged urban dusk gusting through the doors, he'll wash it away again with tepid sips from a paper water-cup. His jaws clenched, Zack remains altogether unmoved by the spectacle of Quint's final rendezvous with his nemesis – Quint, sliding inexorably down the slippery deck and into the Great White's gaping maw . . . *You will please be doing the rinsing now*, as Missus Uren, Busner's French dentist puts it, caught up as she is in the continuous present of those *without fluency* . . . The pink threads spool away into her dinky sink, leaving behind the grit of rotten enamel and the glint of amalgam. Outside, beyond the shaggy hedge, East Finchley would . . . *get on with it*, unimpressed by his self-restraint, by his *not biting the hand that makes it possible for me to feed*. That, Busner thinks, is Jaws's problem: he can't get it into his polypropylene head that he can't get the Orca into his polypropylene head. He doesn't really want to chew the rubbery old fisherman – *who would?* He wants revenge on the whole of humanity for fouling his clear waters with their filthy chemical effluents, and punishing his hearing with the whining of their propellers, and hacking the living fin from his back to shred it into their grisly soup. Five years before, revolving in the LSD's dinky sink *with nothing to hang on to*, he'd still managed to grasp this: the punishment meted out to Claude Evenrude and the men of the USS Indianapolis had been a collective one, with the sharks as Mother Nature's revengers, summoned from the deep in anticipation of a blow that was yet to fall . . . *a bomb that was yet to drop.* As Mark has lectured him, they circled the hundreds of shipwrecked men mostly out of curiosity: *Sailors are not their table d'hôte* . . . They couldn't comprehend how it was possible for these fleshy masses – mere *roister-doisters* – once

361

prised from their steel-plated *shell bed*, to so toxify their ocean. Busner understood all this at the time, but, in common with so many insights bestowed on the psyche *through the rainbow door*, it took only a sudden shower to expose the pot of revelation for what it truly was: *grit of rotten enamel and the glint of amalgam – fool's gold*. – Hooper and Brody kick out for the shore, buoyed up by wreckage . . . *courtesy of the props department*. Poor Jaws, *he's so much trayf* . . . in their churning wake . . . *the afterbirth of an emotion*. Busner cannot stand it any more: his perfidious teeth bite down on the truth — but it's they that crumble and he who cannot swallow the *corny bits*, so spits them into his hand *better out than in* and looks first for a suitable receptacle, then to the window. *A young angel* . . . is standing there. Busner can see only her head and shoulders – the rest is hidden by the nets, *nylon wings* spreading out from bare *bird bone* arms. He registers her curly hair, the yoke neck of her school-uniform dress, and infers the life fluttering inside her from her breath blooming on the windowpane, but *she's an angel all the same*, because her skin, her hair, her clothing – all of it is covered in *the abstraction of heavenly dust!* She knows, he thinks, she knows each and she sees all. The angel raises her hand and rubs a patch of clarity in her *holy expiration*, to which she applies her curious eyes. Zack thinks, Any and all human groups are like this: psychic structures into which some individual flies . . . *a Jenny Neutrino* who strikes others so hard and fast *she splits* . . . and bits of her fly into other psychic systems, so they also fission . . . *a chain reaction spreading through the city*, reducing it to *anomie* . . . *and hopelessness*. He yawns – and when he looks back at the window the girl's gone, while Claude's saying, They called the Indy the clipper ship – not on account of carrying tea round the Cape or anything like that, but because the doc I sacked down with performed hundreds of circumcisions on the green-hands and the swabbies. Why? Fuck knows, that was just the way of it then, it was a fashion: peckers will be worn shorter and pinker for the season . . . Anyway, he was ridic', the sawbones, kept going on about his system – thought as a logistics man I might appreciate the mechanics of the procedure, what he needed in the way of anaesthesia, equipment and so on. Man lay back on his bunk with his eyes shut and came out with this hogwash – I utilised the opportunity – good logistics man I was – to relieve his medical kit of some anaesthesia I needed: sodium barbital – straightened me out well enough, so's when we were hit I'd a semi-clear head. Before that, though, it was censorship time. Chief had a whole bunch of these V-mails and he said to me, what I want you to do, Genie says, holding out the little plastic cup with the two Stelazine capsules jiggling in it . . . *Mexican jumping beans.* Quint – which is what she calls the *old scrag-end* sitting in the vinyl-covered institutional armchair by the open window – does nothing. Genie delivers her prepared speech again: I'm no longer allowed to give you this medication, the terms of your care plan mean you have to take it yourself, and that's what I want you to do. She looks again at the clipboard she holds in her other hand, although she already knows what Lawal, the night concierge, has written beside Quint's name: Staff wrote here you refused to take your medication yesterday evening, so if you refuse again now I'll have to call Missus Perkins. *Rust rasps in a rotten drainpipe . . .* it's

Quint clearing his throat. The room's about the size of two average bathrooms joined together in an L-shape. The upright is both a kitchenette and the passage leading to the front door – off this there are two other, narrower doors, one opening into a minuscule bedroom, the other out of a tiny toilet. Despite the open window the atmosphere in the cramped space is foetid: stale old-man sweat, a smidgeon of urine, and the composting reek of an un-emptied bin full of food scraps and used tea bags . . . *not my responsibility – his*. Quint clears his throat again, then croaks, I'd oblige, young lady, if it weren't that I'm gonna give birth soon to this darn shark spirit – up in my pit here . . . He pulls at his towelling dressing gown where it's bunched up under his arm . . . see, it's all swole up. – Genie's always taken aback by Quint's sweetly reasonable tone, and his accent . . . *very posh American*. Quint whickers gently to himself: Houhy-hn-hn-mm . . . and says: Missus Perkins doesn't scare me. My ass has been a pincushion since '45 – there's nothing she can stick in there hasn't been stuck already. – This is a long speech for Quint – Genie's impressed. The old man is usually too shaky to speak at all – many of the residents have the tardive dyskinesia associated with long-term use of anti-psychotics, but all the staff simply call it *the shakes*, and of all the *shakers* on Genie's roster, Quint is the *shakiest*. She sets the little plastic cup down on the filthy surround of the filthier sink and sighs. The staff call it Lincoln Warehouse: because what they do here is keep the residents – mostly former long-stay mental patients – stacked up in these miserable compartments. It wasn't what Genie had had in mind when she'd thought about . . . *the caring professions*. Still, what chance did she ever have of a decent job without qualifications? *A couple of poxy CSEs don't count, you stupid little cow* . . . Mumsie's death mask spits at Genie from the damp wall of a gloomy half-landing on a staircase that switchbacks down into the cellars of her memory. Beside it hangs Cutty's death mask – but Hughie's has fallen off and lies on the scuffed floorboards. Mumsie's death mask starts to sing: *Stu-pid Jeanie's got no brai-ns, Soon she won't 'ave no vei-ns* . . . Genie rubs the crook of her elbow – she hasn't stuck a needle in her arm since *25th October 1995* . . . and then it was only *a jelly some muppet off the estate give me*. But the scars are deep and it's taking *a fucking age* for the liquorice bootlaces to fade from red to black to brown. She sighs again – and tries again: It's not just a matter of a depot injection – they won't let you stay here if you don't get your act together. Quint whickers again, Houhy–hn–hn–mm . . . – He's biddable enough so long as things are done for him. He sits and he reads, any old paperback will do: a thriller, a Mills & Boon romance or a textbook. Before the new care plans were introduced requiring staff *not to care*, and she was ticked off for doing it, Genie would stop by the Sue Ryder shop on the Mile End Road before she took the tube and pick up a book for him for a few pence. It amazed her – who'd never got into the habit of reading – how Quint could lose seconds between the lines, turn pages into minutes, interleave chapters with hours, and so fold the whole day into a Maeve Binchy or a Colin Dexter. She'd visit first thing in the morning, and whenever she passed she'd . . . *pop my head round the door* and see him there, in his chair, his heavily hooded eyes roving along the lines as his thin lips moved. She asked him once:

Are you saying the words to yourself? But he preferred not to reply. – This was soon after she'd started the job, and everything about work was still a novelty: getting up in the morning, showering, setting off to spend the day somewhere else . . . *just like any normal*. The other staff were mostly Filipinas who laughed behind their hands when they found out Genie had been assigned Quint. The most approachable of them, tubby Marcia, said: He's a creep, that one – I never seed it, but before they say he put his hands on plenty girls . . . grabbed at us – grabbed up us skirts! As she'd said this, Maria's hands went to the big wooden cross hanging round her neck on a length of dull chain – forsaking it, they went to the pockets of her pale-blue nylon uniform tunic, which were patted down . . . *to check she ain't lost her faith*. If Quint had perved on the women, it must have been a long time ago – he was very old now, *well into 'is eighties*, although his exact age was frustratingly absent from his notes, as was a lot of other basic information. Quint had also lost his hair, apart from a tatty fringe left behind on his nape that, before the new care plan, Genie would trim with nail scissors. She washed his juddering torso as well: sponging the deep and angry sockets of his neck and collarbone, the slack cordage of his muscles and tendons . . . *he oughta be dangling offa cross*. It awakened in her an odd tenderness – the same combination of protectiveness and anger she felt towards Pippa when she was a toddler. At these times the old man seemed weirdly familiar to her. Poor little sausage, Genie would say as she screwed the sponge into his armpit. His hand flailed, and she felt his timeworn skin . . . *thin as rice-paper* . . . snag on his bones . . . *like it might tear*. She stared into his peculiar sea-green eyes and they sucked her down into their depths. *Those eyes* . . . so watery . . . but *they burn* – not with lust, but, she suspected, with memories too traumatic for him to find the words for. And of course Quint seldom spoke anyway – unless it was to thank her with great courtesy for whatever small task she'd done on his behalf. Thank you kindly, ma'am, he'd say – and sometimes he'd struggle to rise from his chair, rocking back and forth so he could make a grab for the Zimmer frame that was inches away. When she'd ask him, What d'you think you're doing? he'd collapse back, wave his feathery hands and croak out, Door . . . Open the door for you, ma'am. It'd become, she thought, a sort of joke between them – although, when she considers it, the joke's on someone else altogether, because now she's no longer allowed to give him his medication, Quint, *a naked, white blob* . . . is . . . *coming out of his shell*. Pointing at the cup with the Stelazine in it and the one beside it half full of Chlorpromazine linctus, she chides him, Make sure you get it down you, but she knows: *He'll do nothing of the sort* . . . Doubtless Missus Perkins, the psychiatric social worker, would have *a thing or two to say about that*, but Genie . . . *couldn't give a shit*. So what if the old man didn't take his medication – so what if he ranted and raved? There was no one to hear him except other ranters and ravers. As for jumping out the window – it was too small and he was too feeble. Besides, Genie had a more positive motivation: as the old man's mind *dried out*, snippets of his past were coming to the surface: *my ass has been a pincushion since '45* . . . that made her feel . . . *like we're related*. After all, she'd been a pincushion for a long time . . . *and a punchbag* . . . *and a fuck-rag* . . . yet she too

367

had come alive. On good days, days when Pippa didn't cry on the way to school, days when Genie didn't awake to the gnawing realisation that, despite *all the work I've done on myself*, this terrible, remorseless creature was still inside her, one that, no matter what she threw into its vicious jaws . . . *booze, gear, pills, fags, cocks, food – fucking oxygen cylinders* . . . would remain *ravenous*. No, on good days Genie felt alive – and happy to be so. She'd stop at the Bengali shop by the tube and admire the display of fruit and veg' out front – the tapering white radishes and the sharp ribbing of the jhingas – she'd savour the citrus tang of a shaktora, and when one of the shop boys came out she'd say, Bhalo houk thumar, then delight in the smile that overtook him. On good days Genie cried – not bitter tears of self-reproach but ones of . . . *joyful sadness*. As the tube battered through Stepney Green and Whitechapel, then stopped at Aldgate East to *throw up* its breakfast of commuters, Genie would be immune from the nausea she used to feel: the frowsty girls who'd rolled straight out of bed *into their dirty knickers*, the put-together ones who'd been *up since the crack putting on slap*, the spotty boys in Next suits with drunken buttons, the flash getters mincing along the carriage in their penny loafers – she loved them all, she admired them all, because weren't they doing the same courageous thing as she . . . *getting up on deck and reporting for duty*. And on good days Genie also loved the city itself – loved the gummed-up grooves on the carriage floor, loved the grot-filmed windows through which she could see nameless hunks of abandoned machinery and piles of long-forgotten coal. If she squinted, she herself would come into focus, floating through this underworld: her wild hair tamed and sensibly styled, her plain leather coat and clean white blouse. She didn't look like anyone much *and that's good* . . . because the important thing was that, like the city – which was bloated with all the rotting memories of its gross and heinous acts – *I'm still alive* . . . not dead like poor Hughie, poor Cutty, poor baby Philip . . . *and that sad cow*. Alive, so able to appreciate – in common with the Bengali women on the estate *who brought me back from the bloody dead* – that, although she might feel like a *probashi*, with every day that passed this *bidesh* became *my London*. – That morning, getting out at Embankment and walking up Villiers Street, Genie shushed through the *wet bracken* of discarded newspaper supplements and heard the celebrants' tipsy cries as wind soughing . . . *through ashes and oaks*. Wending her way through the back streets of Covent Garden, Genie entertained the possibility that she really had returned home *to London*, and all the familiar mysteries of the copse: its sinuous paths of fine sand, its shady dells and sunny clearings. Genie experienced . . . *the wonder*, and refused to let it dispel even when those dells were, on a second look, occupied by shop girls setting out scented candles and pot-pourri. *This can be a good day – it can!* Genie had awoken in Flat 27 at Jebb House, switched on the radio and, instead of a hysterical DJ telling her some pop star *'ad flipped 'is wig*, heard there was a new prime minister, one only *a couple of years older than me*, whose fluffy brown hair and startled eyes always made her think . . . *Where's the boy who's lost his sheep? He's over in the corner with Little Bo Peep, a-haaa, al-riiight* . . . – Standing before Quint, gripping her clipboard, Genie tries to hang on to the *good day* even as his yellow, horny feet tap at the lino, and his sunken chest lifts and lets fall the candlewick bedspread wrapped around it – tries to, yet cannot . . . *it slips through me fingers* as the old man sings, Black water ri-sing, comin' in my windows an' doors . . . a pause, then he creaks on: Black water ri-sing, comin' in my windows an' doors . . . Another pause – far off in the depths of the building Genie hears the crash of the arriving lunch trolleys and a garbled curse, Fucking trolley! Summoning himself, clutching the arms of the chair with frantic fingers, Quint forces out, I had a dream la-ast night, babe, not a mule in my dog-gone stall . . . – The mystery of the old man is in all of this: she's never heard him sing before, yet she recognises his voice – and although this voice breaks, it does so *tunefully* . . . while as for the expression on his beaten face, it's . . . *beautiful*. What's that you're singing, Genie asks, is it the blues? But he's collapsed – and so have his features – into a sullen grimace. Genie, feeling a quickening in her belly, realises . . . *this is where it's all been heading*: the angry pity she'd experienced as Pippa's fingers slipped from her own, and her small daughter disappeared into the uproar of the playground – the strange tension she'd endured on the tube, her mouth *eggy-tasting*. When she got out at the Embankment, despite it being a *good day* . . . the sunlight was really a tacky deposit on every surface . . . *dried spunk*. As she turned off Endell Street and walked up Shelton Street towards Lincoln House, its odours *hurried out to meet me*: the gases of gut and gizzard pushing against the wire-reinforced door glass – the meat-steam from smoked lungs straining through the sepia nets puffing out of its *slitty windows*. In the basement, where Genie punched her time card, the coffee's *instant bitterness* caught in her throat. *All of it!* was leading to this: *My period — my monthlies . . .* If, that is, any month could ever be so long — because the last time Genie remembered feeling this way was before she fell pregnant with the twins, back when she was first with Cutty *and he flushed my pills down the bog,* saying it was to stop her going on the game . . . *but I wanted to stop!* Cutty – Cutty by name, mostly *cut about by others' evil natures.* His face was before her again: the razor scars on his handsome cheeks underscoring the wide-eyed innocence of *his madness.* What, me? those eyes seemed to say, every time his mouth opened and the paranoid words ran away from him: *You – you fuckin' whoo-er, yous tryin' t'poison me! I seen you – I seen you put poison in that mash there!* This was when the three of them were living at Jebb House, Cutty stopping with them two or three nights a week, then heading back West to get his injectables script from Doctor Dahani. His injectables script and methadone for both them, together with the half-ounce of gear laid on weekly by Welsh Taffy, which Cutty served up to a string of City traders he'd managed to hook. I seen you! he'd cried, his thick black hair *electrified . . .* his broken teeth bared, his scars . . . *bright white – near silver.* And the baby, who'd been strapped into her highchair *screamed* as she took fistfuls of beans and mash from her plate and squeezed them *in 'er dolly 'ands.* Standing in the grimy little kitchen, listening to the wind whistle through the furred Vent-Axia, Genie had forgiven him: she knew what he'd been through in Barlinnie – the beatings from fellow inmates as well as the screws, the punishment block where his shit went out in one cardboard dish and his food arrived in another, food that was indeed *laced with tranks so strong I shat*

371

mesel'. Look, Cutty, babe, Genie had said, approaching him so-slowly, her hands – one of which still held the potato-masher – in plain view. Why don't I juss swap these two plates round, yeah? Then, if there's any poison in your one, it'll be me as gets it, yeah? I'll be like your . . . food taster, yeah? – Cutty had stared at her, his eyes narrowing and narrowing until all the innocence had been wrung from them and there was nothing left but cold black suspicion. I never thought ye had it in yous, he said. I never thought ye were that devious a bitch . . . His fear smeared from one plate of sausages, beans and mash to the other identical one, and he muttered: To be vicious enough to poison yer old man, thass lower than any slime's gone thass still human. But to poison him by trickery – 'cause you switched them plates, didn'tcha, bitch, issa double-bluff – thass diabolical . . . diabolical, that is . . . He hadn't finished speaking before he grabbed the baby by the webbing binding her to the highchair and, making horrible guttural noises, began to drag her and it along the passage to the bedroom, swiping at the charged air with his fork, sending mashy pebbles dashing against the walls. The highchair's rubber stoppers squeaked on the floor of pine-effect laminate he'd begun laying when he was high on crack but *given up on when 'e came down*. The final dumb incon-sequence to float through Genie's head before he slammed the door shut was that the fork with which Cutty was about to kill their baby was one of the ones with the bright blue plastic handles Debbie had thieved on the Butlins holiday . . . *it's come a long way*. Things do better than people . . . Genie had thought, looking about her wildly at the few sticks of furniture from the Dudswell cottage that she'd got off Mumsie . . . they last longer – they don't mind lying in skips or being kicked around the streets . . . have no feelings 'bout breaking or being broke. She had pleaded with Cutty through the door, from behind which came low-pitched grunts and high-pitched wails. The expression she'd heard on the news whenever there was a hostage situation kept spooling uselessly before her eyes . . . *trained negotiators . . . trained negotiators . . .* Finally she tore herself away, threw herself down four flights and ran the five hundred yards to the nearest pissed-in phone box. This much she remembered: it'd been a drizzly Friday evening and through the *bent bars of the cage* she saw the Bow Flyover rearing up beside her, one carriageway frothing with red brake lights, the other streaming with white headlights. Her ten pence only bought her a few minutes of Mumsie's pissed maundering: No, no, she couldn't be expected to come over and deal with Cutty, she'd done her time with delinquents – 'sides, it was Genie's problem, all Genie's problems were hers and hers alone. If Mumsie had spoken Sylheti, she'd probably have said, Ar khoyo na, amar janre dori-layse, Old age is getting to me, *'cause it was*, and, much as *she always done all she could to make me feel like shit*, time was *she'd've come running for the sheer drama of it an' the promise of an ambulance to chase* . . . Genie had hung up. She hadn't any more change – there was no one on the pavements and a low, evil wind blew rain and exhaust fumes into her face as she ventured out into the stalled traffic, tapping tentatively on windows, receiving blank stares. It was then, and only then, she discovered she'd left the flat without her shoes, and that her tights had shredded on the *cold, wet and oily tarmac* . . . — Throw de darkie in de coal hole, throw de tar baby in dere too, Quint whispers, and Genie's appalled to feel the touch of his mind on hers . . . *like we're connected*. She goes over and squats down by his chair: D'you know something, matey? she asks. Is there anything you want to tell me? Quint's raw old eyes are full of tears – a muscle leaps in his sunken cheek. For a moment Genie sees herself as she imagines he does: an amorphous shape, armed with teeth, circling him . . . *not attacking – only curious*. His dry lips part and out rustles, Ho darkies, hab you seen de massa wid de muff-tash on he face . . . His hand floats up from his lap and Genie snags it in her own – it's light and dry . . . *parrot food*. Gimme the book, Quint says and, leaning in towards him, she asks, What book? so gets *a nose-full of sour rot* for her trouble, together with a single word: Jaws. She snorts, gets to her feet and goes to rummage in the plastic laundry basket jumbled with paperbacks that lurks at the bottom of his cupboard, beneath a sad rack of frayed shirts and stiff suits . . . *charity-shop rejects*. Genie finds the fat paperback, but when she gives it to him he beseeches her again: Pen – gimme some kinda pen, and she says, Only if you say please – pretty please. – In the corridor she thinks, Marcia or one of the other girls might have a Tampax . . . Her sensible shoes *black jobs from Clarks* sound on the patterned swirls of the institutional lino: *Boom-boom, boom-boom, boom-boom* . . . and the submarine orchestra gets going, horns oompahing bubbles, bowing arms reeling in fathom by fathom the all-consuming years. — That evening on the Bow flyover it'd been a different sort of instrumental: a soapy opera that had climaxed with its pathetic bubbles popped by drum-beats: Boom-boom b-b'b'boom! and the jingly sentimentality had jangled inside her as she dragged her torn feet back to the phone box and dialled 999. She'd given them Cutty's proper name, so *when the Old Bill came they was mob 'anded*: armed clones wearing bullet-proof vests and crash helmets. There was no sign of any negotiators . . . *trained or otherwise*. They smashed in the bedroom door with a special battering ram – which seemed to Genie *overkill* – then charged inside. One of the coppers brought his gun butt down on the fork-wielding hand – Cutty screamed, and carried on screaming as they hauled him away along the landing. Meria Amal next door said nothing, only stood there in her dainty white robe, her mouth a perfect O. It'd taken ages to calm Pippa down – Genie gave the poor little sausage a cold greasy one to suck on while she picked at the beans stuck to the lino. Absent-mindedly popping one in her mouth, she glanced at the works in the tumbler by the empty baked bean can, the *meanz cuntz* hadn't noticed them – or the scraps of sooty tin foil on the floor, or the pill pots and linctus bottles in the bathroom . . . *s'pose they got their priorities, same as* . . . – Two months later Cutty was dead. Mumsie *beat 'im to it*. Debbie wrote from Nottingham *she felt no pain*, which was . . . *a lie*, because all Mumsie had ever felt was pain – other people's pain as she expertly probed their sensitive spots to cause them . . . *more pain*. She felt no pain, and Genie pictured *the lucky cow*, stabled in a curtained booth at the end of the ward where she was fed plenty of . . . *pure 'eroin*. Debbie wrote: *I would've called you if you had a phone* . . . A phone! The very idea of it! With Cutty on a restraining order, Genie was reduced to her benefits and her script. She ended up doing weird bits and pieces with the pond life off the estate . . . *spawn* she allowed to drift into the flat once she'd dropped Pippa off at nursery. They brought travel sickness pills, which, crushed, filtered and shot up *together wiv a jelly, took you for a little holiday*. Genie would get back to the flat to find she'd spent the whole morning standing in front of the cupboard in the bedroom – a cream-and-gilt-painted thing Cutty had found in the street and humped home. But Genie hadn't been staring at the fancy cupboard – she'd been gazing out from a sun-drenched terrace over a sparkling sea, and her skin was tanned and oiled and smooth, and she held a cool glass in her hand that dripped with condensation. When she brought it to her lips, the back of her throat flooded with . . . *peachiness*. There were quite a few lunchtimes when Genie didn't make it to the nursery by pick-up time, and Meria Amal brought Pippa back with her own kids. She spoke to Genie, the hem of her scarf held across her mouth: You're going to be losing that child . . . *'cause she thought I was pagol – mad. She thought Cutty done sadutona on me* . . . Frozen in the corridor of Lincoln House, feeling the sickly quickening in her belly, Genie supposes *it might've been true* . . . and, if so, it was *the curse that keeps giving*, because now Cutty's dead she thinks of him with such piercing sadness . . . *it's almost love*, while in her otherwise painfully clear mind there's this small and dirty cloud *boiling*, its wisps and puffs shaping features – *sometimes Mumsie's*, other times *Hughie's*. At the end of the corridor a body is *X-rayed* against the window – it's one of her fellow care workers and Genie calls out, Oi, Rose, you gotta pen I can 'ave a lend of? — which was what she said to Father John the day they buried Hughie in the churchyard at Flixton. The other mourners had squelched back into the vicarage, leaving her kneeling by his open grave. In spite of her ringing shock . . . *a death blow, deffo – I saw stars* . . . she couldn't choke down her sarcasm, which was as *bitter as the puke* Hughie had drowned in. Father John and Father Dick, who'd looked after her poor mad brother in the last months before he died, were *un-be-fucking-lievable*: a pair of priestly pooffters who ponced about in weirdo brown woollen robes with bead belts from which hung hefty wooden crosses. They offered teensy glasses of sherry to Mumsie and the gang from the Plantation. Genie overheard Father Derek saying to Val Carmichael as he tipped the decanter, I can absolutely assure you it isn't South African, and Val bitching back, I couldn't give a fuck if it was made in Nazi Germany, mate. Couldn't give a fuck, because he and the rest of them were shamelessly topping up their glasses from quarter-bottles of vodka they'd brought with them. Out in the rain the black water trickled down on to Hughie's coffin . . . *plipetty-plopetty – poor little weed* . . . Genie took the pen Father John handed her and, hunching over to shelter it, wrote shakily on the cheap crappy card, Love you forever . . . before letting it flop down on to the other drenched offerings. A couple of peasants were waiting under the yew tree, and as soon as Father John had helped her to her feet they came forward to begin their . . . *muck-spreading*. – In the cold and dusty vicarage Genie shivered: the dead were boring up through the saturated ground, their wrinkled white corpses compressing, then stretching out as they *slinkied* beneath the foundations, Val Carmichael's *evil Punch face* hanging in the gloom . . . *waiting for them*. There'd been

377

as many as twenty people in the room, yet they were so hushed Genie could hear the rain shushing down outside, and *it might as well've been falling inside* – falling on the poofs' crappy knick-knacks . . . *anyone as thinks they're all natural interior designers shoulda seen* the painted plaster Saint Francis with *Tweety-pies* perched on his outstretched fingers, and the collection of bamboo back-scratchers hanging from nails hammered into the wood panelling, and a disgusting ashtray which was *close to the bone, given 'ow Hughie had died*: a glazed-brown pottery bed with a glazed yellow skeleton lying on it. Fags were to be stubbed out in the socket between its ribcage and its pelvis – its skull lay grinning on the glazed pillow, and the bedhead headstone read, *R.I.P. POOR OLD FRED HE SMOKED IN BED*. Genie had watched the raindrops running down her mother's drained white face. When she'd come in from the graveyard, Mumsie'd looked at her – eyes drinking in the unzipped and mud-spattered parka, the white nylon blouse soaked see-through, the back spidering of her bra – and she'd spat: *Like a virgin – all fucking wet for the very first time* . . . — Ten years ought to feel like a long time, but to Genie it's . . . *none at all*: the hurt remains . . . *livid*, the outline of a hand . . . *burning across my cheek.* Holy-rollers Genie knows who've cleaned up from drugs and booze pronounce pieties such as *Holding on to a resentment is like drinking a cup of poison and expecting the other person to die* . . . but, although Mumsie's dead, the poison still . . . *burns inside.* Genie holds the biro Rose has given her . . . *tight* and runs the fingers of her other hand along the tiled wall as she boom-booms back along the corridor to Quint's door. — Everyone had heard what Mumsie said.

Outside the rain kept falling, the sludge was shovelled into Hughie's grave, and Genie's *Love you forever* disappeared *right away* beneath the shitty torrent, the eyes of the cartoon beastie on the front of the card – two black plastic beads in celluloid pods – *rolling in agony*. Everyone had heard what Mumsie said, but none of them reacted because they were all as shocked as Genie – their brassy, tarnished faces *ringing* with the impact of his discovery: Hughie's singed and battered body in the ashy carapace that had been a sleeping bag, lying on the bare concrete floor of the old sweatshop in Greatorex Street. The vomit he'd choked on was crusted in his hair. The pathologist hadn't been able to determine whether he'd died *by drowning or burning*. All Hughie's friends . . . *heard what the bitch said* . . . They stood there: the girls in their carefully assembled black funeral costumes, the boys coming on *like trampy spivs* in ill-fitting old sharkskin suits they'd *picked up in Oxfam for a tenner*. Father John and Father Derek sailed among them, smiling hesitantly, pouring sherry and encouraging them to share their memories of the dear departed while outside the rain snare-drummed on his grave . . . *Ashes to ashes, funk to funky, we know Hughie Gruber's a –.* Except that he wasn't – he liked a bit of puff . . . *who doesn't*, enjoyed a drink . . . *who doesn't*, loved to plunkety-plink on his acoustic, *My girl don't stand no cheatin', my girl, My girl don't stand no cheatin', my girl . . . My girl don't stand no foolin', when she's hot there ain't no coolin', My girl, sweet little sugar is my girl* . . . Hughie's voice was high and pure, no snide hint or lusty grunt ever fell from his *dear, dear lips* . . . only innocently *dirty chortles*. He'd had girlfriends, of course – there was one at his funeral, a stick-thin-thing in black

Lycra with a painted Sindy face who reeked of tiger balm and . . . *didn't look like much of a goer* – but then how far could Hughie have gone, what with *the precious crown jewels still clutched in 'is Mumsie's hand?* Oh, Mumsie! She'd been so bloody proud when her darling boy went to Cambridge! It justified all her favouritism . . . what *she called faith in 'im.* What a joke – he'd only applied because his *beloved older sis'* was living there and, unbeknown to him, *'cause we all conspired to keep 'im in the dark*, getting her beer money by *yankin' the 'andles in Delilah's Massage Parlour.* There are, Genie thinks, so many Delilahs in this world – but so few Samsons. Hughie though, Hughie'd been one of the Samsons . . . *outta the sweetness came forth weakness* . . . – The signs had been there from the time when he was little and *too soppy by 'alf*: crying bitterly when they happened on a blackbird's rumpled corpse, or pointing out to Genie with wild wonderment the quicksilver raindrops poised on a leaf. – In his first term at the University he went and hacked off all his lovely hair – *said 'e was a sadhu, but 'e looked like a skinhead saddo* . . . His new college friends told her where to look for him – Hughie always made friends wherever he went . . . *so open, so blindly trusting – funny too* . . . She found him in the chapel, trapped between two pillars, staring up at the figure slumped from the cross *like 'e knew what was coming.* That first time he was a week in the local mental ward, then he was himself again – except when, after his death, Genie came to consider it properly she knew that the adult self he'd grown up into *was the crazy one.* The next time they found him wandering around Grantchester Meadows *starkers and buzzing*, flinging his arms round the glossy-black bullocks' necks *and kissing 'em.* Genie had been gone by then, she was . . . *down in the Smoke – chasing the fucking dragon*. And Mumsie, having taken a job in a school in Leytonstone, had bought the house off the Roman Road – *going back to my roots*, she'd called it . . . *like she was fucking Alex Haley*. Hughie had told his rescuers he was bending down *to kiss the green serpent snaking beneath the trees*. His mouth had been full of mud, they said . . . *and there were flowers in 'is mind*. It was too much acid, 'course – but too much of . . . *everything else as well*: too much sensitivity, too many thoughts. Now all of it was gone . . . *steam offa piss*. . . and only those living ghosts had been left behind at the vicarage, spirits who silently sipped their vodka-laced sherry. Young people's funerals . . . *and I done a few* . . . were always sick and tired and stunned. Old people, they grew weaker and weaker, until by the end they were making only the feeblest of motions and so slipped gently below life's surface, *leaving 'ardly a ripple*. But the young – they thrashed about and *kicked off*, punching their way out of the life they'd so recently *'ead-butted their way into*. They left behind this choppy soundsea: *Blah-blah-blah* . . . *Terrible business* . . . *Awful for his mother* . . . *How're you getting back to town?* — Because after all . . . Genie thinks as she pushes open the wood-effect door and smells the old-man smell and sees the Clozapine in its little cup by the sink, and sees the *old motherish* man by the window in his shawl with his paperback . . . it's always the others that die: always Hughie and Cutty and Mumsie and David Martin and One-Armed Mickey. After they've *gone under* life flows in again so smoothly and rapidly, its surface unbroken, because really . . . *there's nothing down below at all*. – Quint peers at her. His chemical

381

trembling is transforming into something else: the normal tremor of old age. His fingers fidget, his desiccated lips are chafed, the long white hairs on his Adam's apple *wiggle*, he mutters and twitches – yet all this animation is pleasing to Genie. For the nine months she's worked at Lincoln House . . .*'e's been scuppered*: a burnt-out shell of a man, his carbonised face on the point of disintegrating *into ashy bits*. If she had a cold or anything else that was catching she wasn't meant to go in to see him – *Agrunyou-something-or-other*, Missus Perkins had called it, and said: His immune system is compromised – he can't fight infection. Yet he's *pretty fucking feisty now*, and this after only a couple of days of the new . . . *careless plan*. Genie hands him the biro and Quint says, Wrong kinda fuckin' pen, girlie – too sharp, it'll tear the pages here. I need a f-f-f –. Felt-tip? she suggests, and his expression is one of furious gratitude. If I'd a f-f-felt-tip, he says, I'd felt-tip in the mornin', felt-tip in the evening too – I could plot the ballistics of heavenly orbs and figure out the Godly integrals right here. He indicates the Jaws lying open in his lap. Genie sighs, But Mister Evenrude, y'know I'm not meant to get stuff for you any more. I've money, he croaks, if that's what it'll take, you chiseller – there's money in my pants pocket, over there . . . Genie thinks: He's a hold on me – and I don't get what it is. She says, Well, now, it just so 'appens I gotta go to the shop anyway for a . . . woman's thing, so this time I'll fetch it you . . . Then, standing in front of the cupboard door, she hesitates and is back yet again in Jebb House . . . *fucked on Cyclizine* — talking to that other cupboard. Knowing if she could only bring herself to yank open its door, Mumsie would be lying inside, curled up *like a pussy cat*, with a blissed-out expression on *'er savage old face*. – Debbie had written that they had *withdrawn care* from Mumsie, who'd abandoned her two-up two-down off the Roman Road and gone up to Leicester to be cared for by *Little Miss Hoity-Toity*. Yes, yes, they'd *withdrawn care* and given Mumsie *a lovely big hit of gear* and another *annanother* . . . until she . . . *was well and truly under*. Genie hadn't gone to the funeral: on the day she'd sat on the edge of the bed, looking at Pippa sleeping in her cot . . . *'er crappy little nappy* . . . *'er scrawny little legs* . . . and fought hard to prevent herself from picking her up by them and *dashing 'er 'ead against the wall*. – *I'm not going to say anything about your behaviour* is what Debbie had written about Genie's behaviour. – But she still *did the business* . . . two months later a solicitor sent a banker's draft for three grand. Genie spent Mumsie's legacy *as she'd've wanted me too – no!* Mumsie couldn't imagine herself dead – because then there'd be *no more pain for her to cause* and *no more cock, no more drinky-poohs*. A grand went to Cutty . . . *to fuck right off out of it* . . . another on debts and rent arrears. With some of the third Genie bought a few bibs and bobs for Pippa and the flat. The balance she spent on . . . *getting fucked up*. – A month after that she was still fucked up: it was spring and they were out walking by the canal. Pippa wouldn't go in her pushchair: *she 'ad a plastic figure-thingy of Ronald McDonald* . . . and kept putting . . . *its 'ead in 'er mouf – givin' it 'ead*. Genie saw a magpie perched on a plastic bucket stuck through the torn mesh of a chain-link fence. She looked away to the canal, scummy with oil and wood chips. She looked at *another planet* . . . that was Canary Wharf. She looked back: the same magpie was pecking at the stalks of some freshening foliage. She said to Pippa, Stop slobbering on that thing – and looked again: the magpie was sitting right beside them on a concrete post and giving Genie *its glittery eye*. An omen – that's what it was. She yanked Pippa along so fast the toddler tripped and fell . . . *gravel sticking in the soft palms of her 'ands*. Genie forced her into the pushchair and ran on, its wheels skittering, snagging, while the baby *didn't know wevver to laugh or cry* . . . – On the tube Genie sat, stunned: it was a Sunday afternoon and the carriage was nearly empty, but even the few passengers there *were ghosts to me*. They changed at Victoria – on the Circle Line Genie thought, This is fucking purgatory – purgatory. She could feel the methadone ebbing from her cells – and picture the bottle of linctus in the fridge back at Jebb House . . . *glowing like a radioactive pile*. They would go on like this, round *annaround* . . . the Circle Line . . . *from 'ere to fucking eternity*. And wasn't that the truth about all her relationships: if they'd endured at all, it was only because *I went round annaround*, because the second she got too close to anyone . . . *Boom! It blew up in my stupid face*. Genie skidded Pippa along Spring Street, past the costers' skeletal barrows – there was a rotting peach, a crushed banana, a scurrying mouse . . . *a dying man*. The lifts never worked so she folded down the pushchair and dragged Pippa up the stairs of Gargery House. So many houses, she'd thought: Jebb and Gargery – Aziz House, where she went to get her benefits. Geale House, the health centre – Ventris House for the DDU. All these houses – *but no fucking home*. — Long after that, when she began working with Meria Amal and the other Bengali women, they translated for her the song they sang as they pulled up the summer-softened chunks of tarmac from the car park behind St Olav's . . . *and even strips they rolled like turf*: How can I accept that my husband has gone to London? I'll fill up my suitcase with dried fish, All the mullahs – ev-ery-one has gone to Lon-don, The land will be empty – what'll I do? We sang this in Sylhet, said Priya . . . *who's all of four-foot, but a live one* . . . When we were desh – at home in northern Bangladesh. Then we thought bidesh – here – would be a paradise. How could it not be, when the probashis sent back all this money? We sat down by the Surma and sang: When my brother goes to Lon-don, he'll give orders at the tailor's, He'll make a blouse for me. Then there's the bit from the beginning again. The refrain, Genie said. Yes, the refrain: How can I accept that my husband has gone to London . . . Now you're 'ere, Genie had said, picking the asphalt from her callused palms, and is it the paradise what you thought it was gonna be? Shamila, who had a wall-eye and *screwy teeth*, laughed bitterly. It'd be some kind of paradise, she said, if my husband stopped fucking all the crack whores in Banglatown, went back to desh and left me and the kids to get on with our lives. — This time, because they didn't *'ave a live one*, it took the Old Bill ages to come. Pippa sucked Ronald's head – Genie cadged a fag from the bloke who lived next door, an old Irishman in string vest and slippers who said, no, he hadn't seen Cutty in days, and yes, Genie had probably done the right thing by calling the guards. – When they did finally pitch up, it was a solo woodentop and couple of paramedic types. Was it possible to be shocked . . . *inside of being shocked?* Because, although she'd been expecting it, *I was still shocked* when the copper kicked the door in and there it was: *a single magpie* lying on the floor on its side, not looking peaceful *or anything much* – only very dead. Genie had been so shocked she forgot for a long time to take Pippa away, and the little girl *was stood there seeing what no kid oughta see – her dead dad.* — Quint says: Well, girl, you going, then? Are you gonna get me that f-f-felt-tip? I tellya, girl, the sacred orbs can't wait – the letters can't wait. There'll be a hullabaloo if'n we don't tell Lulu. – Genie opens the cupboard at last and finds a few coins in the pockets of the dirty old trousers hanging there. The empty hangers tinkle airily – and suddenly she's striding along the corridor, her thoughts *tinkling airily* as she anticipates the sunny streets and the holiday atmosphere . . . *a landslide victory*, that's what everyone was saying. — That's what Genie's recovery had been as well: *a landslide victory* . . . All that summer, two years before, she and the others had shifted tons of tarmac and earth and rubble off the site – *sliding the land by fucking 'and*, because Geoffrey, the vicar, being a decent bloke *and no perv*, had offered it to the Bangladeshi women for nothing, so they could build a community centre. They crawled about *on our 'ands an' fucking knees*, until at last the council was shamed into sending a digger and a couple of hardhats, who mostly sat in their corrugated-steel hut, smoking fags and . . . *doing fuck all.* Meria Amal, Priya, Shamila and Genie – all the women took it in turns to look after Pippa together with their own children. Pippa began speaking a few words of Sylheti – which was . . . *sorta cool.* Genie went every day to badger them at Ventris House, 'cause *you don't get nuffink in this world unless you make a stink.* Walking along the Mile End Road on hot summer afternoons, all the Bangladeshi girls coming from school in their dark robes and their white head-scarves . . . *button-bloody mushrooms sprouting up all over*. Genie's drug worker was *a drowned rat* with a brown beard and a lazy eye that *knocked off altogether* when he was stoned – and that was a laugh: a drug worker who was . . . *working at 'is own 'abit*. He was called Dermot, and seemed to have no sense of his own ridiculousness. Genie said to him: You're gonna open your door and find me sitting out here, on this chair, reading this claptrap about clap every fuck-ing day 'til you get me my detox. Eventually Dermot did better than that – he got DSS funding for residential treatment. Meria Amal said: I'm happy to have her, Genie, but Faisal will be unhappy if she doesn't cover her hair in the street. – The last thing she saw before she got into the car with Geoffrey, who'd agreed to drive her there, was Pippa, *another button mushroom* sprouting from the balcony of Jebb House. – The treatment centre was a big slab of sandy stoniness dumped down in sodden Wiltshire fields: the summer had *gone off*, and curtain after curtain of rain swished in drenching succession between the dining-room windows and the hills that rose up two or three miles away. The other junkies were either Bristolian DSS types who burbled *a load of bollocks* or posh totty whose mumsies and dadsies brought them cashmere woollies when they came to visit – woollies the cuffs of which they chewed as they lounged on broken-down sofas and . . . *uneasy chairs*, twirl-ing the ends of their luscious hair and negatively *ya-ya-yaaing*. No one came to visit Genie – no one but Meria, Geoffrey and Dermot knew she was there. In the gloomy dining room, where portraits . . . *someone dead's ancestors* . . . looked grimly down on the human wreckage drifting about the Formica tables. Genie ate with the alcoholics, who were either red-faced salesmen types . . . *quarter-bottle of voddie an' extra-strong mints in the glovvie*, or genteel old ladies . . . *walnuts pickled in gin*. The old ladies remained pickled even after their detoxes, and behaved as if they were on *a fucking P&O cruise*, gossiping about all the amusing things said in the therapy groups, *like they was some sorta entertainment*. They were kind enough to Genie . . . *took me under their bingo wings, showed me 'ow to use a fish knife*. One afternoon in group, death – which went by the name of bereavement – reared its zombie head, and Genie found herself choking out that . . . they'd done an autopsy on Cutty – just like they'd done one on Hughie. They'd cut up Cutty – *what a laugh* – but Genie wasn't laughing, she was crying, crying hot salty tears. After the autopsy there hadn't been a funeral – his body was donated to a teaching hospital by his family. Donated! That wasn't a laugh either . . . *basically they just dumped 'im*. Genie sobbed *on annon*, imagining some cack-handed medical student taking a scalpel to Cutty's razor scars and *opening 'em up again*. The student not knowing a thing about Cutty – how he could do the Times cryptic crossword in an hour, or that when he hadn't been too *off 'is nut 'e was a decent father – no, for real*. Genie cried hot salty tears and *shared* . . . Cutty's remains . . . *with the group*. His younger brother had come to see her a couple of months after it happened. Their parents were middle-class Glasgow Jews – both psychiatrists . . . *which was ironical* – and they wanted no part of Cutty, alive or dead. The brother was quiet and diffident – he'd looked around him with ill-concealed pity at the chipped and bashed furniture, the carpet off-cuts laid on the rancid floor, and Pippa's small collection of toys – mostly give-aways with unhappy meals that were kept in a milk crate. He couldn't see the earwigs that wiggled out from the kitchen waste pipe, or, because it was too early in the year, the flies buzzing in the bathroom, or the cock-roaches moseying in from the rubbish chute opposite the front door to *infest this house – 'cause I been on the pinball, And I no longer know it all, And they say that you never know when you're –*. Cutty's younger brother told Genie they'd done an autopsy, and it wasn't the resounding smack or the screeching coke or the gasping Physeptone or the snorting Tuinal that had silenced Cutty . . . *at least not directly* . . . but a well-spoken heart attack talking its way into the flat. Cutty's magpie body had been . . . *thieved from me* – the medical student who inefficiently hacked him up had probably thought he was only some *dumb crim' or mental defective.* — It's sunny outside. The faecal fetor and acrid bleach of Lincoln House cling to Genie for a moment – then disperse. Everyone she passes as she walks along the road towards the little convenience store on Bow Street wears the same slightly dazed expression: the *historic landslide* has slid under their features . . . *making 'em all soft and wonky.* Since taking up with the Sylheti women Genie tries not to think of smelly Pakkis running dingy little Pakki shops – but it's difficult, given that Meria and the others speak as poisonously about Pakkis as they do about Derek Beackon . . . *and his Nazi slime.* It is, they say, a matter of izzat – honour: the war crimes of the past cannot be forgotten or forgiven. This much Genie does understand, because she dimly remembers the pot-bellied kids that George *and those other hairies* did the fundraiser for in New York. Sporting their cheesecloth smocks and Moroccan burnouses . . . *who the fuck did they think they were – Guardian angels?* – Mars Bars and Kit-Kats, the thousands of tiny stabbings crisps inflict on *ready-salted gums.* Genie takes the lightweight and light-blue cardboard box from the top shelf and at once feels . . . *sorta unburdened.* Acceptance – nowadays everything is about acceptance. Ibrahim, who runs the shop, looks embarrassed when she puts the Tampax on the counter next to the stack of early-edition Standards with their . . . HISTORIC LANDSLIDE*!* headlines below the faces of the Happy Couple, newly-wedded to power and garlanded by plastic Union Jacks. Mumsie used to say: *For an ugly Imperialist warmonger the Brit state does 'ave the prettiest flag* . . . But then that was Mumsie, who, *for a black-hearted cow, had a pretty face.* Genie supposes Ibrahim thinks her too old to have this sort of curse – but then what does he know: Pakki boys grow up *fumbling in the dark,* believing women's bits are *dirty bloody holes,* all they want are . . . *angelic fucking virgins.* She smiles: How're you today, Ibrahim? Yeah, yeah, mustn't grumble, Genie, mustn't grumble – new gov'ment, innit, brave new bloody world –. His revolving eyes lock on to the Tampax, he flutters his long eyelashes and blushes . . . *a pretty sight – 'e's a pretty boy.* She saves him from himself: Gotta felt-tip pen, Ib' – not a Magic Marker, but nothing too fine either? He says, I've just the thing, and tips forward on his stool to rummage under the counter, where he keeps the boxes of phone cards. Genie sees the label curling up from the waist of his jeans, and the thick, black hairs *felt-tipped* in the dip of his spine. Her eyes go to the rows of Mayfair, Parliament, Park

Lane and Rothmans. — The last cigarette she smoked was on the terrace at the treatment centre. It was the one Sunday afternoon she'd had a visitor of her own. She'd made her visitor a piece of toast . . . *and two for me.* A few minutes later she'd made two more for herself – larding them with big mounds of glistening jam from the litre catering tin she had to restrain herself from *plunging my hand in, scooping it up and guzzling it down.* Sitting on the terrace, dismembering conversation with him – tearing off arms of memory, legs of reminiscence – and watching him fussily anoint the corner of one of his pieces with butter, then a little honey, then tuck it slowly in his mouth, Genie felt the hard ball of undigested bread swell in her own shrivelled stomach. She'd only finished her detox the week before . . . *and the hunger was fierce.* She wanted to *eat every-fucking-thing:* chew up the genteel old biddies with their Victoria sponge-brains, suck down the Bristolian fuckwits drivelling their newfound dogma of *sharing and trust.* Her guest sipped his tea, nuzzling his wet lip wetter with the rim of the cup. It was the first fine day in weeks, and they'd had at least this to enjoy: *passing clouds* . . . Genie got out her mingy, crumpled pack of ten Embassy and, brightening, he said, I say, d'you mind if I bum one of your fags? It made perfect sense at the time: why give up all those addictions and hang on to this one . . . *in many ways the worst of the lot.* But by the same token: why let go of all those dull hatreds and hang on to this one . . . *the sharpest of them all.* – But she does hang on to it, and when she walks around Covent Garden she often imagines she sees him – sees him in Great Queen Street, peering at the window of the shop that sells Masonic regalia. Or, if she uses the public toilet in Lincoln's Inn Fields, when she comes out she sees him again: a tall, stooped figure in a hairy tweed jacket who examines the list of opening times attached to the railing outside the Soane Museum. *Why not?* If Kins were to come to London . . . *that'd be the sort of thing he'd do.* — Apart from the one devastating remark . . . *which touched me for the very last time, I wish* . . . Mumsie had been on her best behaviour, passing out pleases and thank-yous, giving sidelong glances at her Plantation cronies . . . *to make sure they kept in line.* The rain continued to fall – and Genie watched it fall, propped up by the window. She fidgeted with an ivory shoehorn, pressing her eyelids and cheeks with its cold curve, then using it to lift the sodden cloth from her cold neck. Kins came and stood beside her. For a long while he'd had the good sense to say nothing at all – but then he cleared his throat: Harrumph! *the stupid, loud, clumsy fucking clod* . . . She squinted sideways at the shammy leather of his old faker's neck and had *a creepy feeling* . . . it was *part of me* stretched between them, a translucent wing *of me 'an him.* When Kins scratched his neck with the backwards-upwards fingerflick that she remembered from her childhood and that . . . *still disgusts me,* Genie felt it. Harrumph! Kins cleared his throat again *annagain* . . . Your mother, he'd said, she doesn't mean anything by it – we're all very upset, of course . . . We must be kind to each other. Genie said nothing – only stared at the sodden garden, and the sodden garden roller, its rusted drum tied down by weeds, and beyond this . . . *the sodding graveyard.* The older I get, Kins continued, the more I believe that kindness is all we have –. Are you fucking mad? Genie had said — and she said it again on the treatment centre's terrace as he *bum-sucked* on his bummed fag. Kins winced. How old would he be now? At least seventy-five, probably more. It'd been kindness, she knew – kindness alone that had made him take the trouble to discover her whereabouts. He'd said: I looked in on Missus Amal, a lovely lady – very . . . vibrant – which was Kins-speak for dark-skinned – and little Pippa, she's doing awfully well. Genie rose abruptly, her knees banging the table legs – the cups and plates rattled, the sky wheeled, at an adjoining table a man in a loud tie muttered, Steady on . . . She wanted to stick out her tongue and stub out her cigarette on it – to embarrass him and spite herself. Kins sat there unruffled, his soggy red cardboard face bulging with all . . . *the stuff inside 'is 'ead.* She'd always assumed he was an alcoholic – what'd he ever done with Mumsie except *match her, glass for glass.* But now she had the same weird sensation that she'd had at Hughie's funeral: she *squeezed* his Victoria sponginess with her eyes and saw . . . *it's saturated – 'e's full up.* It was a calm saturation – *for 'im the war's over.* Besides, alkies never came anywhere within five miles of treatment centres, not voluntarily . . . *it's like vampires and garlic.* She ground her Embassy out on the terrace, and with her trainer's toe carefully manoeuvred its dying end into a crack in the paving. She stalked back inside for more toast and jam. When she returned, Kins asked, Are you all right for money? and Genie laughed . . . *like a fucking drain*: thick, sewagey gurgles of waste merriment. Let me help you out with a bit, he said. Y'know my boys are all grown up now and financially independent, and my wife and I have relatively simple needs . . . A ridge of thick cloth rose up behind his ruddy head, the tufted tweed *growing* . . .

out of the sparse hair. Kins's moist mouth had been lopsided with the ingratiation . . . *he calls kindness.* Genie thought of a picture Geoffrey had hung up in the vestry at St Olav's: blokes in fancy armour with little tutus of chain mail, hanging about propped on their spears and swords. They had page-boy hair-dos, and in among them, *casual, like it's no big deal,* were guardian angels, who were much the same as the knights apart from their floor-length wings – wings the painter had done with fiddly care, every feather picked out . . . *individually with Melawotsit lotion.* When she went in to make tea for the women workers – the way they liked it: bags, sugar and condensed milk, *all boiled up together* – Genie spent the waiting time admiring the brushwork . . . *'cause I was always crap at it . . .* and searching for the precise point where the angels' metallic armour turned into shiny feathers. *Him! My guardian angel – the very idea!* Yet, when she considered it, Kins had always been there . . . *hanging around,* not saying too much – not exactly helpful, but absorbing the very worst of Mumsie's electric anger . . . *earthing her.* Genie shifted in the heavy garden chair – her jeans were getting tight. Soon, she thought, I'm gonna start farting like a trooper . . . She laughed, and Kins had said, What's funny? And she said, I'll tellya what, see, it's all about honesty in this place – sharing honestly and telling everybody – all day, every sodding day – exactly how you feel about 'em. Well . . . let me tell you honestly, Mister Peter-bloody-De'Ath, I've always – and I mean always – hated your fucking guts. – He sent her two hundred quid. A cheque was waiting for her when she got back to Jebb House, together with Pippa, who chirruped, Tumaray dekhya kubh kushi oiysi, and

Genie said, What's that when it's at 'ome, then asked Meria's husband if he'd cash it for her. – Kins's letters kept on coming, together with small amounts of money enclosed . . . *nothing big – twenties, the occasional fifty, it weren't like I was living offa 'im.* Eventually one came that said, I don't recall if I've ever spoken to you of my brother Michael . . . and Genie thought how ridiculous this . . . *turn of phrase* was – and then how strange it was to have it *wallowing about* in her mind, this . . . *turn of phrase.* She let it wallow for a while as Kins *carried on at me* from the naff notepaper: He's been dead for some years now, but the homes for disabled ex-servicemen he set up in the sixties are still going. I'm afraid they've changed a good deal – their ethos and that sort of thing – especially since the London one's been obliged to take local government funding . . . Kins pauses, pen gripped tight . . . *in my hamfist.* Will she understand all this stuff about ethos, he thinks, and is it strictly relevant? Then again, calling her attention to funding could be *rather tactless.* He looks to the small window of the cubby-hole he calls his study and stares vacantly at the roundel of stained glass his wife has hung there, a souvenir from Iona . . . *kitsch, really*: the saintly head with a pale-mauve halo through which daylight blearies. It stirs in him not higher thoughts but memories of lower things: his own clamorous diarrhoea in the lavatory of the bed and breakfast where they stayed before taking the ferry from Mull. Maeve had heard and said, I hope you're not going to spoil everything – which was always her gently oblique way of chiding him for having drunk too much. Kins admonishes himself: Don't be ridiculous, Jeanie's perfectly bright – simply unlettered. Moira always said she was the brightest of the three, and it was only the problems with her ears as a baby that'd held her back. Kins grips the biro tight, his hand aches from the pressure he applies to the page. *Sirbert's letters were always the same*: sheets of mirror-written Braille Kins used to run his fingers over, marvelling at the pressure that this *prosaic Leonardo, well into his eighties*, continued to apply to his elder son. Kins thinks of his father's funeral — there hadn't been many people there: Missus Haines, the housekeeper, Kins and Maeve, Michael – who was already ill. *Served him right* . . . although Sirbert hadn't needed to push people away . . . *they kept their distance*. Towards the end the old man had become *really rather vicious in his bigotries*, sitting in the Blackheath house, slowly being absorbed into the pile of junk he'd amassed: the old golf clubs and car manuals, the lab equipment and the prototype hearing aids, all of it scavenged from a civilisation that *has yet to succumb to an apocalypse*. At the cemetery in Nunhead the undertakers brought a folding chair to the graveside so Michael could sit, his father's long coffin before him . . . *I struck the board, and cried, No more!* And there'd been, Kins thinks, cherry blossom – and a single magpie pinching a glittery remembrance card from an adjacent grave as he bent to scatter a few clods . . . *in the hole*. Bumbly, Sirbert then Michael – all helped down into the ground by solid and unsmiling men who a generation or two ago would've seen themselves as *artisans, planing their beech boards*, but probably now regarded what they did as *a service industry*. There was the long, tawny cemetery wall, beyond it the red-brick superstructure of a block of thirties flats, with the spring sun warming its tiled roof. There was all this . . . *solidity*, yet Kins had had the disagreeable sensation that Sirbert was being ... *buried at sea*, the long coffin pushed out from the ship's side over the roiling waters and pausing there for a moment as its occupant struggled inside, shifting his weight so as to *slide it back on to the deck of HMS Pinafore*. Bumbly's brother Martin had been a remittance man. Family lore had it that when he was dispatched to Canada before the First War, his ship had sailed up the St Lawrence, and on arrival Uncle Martin had seen at the dockside a large hoarding proclaiming CANADA DRY. He hid in his cabin but was forcibly ejected by the stewards. In the late fifties Kins had travelled to America on a sabbatical. Responding to a plaintive postcard, he met Uncle Martin at that point on the Canadian border where it bisected the bridge over Niagara Falls. The bridge was beautifully engineered ... *and tremendously stable*. Uncle Martin shook terribly – he was shaggily bearded and several of his fly buttons were undone. Down below tons of water shattered on the rocks ... *and then tons more*. The remittance man uncorked one of the two bottles of bonded liquor Kins had brought him and drank down a quarter of it there and then, ignoring the tourists' clucking disapproval. After that Kins never again ... *entirely let myself go*. – At Michael's funeral the church had been packed ... *Seldom has a man been so widely loved*, said the principal eulogist, and Kins had cavilled: 'Though not especially deeply ... The man at the lectern was a prominent politician of liberal inclinations who drank heavily and dressed loudly, but for this occasion ... *he wore a very sober suit*. The flowers on the coffin and by the shallow step dividing the nave from the chancel looked to have been *unloaded rather than arranged*, while the mourners manifested a dutiful air – a response,

Kins suspected, to his brother's own loveless *and faithless* devotion. Michael had tried to extract a spirituality from diligent charity . . . *but transcendence is a by-product, Ape*. Most of the congregation had been long-stay inmates of the Lincoln Homes – many were . . . *minus a leg or two*. Taking his turn at the lectern – *Un-der-neath the arrrr-ches!* – staring out over their resolute and traumatised faces, at their maimed bodies folded and pinned into martial dress, a forty-year-old ejaculation rose unbidden to his lips – and he nearly cried, *What the bloody hell have you got that on for?* — Kins has borrowed several sheets of Maeve's notepaper to write on – they're the faintly unsettling pale yellow shared by early-spring crocuses . . . *and winceyette sheets in B&Bs*. Each of these sheets is decorated in the top corner with a sprig of holly and a robin redbreast. He hopes Jeanie will find this stationery less *antagonising* than the stuff he normally uses – as an emeritus he's still supplied with the University stock, with its *offensively municipal shield*. Pausing, it occurs to him, *I really haven't a clue*: it could be Jeanie will magically divine the sort of thing Maeve usually writes on it . . . *O, Jesu, I feel thy spirit in that gull, That soared across the Sound of Mull* . . . She would certainly laugh bitterly and hard if she were exposed to this doggerel . . . *which would be unkind of her – and a mistake*. Maeve's faith is a deeply practical matter . . . *can-do, Americans would call it*. Two nights a week she waits for the phone to ring. When it does she listens carefully to whoever's on the line. If it's appropriate, she'll offer useful advice . . . *compassionately*. Kins knows better than to ask her what the callers say . . . *she's bounden to be silent* – although when they were younger, *and I was drunker*, he felt the occasional urge to grab the receiver and shout into it: Kill yourself, for Christ's sake! He also *groundlessly* resented the meals she cooked for ailing or elderly neighbours – as he'd once been jealous of the neglected children she'd added, on an ad hoc basis, to their own brood. *That's all changed now* . . . He understands – and approves of – her rooted existence, although he knows he could never have properly shared it. As for the kindness Maeve has shown him personally: he's always appreciated it, but now . . . *at this late stage, as we bumble about the bungalow* . . . he reveres it. Such self-sacrifice . . . *she knew I never loved her passionately – she knew about Moira* . . . was of the same order of cliché as her verse . . . *nothing short of saintly*. The sliding door that seals off Kins's book-lined nook from the living room opens, and there, in one of the gaudy form-fitting tops she favours, is Maeve . . . *with her drooping belly and her pendulous udders*. Kins sees her cast into a hungry slit-trench with others of her genteel kind, together with Brockleby's beloved Friesians . . . *in an agglutination of hooves*. Smoke billows over the jigsaw of *their tops and hides* while off to one side stands a bright-yellow digger, beside it donkey-jacketed workmen *who smoke as well* – part of a proletariat . . . *I once, laughably, believed I had some solidarity with*. Maeve holds a serving spoon – this, and a small gold cross on a chain round her neck, *catch the light*. Her *close cognate* once said to Kins . . . *You never forget the smell of burning human flesh*, which at the time he'd marked down as *typical hyperbole*. He hadn't been to Moira's funeral. He thought it best not to distress Debbie, *who's very highly strung* . . . a formulation that ill fits the truth . . . *she loathes me*. Smelling the distinctive *beefysoapiness* of Maeve's soup stock, Kins wonders if

Moira *smelt her own flesh as it burnt?* – The continuity announcer in the kitchen says, Now the World at One . . . and Maeve says, When you're done with your letter, I'll dish up. – During lunch she chats about a forthcoming jumble sale at the church hall, while a reporter speaks over her, saying it's impossible to estimate the numbers of the slain, who lie all over the muddy-red lanes of Kigali and are strewn across the green hillsides . . . *fresh laundry scattered by the wind on a flappy-wappy day.* Kins has seen the images on the television news – he says, That's nice, and Maeve says, Do you like it? It being a china marmoset . . . *or perhaps a mongoose* that shares the small table they sit at – along with the cruet stand, illustrated place mats she bought in Bridlington, a variety of china, their polished cedar-wood napkin rings, their painted glass tumblers . . . *there's no end to it all – the stuff.* He carefully cuts a section from a cold roast potato, topples it flat with the tip of his knife, puts a cucumber sliver on top of this . . . *the seed pods are Ceres's corona* . . . carefully applies a layer of salad cream, then fork-lifts the *pathetic smorgasbord* into his mouth. I'll keep on exactly like this, he thinks, until . . . – Maeve has thick and full-bodied hair . . . *fat hair* that's grey at the roots *where the henna's grown out.* She has a heavy, sensual face – the mouth wide, the top lip dimpled, the lower one curled. Her nose is . . . *predatory.* She also has a prominent brown mole at the corner of her jaw. When the boys were small enough to be embarrassed, she agonised over whether to have it removed. Now the boys are *removed* . . . and her weight-gain has overwhelmed the mole: soft powdered flesh *sliding down on top of it.* From time to time Maeve attends Weight Watchers in Stevenage – Kins thinks for the socialising. At night she cleans her dentures with a toothbrush before combining them with two parts Steradent tablets and one of water in *a bombshell* . . . she carefully places in a cabinet, in the bathroom she's filled with polished conch shells, scallop shells, convoluted sponges and a sailor doll she bought in Brighton in the mid-sixties, whose white bell-bottoms, tunic and dish hat have long since faded to the same sickly green *as his synthetic face.* Surprisingly confident in her body, Maeve always enters their bedroom entirely naked, her breasts and belly swaying around the *storm cloud* of her pubis. But she keeps her hand tightly clamped over her slack lips and caved-in cheeks until the bedside lamp is out. In the darkness – which is utter – Kins hears the bombshell bubbling in the bathroom cabinet, the Steradent tablets' effervescing amplified by its fibreboard into a tidal race that gradually ebbs, even as he himself . . . *slips down the wetted and re-wetted sand into the sleepy sea.* – His own teeth are a disaster. He sees his dentist, Mister Eckersley, *out of a perverse loyalty* – which is what, Kins acknowledges in insightful moments, has ordered the remainder his life . . . *once my fundamental disloyalties are subtracted.* Eckersley is as old as Kins, and surely would've retired by now as well, were it not the tinkering he does with his obsolete equipment in his ill-lit surgery is *much the same as anyone else's retirement* – a hobbyist in his shed . . . *or Sirbert, for that matter.* To be fair, Eckersley doesn't pretend there's much he can do: from year to year the proportion of weedy gum to eroded tooth increases, Kins's crowns are cemented and then washed away . . . *You can rinse the briny for me now* . . . At least there isn't much pain, so long as Kins avoids anything requiring *a proper bite.* – On the days Kins goes into town to visit the valetudinarian dentist, he walks through the woods skirting Hemel to Apsley Station, takes the train into Euston and walks on from there to the northern end of Wimpole Street. Every time, he remembers the same long-ago morning: waking in the bombed-out house on the west side of Fitzroy Square, Timofei bringing one of those thru'penny cartons of milk they sold back then and making tea for them on a spirit stove in the corner of the room with the sooty nets and the perished, rose wallpaper. Or at least he thinks he remembers this. It could be the memory, *like Eckersley's handiwork*, is only . . . *a partial reconstruction*. If so, *it'll do*, because, now that Kins is faced with this – the fatty soups and the cold-meat lunches, the steamed-fish suppers and the Lincoln biscuits dunked in front of the nine o'clock news – he understands that all the rest – the thousands of students that have *passed through my mind – my own children, too –* has constituted no progression at all, but only been . . . *a sort of filling*. The long, painfully bright days, when he'd lain in the hedges and copses of Lincolnshire, Cambridgeshire and Hertfordshire – the shorter nights, when he'd cooled his heels on the icy stars strewn beneath his feet. All that strange time, when he'd schooled himself to shun *lest I be shunned*, it was this: *the long walk into captivity* that had been *mine and mine alone*, the sole portion of his life he'd managed to grasp and hang on to . . . *entrails* of self-knowledge and self-forgetting that now lay *in thick loops and coils* around the bungalow, tying together the toby jugs and embroidered cushions Maeve bears back from bazaars and car boot sales. *But who is that apart? His path disappears in the bushes, behind him the branches spring together, the grass stands up again, the waste land engulfs him –*. Is it Jack Clarke you've been replying to? Maeve now asks – she'd seen another letter from him arrive that morning and . . . *she knows the bad effect they have on me*. No, he says, dabbing the salad cream from his lips, I'm writing a note to Moira's Jean suggesting she might go to work at Michael's London place. Oh, Maeve says, poor little Jeanie. Kins dutifully rolls and inserts his napkin in its ring, knowing as soon as he's gone Maeve will repeat the operation. There is, he believes, great comfort to be had for the both of them in the long impasse of their marriage: not going anywhere is by definition . . . *a respite*. He thanks her for lunch and places his plate, beaker and cutlery on the draining board. The only time in his life that he actually did any washing up was when Moira and the children were still at Dudswell – then, in a craven attempt to be the new man she said she wanted, Kins had ministered ineptly to Jean and Hugh, preparing breakfast for them and tidying up a bit after they'd left for school. Coming down from her bedroom, hung over and *caustic as vomit* in her fluffy dressing gown, Moira had railed against him: *You – you're as yellow and sticky as the yoke on that plate. You can't get it off – and you'll never get it off you: while you were pissing about in London better men than you were dying in their droves – innocent women and children too*. In his hand Kins holds *forever* the egg the oddmedodd woman gave him on the morning he was released from Louth police station. He has only to clench his fist to smell anew its richness of nutrition and fertility, and to feel its heat passing through his skin . . . *into my flesh and bone*. Jack Clarke's letter lies opened but unread in the wire tray on top of the half-sized filing cabinet in Kins's cubbyhole. Jack is old now *of course* – sick as well, while his long-festering resentment *cramps his hand, malforming all it writes.* There is, Kins thinks, something rather unfair about the effort he has to put into deciphering the abuse Jack directs at him . . . *through the picture window* from *God's waiting room* in Torquay. Kins has had to wear *a mask of effacement* so as to slip past all the snares set and nets laid by society – the Loyal Toasts and Remembrance Day parades, the more subtle and diffuse conventions calling upon the individual citizen to *express pride* . . . and thereby to enlist his own murderousness in the cause of the State's. The long walk has continued throughout his life: he has lain up in the daytime, hiding inside his pedestrian career – after all, what else would be expected of a sociology lecturer at a provincial plate-glass university but such a nondescript and wet socialism? *A Gannex ideology* . . . slung about his shoulders as a protection against the persistent drizzle of capitalism. *Vote! Vote! Vote! For Mister At-lee! Punch old Churchill on the jaw! If it wasn't for the King, we'd do the bastard in* . . . By night Kins forced himself to *go on* . . . accepting profound isolation as the price for making any progress at all. *Objectively* he understood there was a place for him with the duffel coats and the kitbags – he might've walked on . . . *to Aldermaston, then Greenham Common,* but faith, he believed, was not so readily transferable – there could be no *démontage*, the machinery of conviction crated up, shipped out and . . . *put to another use.* He remained *all at sea* . . . with this cry ringing in his ears: *Sauve qui peut!* To be shunned were he to *break the surface* – this was to be expected – but to be *shunned by the shunned?* Well, this seemed . . . *very hard cheese indeed* . . . *The cushy billet that your father's influence secured you disgusted me then and disgusts me to this day! While I suffered imprisonment in Wormwood Scrubs and abuse at the hands of warders and inmates alike, you, by reason of your upbringing and connections, sailed through the war as* <u>*free as a bird!*</u> Jack Clarke's vehemence wheezes through under-linings and exclamations – the emphysema keeping him trapped in a sitting sprint is not his only *chronic obstructive disease*, but Kins wearies at the idea of trying to clear away his former comrade's *dense delusions*. He's written to Jack *at length, several times* – he's tried, fruitlessly, to obtain copies of his own and Michael's tribunal decisions, with a view to proving what everyone who ever had dealings with Sirbert soon learned: *His probity was absolute – and punctilious.* If Kins could've been exculpated, he knew this wouldn't appease Jack, who remains *stuck in a counter-factual past*, one in which he didn't run his Exmoor smallholding into ground that had been *poor soil to begin with* . . . and latterly *whisky-sodden*. In this sunlit Cockaigne, Jack had won the fair and bounteous Annette – not, as he insisted on maintaining, been robbed of her by Kins, the *scheming Lothario*. Maeve and Kins received a round-robin letter from Annette every Christmas – this was littered with names such as Boffo Teaser, Pride of Whitby and Lord Monboddo, the fox terriers she'd taken up breeding since her retirement after a long and *probably perfectly fulfilling* career as the headmistress of a girls' grammar in Staffs. In the photographs Annette enclosed, the terriers' sharkish muzzles wreathed her own unsmiling one – she'd never married, and Kins thought *meanly*: They'll turn on you some day, your canine children, and tear you to shreds. – Although really he was thinking of his own boys . . . *the Butcher, the Baker and the Candlestick Maker* . . . This being how he mocked them in the most secure cubbyhole of his mind . . . *Maeve must never know.* The Butcher detoured to visit them when he drove from Cheltenham to see his masters in London. In winter he wore well-tailored overcoats of cashmere or still more exotic wools – there was never any dandruff on his velvet collars. He'd park his sporty little German car in the drive behind his father's ancient Rover, then come in to sit at the kitchen table, eat his mother's banana bread and inquire after her jumbling. The Butcher's closely shaven face was *rather pink*, and, although his mother never seemed to notice it, Kins could see through his expression, which was mixed with *two parts interest to one of filial concern* – concern that evaporated when he saw his father pottering by the drinks cabinet, bottle of Gordon's in one hand, Martini in the other. Bombshell? Kins would ask his eldest son, and Jonathan invariably snarled, Not when I'm driving – you should know that . . . *with all the emphasis on should.* On occasions when he'd detonated one bombshell too many, Kins needled the Butcher: I shouldn't've thought you spooks get your paws on quite enough of the public purse to afford BMWs and Savile Row tailoring – is there anything you'd like to confide in us? P'raps you've some secrets of a personal rather than a political nature? – Over the years Jonathan's once visceral contempt has grown more rarefied – during his furious adolescence they'd re-created other battles – Londonderry, Goose Green, Orgreave – and he'd squared up to his pacifist father, his fists raised. To deflate him, Kins would say, Come along now, old boy, I'm just pulling your leg. He doesn't say it any more – he feels no need to mollify Jonathan since the *turkey shoot* on the Basra road, a slaughter that in some indefinable, yet for all that real, way he's convinced his son *had a hand in*. And *having a hand* is surely what it's all about – Kins has never felt that homoousian unity, *the flesh-of-my-flesh*, with the Candlestick Maker, the Baker *and certainly not with the Butcher* that he knows he ought. Worse, he has this sympathy for others – for Michael . . . *for little Jeanie too*. The Butcher is, Kins believes, the victim of a double-bind far more exacting than that imposed by his ramshackle upbringing: the red-brick semi in which everything was *present and correct* . . . except for his father's soul, which was intermittently and confusingly . . . *AWOL*. Not much given to psychologising, Kins nonetheless has *a hunch* his eldest's willingness to *fight for the old cunt* in secrecy might relate to his own compartmentalised life. *Fuck you, fuck you, fuck cur-i-osity* . . . Jonathan has never evinced – but what if he had? How could Kins have explained this to him: Moira, on her hands and knees, cleaning out the inglenook fireplace at the cottage, her bottom switching back and forth lasciviously, in time to her raucous obscenity . . . *fight for the old cunt, fight for the old country!* as the ashy dust rose. — That morning, the sunlight dazzling through the diamond mullions . . . *I couldn't control myself*: he'd pounced on her, and *she'd been delighted* by the violent passion she'd provoked even as . . . *she beat me about the head with the filthy brush!* They'd dragged each other by the hair into the poky scullery with its flaking plaster and cobwebbed empties, Kins had lifted her skirt, torn down her underwear and . . . *had her* – a quick and savage *knee-trembler* that climaxed *for the both of us, I think* when *one green bottle did*

accidentally fall and the shattering glass was the *blitz of our orgasms.*
Because that had been the way of it between them . . . *for more years
than I ever wish to forget.* If Kins wanted Moira he had to . . . *Fight
for the old cunt, fight for the old cunt* . . . He wondered then – and
wonders still as he unscrews his pen and resumes his letter to her
daughter – if she made her other lovers behave in this fashion, or if
it was only impotent him she took such pleasure in antagonising.
Not that it happened often: maybe five or six times a year *on
average* . . . in the thirty or so *we consorted.* Kins had found it hard
to understand why it was that *I persisted* with a relationship that,
realistically speaking, was little other than *abusive.* Now that
Moira was dead, however, he could see its entire course laid out in
front of him: another *long walk into my captivity with Maeve –* who
intuited that his fleshly infidelity was *meagre and incidental to the
drama,* while she tolerated him as a cack-handed supernumerary
during pregnancies, confinements and feeding times. His elbows
on a sodden beer mat in a local saloon bar, Kins had once heard
this miserable dispatch from the front line of the sex war: *A man
doesn't pay a prostitute to have sex with him, he pays her to go away.*
This, surely, had been how it was between him and Moira, with this
forlorn permutation: *I paid her to tell me to go away . . . Dear Jeanie,
here's a little something to help you get back on your feet, and to go towards
anything Pippa might need for her new school. Things are very quiet at
my end, it's really rather amazing how long you can drag out a single
round of golf if you try –.* He stops and has the wild notion of tearing
the unfinished letter to pieces. *She doesn't want to hear this rubbish –*
rubbish verging on a . . . *confession.* He looks about desperately at

the shelves lining his cubby-hole – shelves stacked with peeling old plastic-covered ring-binders and superannuated textbooks . . . *One Dimensional Man* – then, exhaling with a long shudder, he resumes: *Anyway, as I was saying, my brother set these places up, and it occurs to me that now Pippa's in school most of the day you might want to think about a little work. When I saw you at the clinic you said you might be interested in counselling, or at any rate something in that neck of the woods* –. Again he stops, appalled by this trope, and envisions himself stark-naked, standing chest-high in sopping bracken, a rope in one hand, all about him squat and shaggy Forestry Commission conifers . . . *slouching in the grubby mist.* He releases another shuddery breath and considers: P'raps it will end like this – another suicide defeated by the practicalities. He puts his pen to one side and gets a pack of ten Silk Cut out of the desk drawer. It's a sort of paradox, Kins thinks, that he began controlling his smoking and drinking at about the same time he retired, and so no longer had any real need to. Only . . . *sort of,* because the initial impetus was supplied a few years before by Sirbert's death – after it Kins could no longer bear all the *clutter of intoxication* . . . nor the spectacle of ashtrays . . . *overflowing with dead thoughts.* — After the funeral the De'Ath brothers spent a long weekend together at the Paragon house. To begin with, they attempted a dispassionate cataloguing of the ballast their father had taken on as his *sharp prow of a nose* cut through life. Soon enough they were defeated: there was quite simply . . . *too much of it,* and it was too heterogeneous. Their father's phenomenal obsessions – the radio equipment, the hearing aids, the optometrists' lenses, the laboratory beakers and retorts, the woodworking tools – were mixed in *willy-nilly* with their mother's flimsier sentiments: she'd left no christening card unbound or lace pillowcase unbundled. No sooner had they succeeded in gathering together all the golf clubs, balls and tees than they would light upon a cache of hundreds, if not thousands, of score cards. Byrnes, Michael had read aloud, J. F. Byrnes. Whoever he was, Sirbert soundly thrashed him in Bermuda in '45. That'd be Roosevelt's turncoat southern Democrat, Kins observed drily. He was director of their Office of War Mobilization – then Truman gave him the title of Assistant President. There can't – he laughed abruptly – have been a senior politician or bureaucrat from any of the Allied powers – barring the Soviets, of course – whom the old man didn't humiliate on the course after intimidating them across the conference table. – Upstairs in the attic the brothers disinterred their fossilised nursery from beneath several strata of the more recent past. Inhaling must and linseed oil, they dug into back-of-beyond numbers of the Magnet and pulled up squash rackets *thumb-screwed into their presses for half a century*. Michael began to speak, a little, about the wars they had fought as children – the chipped Scots bugler . . . *he'd cherished*. But then he threw up his hands: I've no stomach for this, Ape. I vote we get someone in to clear the lot, flog it off and divvy up the balance once they've covered their costs. And Kins, thinking of the modest bungalow on the outskirts of Hemel – of which Maeve had already said *I've set my eye on it* – and factoring in the emotion required to empty their own semi full of redundant family life, threw up his own hands: You're right, Ape, after all reminiscence is a by-product of serendipity – you can't simply extract it from the past through an industrial process. – They spent no more than five minutes wandering the gloomy reception rooms – it'd been sufficient for them to snatch up enough souvenirs *to last the balance of our lifetimes*. Michael took only a cigarette box in the form of a silver-plated lighthouse, an ugly bibelot Sirbert had received in his capacity as one of the Elder Brethren of Trinity House. When Kins queried this choice, Michael only *shrugged his shoulders* because . . . *he must've known he was already heading for the rocks*. Kins chose some evidence of his father's punishing mental callisthenics: a few of his extramural degree certificates and the typescript of The Substantiality of Consubstantiation, a monstrous work of synthesis that, beginning in the sixties, had occupied Sirbert's final years. The book was his attempt to reconcile the Romish and Reformed churches within the context of the then fashionable existential phenomenology . . . *I'd no idea he knew anything about*. Bundling the fusty pages into a cracked leather portfolio *of comparable redundancy*, Kins solemnly swore to himself he'd do what was necessary to secure a publisher for the magnum opus, a task he very soon acknowledged – *Dear Professor De'Ath, I am returning your father's manuscript, which, while interesting . . .* – was beyond him. Unless, that is, he was prepared to spend the remainder of his inheritance on having it privately printed, and . . . *what would be the point of that?* — Lodged in his cubby-hole, Kins has an apprehension of time slowing down around him: he has entered the eye of a temporal storm. The milkman who left the Express Dairy . . . *aeons ago* piloted his electric float at supersonic speed along the somnolent suburban streets, *the boom echoing over the rockeries.* When he reached their cul-de-sac, and leapt down to fetch one gold-top and two red from the crates, the inertia spreading out from Kins's mind gripped him. The milkman waded a few steps through this time-treacle before coming to a halt on the garden path, teetering, then toppling over . . . *it's taking him hours to fall.* He's falling still – while the spilt milk has long since seeped away, and, although several times during the long morning of *our retirement,* Maeve has speculated, I wonder what's happened to the milkman? she's done nothing towards finding out, not so much as raising the blinds, *let alone opening the front door.* Kins sighs acridly – Maeve would prefer it if he didn't smoke in the bungalow, but then *there are many things she'd prefer.* He rereads the last line he penned: *especially since the London one has been obliged to take local government funding* . . . and laughs mirthlessly. The English language, he knows, with its superfluity of vocabulary, presents any moderately well-educated user with near-infinite means of expression . . . *Be that as it bloody-well-may-be* . . . For Kins, all sentences, no matter how far they may travel, always wheel round before homing in on: *local government funding.* During his academic career he wrote three books on the subject – the last of which achieved the status of a set text in certain universities . . . *not here, though, in the Dominions.* Local government funding has never interested him that much *per se,* rather, it had been a niche he'd spotted in the bland cliff-face of his subject, one he scratched his pen away at with sozzled persistence over the years, thus carving out *tenure.* I don't think, Sirbert used to chide his eldest son, I've ever in my life observed such a determinedly consistent wastage of ability as yours.

My own intellectual interests lie, as you know, in the realm of the synthetic, while my analytic powers are indefatigable – I could no more prevent them from processing data than I could . . . than I could . . . It had been a rare moment of speechlessness on Sirbert's part, and Kins felt he'd done well not to offer up: Than you could coin a metaphor, or any other figurative language. Anyway, Sirbert had resumed, that's by the by – you, on the other hand, excel at theoretical analysis, and here you are, well advanced in middle age, and an academic at a minor university, teaching a pseudo-science that really doesn't require any great breadth of mind, let alone focus. Is it your dipsomania? Is it this weakness that's so hamstrung you? Kins had shrugged it off. *We never talked*, if by talking is implied an exchange of feelings, *we only swapped information, took argument-ative tricks, made opinionated bids – those were our conventions, that was our contract.* And although he remained *eternally grateful* for the forbearance his father had displayed during the war – *better than forbearance – true tolerance*, as the old man grew more and more casually bigoted, reverting in his dotage to a purblind Edwardian perspective, from which he dimly perceived that London was filling up with wogs, blackamoors and shonks *whatever THEY may be –* so Kins protected his inner self, one he saw as possessing all the characteristics his father inveighed against: *a tiger*, roaring at a palm tree, at the top of which crouched *Little Black Kins*, wear-ing a girly grass skirt and *scoffing Scotch* . . . It would've been well beyond Sirbert's vestigial imagination to have seen the world *the way I often do*: as a complex structure of mown verges, cleared drains, tarmacked roads, electrified traffic lights and, *industrial action permitting*, regularly removed bins – all of it held together by the *local government funding* that, while invisible to everyone else, Kins can see perfectly clearly *when I'm a bit blotto*. – At Michael's funeral he had been … *more than a bit blotto*. He'd struggled through his own short eulogy and left it to the burgundy-faced politician to do the career review: Michael's distinguished war record … Most missions flown … DFC and Bar … Youngest Group Captain … The Hiroshima epiphany … The experiments in communal living … The charitable homes that grew out of these … – Hearing his brother so anatomised, Kins wanted to cry out, You make it sound so bloody simple! but could think only of Michael's final earthbound moments. He'd eaten at a cheap Chinese restaurant in Soho – one he'd gone to for many years, purely on the basis it occupied the building where there'd been a British Empire Restaurant during the war … *the two of us patronised*. Not nostalgic or sentimental exactly, Michael had shared this characteristic with Kins's teeth … *so bloody sensitive*. No doubt this quality had informed *his final bites* … Five years have passed, yet still Kins cannot tear himself away from this last supper: the sweet-and-sour pork balls, the rice grains strewn across the utilitarian tabletop – and Michael, chewing it all over, and quite possibly remembering — the evening during his first leave when they'd heard Myra Hess play at the National Gallery. Walking out from under its sugar-shaker domes, they'd seen the searchlight beams of the batteries in St James's Park stroking the low clouds' grey bellies and the greyer ones of the barrage balloons – a sight of such unearthly beauty they stood there arm in arm for sometime.

Under the influence of the Brahms, Kins had disinterred a God he hypothesised might in fact be *a bit like Myra Hess* – in appearance, at least: mannishly handsome in profile, with a broad low brow and powerful upper arms sheathed in black silk. God was . . . *immanent*, certainly, why else would his immaterial fingers arrange this dramatic light show, compose these thrilling and explosive chords, and direct *all these extras* to scatter across the doomy square, so abetting *the little house painter's Gesamtkunstwerk?* — In 1952 Kins had been in digs in Nottingham, teaching evening classes for the WEA to men from the bicycle factories who called him The Prof, and took diligent notes about Weber and the puritan work ethic. He'd little to do in the day but walk the streets, or haunt the public library – at lunchtime he'd eek out half-pints of wallop in pint glasses. – One crisp autumn morning he took the local stopper to Matlock, then walked on along the river and into Lathkill Dale. The damp grass and bracken soaked Kins's flannels and after this his socks – the stream trotted along beside him, and the walls of the modest limestone gorge, with their perpendicular joinery of embrasure and shelf, suggested to him the furniture of *a natural public library* . . . Evidence, if any more were sought, of ubiquitous . . . *local government funding*. By the time the sun was at its zenith, the stream had dwindled and disappeared underground, while the chunk of Wensleydale in his jacket pocket had fallen apart in its own sweat. He sat on a rock, everted the pocket and sucked at its seams as he looked about him . . . *rather madly* at the trailing ferns scintillating with moisture –. Suddenly a man was there, trudging stolidly down the hushed defile, wearing old-fashioned leather gaiters and a well-worn tweed coat. Kins thought of Williams's words: *They'll be coming for me any day now and it's the fucking glass-house for me – how d'you think I'll stomach that, eh? Least you can do is be free for the both of us* . . . Then he noticed the collie the man had cradled in his arms. The dog was dead – of a heart attack, the farmer explained: They'll run and run, yer can't stop 'em – but 'e were exceptional, should've stopped back home by the fire, but 'e insisted on coming with. One second 'e were running – next 'e were stone dead. Any road, it's a good way to go, 'appen y'ull agree? The man's philosophical attitude was, Kins thought, confirmed rather than belied by the tears streaming down his wind-worn cheeks – a weeping that silently continued, unremarked by either of them, as they took it in turns to carry the body back down the dale. The dead dog was still warm and . . . *beastly heavy*. Shifting its awkward weight in his arms, pressing its matted fur to his own soft cheek, Kins felt privileged to be having a part in this small drama, one with the sweet animal reek *of authenticity*. That evening, on his way to the Institute, the paper-sellers were crying, A-Bomb Test! A-Bomb Test! The photograph showed a filthy ball of exploding dirt that was formerly one of the Montebello Islands off western Australia. When his students had assembled, a gawky bat-eared young fellow called Weaver – Kins had pegged him as *the brightest of the bunch* – seemed to be voicing the sentiments of all when he said, It makes Britain great again . . . Kins, by then long used to *silence and exile*, kept his lack of bellicosity to himself, only observing gnomically, The poet wrote, No man is an island, entire of itself, every man is a piece of the Continent, a part of the main – but what is Man when he can destroy an entire island? Kins felt the dead collie's paradoxically heavy phantom to be still hefted in his arms. Looking at his earnest and patriotic pupils, he thought, Nature will have its revenge on us all – there can be no apologia pro vita nos. Our shackles will bite into our shins – when the boat casts off and sets course . . . for the Isle of the Dead. The following spring the Rosenbergs went to the chair. — And when Michael's boat cast off? *No!* In his cubbyhole Kins grinds his fists into his weepy eyes. To gift his brother such an elegiac last supper was *pat – cod – rot – shit!* The truth was Michael had been burdened by his duties: the ceaseless fundraising and glad-handing, the monstrous intractability of petty administrative tasks . . . *which I understand well enough from convening the Department.* He would've been weary – *no doubt* – and the food probably left his mouth sweet but his belly sour . . . *and griping.* His brother had taken a flimsy toothpick from the glass full of them that arrived with his bill, then, buttoning his overcoat, shouldered his way into Wardour Street, only to be struck down by this *bombshell: a filthy ball of blood mushrooming in his brain.* This was a busy weekday lunchtime, so the sight of a man having some sort of fit in the gutter was, Kins supposed, *not that unusual.* At any rate, the ambulance man he spoke to let slip: The traffic was diabolical – took us twenty minutes to get there, but 'e was alive when we did . . . Twenty minutes during which *no one had touched him – held him.* A coat was chucked over his discarded body, but its owner regretted this degree of contact . . . *as if a stroke were bloody contagious!* The ambulance man had said this to Kins as they smoked and chatted in the UCH loading bay. The automatic doors to Casualty slid open, releasing a warm fart of antisepsis into the filthy forecourt – and the ambulance man went on: When I tried to give it 'er, she asked me to fetch her keys and what-not out of the pockets, then get rid of the thing . . . *Twenty minutes!* During which he lay twitching on the hook, landed half on and half off the pavement, and looking up at the thin greyish line of the sky . . . *Nature had its revenge*, because, while the things that men and women do and say in this world may be evanescent, *including our denials of God, our consciousness of them is . . . eternal.* Oi, mate, the ambulance man said, you're not one of those blokes who's gonna make a stink, are you? I'm sorry for your loss an' all that, but I seen heaps of strokes like this and I can tellya, your brother didn't stand a chance. Over his olive-drab shoulder, Kins saw the exposed compartment of the man's ambulance, a . . . *sort of grotto* tricked out with cylinders and syringes and tubes and mysterious electrical equipment, in which he and his colleagues worked hard to . . . *snip away at the odds*, while all the time they were being rigged by changes *in local government funding*. – She hadn't really understood what the fuck Kins had been on about until she got stuck in, but now she saw it everywhere she looked – penny-pinching of the meanest kind. Lincoln House's kitchens had closed the first month Genie was on the job, and the residents unable to fend for themselves now had their meals delivered by the same contractor that did meals-on-wheels for the local authority. Gidlow, the on-site administrator, had moments *when 'is conscience troubles 'im*. One day, when they were standing in the empty basement, looking about them at the tarnished zinc of the old equipment, he admitted to her the savings were . . . *bugger all*. On top of that, the private contractors did everything they could to *shave off a bigger profit for themselves*, buying three-day-old veg' from wholesalers: blighted potatoes and wilted greens. As for the meat, it was *probably cat – definitely horse*. The tepid sludge arrived in compartmentalised trolleys that were taken up in the lifts and wheeled at speed from flatlet to flatlet – the residents shuffled to their doors, took their plates, shuffled inside again . . . *like in the nick*. Their soap was greasier, their toilet paper harder, their heating colder, their light bulbs dimmer. In winter the place was . . . *like a fucking morgue*, and the only reason anyone ever went to the communal living room was to . . . *scarf the tea bags*, which were delivered once a week and disappeared in minutes. But all this material want was as nothing compared to the *withdrawal of care*. Tucked in by the giant wheelie bins stuck in the crook of Shelton Street, Gidlow smoked and reminisced: When Mister Lincoln was alive this place was . . . well, not exactly a happy ship – how could it be – but we spent time with the residents, and they spent time with each other –. Always in and out of each other's flats, were they? Genie interrupted, and Gidlow, a fleshy but handsome man in his fifties with weirdly permed brown hair she suspected of being *a wig*, laughed shortly: Yeah, always in and out they were – 'course, a lot of 'em were disabled ex-servicemen, and they 'ad a bond. I swear, to hear 'em bang on about the war you'd think it was the happiest time of their lives. He took a final loving drag and dropped the butt into the gutter. For a moment Genie wished she could pick it up and . . . *suck passionately*. Beyond the peaked roof of Lincoln House rose the dull robotic bulk of the Cable & Wireless offices. They both contemplated its mirrored windows, and Genie wondered if Gidlow was thinking, as she was, about how all the busy worker bees in there were sitting in their *pressed boxer shorts* and their *Knickerbox undies*, tapping on keyboards, or tripping along to meetings in glass-fronted conference rooms – how all of them were *connected up* to a wider world, while inside Lincoln House *the lines're all dead*. — Genie stands in the hallway of Lincoln House. Plastic-encapsulated notices warning of bacteria . . . *and thievery* are pinned to noticeboards. Lunchtime is over, the clattering has died away, and the building is drifting into the long afternoon, floating on a thick slick of *Stelazine, Haloperidol and Largactil.* The contrast, after the shiny happy hubbub of Covent Garden, is, as ever, *enough to make yer go loony* . . . if, that is, you aren't *loony to begin with.* – She heads for the disabled toilet by the stairs and bolts herself into its confinement of tile, bleach and . . . *the ghosts of dead turds.* She usually uses the ordinary *bogs* . . . because every time she sees the bright-red emergency cord in here . . . *I feel like yanking it,* and when someone eventually comes – which would probably take *for-fucking-ever* – explaining: *I've given birth to a dead baby – that's why there's all the blood. I've put it in there – in that* SANITARY BIN, which is what she concentrates on, as bow-legged, she scratches at herself with the cheap toilet paper, then presses home the applicator. Genie feels its sharp cardboard edges *cutting into me* . . . as she slowly . . . *shoots meself up* with the tampon. *Bunged-up proper, now* . . . *Bunged up prop–*. Genie takes the stairs back up to the third floor and strides along to the door of creepy old Quint's flat with the felt-tip she bought him held like *a flick-knife in front of me* . . . It's a posh one – a Sharpie that cost a couple of quid more than he had, but she wants him to be pleased – *pleased with me* . . . Although why she should've chosen to care for this dirty-minded old man, rather than one of the more deserving residents, *is a mystery.* Gidlow said Quint had been at Lincoln House *for time out of mind* – at any rate since before his own. When he had started working there, the rumours about Quint already had the dusty quality of legends, for so long had they been decaying behind the plasterboard walls and above the lowered ceilings. Evenrude, Gidlow told Genie, had met Michael Lincoln in the war. They didn't serve together, obviously – given old Claude's a Yank. But when Lincoln's Lancaster got shot down in a raid, it was Claude what saved 'im, landed his seaplane or whatever alongside 'im an' pulled 'im out of the drink. Stands to reason a bloke never forgets something like that, and when Claude lost 'is marbles in the seventies, Mister Lincoln was on hand to do the right thing, 'cause that's what he was all about, Mister Lincoln, doing the right thing. – Genie wonders if she's doing the right thing . . . *Little Miss Muffet, sat on her tuffet, her knickers all tattered and torn, It wasn't a spider who sat down beside her – it was Little Boy Blue with the horn* . . . There are no locks on the residents' doors, and even if there were, it'd take Quint *about a day* on his Zimmer to reach his. She shoulders her way into her unchanged mental picture only to find it . . . *ripped to shreds!* He's standing in the middle of the room, his dressing gown and pyjama top are lying on the floor – and he's wrestling with a suit jacket he's managed to extract from the cupboard, struggling to thrust one slack *turkey wing* into an armhole. The jacket's fabric shines . . . *sharkskin,* and Quint says, I can smell

421

you, girlie, you've come on – best keep that clown's pocket of yours outta the water. Genie says, What you talkin' 'bout – you're disgusting! and would leave him to it, were it not for the fascination he exerts, buttoning the sharkskin jacket over his sagging belly, picking up the thick paperback and sitting back down . . . *pompously*. Genie can feel the tampon inside her sitting . . . awkwardly. Quint snarls: Got the felt-tip? She stands behind his chair as he flicks through the book's sun-faded pages and imagines it resting on the tanning thighs of some . . . *Sandra or Bernice*, adrift in Majorca for a week or two of . . . *sangria and blow-jobs*. Quint natters as he leafs: Man lay back on his bunk with his eyes shut . . . came out with this guff . . . I utilised the opportunity . . . to relieve his medical kit of some anaesthesia . . . sodium barbital . . . When we were hit I had a semi-clear head . . . 'fore that it was censorship time – Chief had a whole bunch of these V-mails . . . He said to me –. He stops, uncaps the pen and, with a neat dab, eliminates a single word, then leafs on, stops, does the same again and again *annagain annagain* . . . Genie says, What're you doing? The old man doesn't reply, only increases his pace: licking his index finger so he can flip the pages faster, scanning the lines with frenetic jerks of his head, submerging the forbidden word beneath *black ink blots*. There's no sign of his shakes now – unless, that is, the entire repertoire of actions – flip-scan-dab, flip-scan-dap – is . . . *a single complicated tic*. What're you doing? she asks again – although she knows by now . . .'cause 'e said so 'imself: *it's censorship time*. That's what he's doing: censoring every single shark from his copy of Jaws. This may be the snafu at the end of the world, Quint mutters as he dabs, the felt-tip squeaking. But how could I know 'til I read it exactly how convincing it would be –. If it's upsetting you, Genie interrupts, you shouldn't do it, and she reaches down over his shoulder to grab for the pen but, shrugging out of his own now useless life-vest, Claude tears himself from Gorecki's embrace, propels the murdered kid's one before him as a float and kicks out for the wave crest beyond the wave crest beyond this one – a crest beyond which he can see the familiar snowflake-patterned wallpaper of the Concept House's hallway, and, stuck to this by its gummed flap, an envelope across which he himself scrawled . . . *hours, maybe years before* . . . Faithful Yet With Beast. Where's Claude gone? Busner is *querulous* . . . No – worse than that, Michael thinks, he sounds frightened. I don't know, he answers, maybe to the lavatory? The psychiatrist slumps back in the sofa – he's perspiring and his hair is a mess, although his eyes have regained focus and Michael has the impression *he's returned from wherever it is he's been to*. Busner reiterates: Where's Claude gone? I – I don't think it's a good idea for him to be alone at the moment. What Zack really wishes to express is that *I don't want to be alone at the moment!* Lesley has evaporated, and now Claude – while the girl-angel at the window has vanished into the fiery furnace of the afternoon sun. The only ones left in the living room are Kit, his guardian and Roger, who's *worse than useless*. Zack rather wishes he could drag Radio-bloody-Gourevitch up from his stupor *by the scruff of his rollneck* . . . and give him a . . . *sound talking to!* – Now that the sedatives have started to take effect, and the kaleidoscopic whirling of *memories, dreams and God-awful reflections* is winding down, the *ecstasies and the agonies* of the trip are giving way to the security of well-worn irritation . . . *cosy as carpet slippers*, a pair of which Roger keeps in the back bedroom he intermittently shares with his protégé, together with some other stuff: a cache of tatty folders crammed with off-prints *of his charlatanism*, and the portable typewriter he uses to bash out front-line dispatches from *the front lines of the mental health war*. Mostly, however, *Rodge isn't here either*: he's off opening his latihans at a Subud, or stuffing his face in Cyrano de Bergerac, or attending some other . . . *love feast* where he *crashes out on the bones of his repast*. Lord knows what his square and demure wife thinks about that. On the rare occasions when the Busners and the Gourevitches have dined together, *chewing dead meat* at the Great American Disaster on the Fulham Road, Caroline seemed altogether unconcerned: touching her glassy bangs with perfectly varnished nails, maintaining a brisk patter of inconsequence while her husband sniggered and yawned and scratched over his wooden trencher, parping out the tomato ketchup, leering at the waitresses, bawdily commenting on a framed front page of the New York Times hanging by their table that showed the Hindenburg's New Jersey conflagration – *Wow, man, lookit the big burnin' titty!* Caroline had only said, Jesus, Roger, you're such a goddamn baby – implying she was fully prepared to indulge this *and carry on breast-feeding him indefinitely*. – The portable typewriter sits up there, a white plastic jaw implanted *with black teeth*, and every time Zack passes by on his way to the bathroom, he peeks inside and observes it biding its time . . . *waiting patiently* on an orange box, with Claude's books scattered around it in a circle on the floor. Really, what do Rodge's writings really amount to? They're only the *cannibalisation of the recent past*, the revolutionary moment *gobbled up to be regurgitated* in the form of pathetic stoned musings . . . *luncheon meat torn by kazoos.* – Lesley must finally have managed to *relearn the conceptual apparatus of recorded sound*, because electric guitar comes *footling melodically* from the speaker, while *a dusky voice husks*, Down the street you can hear her scream, You're a disgrace, As she slams the door in his drunken face, And now he stands outside, And all the neighbours start to gossip and drool . . . – Jumping up, Busner says to Michael: I-I rather think I heard someone at the door! – Which comes out as . . . *a series of doggy yelps!* Immediately Zack is at the front door, but, as he reaches for the latch, it swings into his terrified muzzle . . . *Meehan's coming in!* He's gathered together his *strike force*, Sergeant Sealy, the Community Relations Officer, and Mister Freeson, accompanied by . . . *heavy bombers, mobile artillery, a thousand helicopters, ten thousand men* . . . and all of it under the command of . . . *Miriam!* Who steps straight into her husband, a supermarket bag in one hand, her handbag and keys in the other, and an expression of such alternative preoccupation on her face . . . *school fees and gas bills, shoe-fittings and Green Shield stamps* . . . Zack recoils into *some further semblance of sobriety.* Oh! they both exclaim – and, spotting Mark and Danny behind her, dark shapes mutating *into further semblances of me – semblances of her*, he carries on: Um . . . I don't know – the boys, p'raps? But Miriam has already smelt the *room notes* of Lesley's joint and hears *Jimi's guitar ones* . . . so, turning to her sons, she says, You better go next door, boys, I need to have a grown-up talk with your father. Ah, yes, Zack splutters, I think the others are all in the garden – I'd better . . . and he barges past her. Hello, boys, he says cheerily, shutting out for a moment the vast and *aching-to-be-filled* void that's hiccupping over his head. Why, he thinks blearily, doesn't it all – houses, hedges, cars, dustbins – fall up there! He sees that Mark . . . *the young Mars* . . . holds an Airfix Superfortress in one hand and an Airfix Lancaster in the other – he notes that Danny is *sucking amber* . . . a traffic-light lollipop in his sweet little mouth . . . *time to stop – or to go*. He thinks of how sibling means drinking-from-the-same-stream *in Latin – or possibly Greek*, and he *draws a bead* on Mister Meehan, who's coming out of his own front gate – only to relax when this *enemy* raises his hand in an acknowledgement, *swearing volumes* about how he's *pleased to see you wid de fam-ee-lee*, so Zack waves enthusiastically back. – Danny says, We want to watch Jackanory, Dad, and there's no telly in the other house, and Zack says, Well, if you'll give your mother and me a few minutes I'm sure we can sort something out –. Then has a vision of himself dragging the Kid by his ankles from the living room of 117 and *dumping him by the back fence*. – Once he's let the boys into 119 and heard an *oddly convincing* paterfamilias's voice tell them, Behave yourselves, Zack *rematerialises* . . . in the hall . . . *faithful yet with beast*. Miriam must, he thinks, be in the kitchen – but, before following her there, he peeps into the living room and hears . . . castles made of sand, Fall in the sea e-ven-tually, and sees that Roger's gone. Michael Lincoln and the Kid are alone . . . *and then there were two!* Miriam is indeed in the kitchen: she has a jar of sandwich spread in one hand and the *bread to spread it on* in the other, Oscar . . . *who adores her* . . . is rubbing against her

426

stockings . . . *I can smell the static – it smells like the rasp of my unshaven cheek against her thigh* . . . Zack pulls out one of the chairs from the table and sits down heavily. My, Miriam says, it's all rather spic and span in here – have you been having some sort of a renaissance? Her husband's conjecture is . . . *an implausible helicopter, beautifully drawn – but too heavy to fly* . . . that nevertheless touches down perfectly on the well-wiped tabletop, synchronous with the understanding that *she means it figuratively*: although it's that long ago . . . *centuries, at least* . . . since he and Roger and Lesley tidied up the kitchen. D'you want me to get Roger? Zack plucks out of the air . . . I mean, if we're going to discuss winding things up here, I think he probably ought to be part of the conversation. She looks at him nonplussed, and this anxious shading to her face – which, with its pale skin, dark straight brows and finely modelled nose, occupies *the exact point where severity, beauty and plain prettiness meet* – jolts him: he has, Zack realises, fallen into his usual misapprehension . . . *that she is me and thinks my thoughts.* Miriam says, Why the hell would I want to speak to Roger about this? I've driven all the way over here on a school day to tell you something awfully important about us, Zack. She clutches the bread tightly, breathes the words squeakily . . . *a doctor has her by the balls* . . . I've fallen pregnant again. – However vertiginous his own *freefall*, he manages to get up at once, go to her, take the bread and the sandwich spread, put them on the kitchen unit and embrace her, kissing first her hair, then her ears . . . *Can she hear the automatism of my actions? The clockwork conditioning making me say*: That's wonderful news, Miri, I'm so happy . . . Oscar nuzzles between them . . . *a furry baby – trying to get in on the act*. Zack feels beneath his palms the otherworldliness of rayon, beneath this her shuddery back . . . *She's crying – it's only to be expected* . . . Zack would like to cry too – cry for his own detachment . . . *the poor ickle orphan boy*, because acid or not he recalls clearly: It was like this when she told me about Mark and Danny. On both occasions I went through the requisite motions of joy-at-the-miracle, but it wasn't a new life I felt stirring inside her – it was my own gestation, recapitulated. He re-experiences this metempsychosis now: the hydrocephalic brow of his foetal self, its vestigial limbs, its premature thumb-suck and the neon-blue delta of arteries worming over its fontanelle. He sees this me–him, floating in a glowing caul against a backdrop of deep space and unwinking stars. He hears the kettledrums roll, realises the seat of his imagination . . . *has been buggered by Pinewood!* and tries to summon the will needed to repress his giggles, as he's overtaken by *Waa-waa-waaaa! W'Waaaa! Boom-boom, boom-boom, boom-boom! Waa-waa-waaaa! W'Waaaa! W'waaaaa!* Feeling him grow rigid in her arms, Miriam thinks, Wood – dead wood. Her husband may've bathed this morning but the sweat of intoxication reeks in the crook of his neck . . . He's the real baby – already utterly unable to share the responsibility, and I'm a bloody fool, a bloody stupid fool . . . She unburies her face, and there in the kitchen door, staring at her with an expression she's never seen him *wear* before, is *the Creep!* who takes the tin opener dangling round his neck and, with his eyes locked on hers, slowly opens out its corkscrew attachment, then *obscenely screws it* into his *stinking ruin* of a mouth, unscrews it and runs its wet tip across his scraggy throat. It's crypsis, Miriam thinks, that's the form his psychosis truly takes. All this time we thought he was the predator, but that's not it: he's evading the predator . . . by blending in . . . Feeling her stiffen in his arms, Zack thinks, I'm wood – wreckage, bobbing on top of her hormonal sea. What, after all, is male desire? We rise up to a peak, break foaming, rise again. Whereas they – they have this terrific liquid inertia, so heavy and slow to move. We're the wind – they're the curr–. Miriam has broken the embrace, and her familiarly strange face has assumed . . . *that expression*: profound irritation with her own *great competence*. What did you mean, she says, by winding things up here? Oh . . . really, Zack splutters, d'you want to go into it right now? From the garden there comes *the antistrophe* . . . Eileen's, Irene's and Maggie's voices all . . . *rising and falling*: Podge! Po-odge! Podgie, sweetie, where are you, love?! Po-odge! Overcome by this, and by a premonition of the months to come, anxiously checking the front of her panties and seeing . . . *spotting*, Miriam sinks down on a chair. What – she tries another angle – the bloody hell has been going on here? I mean, drug-taking, pretty obviously – but what else? Zack constructs several fabrications in his mind before . . . *castles made of sand, Fall into the sea im-mee-diate-ly* and he's resigned to the truth: Roger and Lesley gave some of the others LSD – and took it themselves. What about you? she demands, and he's ready *with this tetchy self-righteousness*: Me? Me? Oh, I'll jolly well tell you what happened to me, the irresponsible idiots spiked me – gave it me without my knowledge. He sits down opposite her . . . I tell you, Miri, it's been an absolute nightmare, but I managed to take some sedatives, so the worst of it's abated. Into this *safe little harbour – she rams*: You?

You managed to take some sedatives – what about the others? Who exactly did they give this stuff to? Po-odge! Podgie, darling, where are you love? Don't hide from us – please! Irene's standing immediately outside the kitchen window, her hands cupped . . . *a bony megaphone.* Miriam says with *the bureaucratic manner of an Eichmann*: Podge, who appears to've gone missing – tell me who else, Zack, or do I have to wring it out of you? *Vee haff vays of making you tock!* Before he's *broken* . . . he tries to fasten . . . *a damp scrap of amour propre around my sagging belly* by rising, fetching the kettle from the hob, filling it . . . *how readily water washes things away – it's what it's for, surely* . . . and clashing it back down on the blackened prongs, at which point he does indeed . . . *tock*: Yes, well – Podge, but she seems to've been handling it . . . pretty well. She's stayed in her regressive baby persona – the one she calls Fiona – talking gaily about going through the rainbow door . . . That . . . sort of thing. And, um, the Kid – they gave it to the Kid, and he's . . . well, he's not doing so well. He's in the living room in . . . rather a bad way – but luckily this chap Lincoln turned up, his guardian, y'see, and I think he's doing his best to – the gas ignites with a Whumph! – reach him. Tea or Nescaf'? Ignoring this pantomime, Miriam remains implacable: And? What about Claude – were they stupid enough to give it to him? Were they, Zack? Busner stands with the jar of Mellow Bird's in one hand, a teaspoon in the other . . . *all this holding things – if only they'd float.* The moodiness lilts on from the speaker in the front room. In there are . . . *Creeps – lots of him*: three Claudes lined up primly along the sofa, two more sitting on the floor, a third flung down on the mattress . . . *and more*: Claudes dangling *by their army boots* from the ceiling tiles and clustered along the cornices . . . *Throw de darkie in de coal hole* – Claudes are a-censoring in the hall and ranged up the stairs, Claudes are in the back bedroom typing, and in his own one . . . *horsing about in my bed*. Claudes in the bathroom, juggling with bath cubes . . . *Fort – Da!* Claudes tuning their trannies and fiddling with their amulets . . . *Oh roister-doister little oyster, Down in the slimy sea* . . . Claudes higher still: up on the roof with General Shoemaker, importuning him: *Got any bob-a-jobs for me?* Claudes leering and jeering. For, although the memory of whatever it was he heard the two men discussing when the LSD *had me in its grip – mangling with my mind* has already retreated, it's left in its wake this very solid apprehension: All this time, when Busner thought he was observing Claude, *really it was Claude who was keeping a coldly curious eye on me*. He shudders, feeling the rough skin of Claude's psyche *scccraping* past him, as the *beeg feesh* circles below the surface of the apprehensible world. *When will he charge from below at these merely superficial events?* Well? Miriam insists, Were they? Wearily Busner concedes: Yes, they did give some to Claude, but here's a funny thing: it barely seemed to affect him – on the contrary, for the past few hours he's been making more sense than I've ever heard him make before –. Po-odge! Podgie, pet – come on now, Podge, don't be a silly-billy, this is no time to play hide and seek. Miriam, who's holding Oscar's wounded muzzle between her hands and thighs, tut-tuts over this, over that, over . . . *bloody everything*. She says, Don't you think you should help them find Podge, Zack? You may believe Claude's perfectly lucid – but a moment ago he was right over there and made an absolutely filthy gesture at me. Busner turns – and the green Claudes thronging the hallway change to aquamarine, to cobalt-blue, to blue, to silver-blue, to silvery, to silver-white, to transparent – the particulate wave *gushes through my head, how readily water washes things away.* He staggers, collapsing back into the chair opposite his wife's. How, he thinks despairingly, can a bird be mellow? while saying: In a moment, dear, I need to collect myself a little . . . *a dangerous locution,* because no sooner is it out than he sees his own severed head set on the enamel-topped bench, and Claude preparing to attack the raggedly exposed windpipe with *one of Roger's scalpels!* Anyway, Busner gasps, with a new little one on the way . . . Claude . . . Roger . . . I meant what I said . . . before you quite rightly pre-empted me . . . This ghastly episode has confirmed it: it's time to wind up this, um . . . experiment in communal living. I – I don't believe any of the Concept House's residents are . . . significantly less distressed than they would be anywhere else – if they are, it's only at the cost of those around them being markedly more . . . distressed. Y'see – he brandishes the teaspoon authoritatively . . . *nearly my old self* – the overall quantity of, um, distress remains the same, y'know –. *A giant bog brush!* shoots through the back door, it . . . *scrubs round,* only to reveal that it's *Maggie's head in curlers.* Maggie's face says: Oh, hullo, Miriam, didn't know you were here – have you seen Podge, Zack? She's gone missing and we're all getting a bit worried. A bit worried is, Busner thinks, what Maggie is all the time – her anxiety given tangible form by a ceaseless but controlled agitation: *knitting two, purling three, casting off, crocheting, fiddling at her hair with pins and rollers* . . . Miriam says: We'll be with you in a minute, Maggie dearest, Zack and I are just having a rather important chat. Maggie's head is withdrawn, and they hear her clambering over the broken fence into the garden of 119, calling out: Podge-ie! Podge-ie! I'm glad, Miriam says, you've finally begun to see sense – look at this. She pulls a folded Evening News from her handbag and spreads it on the table between them: FOUR DEAD IN KENT STATE SHOOTINGS shouts over a fuzzy photograph of crumpled bodies and kneeling, keening girls. Oh, I say, Busner says – and Miriam snarls, Oh, you say, do you – you say. Well, I say this is where all your libertarianism has been headed – these poor children gunned down by the National Guard, those other idiots blowing themselves up in New York a few weeks ago – this place, with its mentally ill patients – which is what they most certainly are, Zack – running amok. You need to grow up and take some responsibility for things right now. Right now, Busner echoes absently, for all he knows is that *it's true – this is the watershed*. He tries to . . . *stay in the moment* . . . but can't shake the last few *jewelled arabesques* from behind his eyes, *Godly integrals – Satan's differentials* . . . the solution of which tells him *time – like identity – is a relative concept* . . . since directly before he gains the final wave crest and reaches the safety of *dry linoleum*, there's a sharp blow to the back of his neck. Claude stops swimming, goes under, comes up spluttering, Wh-Wh-What the fugg! The Chaplain's salt-encrusted moustache is . . . *in my face*, the Chaplain's hand is . . . *round my throat*, while the one wielding the Very pistol torn from Claude's belt is raised up to . . . *do it again!* You're. Not. Getting. Away. So. Easily, the padre pants. I. Saw.

433

What. Happened. Back. There! The mirage of the suburban house decades away crumples into the unceasing watery heave and Claude realises: I'll always be here . . . always. If I die and go to heaven, heaven'll be an ocean and there'll be assholes same as this one floating about in it, waitin' to stick it up my keister. What. Do You. Care, he gasps back in the Chaplain's face. What's. Gonna. Happen. To. Me – I'm. Gonna. Die. Isn't. That. What. You. Want? – There's no fixed point of any kind in this ever-changing, never-changing water-world, over which flies a dispersed flock of raucous seabirds. There's certainly *no firm ground* for this *sophomoric debate*, the kind of *bull session* Claude remembers having with his Columbia class men in the corridors of Buell Hall before *I began seriously cutting classes*. There's satisfaction, however, to be gained from the insight – no matter how fleeting, for it's *slapped out of me* by the next wave – that the Chaplain may actually *drown too* in the very process of calling Claude to account. He's plainly at the limits of his own endurance: all night Claude heard his voice, ringing out over the men's whimpers and wails – sometimes from nearby, then from way off: *Ego te absolvo a peccatis tuis, in nomine Patris . . .* By dawn he'd acquired the strange fruit of all these absolutions: a necklace of thirty or more sets of dog tags, their chains tangled round his straining neck. Claude theorises the Chaplain must believe so strongly in the afterlife he imagines these useless hunks of nickel to be *amulets in which the souls of the skin angels are preserved*, or perhaps he thinks they're *radios over which he'll be able to hear the faint voices of the dead* telling him what to expect as soon as he gives up paddling *and joins them*. But no – *no such fucking luck*:

for providentially, *as he'll see it*, a life-raft comes scooting down the face of a wave, and, snagging the rope trailing from its thwart, the padre pulls first his own *miserable clanking carcass*, then *mine*, into . . . *the raft of Medusa*, which is some ten feet by four of canvas stretched over a balsa framework. It sits low in the water, floors awash, so the two dead bodies on board wallow in this bilge, while the five live ones are obliged to stand up *on tippy-toe*, hanging over its sides. – There's some muttering from these *Amos and Andies* as the Chaplain and Claude are *piped aboard*. But the Marine master-sergeant – who *fancies himself as Nimitz* and *has a jones for the habit of command* – spots the Chaplain's silver crosses and so quells the mutiny. Within the first five minutes they're on the raft, ten times as many other boarders are repulsed: the saved have armed them-selves with paddles, boat-hooks and spars from the wreckage – and with these they stab at chests and crack heads *unmercifully*. The Chaplain's bedraggled blond moustache no longer hides the *irresolution* of his lip – *he's on the ropes* – so Claude rides him: What the fuck didja do that for? You b'lieve I killed that kid – so lemme die, isn't that punishment enough? The Chaplain's eyes are swollen and unseeing, his hands are *puffed-up baseball mitts* – although dying, he summons the *spiritual fortitude* to *weigh me in the balance*: Suicide, he whispers, is a kind of murder, man – it's a sin, a mortal one. Claude shakes the Chaplain's head – but he's not to be silenced. He preaches on, even as his congregation deal out savage blows, and his sermonising becomes his own death rattle: It's not for you to decide when you die – no man has . . . that right. You . . . you – you'll die in God's time, not your own. Your judgement . . . when it

435

comes . . . and it will . . . will be in heaven, not here on earth. – Claude would enjoy pointing out to the padre the utter fatuity of this particular expression – given the circumstances – but the opportunity is denied him, for within minutes the Chaplain has gone to meet his Maker . . . *presumably another fuckin' Boston Irish cut from same musty jizz-stained cloth,* and a short while after the sun's rim nudges the horizon. When the killing begins in earnest, Claude has a ringside seat, one from which he can see the swimmers in the water cling together, then fall apart as the waves . . . *rock my soul in the bo-som of Abraham.* To begin with, it's the dead they take, which is *entirely reasonable:* the listless corpses are instantly reanimated, their sightless eyes take one last look at the fading light, their arms jerk up to signal . . . *Time out!* then they're gone. Soon enough attention shifts to the living. Initially, it isn't clear to Claude why one man is ravaged and the one beside him spared – then he under-stands: those who've kicked off their shoes are attracting suitors with the white flash of their *tootsies.* Those who've shed their pants are still more appealing – and those who're *bare-assed naked* are the most of seductive of all. Claude almost wishes the padre were still in the land of the living . . . *or should that be the Island of the Dead?* . . . so he could draw the holy roller's attention to this phenomenon, which might be down to murderous lust, or prissiness . . . *it's hard to say.* Instead it's time to say . . . *So long, farewell, Auf Wiedersehen, adieu.* Claude's shipmates are getting restive, they've slung the other corpses overboard and now it's *Chappie's turn to take a bow* . . . over the gunwale . . . *Adieu, adieu, adieu!* But before he goes Claude removes four or five sets of dog tags and puts them round his own neck. The master-sergeant says, Whaddya want those for, fly-boy? And since it's a civil enough inquiry, Claude answers: Luck, maybe – or they might talk to me – he presses a tag to his ear – tell me what the fuck's gonna happen. The Chaplain dives straight down, drawn head-first by the deadweight of his mementoes – he gets a little goosing . . . *his ass pinched – but what's a girl to do?* Anyway, this doesn't last long – he's made it through the crowded *chow line* . . . and is gone. Claude watches him sink for as long as he can see his twirling feet – it's a peaceful enough sight, and a distraction from the swimmers' shouts and screams, which are *frankly rather overdone – vulgar, sobbing, maudlin rummies pleading for mercy in the tank.* Claude's confronted by one fellow who manages to grab on to the raft – every contour of his face is defined by a desperate yearning – then his body shivers and shakes, reaching . . . *a climax*: the blood pours from his eyes, his mouth, his nostrils, he goes limp, lets go, lazily up-ends . . . *a cork* . . . from the end of which protrude *three . . . four* white vertebrae. The offal slick spreads out across the water, replenished *for a time* by the pumping of the half-man's heart. – Anywhere Claude directs his gaze there's more of the same . . . *to feast my eyes on*: arms are taken off at the shoulder, legs at the knee or crotch, heads at the neck . . . *kinda merciful, really.* Try as he might, Claude finds it difficult to maintain the necessary detachment – appreciate the spectacle for what it is: *a Saturday night fish fry* . . . attended by . . . *jigging jig-a-boo diners*, who're such *jive bunnies* . . . they can hop, dive and eat . . . *to their cold, cold hearts' content* all at the same time. He guesses it might be time for *a few more vite-a-mines* . . . after all . . . *if you gotta Johnson you oughta*

437

give him a little Johnson's waxing, eh, Molly? Where'd you put the stuff – *in Fibber McGee's closet?* There are two more of the syrettes in his shirt pocket – but, while his shipmates are mostly distracted by *show* *time*, there's one big lunk – a Hoosier, to judge by his honking – who can't take his eyes off Claude. *Maybe he's a hop head too – could* *be he's made me.* – The big circle of swimmers the Chaplain managed to tie together drifts away from the raft, attracting as it goes more and more desperate men, who grab on to the writhing mass of their comrades . . . *in arms.* Safety in numbers is one of the many delusions, *like truth, justice and the chain of command*, that have been torn apart and scattered on the waters. When the setting sun's last low-angled rays lance into the bloodied waves, a furious mêlée engulfs the group, seemingly *from within* – arms throw punches, legs kick free and bodies are lifted clean out of the water and slung . . . *every which way.* The master-sergeant, *who probably enjoyed* *counting them off the LS at Iwo Jima*, takes a perverse pleasure in doing the same now: synchronising his watch with the feeding frenzy, he remarks to the others, We-ell, that's maybe fifty of the poor bastids gone in the past ten minutes. This intelligence Claude snickers at – because, what with the distraction, he's managed to *take another shot in the* leg. Soon after, the night falls on top of them: banked-up masses of cloud blowing up from the south cover the *bare-ass moon* . . . and the dinner-and-dance crowd *slink off back to* *the depths.* For a long while the six men in the raft can hear the remaining swimmers hollering and beating the water with their hands – and if Claude weren't so sweetly drowsy, he'd tell them to cut it out because it's interfering with . . . *my nod* . . . *Oh roister-doister l'il oyster, Down in the slimy sea* . . . – At last, *mercifully*, the wind gets up and the raft spins away from them, sliding up on the acclivity of each wave, poising for a lurching moment, slip-surfing down into the next *hateful trough*. Claude, his arms hooked over the side, his back cushioned by the kid's life-vest, his legs rolling in the cooling bilge water, is perfectly content . . . *you gotta take your ease where you can*. One hand is *down my pants* . . . and the other *leafs through a Nick Carter*. Pop has one of the newfangled radiograms, teenage Claude carps, but he won't lemme near enough to adjust it, so all we get to listen to is the Hot Five blowing in a blizzard of interference. – Long past midnight, two of the *dumb Prairie polliwogs* get a powerful notion to drink their own urine. Claude looks on amused as they kneel before one another in turn and cup their hands to receive *the trickled libation*. The master-sergeant . . . *such a prude!* . . . is disgusted: What're you morons playin' at? he barks. Doin' that'll drive you as crazy as guzzlin' seawater – break it up, now! But he's too weak to intervene – and before long the big Hoosier and *his mule-skinner pals are getting in on the circle-jerk*, slurping up whatever droplets they can – licking their fingers too . . . *mmm-mmm*. Claude wishes their apple-pie moms could get an eyeful of this . . . *faggish behaviour*. When they're done, they collapse back against the sides and . . . *that's worse*. All there is to look at are their swollen, oil-stained faces and their white teeth when they open their mouths to *Happy talk, keep talkin' happy talk* on the subject of rescue. Claude has no illusions: If they were gonna find us, he thinks, they would've by now – it's been over twenty-four hours since the Indy went down. Distress messages would've been radioed to Guam before the ship was abandoned – and they're at most a couple of hours' flying time away. *No!* Claude holds fast to this *prophetic hairball*, its fibres thick with *bile*: We're a sacrifice, an offering to Neptune or Poseidon or whoever the fuck he is. Such detachment is possible so long . . . *as they let me alone*, but maybe an hour before dawn, conditions on the raft *take a turn for the worse*. For sometime the urine-drinkers have been silent and eyeing each other suspiciously, now the master-sergeant says, I dunno what you got there, sailor, but if it's K-rations you oughta share some with your shipmates. Tucked up in his warm narcotic bed, Claude thinks, Who cares? It ain't like the big Hoosier's got a chateaubriand and a glass of fine Tokay – it ain't like he's got hash browns, eggs sunny side up and a whole mess of bacon. But the master-sergeant doesn't take this live-and-let-live approach, he's got *Camp Pendleton stuck up his fuckin' ass*, and he says: That's an order, sailor, then, when the Hoosier goes on nibbling just the same, there's a dull gleam and the master-sergeant says, This here's a Ka-Bar fighting knife, near 'nough ten inches of tempered steel, sailor. It's property of the United States Marine Corps and was issued to me for the sacred pursuance of my command. Claude would like to point out to the master-sergeant he's outranked . . . *if I could be assed* . . . then mock him: *Property . . . Sacred . . . Pur-su-ance!* What kinda damn-foolishness is this? But the Hoosier beats him to it: Oh, ma-an, can you hear yourself? Boodlie-property, boodlie-USM, boodlie-sacred, boodlie-command – why don't you shut-the-boodlie-fuck boodlie-up? – When the two men begin to fight, it's so slow and clumsy the others pay it no mind. Claude almost admires them: to peck away so . . . *the Woody-Wood Pecker-heads* . . . at their dumb pecking order shows a *degree of conviction.* Claude remembers amateur bouts at St Nick's Arena . . . *West 66th and Columbus* . . . Tough Puerto Rican and Bajan kids *sockin' the shit outta each other for ten bucks*, the peculiar smack-squelch of padded leather hitting flesh, their squeaking boots on the tight canvas, their own grunts and the gentle patter of blood *on the worn boards.* This was a different variety of roughhouse: the sodden bodies grappling on top of each other, the slack canvas inches deep in water, and the lighting so bad *you can't see the action*, only the result: the master-sergeant's KO'ed corpse rolled over the side, followed by the bodies of two others who'd died in the night. The Hoosier and his pal lie back to savour the *remainder of their repast*, which is . . . *bupkis*: salty Spam and a few crackers. Claude considers whether to congratulate them – it takes some robust self-belief to muscle in on the action when there're so many other, sleeker, heavier-weight contenders around – but then they turn their attention to him: I say, loo–tenant, the Hoosier whines, and his stooge joins in. I say, loo–tenant, the Hoosier needles, how come you're down here in the sea with all us sad swabs? How come you ain't up there with your pals? I seed 24s and 29s coming over all day – seems like maybe they don't love you. That surprise you? Really, now? – Claude's disinclined to answer . . . *I prefer not to* . . . because, when all's said and done, *there are a thousand million questions about hate and death and war.* Instead the smarter option is to give the Ka-Bar fighting knife a wide berth . . . *slide by the hat-check, wait for a cab out front* . . . Where it's cold and grey and almost silent to begin with,

441

save for the *holy rollers'* hissing: *Forgive us our tressssspassses, asss we forgive those who tressspass against us* . . . But as soon as the sun pushes above the wave beyond the wave beyond this one, Claude feels the warmth ebbing from the ends of his fingers and toes. He gropes up under his life-vest . . . *No! No! Jesus, no!* The last syrette is *a useless scrap of tin* – it must've been burst in the night by the first or the ten-thousandth concussion as Claude was thrown against the raft. Now pain is everywhere in the sea . . . *the sea is pain* . . . and blanched body parts swirl in it, stirred by the long tendrils of a man-o'-war jellyfish – while the holy rollers who're still alive greet the dawn with a rousing chorus, *'cause we're the worms.* – The first hit is so spectacular Claude experiences *a kinda awe*: a man is lifted clean out of the water and comes water-skiing between the others, a broad wake curling behind him, red, red flounces all over his sambaing body as he *wing-walks down to Rio.* After that the Katzenjammer Kids *zip it* and await their turn with sullen resignation. No one's minding the store any more . . . *now that the padre's amscrayed*, the men tied together in the water slowly unravel, as first one is winkled out of his life-vest – then another is *asked to dance.* Yet still *poor Claudine* remains *a wallflower*, her bare tootsies *a–twinkling*, her salt-encrusted, oil-smeared face *too ugly* to attract any suitors. She pals up with one girl who spews up blood, then *jitterbugs under* a second, who calmly *unhooks her own brassiere* . . . then, with a relieved, grateful expression, *offers her body to the football team.* – The sun's right up when the last of the MS ebbs from Claude's veins. His eyes widen and widen . . . *great dishes focusing all the rays* . . . *on to exposed nerves.* Sight, Claude realises, is pain . . . *always has been*. To look upon the adorable face of a new-born baby *is as hurtful* as it is to contemplate the huddle of men he's floating towards, who've *still got the spunk* to whoop and holler and flail the water. Floating into a patch of lucidity, Claude estimates there are maybe two hundred left alive, and – good logistics man that he is – he figures that with each one who goes the odds diminish for all those who remain. It should *consternate* . . . but it doesn't. *Wehe dem Fliehenden . . . Welt hinaus ziehenden!* If Pop were here, Claude would share this dope with him: The odds don't matter, 'cause no matter how bad they may be . . . *it's always the others who die*. When the hallucinations begin, Claude joins in enthusiastically: he too can see the railroad tracks laid out around the horizon in a great and scintillating circuit – he also sits, ready to drive to the station and catch a train *outta here* in a stalled Studebaker, *if only I could find the ignition*. He also looks up into the sky and witnesses hippogryphs and pterodactyls escorting vast formations of *skin angels* away to the *plains of heaven*. Some *clever girls*, who believe they have an angle, have figured out their suitors are mostly preceded by pilot fish, so they go for these with their knives, convinced that if they can kill them, they'll be left unmolested. Claude's irritated he's been dragged back down from the wide-open sky to this badlands of bluffs and sinkholes that *won't keep still*. He ducks his head down for the first time since he said so long to the Kid. They're all there: *Ivan Shark, Fury Shark, Admiral Himakito, that Chink shit-bird, Fang . . . the sinister Barracuda . . .* and there's another one he hasn't seen before, one he immediately realises is . . . *my nemesis*. This shark has an enormous swollen white brow, hateful *piggy little eyes*. He charges straight at Claude, travelling so fast his dorsal fin sends up a fine *whip of spray* towards the hot white sky and the sun's *throbbing white-hot disc* . . . The shark wears a threadbare pale-blue regulation dressing gown with CT stencilled on its breast – its skirts flap wildly in his churning wake as he comes on, his button-black eyes slipping and sliding across the swimmers' faces, sizing them up as *meat hangin' on the bone* – and still he aims unerringly for the most defenceless man in the oceanic room, with its peeling wallpaper sky, its dank-grey towelling clouds, its linoleum waves, its bobbing avocado mines, its wreckage of bath cubes and soap bars worn *smooth and dry as cuttlefish under a 40-watt sun* – and as he rises up out of the water it purls away from his forehead in *red swirling curls!* and Claude is gripped by a terrible rage: Better to end it . . . *now! Right now!* Not go on *round annaround!* He tears at the tangle of dog tags about his neck and discovers among them *a can opener!* He fumbles out its corkscrew attachment with swollen nerveless fingers, then lunges at the shark's face *again annagain*, until the blood is full of bathwater and the shark is bellowing for Help! He-elp! HEEEELLLLP! – a cry no one hears at first because *we're all gathered together* in the back garden of 119, looking up at the window of the bedroom Maggie shares with Irene. Irene arches her long back and curtseys to a broken cucumber frame. You are the wind, my darling, she declaims, wind-milling her arms, you are the rain, the sun and the sky. Miriam says through gritted teeth, I don't think that's altogether helpful. Oh! But Zoroaster and Zarathustra, Irene cries, Finnegan and Alice! They've all been through the rainbow door and now it's Podgie's turn! You are blessed, my darling, she calls to Podge, chosen from among all of us spectrum girls! Miriam doesn't think Podge seems especially blessed, sitting there on the outside ledge, her bare legs dangling, her blonde tresses messy, her eyes locked on the railway embankment, and her thin white arms flexing as they take up the strain. I'm ready, she calls down, I'm ready to go through the rainbow door – but you will join me there on the other side, won't you? You won't be a meanie, will you, Rene? A train comes fernicketing along, and under its noisy cover Miriam curses her husband: Do something, you bloody idiot – do something! She's going to jump any second! But Zack only stands there, the jar of Mellow Bird's still in his hand, his *fishy mouth* hanging open, his own eyes . . . *watering*. Miriam frantically considers the options: Eileen is beside them, Barbie Jesus at her breast, absorbed in her fugal feeding state – Clive is drunk and distressed, balling his fists in his Fair Isle, hunching into the shrubbery, then hunching back out . . . *because he cannot bear to miss whatever's going to happen.* As for Maggie . . . *the tricoteuse* . . . on she clickety-clicks – although it's worse than that, because, holding the *yashmak* of her handiwork up over her mouth, she mutters, Jump, and then a little bit louder, Jump. Her eyes are bright with childlike desire, and it can only be crazy childishness that allows her to believe her next Jump! – which is very loud – remains unattributable. Podge peers down at them all: Are you sure I should jump, Maggie? she says. I mean, golly, I do want to . . . And I shan't blame any of you if I'm not lifted up with the Maharishi and Meher Baba and taken through the rainbow door to Sector 6. If I do, um, just bash down on to the patio . . . and I'm all smashed up, I'm worried . . . I'm scared I'll be fat – I don't awfully mind being deaded, but I can't stand being fat . . . Miriam is stricken by all this stasis: shackled to her husband, to the residents . . . *to Barbie Jesus and bloody Willesden* by her own inertia. The fall yet to happen plummets through her imagination: Podge, an outcast from heaven – her streak through these few short feet sickeningly prolonged, giving them time to admire the onrush's artistry as it arranges her hair into a blonde semblance of wings . . . *a skinny angel*. Do something, Miriam begs, or at least say something! – Movements, when at last they arrive, have a provisional feel: No one actually does anything – instead they strive to illustrate the form their actions might take, *were we by any chance to perform any*: Oscar tries to jump up at Clive, his paws scrabbling on the stocky man's thighs – Eileen tries to remove Barbie Jesus from her breast – Irene tries to get a forsythia bush to lift her – Miriam tries to reach the back door to 119. She has clear images of the knob turning in her hand, the chipped crockery on the shelves of the old dresser, the faded Axminster runners in the hall and on the flights of stairs she pelts up, a pillowcase dumpy with dirty laundry on the first-floor landing, the photo-booth strips of Podge striking poses Sellotaped to the wall beside the unmade girl's disturbed bed, and Podge herself, her shock smoothing to relief as Miriam throws an arm about her waist and hauls her bodily back in through the bedroom window – none of this actually occurs, any more than Zack's efforts to catch the falling girl amount to much more than a shuffle forward and a tentative movement to . . . *offer her a cup of Mellow Bird's!* – It's left to Podge, whose elbows *really do* decisively bend, then extend – it's left to Lesley, whose arm *really does* lunge through the window in time for him to grab the back of her dress. *I wonder if one day you'll say that you care . . . If you say you love me madly, I'll gladly be there . . .* Podge dangles from the end of Lesley's . . . *string.* Her tartan mini-dress is a *noose* around her armpits, her bared body thrashes from side to side, rendered all the more shockingly naked by the *scraps* of her underwear, and the plumes of perished mortar and brick dust her heels drum from the Concept House's worn façade. – Now at last . . . *at last!* . . . Miriam's husband sees fit to act: *really passing* the jar of Mellow Bird's to her and stepping forward to stretch up his hands and capture Podge's bare feet . . . *flying fish* . . . and for a moment, before the girl slithers down into Zack's arms, Miriam sees the peculiar look he exchanges with Lesley up above and knows . . . *something sexual has passed between them – all of them.* Since the general spell has been broken, she's prepared to act upon this information *right away* – and would do so, were it not that, as they all gather round and reassure Podge – Of course you didn't look fat, darling – and the girl's sobbing subsides beneath their soothing, a distress call Miriam realises she's been hearing through-out this crisis, but has repressed, rises to a bubbling screech: Help! He-elp! HEL-EL-EL-ELLLLP! and dies. – There's no room for everyone on the landing: they mill about bumping into each other, some ricocheting off into walls, others rebounding through doors or rolling down the short corridor and into one of the two smaller back rooms. Yet others cannon into the banisters and end up as part of the general confusion. There's no room for everyone on the landing, and he can't identify any individuals – only a generality he knows to be . . . *everyone*, because, although he and Miriam reached the bath-room first, and did their best to maintain a *professional demeanour*, *everyone else* was close behind. There are no individuals – and there are no discrete sounds – instead a low hubbub assails him, which could be collective human distress or – and this seems just as likely, given the aqueous light and moist atmosphere – the queasy *quale of seagull-and-seashore*. Nudging up against a man and a woman who, although *sobbed by racks* and loosely embracing, are still managing to revolve in the awkward space, Busner attunes his ears to: Oh roister-doister li'l oyster, Down in the slimy sea, You ain't so diff'rent lyin' on your shell bed, To the likes of l'il ol' me – a signature that calls to his mind a *signer* – and through the open door, sitting on the sag-bag in front of the orange crate supporting Roger's typewriter, he discovers Claude, with the gory corkscrew-cum-tin-opener clotted together with the rest of the bloody pendants on his pathetically stained *and fanatical bare* . . . chest . . . *LESS PASSION FROM LESS PROTEIN – LESS FISH* . . . Shock ebbs away – and surges back: Busner stands on the bleak foreshore of his own consciousness, seeing the red bath-water . . . *Fort* . . . and the white *bivalve* floating in it, sucking in the *protein-rich nutriment* through one orifice and bubbling it out *through a hole corkscrewed in its throat – Da!* Claude completes his couplets: But roister-doister you're somewhat moister, Than I would like to be . . . and falls silent. Completely silent – so silent Zack hears the susurrus on the landing, hears also Michael Lincoln on the phone in the hall: Possibly an accident, quite likely something more serious, at any rate the police should attend. *Attend* . . . it has a decorous sound, it *betokens beadles and dance cards* – but Zack's received these particular attendees enough to know *it won't be like that*. Before they attend there's this awkwardly shaped hiatus – *an elegant spiral staircase boxed in with plywood*, one in which the *predator* remains free to *peck a key . . . peck another . . . peck a third . . .* and sigh: I didn't do it, y'know. I mean, it's not like I didn't want to – I've wanted to stick a shiv in the bastard ever since I first saw him, but I didn't do it. – Claude pecks another key on the typewriter and laughs sourly: It's like, Gourevitch, right, he's such a fucking creep, he always wants to be in on the next thing, he thinks he's so goddamn avant-garde – well, yeah, he beat me to it. Did it to himself before I could . . . — Thankfully the ambulance men attended first. Zack remembers Miriam coming out from the bathroom, wiping her hands bloodier on one of the towels and saying to them as they stood there on the landing . . . *all Blancoed bandoliers and Brassoed buttons . . .* There's a lot of blood but it's actually pretty superficial, the problem will be infection . . . maybe tetanus – that, and getting him out of the bath. – What hadn't been a problem was corralling the residents, who, as soon as the ambulance came clanging down Chapter Road, fled to the end of 117's garden, and remained gibbering there, huddled in the shrubbery, until it was all over. When the Panda car had gone, Zack watched the ambulance men carry out Roger in the sling of their linked arms, his naked body enfolded in their clothed ones, his ravaged throat wrapped in one of Maurice's *wedding winding sheets.* As he was hefted towards the front door, Roger regained consciousness briefly – liquidly whispering, flapping a white hand – and Zack, who'd somehow felt his authority would be reimposed by *seeing them off the premises*, stepped forward to hear this denunciation: It . . . It was Oscar . . . He told me to do it . . . Then they were out in the road, under the told-you-so scrutiny of Mister Meehan and other *helpful neighbours*, leaving Zack staring at the envelope gummed by its flap to the geometric blizzard . . . *Faithful yet with beast*. It's this he completely retains – remembers far better than the plods, one of whom attended ostentatiously by their car, radioing for reinforcements. — Watching Hooper and Chief Brody, pedalo-ing through a shark-free sea, away from the final credits . . . *separating us from them* . . . Busner *takes a stab* at reconstructing the sequence of events. Had he remonstrated with the police who'd handcuffed Claude in the back bedroom, frogmarched him down the stairs and out to the Black Maria? No, it seems unlikely . . . *passivity had been the order of that day*. As for Miriam, once her job had been well done, she'd reverted to type – *the stone age mother* – and kept Mark and Danny safely hidden in their bedroom cave next door. – The onion-seller in his hooped jersey leaning against his bicycle *festooned with weeping waiting to happen* . . . The rag-and-bone man bending down from his seat atop a pile of broken old prams *to comfort his nag* . . . The coal man in his leather jerkin, a grim expression *on his carbonised face* – these are the vignettes Busner can find *behind the small stiff doors* of the nativity calendar, because that's what it had been: *a day of birth and rebirth*. Michael Lincoln went with Claude to the police station – Busner pulled the plug, watched Roger's watered-down blood drain away, and so found the scalpel the yogibod had used *to operate on his own prolapsed ego*. Miriam telephoned to secure

Claude's release, but that had been pretty much the last *we'd had to do with him*. – The final names float up into *the gods: best boys, key grips, electrician's mates*. The film's soundtrack, having coasted into a lagoon of idyll, flourishes a tail-end allusion to the possibility that life . . . *even for Jaws* . . . may be eternal: the basses rubba-dubbing, the kettledrums bumma-bumming, the tuba giving a defiant honk. Mark's been on his feet for a while – and his father sympathises with his urge to be gone: he's allowed himself to be seduced by the rubber shark, and now he feels . . . *sullied*. C'mon, Dad, he says, c'mon. Busner stays slumped in the past: *it isn't over 'til the fat lady sings*. The Kid came down, had a haircut and went back to Uppingham – his ego-death was probably *a good preparation for a career in the Civil Service*. Maggie, Irene, Eileen, Clive and Podge also *disappeared into the system – as have I*, although into a part of it where conformity *is imposed by white coats and straitjackets, rather than by pinstripes*. A year or so ago Busner thought he saw Podge in the day-room of the acute ward at Heath Hospital – there was the same blonde hair, the same babyish voice . . . *I can be a rain-bow . . . be a rain-bow* . . . but when he rounded the back of her blue-vinyl institutional chair, the face, although possessing the same features he remembered, *was puffed up to the point of being unrecognisable.* He'd stifled his greeting – while she'd looked at him with tranquillised eyes that, unable to hold on to his, dropped down into the Bunty lying open on her lap. Backing up, turning and walking away, Busner had grimly concluded that either it hadn't been Podge at all, or else *she was responding well to treatment* . . . because the young woman *trapped behind the rainbow door* was *terribly overweight*. – Dad! Dad! Mark tugs at his sleeve. The last few members of the audience have stood and are stretching in a way *peculiar to the end of matinees*, when people *rouse themselves from waking dreams to this daymare*. Busner shares their discomfort as they battle *with taboo* . . . and the hot, damp underwear *wedged in their groins* . . . *between their buttocks*. He senses also the struggle these minds are engaged in, as they try to resolve this latest, passively engaged-in spectacle with *their more persistent delusions of active control*. – Dad! Ple-eathe, Dad! Mark starts towards the end of the row – the safety curtain is descending, *big and beige and bland*. He calls back: The next programme thtartth in ten minutes, do you want to thee it again? – Getting to his feet, discreetly freeing his own hot, damp underwear, moving towards the exit with the stiff steps *of an accident victim being rehabilitated*, Busner wonders whether he wants to see it again. For now the epiphany *thrum-thrumms* inside him, while his awareness circles it *again annagain*, keeping an eye on his own understanding, lest it prove to be a *more efficient predator*. — He hadn't wanted to see Claude Evenrude again – he'd heard that Michael Lincoln had found a place for him in one of his homes . . . *which made perfect sense*, and in due course, as they stripped the two houses on Chapter Road of their last pitiful sticks – folding and shaking the Indian wall-hangings, hefting the mattresses on to the rag-and-bone man's cart – Zack had boxed up the Creep's books and sent them on . . . *Love's Body*. He hadn't wanted to see Roger Gourevitch again either – but there were things that had to be done, if only in the interests of . . . *preserving continuity*. Roger had convalesced at a nursing home on the outskirts of a Surrey dormitory town . . . *sedation beyond somnolence*. Their talk had been, Zack thinks, stilted and confined to practicalities. He retains only this detail: the scarf wrapped round Roger's healing throat bore a disturbing resemblance to the one Claude had worn on the revolutionary May day. — They stand in the street, father and son. The queue for the evening performance is *champing at the bit*, while cold sleet *cross-hatches the black bones* of nineteenth-century civic pride circling the roundabout. Zack would like to take Mark's hand – but that's . . . *out of the question*. He'd like to have this tangible confirmation he's the same man he was *five years ago, ten . . . twenty*. Because his present awareness is indeed proving remorselessly effective when it comes to *eating up the past*. Some people – Zack supposes, as they hunch up and walk through the drear back to the car – do indeed lead seamlessly integrated lives, rather than experiencing a series of discrete and eminently forgettable episodes . . . *but they're wrong to*. For a generation now – almost the entirety of his life – the photo cubes have been piling up on the sideboards and the slides have been remorselessly *slotted into the carousel*. He improvises a commentary for these images as they go round annaround . . . one that will make the show *as dull as all the rest: This is me lying down in the New Mexican desert – you can't see the flash, only how surprised I am . . . And this is me with the rest of the crew – don't we seem jolly? And this is Hiroshima, where we went for our holidays . . .* The light of ten thousand suns had fixed an image of unspeakable negativity on the collective consciousness forever . . . *and so we never speak of it, we carry on regardless. We get out our keys . . . We open the car door . . .*

We get in . . . We lean across and open the passenger door . . . Our son gets in and we say: Did you enjoy the film? stupid thing to say but sorta thing he always did say, 'cause for an intelligent man he could be . . . very stupid . . . stupid cupid lay off my . . . arseholes are cheap today and that . . . an' that . . . men walking in a ring – round the ring, flowed up and down king william street inna ring . . . up and down the graben too . . . frau komm mit they said – he said, i said i don't speak the lingo, mate . . . lies, all porkies . . . he said . . . he quoted . . . he said, hum-hum sometimes . . . sometimes i feel bad about what we do . . . what we do? we do nothing – nothing, doing is babies done doing dead diphtheria did for 'em . . . chuck 'em in poplar baths . . . chuck 'em in barking reach – reach in there, pull out a dead baby or three . . . doings done doings dead princess alice and done dead never known it, nan said . . . never seed it like that babies floating in on the bloody tide . . . floating in the family way . . . two way . . . family favourites . . . hundreds of the poor little fuckers . . . people up stepney way used it as an excuse to get rid of their babies inall . . . went down in the dark, dropped 'em off . . . black water rising . . . coming in my windscale and door . . . blocks of coconut ice floating in it . . . toffees . . . what's a girl t'do t'get 'erself a drink here? drinky-pooh . . . drinky-pooh . . . ooh, i'm parched – mine's a baby guinness . . . come round don't come round come round don't come round don't come round don't buy their bloody round or buy the round and don't buy me one . . . given up on mumsie, they have . . . no sweet tea . . . no-kay tokay . . . no frat . . . no frat with kraut prats . . . come for a swim in barking reach . . . come down the donau . . . he said she said the film was

454

good – little wifey that is . . . what we do? we do nothing – cocks in cunts it's nothing . . . try pushing one out – try pushing three out . . . inna ring king william street . . . what i want, young lady, is absolute attention to detail . . . patronising bastard . . . into central hall . . . putting on the agony . . . putting on the style . . . putting on the banana boat floating all the while he says this and that boodlie-boo . . . boodlie-bar . . . i'm parched – what's a girl to do to get a drink round 'ere? not in their round not on his round . . . come up on his round . . . all right missus . . . come on his round . . . thought i was a slag – he was the fucking slag . . . all of 'em fucking slags – stick their slag in anything . . . stick it in central hall . . . so gentle – gentle he was . . . never gone out for four years then suddenly schippen in london . . . frau komm mit . . . no – no frat, you prat . . . mitkomm frau . . . well spoken up on his hind-legs . . . impressively passionate . . . knew his way round there – and there – stayed down there forever-and-a-day . . . boodlie-bar . . . boodlie-boo . . . putting on the agony . . . putting on the style . . . girl don't forget that – girl don't forget the tallyman . . . smelt of gefilte fish . . . schmaltz . . . girl don't forget when it's her round, so why d'you leave it out . . . girl pays 'er own way, buys her round, ha! fließen die tränen, mir ewig erneut . . .'less you buy me a baby guinness . . . easily done, no, really – easily done . . . if you wanna go where cock 'n' cunt fitz – puttin' on the ritz . . . in funds then, later . . . didn't seem himself later . . . central hall, king-hall, fat old priestley and fraud . . . name's fraud, come in, fraud, put up yer feet, fraud . . . take a load off, fraud, grab my tits – bite my tits, fraud . . . stick it in, fraud, c'mon, fraud, tell us about the sharks, fraud . . . pity . . . pity poor me . . . gissa orange, fraud . . . gissa lemon, fraud . . . fucking clement . . . fraud . . . down the donau . . . down barking reach . . . up king william street . . . not so strict about frat and bennies in tubes like gum up all night in the donau . . . so hot . . . saw it then schippen . . . stupid horse . . . lay down and died it did on this stuff on the donau laid down dead on a heap of stuff inna barge – i dunno umbrellas and what have you . . . hell of a coincidence . . . him here, me there, with the occupation . . . softly speaking boy . . . jew . . . s'pose . . . done for them . . . . done for them proper never talk again fine figure of a man . . . never . . . never forget the smell of patronising gefilte fish . . . never have to . . . one thing . . . one thing maria never have to . . . come in tokay, okay never have to . . . paid my way . . . five go mad . . . five kill their selves . . . five farthings . . . five of this . . . five of that . . . never forget the tallyman – smelt of gefilte fish . . . never forget hard cheese . . . sweet tea . . . fags . . . what's a girl to do to get a drink round here? easily done . . . easily done . . . nicely-nicely . . . sky masterson . . . so bright . . . what did you think of the film? quotes it bloody ver-ba-tim . . . drinky-poohs . . . drinky-poohs . . . too late too busy too busy too late same thing day after day one in ten go mad, fließen die tränen, mir ewig erneut . . . no one should 'ave to bury their child at the sea with the black water rising oed' und leer das meer . . . no one should know that they don't know but we don't know, do we? why would I tell you . . . tell you what tell you nothing too busy same thing day after day one in . . . one in . . . mad . . . putting on the agony – in the fucking agony . . . i'm parched . . . lift it up good scotch and tokay and

bennies up your blood up . . . frau mitkomm fuck you fuck you
fuck curi– curi– . . . I dunno flowed up and down king william
street in and out of each other's house inna ring . . . in the ring . . .
big house in the ring . . . in the graben . . . fancy clock all done
in . . . broken glass little prick meant to come out and hit a bell . . .
cut his cock off and his balls beaten him one eye out . . . strung 'im
up on a lamp-post an' set fire to 'im . . . smell of burning flesh . . .
never forgot it . . . never forget it . . . forgotten me . . . saint martin's
took a pasting inall . . . get your bloody round in . . . that place
bratislava now . . . maybe i don't know – change my name – your
name . . . all down not to symp' . . . fucking czech partisans . . .
no checkmates . . . no, not me . . . he said traumatic i said you're
making a meal of it, boy, few hours out swimming with the
fishies . . . you should know . . . seen that, seen that three fags for
an iron bloody cross and bodies every which way strung up on
lamp-posts cocks and balls cut off set on fire stick that in your pipe
and smoke it human flesh you never forget the smell of it come up
on me go down they didn't say that then said that later go down
but don't bite seen in him liverpool street up and down king william
street inna ring they were putting it on the agony been inside four
years keeping shtum keeping away from the nazis come out on train
on the train you never forget the smell it's the smell of duffel coats
wet duffel coats all mimsy girls and him up there on the stage talking this boodlie-ba, boodlie-boo, boodlie-test, boodlie-megatons,
boodlie-annihilation and bertie russell up there with 'im . . .
skull-face click-clacking . . . like 'e knew 'im . . . a mother should
never have to do that drop a baby off barking reach see him float

down there in the oil and all that shit down there what they got down there all that shit . . . loved them . . . loved them . . . no love like it . . . swear . . . they know nothing ickle-wickle know nothing . . . need a firm hand no disputing that need a firm hand strict procedures but love also need a lot of love don't know what they're doing . . . we don't know what we're doing . . . oh, jesus – I'm parched . . . what's a girl to do to get a drink round here? you should never 'ave to bury a child in the system . . . not because he's a mental defective . . . come over from the ruskies . . . state of 'em . . . no frat . . . no frat . . . no freiheit . . . gross gott . . . but painted 'em up proper . . . got some sulpha for the worst of it . . . got to . . . had to open up for it . . . but you expect that . . . putting on the agony . . . a mental defective . . . shaved all his hair off said he was a holy man . . . i cried all night i cried . . . i was parched . . . fließen die tränen, yeah, yeah, mir ewig erneut . . . don't care made to care no one been bad that enough to not care held him . . . you don't know, can't know – trauma? i'd give you bloody traumas round and round trauma pushing it out and in a foul mood one goes mad putting on the agony . . . five die . . . ten go mad . . . no mother should have to leave him with the pansies but i couldn't handle him, he was well gone but no mother no son his crown jewels all burnt . . . should hold it in a silky sow's purse not even any balls in there just his winkle maybe not and never thought nothing much of it they done that down our way givvit a little suck and that . . . calms 'em, don't it . . . sang to me that night . . . my girl don't stand no cheatin' . . . fließen die tränen, yeah, yeah, mir ewig erneut . . . always been a sucker for it . . . lovely voice . . . sing this – sing that, come back to

the cottage that time again later it was . . . sing lieder like the fat
bint in the ruins of the adlon said she's been a pg . . . cut her hair
off . . . addabei . . . addabei . . . addablues . . . show tunes, happy
talk – please embrace me, sweet embraceable you . . . sing anything . . . lovely voice got his whole hand up me once i swear fingers
in my arse too i said i'm not a fucking glove puppet . . . i've had
a bloody kid, i have . . . left debbie back in poplar went on the
razzle . . . up central hall . . . maybe conway hall . . . dunno . . . good
people, though . . . ideals . . . we had 'em . . . he made a mud pie,
sweet thing with green eyes couldn't really talk much but names
change lovely boy . . . pressburger inna jeep . . . plenty of fags and
upsie-upsie that time what with the bennies and the fags and the
okay-tokay . . . what's a girl to do to get a goddamn drink in this
lousy saloon . . . wild boys . . . quis custodiet ipsos custodes, he said
when he got back with her from berko carnival, i said kiss custard
sick custard . . . we had a laugh . . . we do have a laugh 'though he's
a mournful sod . . . all mournful sods really, all don't know how
thin it is . . . it's so thin this world . . . turn your head it's gone . . .
it's so thin . . . they walk round inna ring in king william street
don't ever really geddit . . . looking for patterns . . . shapes . . .
making mud pies . . . stringing 'em up on lamp-posts . . . a heap of
broken things . . . mother shouldn't never have to see that, don't
care if she's austrian, bohemian . . . kraut . . . frisch weht der wind
der heimat zu . . . don't care . . . shouldn't have to see that, crown
jewels cut off all burnt in his mouth . . . shouldn't've gone with
'em . . . shouldn't've gone bloody anywhere . . . gone there . . . gone
here . . . clean kitchen surfaces best thing there is sign of an orderly

mind . . . you smile when you smoke cadets . . . you smirk when you smoke marijuana . . . don't mind . . . don't mind a little kif . . . had some in the garden at the cottage, yokels didn't have a clue he says responsible . . . i say you don't know shit, boy, wandering you are . . . you're the wanderer far from home you won't ever get home you wander about go on wandering . . . see if i care . . . in king william street in a ring . . . local authority funding not available – make it bloody available . . . these kids . . . good kids basically . . . need a bit of honest . . . firm hand . . . obviously . . . firm bloody hand . . . did you like the film? never went to the film, stayed in looked through the album . . . never one for snaps . . . old man . . . he was . . . old man . . . fine figure . . . that's the tally-man . . . sort 'im out, girl . . . sort 'im out . . . fine figure bottle of bass . . . bottle of bass on his belly fine man . . . and little jeanie in jeans . . . those inserts sewn up good . . . dab hand . . . got that nasturtium shmatte in berko . . . sewn it in . . . looked the bollocks . . . right bobby-dazzler . . . what's a girl gotta do . . . drinky-poohs . . . no mother should have to do that . . . bury a child she don't know what she don't know don't talk to me about it . . . walk round in a ring . . . he was off in – oh i dunno . . . maybe the hatch maybe friern he went all over . . . he wandered when we came down from yorkshire, couldn't hold on . . . hold on to anything but a skilled man knew his fabrics . . . mutti taught him that and there was money there from the factory, they got it back after the war, i think . . . don't know, though . . . not gonna take it off a man ill like that i pay my own way . . . always worked . . . always smelling of gefilte fish . . . fish . . . hell of a bloody coincidence in the public baths your own cubicle and you could have salt water from one tap which made it all floaty . . . some said they went in there and done it sneaked in hot bath sea water bottle of gin . . . down barking reach . . . no mother shoulda oughta done that to her child . . . hell of a bloody coincidence . . . what you know about it? nothing – fuck all . . . i see him . . . i see you . . . i dunno . . . maybe i done it with my husband too . . . that's what they're for innit? putting on the agony . . . putting on the style . . . he was put up somewhere down by queen's gate – not flash, had to smuggle me in by the fire escape, stood out there with the wind going right up me and when he was at it he talked like he was a madman but he didn't half go like the clappers . . . beautiful singer too . . . cried . . . tears like rain . . . didn't know he'd the mentals then . . . plenty of front . . . years later he comes by the cottage and he's spark-a-loco . . . on about coal holes and muffs and what have you . . . wanted to know . . . said he'd found out from fred egan at the campaign office . . . i said fred don't know shit . . . i don't know neither . . . nobody knows . . . nobody's ever going to know . . . i don't – she don't know . . . she don't know nothing . . . i sit up all night at 'er ears . . . syringing 'er ears . . . she don't know the fucking pain of it, she don't know . . . i don't . . . no mother should have to do that – push it out like that . . . joy? don't make me fine figure of a man the tallyman always smelling of gefilte fish she don't know . . . i don't know then maybe when the little one was dead in her i don't know . . . wish i'd something to tell her but I don't have nothing to tell her, they was all walking round inna ring on king william street . . . patronising bastard . . . did you enjoy the film? i told her

what was what – what she should know all i could . . . debbie . . .
head screwed on tight no need done up proper done up prop–
debbie need none done up . . . drinky-poohs . . . debbie come by
tell 'er that . . . that no more drinky-poohs . . . girl can't get a baby
guinness . . . girl can't get a gin an' it . . . girl gone up the farm
with the gripes got that shit inna jar offa them old witches . . .
drunk it down threw it right back up an' felt better . . . maybe . . .
eats into you – shit-for-brains . . . shit in your drawers . . . where the
brown-paper bags're crumpled up . . . dunno why i save 'em but i
allus do . . . eats into you . . . fine figure of a man . . . patronising
bastard . . . i told 'er best bloody thing you'll ever read tell you what's
what time to resist these thin bastards walking round inna ring on
king william street did she listen . . . don't know fucked off gone
off whoring i think . . . never sure 'bout that but my suspicions . . .
i had . . . she come up the club . . . put it about . . . junkie whore,
val said, i fucking hit him with me knucks . . . the cunt – what does
he know maybe i shoulda told her then . . . when . . . when the
baby was dead in her . . . no, not then . . . when she was littler 'cause
she was smart . . . she kept on at me, kept on asking . . . when will
you pay, says the bitch of . . . well . . . when will you? dunno . . . eats
into you . . . eats into your lungs . . . feel it . . . don't matter what
like they what put in me what they like morphine . . . barbs . . .
i dunno . . . still eats into you . . . eats you . . . teeth, not claws . . .
hell of a bloody coincidence . . . sweet nature . . . gentle . . . held
my hand tight 'cause she was scared and she woulda been . . .
dunno . . . no teeth – that's a laugh . . . she 'eld my hand . . . hell of
a coincidence . . . not claws teeth . . . grows more teeth . . . pull out

its teeth . . . pull 'em outta your belly . . . burn 'em out . . . poison 'em . . . fucker grows more teeth . . . come after you . . . fine figure of a man but 'e 'ad the mentals something chronic . . . singing . . . talking . . . carrying on all night . . . saw him . . . hung up there in brattycoleslaw . . . or pressburger . . . i dunno . . . strung up proper cut his crown jewels off and stuck 'em in 'is mouth set fire to them others too . . . never forget the smell of burning flesh candlestick burnt out and bacon both whole flitch got up from 'ansen's on tick whole flitch . . . fine figure of a man . . . threw 'im in off the wall at barking reach . . . threw 'im in the donau . . . lovely water beautiful saw the lights of old wien . . . then he come up on me with mates an' I don't know . . .'appens all the time cocks and cunts . . . horses and carriages . . . peace in our time . . . when i'm minted that's a fucking laugh when's that gonna be? i don't think so . . . paid my way . . . paid theirs inall . . . paid my way . . . went over poplar, was it? dunno, bought ledger experience . . . no, wing it . . . always good at picking things up . . . pick up clerking . . . pick up typing . . . pick up kraut . . . bit of french . . . mon semblable . . . mon frère . . . what's that you say . . . you like it? pick up teaching . . . pick up books . . . what i don't know ain't worth knowing and it ain't worth knowing what I know neither . . . the old man . . . fine figure of a patronising bastard on king william street . . . he come by . . . pay his way grant 'im that . . . bring a bottle of scotch . . . voddie . . . pack of fags . . . flitch of bacon – on tick, 'course . . . do the cross-word . . . never a cross word between us . . . couldn't be . . . spend all day riling 'im up he'd never create . . . not a creative man . . . 'elpful, though . . . good with pen-pushers . . . push it in never fight old

463

cunt never fought fighting old cunt fucked in the scullery, me? rich? don't think so . . . not jealous never jealous told her never jealous read this . . . read that took an interest she went off on the road whoring . . . oh, what's a girl gotta do to get a drink in this place, me . . . rich? i don't think so went over shoreditch way picking up bits of stuff to run up at home . . . curtains . . . black-outs . . . bit of crêpe de chine . . . chenille . . . dunno . . . run it proper, run it prop– . . . fine figure of a patronising bastard wouldn't fight – couldn't fight . . . flowing round king william street in a ring . . . i told her don't ever depend on them keep your independ-ence . . . never know if they've got the mentals 'til they shoot off, then it all comes out in the wash . . . same thing day after day one in ten go mad one in five kill themselves . . . never killed myself . . . never . . . wanted to lots of times put them in the canal or seconal . . . better than fucking walking down the tow path with their skin hanging off their little backs she had her skin hanging off her little back better off dead like the burning boy . . . crown jewels cut off the patronising bastard in stepney . . . you can have the job . . . i know your old man what 'e done was go down barking reach . . . bollocks . . . you can have the job if you do me a small service . . . small cock . . . small service . . . pay me . . . he . . . pay me . . . laughed all the way 'ome . . . choked 'im off proper . . . three iron crosses for a fag . . . schippen the bastard out . . . go find the hausobermann . . . go find the tallyman . . . go find your co . . . up at the old-fucking-bailey . . . i don't think so . . . no local government funding for that . . . all my poor boys . . . mongols . . . retarded . . . didn't know much then tried all we could

think it could've been better i don't know . . . patronising bastards . . . boysie don't go by the donau, don't swim in there – no
frat . . . shouldn't've gone with them to bratty- . . . bratty- . . .
bratty- . . . no – pressburger . . . eating into his own cock and balls 'e
was . . . all burnt on the floor . . . not in stepney . . . payback . . . not
in stepney offa brick lane . . . poor little sausage . . . burnt sausage . . . crown jewels all burnt in the sleeping bag . . . no mother
should have to go through that . . . she shouldn't've had to go
through that . . . went down saint mary's . . . she'd already gone
they said . . . patronising bastard walking round in a ring on king
william street . . . went down saint mary's sat up all night holding
her hand nice cool flannel on 'er forehead . . . that all right my
love? not in stepney . . . come back round stepney way that's what
they're for . . . innit? putting on the agony . . . putting on the
style . . . he said bit of a bloody coincidence . . . i told him a coincidence . . . coincidence is she don't know and i don't know and you
don't know we all don't know that's the bloody coincidence . . . it's a
wise child – and she ain't one . . . our fucking father fine figure of
a man in wherever . . . over bow way it was . . . up by the canal
there . . . choked 'im off sharpish . . . done 'im up proper . . . done
up prop– . . . what's a girl gotta do to get a drink in this miserable
gaff . . . i'm fucking parched . . . fließen die tränen, yeah, yeah, mir
ewig erneut . . . too fucking parched for that . . . down poplar
baths – or in barking reach . . . or in the canal . . . maybe . . . anything's better than 'aving 'em burnt to buggery like that girl in the
photo 'er skin all 'anging off 'er . . . oh, i dunno . . . speak proper . . .
speak up prop– . . . patronising bastard . . . all the couples form a

465

ring on king william street . . . i don't know . . . she don't know . . .
he don't know . . . he don't know neither . . . the great bell of bloody
bow don't know . . . hell of a coincidence . . . never forget the smell
of gefilte fish . . . dying for a fag . . . here comes a